P9-DXJ-285

Speak No Evil

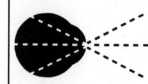

This Large Print Book carries the
Seal of Approval of N.A.V.H.

SPEAK NO EVIL

ALLISON BRENNAN

THORNDIKE PRESS

An imprint of Thomson Gale, a part of The Thomson Corporation

THOMSON

TM

GALE

Detroit • New York • San Francisco • New Haven, Conn. • Waterville, Maine • London

THOMSON
GALE

LIBRARY OF CONGRESS CATALOGING-IN-PUBLICATION DATA

Brennan, Allison.
  Speak no evil / by Allison Brennan.
    p. cm. — (The evil series ; #1)
  "Thorndike Press large print basic."
  ISBN-13: 978-0-7862-9405-3 (alk. paper)
  ISBN-10: 0-7862-9405-1 (alk. paper)
    1. Policewomen — California — San Diego — Fiction. 2. Young women — Crimes against — Fiction. 3. Psychopaths — Fiction. 4. San Diego (Calif.) — Fiction. 5. Large type books. I. Title.
  PS3602.R4495564 2007
  813'.6—dc22   2007003337

Published in 2007 by arrangement with The Ballantine Publishing Group, a division of Random House, Inc.

Printed in the United States of America on permanent paper
10 9 8 7 6 5 4 3 2 1

For Trisha McKay Richins
A loyal and true friend,
and the first person
I trusted enough to read my stories

ACKNOWLEDGMENTS

First and foremost, I want to thank my readers. If you've enjoyed this book, I hope you'll visit my website at www.allison brennan.com to read exclusive content, including deleted scenes, and view book trailers for this and my other books.

San Diego is a beautiful city that I've visited many times and look forward to enjoying again. Though I strive for accuracy, I have taken some liberties with the area for story purposes.

As always, several people have helped with the details in this book.

Jennifer Hennessey, who dusted off her criminology degree; Wally Lind, Dan Pollock, and Patrick Murray at Crime Scene Writers, who are always quick to answer questions on anything from postmortem injuries to tracking sexual predators online; author and nurse Candy Calvert, who answered several medical questions; and

Gary Olson, consultant for the California State Assembly, who once again shared his knowledge of public safety law so I wouldn't have to spend days reading the California Legislative Code.

A special thanks goes to Karin Tabke and her husband, ex-cop and all-around good guy Gary, who always answered their phone even when they knew it was me, on deadline, with last-minute questions that were always more complicated than I originally thought.

My husband Dan and our kids deserve extra-special appreciation for giving me the time to write and travel; my mom, who is truly my number-one fan; and everyone in the Sacramento Valley Rose chapter of RWA, who always answered my most arcane questions while giving me unconditional love and support.

And finally, the people who made this book possible: the Ballantine team, especially my wise editor Charlotte Herscher, Dana Isaacson, Kim Hovey, and Gilly Hailparn, who have all been so supportive; the art department, which gave me covers I absolutely love; my super agent, Kimberly Whalen; and the entire Trident Media Group.

PROLOGUE

At the very beginning, she had seen his face and knew he would not let her live.

She couldn't plead with him, he'd sealed her mouth shut. No way to beg, to appeal to his humanity. He had no humanity. Why hadn't she seen it before? Had she been so blind that when he looked at her she couldn't see the hatred, the anger, the sick lust?

She'd trusted him because she had no reason not to, but looking at him now, she saw the evil he'd hidden so well for so long.

The pain that had kept her awake for two nights had dulled, her body numb from abuse. She didn't think about it, didn't think about him, turned into herself, and remembered swimming at the beach. Or talking to her friends. Or how her mom was so proud of her when she graduated high school with honors.

Burning tears leaked from her eyes.

I'm so sorry, Mom.

He untied her once, to give her a bath. She was too weak to run, too tired to fight. But fierce pain reawakened when he scrubbed her body with soap, making her scream, a deep rumbling in her chest that couldn't escape through her glued lips.

"I need to wash your body," he told her calmly. "Just in case."

Just in case of what? The water hurt, but it also woke her up. Maybe she had a chance. Maybe she could escape. If she could just scream, someone would come. Wouldn't they?

She didn't even know where she was.

He carried her back to the bed that reeked of her blood, her urine, and worse. She tried to get up, to run, but her legs gave way and she slipped to the floor. He gave an odd, coarse laugh at her weak attempt to escape before picking her up as if she weighed nothing and dropping her on the bed.

Then she saw the garbage bag.

No!

She heard herself but no one else could as the bag came over her head. She fought him with everything she had and the bag tore.

Slap.

The pain across her face was nothing compared to what she had already endured, but her strength didn't match his. Another dark green plastic bag slid down over her face. She tried to hold her breath but couldn't. Something else was pulled over her legs. She began to fade. She almost didn't feel him tie up her body. She was light, a feather.

Death was her escape. There had to be something better than this, something brighter, something happy.

A heavy weight covered her body. *Him.* He was on top of her and she couldn't breathe.

Plastic molded to her nose and her chest tightened.

No air . . .

She couldn't fight, but her body tried. Her legs weakly kicked, her fingers clawed at the slick lining.

So tired. Can't.

In the brief moment between life and death, when her body fought but her mind knew there was no hope, an odd peace washed over her.

I'm sorry, Mom.

ONE

Her death had not been easy.

Homicide detective Carina Kincaid stared at the dead, naked corpse of the young woman, avoiding the wide-eyed terror etched on her face. Her mouth was gagged, but what drew Carina's eye was the word *slut* scrawled in thick black marker across her chest. A small red rose was tattooed on her left breast.

The victim lay in a disjointed fetal position, dried blood on her legs and vicious red welts on her breasts, indicating that her murder had followed a sexual assault. In California, that made the killer eligible for the death penalty. One small step toward justice, but it didn't satisfy Carina. This Jane Doe would still be dead.

She glanced away from the body, just for a moment, and watched the waves roll up the beach. Back and forth, calming. Her cheeks stung from the early-morning salt

13

air, but in just a few hours she'd be tugging off her windbreaker as the sun peaked over San Diego.

When she first arrived on the scene with Jim Gage, supervisor of the Forensic Field Services Unit of the San Diego Police Department, they immediately documented that the evidence had been contaminated. Three layers of heavy-duty green garbage bags had been cut away from the body. The park ranger hadn't been able to lift what he thought was trash, so he sliced it open. What had he been thinking?

"I didn't think there was a body inside," he'd said when Carina questioned him.

By the tension in Jim's jaw, it was obvious that he was pissed. But true to form he didn't say anything. He never said anything, which had been the primary reason Carina had broken up with him last year. She could handle his moodiness — she had four brothers, she could put up with almost anything — but his refusal to talk about what bugged him, on the job and off, was a relationship breaker.

Or maybe they hadn't loved each other enough to make it work.

Carina glanced behind them when she heard a car approach. The coroner's van pulled into the empty parking lot and a

14

short, trim, well-dressed Asian man exited the vehicle. Assistant Coroner Ted Chen, the perfectionist. Carina liked it when he pulled one of her cases, even if he made her a bit self-conscious. She triple-checked her reports when he was the responding coroner, afraid to appear the novice despite her nearly eleven years on the job.

"Doctor Chen is here," she told Jim.

"Hmm." Jim finished photographing the body and surrounding area, glancing up as Doctor Chen crossed the sand to where the body lay. "Hello, Ted."

"Gage. Detective." Chen nodded toward the victim. "Was the body found in this condition?"

"The bag had been intact. The park ranger opened it."

"Why on earth would he do that?"

Jim removed his wire-rim glasses and rubbed his eyes with his forearm. "Thought it was filled with garbage and planned on taking multiple trips to dispose of the contents."

Chen shook his head in disgust, his thin lips a tight line. He knelt in the sand, careful to prevent further granules from rolling into the plastic. "She suffocated," he said quietly.

"You mean she was put into the bag

15

alive?" Carina asked for clarification.

"It would appear so, but the crime lab will need to go over the bag to confirm it," Chen said. "See her discoloration?" The victim appeared bluish, almost purple. "No oxygen. No sign of strangulation, and no blood in her eyes or ears to indicate it, either. I can give you a better answer at the autopsy." He glanced at his watch. "I have three autopsies scheduled this morning, but I'll postpone the afternoon schedule to fit her in."

"Thanks, Doctor Chen. I appreciate it."

"I'll have her on the table at two."

Carina nodded, caught Jim staring at her, his face unreadable. "You going to join us?" she asked.

"We'll see how far my team can get with the bag. We're backlogged as it is."

No surprise. Contrary to popular television, most evidence wasn't processed until a suspect was apprehended and a court date set. The wheels of justice also turned the cogs of the laboratory.

Carina forced herself to stare at the victim's face while Chen and Jim prepared her for transportation to the morgue. She looked so young. Eighteen, maybe. Was she a college student? There were two universities within spitting distance of the beach.

Maybe she was still in high school.

She thought about her baby sister. Well, Lucy wasn't a baby anymore. She was a high school senior and smart enough to go to just about any college she wanted. Their parents wanted her to stay close to home; Lucy desperately wanted to move away. But college campuses were dangerous, and Carina found herself siding with her parents on this one.

Fourteen years ago she wanted the exact same thing as Lucy — to get out from under her parents' thumb. But that was before she'd decided to become a cop. Before she realized how truly dangerous the city could be. Before she realized that justice wasn't always swift, and that the system didn't always work.

That some murders would never be solved.

She turned away from the death scene and stared again at the Pacific Ocean, unconsciously wrapping her arms around her waist. It would be temperate today, as virtually every day was in San Diego. Here on the coast, the cool morning breeze loosed a few strands of dark hair from the French braid Carina wore when on the job. The tide was receding, the waves small and playful, pulling back. The shells and rocks reflected

17

the sunrise behind her, the ocean still dark and mysterious. A pair of early-morning joggers, a man and woman, ran on the packed sand.

Had the girl been murdered here on this quiet, clean beach? Or had Jane Doe been dumped?

Carina voted for dumped, but asked the experts.

"Dumped is my guess," Jim said. "There's no sign of struggle, but of course the scene's been contaminated." He visually scanned the area to confirm his hypothesis.

Carina followed his gaze to the parking lot adjacent to this stretch of beach. The highway on the other side was beginning to bustle with morning commuter traffic. Dozens of small, outrageously expensive homes lined the opposite side of the road. A few hundred yards north was a beachside shopping area with several popular restaurants and a bar that catered to the college crowd, which, even on a Sunday night, wouldn't have closed down until the state-mandated two a.m.

That didn't mean the body hadn't been dumped before two, but from Carina's college days as well as her years on patrol, she knew this beach saw heavy traffic until the wee hours of the morning. Before two a.m.

it was more than likely someone would have seen a body-size bag being tossed onto the beach.

Usually, body dumps were done when no one was around, to minimize the killer's chances of being caught.

Though Carina couldn't absolutely rule out the possibility that the girl had been left earlier, logic suggested that she'd been dumped between three and five in the morning. Commuters hit the road early, and by five-thirty traffic steadily passed only a hundred feet away. Sunrise had hit about thirty minutes ago.

"Do you know when she died?" she asked Chen.

He glanced up at Carina from his position next to the body. "Lividity isn't fixed, and it's obvious she's been moved. Her body temperature is 86.3 degrees. But I'm not sure how being wrapped in the garbage bags would affect the loss of heat." He glanced at Jim.

"I'll do some research on that," Jim said. "I'm thinking it would slow it down, but not by much."

Chen nodded. "That would mean she died four to twelve hours ago, but I'd put it closer to four to eight hours because rigor mortis hasn't completely set in. There's still some movement in her larger muscles."

Carina made notes. Ten p.m. to two a.m. Sunday night. He killed the girl somewhere else — in a car? The woods? Someone's house? A secluded stretch of beach? She dismissed the last idea: there were no secluded areas on this part of the coastline, and the police routinely patrolled the area because of the nearby college.

Someone kills her, puts her in their vehicle, and transports her here, to a public beach, where her body would most certainly be found sooner rather than later.

"Arrogant," she muttered.

"Excuse me?" Jim asked.

"The killer. Arrogant. Dumped her body where we'd quickly find it. Convinced he won't be caught, thinks he's smart."

"Dusting off your psych degree, Carina?" Jim teased.

She rolled her eyes and smiled. Jim knew she'd taken all of one psychology class and had never graduated from college.

She walked over to the uniformed officers and instructed them to canvas the area. "Start with the houses across the street. See if someone noticed anything unusual after ten last night up until five this morning. A suspicious car, strange noise. People on the beach. Then hit the shops up the street when they open, focusing on those open past eight p.m., clubs and bars in particular."

As she walked back to Jim and Chen she heard a car turn into the gravel parking lot. Her partner, Will Hooper, jumped out and strode across the sand toward them.

Jim shook his head. "Asshole," he muttered.

"Give it a rest, Jim," she said.

"Sorry, Kincaid." Will approached with a guilty grin. "I didn't hear my beeper go off."

"What's her name?"

"Come on, you woke me at five-thirty this morning. Just because you rise before the sun doesn't mean the rest of us like to suffer." Forty and divorced, Hooper enjoyed playing the field. He was also a good cop, a veteran, and Carina trusted him with her life. He'd taught her how to play hardball in a male-dominated profession, and never once hit on her. Next to her brothers, he was her best friend.

"And? You live ten minutes from here. Did your precious car throw a gasket?"

"Okay, okay. Her name is Monica. And she lives up in Carlsbad, so it took me time to get back down here."

Carina filled her partner in on what they'd learned. She looked back at the dead girl and noticed something unusual around her mouth.

"Doctor Chen, what's that?" She knelt beside Jim and gestured toward a thin, pale yellow substance around the edges of the gag.

"Lipstick?" Will said. "Not that you would know about that." He tugged on her braid.

Carina ignored him. In the increasing sunlight, the gag — a black bandanna — almost shimmered. "I couldn't say." Chen frowned.

Jim took out a swab from his kit and wiped the area around Jane Doe's gag, but nothing appeared to come off. He popped the swab into a sterile tube and closed it. Leaning close to the dead girl's face, he breathed deeply, frowned. Taking prongs, he attempted to remove the gag. It was then that Carina noticed the bandanna wasn't tied. The end was wrinkled, as if it had at one point been tied in a knot, but now it flapped free.

The gag would not budge.

"Glue."

"Glue?" Carina and Will repeated simultaneously. "He suffocated her, then glued the gag onto her mouth?" Carina asked.

Jim shook his head. "I don't think so. I think he glued her mouth shut, then suffocated her."

He had first killed twelve years ago.

That victim hadn't been human, wasn't even a mammal. But he remembered the day with vivid nostalgia as the day he gained a mature self-awareness and an inkling of the darkness inside.

He'd been sitting on the front steps of his house waiting for his mother's friend to leave so he could go inside and watch cartoons. He hated sitting here by himself doing nothing. His mom wouldn't let him leave the yard, but she wouldn't let him inside when one of her special friends visited, even when it was really cold or hot.

He heard shouts down the street. "Get back here, you motherfucker!" an older boy — a bully, Tommy Jefferson — screamed at Jason Porter, the little black kid who lived on the corner in the only two-story house on the block.

Jason looked scared and was running fast, but Tommy and another kid caught up to him and tackled him right there on the sidewalk. His head hit with a dull *whack* on the cement and left a smear of blood. Red dripped down Jason's face as one of the boys pulled him up and shook him back and forth so his head flopped.

The big kids shouted bad words at Jason and pushed him down again, but Jason managed to jump up and run quickly back up the street. The bullies were surprised and raced after him, but Jason got inside his house before they caught up.

He watched the bullies throw rocks at the door until Jason's mother came out, a steak knife in hand, Jason at her side. She used some of the same bad words they'd used on her son.

"Tommy, you touch my son one more time and I'll cut off every one of your fingers, don't you forget it!"

The kids ran off, laughing.

Jason's mother slammed the door shut and the neighborhood became quiet. He was alone on the porch again. He wondered if his mother would protect him from bullies like Jason's mom. He doubted it.

A butterfly fluttered into the yard. It flew from one dying flower to another, searching for something it couldn't find, its black-and-orange wings pumping up and down. When it finally landed on a wilted petunia near him, he leaned forward and captured the creature in his fist. It trembled against his closed hand, the insect's little body moving frantically.

The screen door slammed behind him and

he jumped.

"You can go back in now, kid," the man said as he walked down the stairs.

"When my daddy comes home he's going to kill you."

The man laughed as he got into his truck and drove away.

He pouted and thought about what Jason's mom said. Maybe next time that man came over *he* could cut off all his fingers.

Something caught his eye on the sidewalk where Jason had fallen. Curious, he crossed the dry lawn and squatted. On the rough surface of the cement a layer of skin and some blood dried in the summer sun. He pictured Jason's bleeding face and the large scrape on the side of his head.

Cool.

Something moved in his hand. He looked at his closed fist, then opened it just a bit, a bug curled in his sweaty palm. He picked it up by a wing and it tried to fly away. Grabbing both the butterfly's wings, one in each hand, he watched the legs and antennae frantically reaching out, trying to get away.

He was fascinated by the struggle. So much movement, but it wasn't getting anywhere.

Slowly, he pulled the wings from the body of the bug. One came off clean, but the other tore. The dying bug fell to the sidewalk, its body jumping, squirming.

He stared, fascinated and detached at the same time, until what remained of the butterfly stopped moving. It took several minutes. Peering closely, he realized it wasn't dead. He pushed it with his finger; it jumped once, twice, then stopped.

He brought the pieces of the butterfly into the kitchen to find an old jar to keep them in.

The bug was not much more than dust twelve years later, but the old mayonnaise jar still rested on his nightstand.

It had taken him nearly two hours to remove all traces of the slut from his bedroom. He wrinkled his nose in disgust. He hadn't realized she'd be so messy. She'd shit in his bed and the smell was god-awful. Why'd she have to go do that? He'd taken her to the toilet several times a day.

He'd bought the sheets and blanket especially for the weekend, so he stuffed them into a thirty-three-gallon trash bag. *Heavy duty.* What a joke. The slut had torn the first bag when she tried to get out — he'd needed to use three just to make sure she couldn't break them.

Every detail had been carefully planned.

He washed her body, getting rid of any evidence of himself, though he'd taken great care all weekend. He wrapped her in the plastic bags so he could fully immerse himself in her death, at the last minute putting a blanket on top of her body.

Then he laid on her, holding her tight. She bucked beneath him, her body fighting for air, to escape. For a long minute he lost himself in an odd state of hot ecstasy and cold fear.

It really didn't take that long for her to die. In fact, it was rather anticlimactic. After two days of taking her to the brink of death and back, trying to figure out what made her scream and what didn't, her death was . . . boring.

She died too quickly and he was left unsatisfied. It made him angry. Next time he needed to think of something else, maybe an airhole in the bag. Something he controlled. Or maybe he'd do it like the movie, except he'd wrap her in some sort of plastic wrap. Most of her, anyway. He'd think more about that. It would certainly keep her clean. And if she shit, it wouldn't get all over everything.

He'd watched all those forensics shows on television and he was paranoid about the cops finding him with all their tricks. Otherwise, he would have used his hands. He'd wanted to, just like the film. Squeeze, release, squeeze, release. Give her just enough air, then cut it off. Make it last. Much more satisfying. At least it *looked* more satisfying. He didn't try it with the slut. He had *wanted* to, but it was safer his way. Keep a barrier between them. Minimize contact. The plastic wrap idea might work.

He sprayed disinfectant around his room, scrubbed spots he could barely see, flipped his mattress. Put her clothes in the garbage bag along with the sheets.

Safe. What would happen if he'd left his DNA on the body? The police had no reason to take samples of his blood or hair. Didn't they need evidence? Something to connect him? At least that's what he picked up from television. If they had his DNA, it wouldn't do them any good unless they had other evidence against him. Then they'd need a warrant and all that stuff. He'd never been arrested, so it's not like a computer would flash his name and address.

At first reality had been so much better than his imagination, but then . . . it didn't feel right. He must have done something wrong: when she'd died, he didn't feel the rush of power he was so certain he'd feel.

What could he have done different?

With that thought in mind, he drove thirty miles and looked for a neighborhood that had Monday trash pickup. A quiet neighborhood where no one was out. He found a perfect one, where the trash cans were in an alley. He threw the sheets and clothes and everything the slut might have touched into a half-full garbage bin.

He had thirty minutes to get to class, and the garbage truck had just rounded the corner.

Perfect timing.

TWO

"Glue." Will shook his head. "I can't believe the bastard glued her mouth shut, then did those things to her."

They'd parked near each other in the garage adjacent to the police station and walked inside together. It was close to eight, nearing shift change, and uniforms were coming in from patrol. Carina waved to a few of her friends, though when she'd made detective last year after ten years as a beat cop, some of the guys had given her the cold shoulder. Hell, not just the guys. The other women on the force were twice as bad.

It was like starting from square one all over again.

"He tortured her," Carina said to Will. "Gluing her mouth shut, raping her, suffocating her. This guy is sick."

Will looked both ill and angry. "We need to run a search for similar crimes." They sat down to start plugging information into the computer. Carina's phone rang.

"Kincaid," she answered.

"Dean Robertson here." Dean was now in charge of Missing Persons, though when she first joined the force eleven years ago he'd been Carina's training officer.

"What's up?"

"Heard you found a Jane Doe this morning. She matches the description of a possible missing person."

"Possible?

"I had a strange visit Saturday."

"Saturday? I thought the chief told you no more weekends."

He grunted. "You going to turn me in for working unclocked hours?"

"Me? You said Friday, right?" Dean had been known to work off-the-clock almost as many hours as his regular shift. Never married, he'd told Carina once over beers that he couldn't *not* work. *There are missing kids out there, Carina. Their parents deserve to know whether they're dead or alive.*

Yeah. They did.

Dean continued. "This guy comes in. Clean-cut, late thirties, maybe forty. Wanted to report a missing person. Female, eighteen. Matches the description of your Jane Doe. The desk sergeant took the information at first, then bumped it over to me when the guy got all huffy that we weren't doing something right away."

"How long had she been missing?"

"Less than twenty-four."

"His daughter?"

"Nope."

"No?" She wrinkled her nose. "What's his story?"

"He claims they were friends. That he suspected someone was following her and had told her to watch herself. She hadn't taken him seriously."

"Why'd he think she was missing?"

"She didn't go online Saturday."

"Online? As in, computer?"

"Yep. That's how they met — through a computer class at UCSD." Concern laced Dean's voice. "Something's weird about this, and since the girl's basic description matches your Jane Doe, I thought you might want to follow up with her family."

"And the guy?"

"Steven Thomas. I'll send up a folder with all the information."

"What's the girl's name?"

"Angela Vance. Goes by Angie."

"Thanks Dean. I'll let you know what happens."

Carina had just finished telling Will about the call when a secretary dropped Dean's folder on her desk.

She opened the folder. No photo. Angela "Angie" Vance, eighteen, blond hair, brown eyes, approximately five feet five inches tall, and 115 pounds. Her Jane Doe was five feet four and a half and 120. Angie was a freshman at UC San Diego with an undeclared major. She lived with her mother and grandmother downtown.

"What's wrong?" Will watched her closely.

"What's this Thomas guy's interest in a girl half his age? He told Dean they were friends from school, but . . ."

She logged onto the DMV database and pulled down Angie Vance's driver's license photo. She stared at the bright smile and short brown hair. Her vic had longer, blonder hair, but the photograph had been taken more than two years ago. Carina's chest tightened. Women change their hair color all the time. The face matched their victim. She showed Will and he concurred. Angie Vance could be their vic.

"I'll run Thomas," Will said.

"Let's do it from the road," Carina said, jumping up and throwing her light-weight blazer over her black T-shirt. "I want to check out Angie Vance's house and see if we can get a recent picture of her before we talk to her mother."

Angie lived in a small, postwar bungalow in North Park, an old neighborhood in Central San Diego. It was noon on Monday and Carina suspected no one would be home; she was wrong. Angie's elderly grandmother directed them to Angie's mother, Debbie, who was working as a waitress at Bud's Diner near the highway. Grandma also supplied a recent photograph.

During the short drive to the diner, Carina stared at the photo. It was of mother and daughter, both wearing burgundy sweaters that offset their fair skin. Debbie Vance had brown hair and Angie extensive blond highlights. The older woman had been pretty in her day, but in the picture she looked a little gray and worn, though happy. Her daughter was beautiful, with long shiny hair, curled for the photograph, eyes tastefully made up, and a warm and inviting smile.

Now Angie was dead. Jane Doe and this pretty girl were one and the same. Carina closed her eyes, putting herself in Debbie Vance's shoes. Knowing exactly how the woman would feel when told someone she loved was dead. While Carina was pleased to have a quick identification of the victim, she dreaded having to break a mother's heart.

The call on the radio confirmed it. The coroner ran Jane Doe's fingerprints in the system. Nothing in the criminal database, but the Department of Motor Vehicles popped up with her driver's license. Angela Vance.

Bud's Diner looked like a greasy spoon on the outside, but once they stepped through the doors the rich aroma of a real country breakfast — sweet syrup, salty potatoes, sizzling bacon — reminded Carina that she hadn't eaten.

"Take any table," a waitress said as she poured coffee with one hand and put down a plate of butter-drenched waffles.

"Is Mrs. Vance available?"

The waitress looked up with a frown, but didn't need to say anything.

"I'm Debbie Vance."

Carina might not have recognized the short, chubby woman of about forty, her cherubic face bright from the heat of the kitchen. But the warm smile was the same as the photograph. Debbie Vance came around from behind the counter. "And you are?"

"Detectives William Hooper and Carina Kincaid, San Diego Police Department," Will said. "Is there a private area where we can talk?"

Debbie Vance slowly nodded, her expression confused, her eyes asking questions she didn't voice. Knowing something was wrong, but not wanting to ask for fear the question would bring a tragic answer.

Carina remembered the feeling.

"This way," Mrs. Vance said tightly.

She led them through the kitchen to a small, crowded office that had no door. She looked around for three chairs, but there was only one. No one sat.

Carina asked, "Mrs. Vance, when was the last time you saw your daughter?"

Her lip quivered. "Is something wrong with Angie?"

Carina didn't say anything, and Mrs. Vance continued in a rush, looking from Carina to Will. "Friday morning. I was leaving for work when she got up to go to classes. She goes to UCSD, you know. On full scholarship. She's very smart, straight-As all through high school . . ."

She took a deep breath. "She goes out with friends on the weekends, and I work early and go to bed early, so I don't really keep tabs on her anymore. She's eighteen, she's a good girl, never got into drugs, I didn't think I needed to watch — oh God." Her voice cracked. "I heard her come in late Friday night, after one, but when I checked on her Saturday before I left for work, she was already gone."

Mrs. Vance searched their expression. "What's wrong? What's happened?"

Mothers always know.

Carina took her hand as Mrs. Vance sat heavily into the only chair. Will said in a quiet voice, "A body was found on the beach this morning that matches Angie's description."

Mrs. Vance stared at them, shaking her head. She'd asked, but she didn't want to hear. Carina didn't blame her. No one wanted to hear when someone they loved and nurtured was dead. "No, I would know. It's not Angie. You don't *know* it's her, right?"

Carina didn't tell her the DMV prints matched. It seemed too cold. Instead she said, "When you feel up to it, we'd like you to come down to confirm her identity."

"Right now. Right now. It's not her." She closed her eyes, took a deep breath, said, "What happened to the girl you found?"

There was never an easy way to tell a parent their child was dead.

"She was murdered, Mrs. Vance," Carina said softly.

"Someone killed her? On purpose? Who?"

"We're doing everything we can to find

out," Will said.

The waitress with the waffles — her tag said Denise — pushed herself into the small room and Mrs. Vance turned to her, sobbing. "They think my Angie is dead."

The two women embraced and Carina steeled her emotions, willing herself *not* to remember the agony and pain of losing a loved one to violence. When the two women separated, she asked, "Mrs. Vance, does Angie have a close friend we can speak with? Maybe a boyfriend? Someone who might know where she went Friday night?"

"That's what happened," Mrs. Vance said with a certainty that wasn't as evident in her shaking hands as it was in her voice. "She was with Abby and Jodi. They have an apartment near campus, she's always staying there." She scrawled the names and an address and phone number on the back of a guest ticket. "Maybe Kayla, but they're not as close as Angie and Abby."

"What about her father?"

Mrs. Vance shook her head. "Carl left years ago, when Angie was not much more than a baby. He — We don't keep in touch anymore. He remarried and moved out of state. Doesn't even remember to send Angie birthday c-cards." Her words ended in a sob, which she swallowed back, putting a stoic expression on her face. Holding it together.

"She'll be back today, after class." Denial.

"Do you know her boyfriends?"

"Angie wasn't steady with anyone."

"She never talked about boyfriends with you?"

"Yes, but not in detail. She doesn't have a regular fellow. She's too young for that, and that's fine with me. I always tell her —" she stopped suddenly, looking lost.

"Mrs. Vance?"

She shook her head, gave them a half-smile. "I was just thinking. Everything is going to be okay. You're wrong. The poor girl . . . she's not Angie."

"Mrs. Vance, do you know Steve Thomas?"

"The name sounds familiar," she said. "I think she talked about him around Christmas. Or Thanksgiving. I think they went on a couple dates, but it wasn't serious. Why?"

Will evaded the question by asking about any other casual boyfriends. Mrs. Vance couldn't think of any boys Angie had been seeing recently.

Carina didn't have any more questions, not right now. She knew she'd have to face Mrs. Vance again, at the funeral, possibly at the house collecting evidence, asking more questions. She certainly wasn't looking forward to any of it.

She would much rather interview suspects and witnesses than talk to the victim's family.

Will handed Debbie Vance a card with the coroner's name and address. "If you can come by sometime today to identify the body, we would appreciate it. Just call this number and tell them you're coming. They'll have everything ready. You don't even need to be in the same room, they'll show you on a screen."

Her lip quivered but she nodded. "I'm sure it's a misunderstanding."

When Will and Carina were outside, Carina took several deep breaths before getting into their car.

"Cara, are you okay?"

"Just give me a second."

It was the quiet anguish that got to her. The pain in the eyes. The firm denial even with the internal knowledge that the police wouldn't come ask her to view a body if they weren't nearly one hundred percent positive of the identity already. Because there was always hope.

She squeezed her eyes closed and tilted her face to the sun. One. Two. Three.

Better. She tamped down on her own pain

and frustration, and turned to Will. "I want to talk to Steve Thomas."

Steve Thomas's oceanfront apartment was within biking distance to the university, as evidenced by the wide and well-used bike paths along the highway. There were eight units, four on top, four on bottom. A dozen similar apartment buildings took up this stretch of the highway, half a block from the beach. When she'd been in college, one of her boyfriends had had a place out here, about a mile away, similar to Thomas's apartment. Ocean access justified the outrageous rent.

On the south side of the building, college-aged men and women walked on the path connecting the street to the beach. It was a Monday in February, but if you didn't have classes the San Diego beaches were incomparable virtually year-round. Surfers would be out en masse — the temperature promised to be eighty-two today, and while the water was cold, wet suits made it tolerable. Invigorating.

Sometimes Carina missed the carefree life she'd enjoyed in college, when she could drop everything and pick up her surfboard. When was the last time she'd hit the waves? Five, six years ago? She and her brother

41

Connor had gone out before a big storm, nearly wiped out. Even though they were adults, her dad had been furious. They'd had a blast, though. It had been worth Dad's stern lecture.

She was so out of practice now that she didn't dare go out under the same conditions. Even today's tame waves would be a challenge.

Their radio beeped. "Hooper here," Will answered.

"Sergeant Fields. I have something on the Thomas guy."

"Shoot."

"He's clean, except for a restraining order."

Carina raised an eyebrow at Will.

"Anything else?"

"Oh, yeah," Fields responded. "Angela Vance, the girl he reported missing, put it on him three weeks ago."

THREE

Carina and Will approached Thomas's apartment with caution, but he wasn't home. They called in a patrol to check the area every hour and notify them when he returned.

She said to Will as they drove to the university to locate Angie's friends, "We'll play nice until we can build a case."

"Think he's the one?" Will asked.

"Don't know, but she was obviously scared of him. And what's a thirty-nine-year-old man doing following eighteen-year-old girls?"

"Don't look at me!" Will exclaimed. "I like my women past the chewing-gum stage."

Carina smiled. "I wasn't making a moral judgment on your sex life, Hooper. It's just creepy, you know?" A quick run in the system showed that Thomas had no known occupation, though he received a pension from the U.S. Army. The desk sergeant was trying to dig a little deeper into the guy's military records to see if there was anything else worth knowing. And just because he didn't have a job on record didn't mean he wasn't working somewhere.

The college administration gave them only a few minutes of frustration before handing over Abby Ivers's schedule and a copy of her photo ID. Will asked about Steve Thomas, confirmed that he was also a student, and sweet-talked the secretary into peeking at his schedule. Carina didn't like to play loose with the rules — evidence could later be thrown out in court if they screwed up in the field — but if Thomas was on campus they could track him down.

It would be nearly noon, when Abby's English lit class would end, so Will and Carina grabbed hot dogs at the student union and munched while watching the doors of the building.

"So Angie Vance was last seen Friday morning," Will said.

"But her mother heard her come in late Friday night."

"Though she didn't actually see her."

"Steve Thomas comes by the station to file a missing persons report on Saturday morning. Why would he do that?"

"To throw suspicion off himself?"

44

"That's stupid."

"Who said killers were smart?"

Carina frowned. "The murder was sadistic."

"Maybe he raped her and she suffocated and he panicked, dumped her body."

"Hmmm." It was a thought. But why the elaborate setup? The glue? The garbage bags? The public beach? "What do you think about calling Dillon for an informal opinion?"

"Couldn't hurt, if your brother has the time."

"He always makes time for me. What's family for if we can't bug each other at all hours of the day and night?" She took another bite out of her hot dog, swallowed, and said, "I'd like to hear what Doctor Chen says. Friday night to Monday morning? That's a long time. If we believe that she was home on Friday night, that's a full forty-eight hours before she died. Where did he keep her in the meantime?"

"If it's Steve Thomas, not in his apartment. The walls in complexes like that are paper-thin," Will said.

"Maybe he glued her mouth shut to keep her from screaming." The case was giving her the creeps. She much preferred a clear-cut domestic violence or gang shooting.

Angie's murder didn't fit into anything she'd seen before, so she hoped Dillon had some insight. Her brother was a forensic psychiatrist, and this case would give his psychiatry degree a workout. She'd call him as soon as they were done here.

Carina watched students start pouring from the building. She hadn't particularly liked college; she was too active, too antsy, and she ended up dropping out with only a year to go and joining the police academy.

But there were other reasons for that decision.

"Over there." Will hit Carina on the arm, tossing the last third of his hot dog in the trash. Carina followed suit. "That looks like Abby."

Abby Ivers was a cute, perky blonde in a tight T-shirt and low-waist jeans. Deep dimples sliced her cheeks, and her eye makeup was heavily applied.

"Abby?" She introduced herself and Will and flashed her badge. "Do you have a minute?" Carina motioned for her to follow them back to the bench where they'd been sitting.

"Sure," she said, hugging her books to her chest and frowning. "I guess."

When they were seated, Carina asked,

"When was the last time you saw Angie Vance?"

Abby's eyes grew wide. "Oh God, something happened," she said all in one breath.

"Why do you say that?"

"Because she hasn't returned any of my e-mails, and her IM is offline, and she didn't journal all weekend. I TM'd her on Saturday night and it bounced back 'cause her cell wasn't on."

Abby sounded just like Carina's sister Lucy.

"TM'd?" Will asked.

"Text messaged," Carina translated.

"Right, so what happened? Did she get in an accident or something? Is she in the hospital? She's okay, right?"

"I'm sorry, but she's dead," Carina said gently.

Abby's tanned face noticeably paled. "Dead?" Her chin quivered. "Wh-what happened?"

Carina gave her the bare minimum story. "When was the last time you saw her?"

"Friday night."

"Where?"

"The Sand Shack. On Camino del Oro, off the beach." Abby's eyes teared and Carina glanced at Will.

He asked in his soothing voice, "What

time did you see her?"

"She left at twelve-thirty, I think. She works there, you know, but got off at ten. Then we just hung out. Jodi and I walked her to her car, but we went back because there was this cute guy . . . did her mom say she didn't get home? Did she get carjacked?" Like many survivors, she was looking for answers. Unfortunately, they didn't have any.

"We're trying to establish when and where Angie was seen. Was anyone paying unusual attention to her? Giving her a hard time? Maybe she had a boyfriend she'd broken up with recently."

Abby blushed and looked down. "Angie had a lot of boyfriends. I mean, they all loved her. But she was particular."

"How so?"

Abby shrugged.

"Abby, if you have anything to tell us, now would be the time."

"There's nothing. Just . . . she broke up with a lot of guys because they weren't *the one.*"

"The one?"

"Like, someone you want to spend the rest of your life with." She diverted her eyes and sniffed. "Angie was such a romantic."

Carina sensed that Abby wasn't telling

them something, but before she could push Will said, "What about Steve Thomas?"

"What about Steve?"

"Was he one of Angie's ex-boyfriends?"

She nodded. "They dated back in November, I think. Maybe December, too."

"But he wasn't *the one*," Will said, using Abby's own phrase.

"No, they weren't even exclusive."

"Abby." Carina remained silent until the girl looked at her. "Is there something else you think might be important? Something about Angie that might help us find out what happened to her?"

"No, nothing," she said too fast.

Before they could push her, a male voice called from across the courtyard. "Abby!"

Carina and Will turned simultaneously and watched a lean, athletically built man with broad shoulders run toward Abby. He was older than the average college student and barely gave them a glance before saying, "Abby, have you seen Angie at all this weekend?"

"Angie's dead!" Abby grabbed his arm and held on tightly, her voice quivering. "Steve, these are the police. They're talking to Angie's friends."

Steve? *Steve Thomas?* Carina watched the man's face closely. He matched the description Dean Robertson had given her over the phone. Dark blond hair, blue eyes, late thirties.

His face tightened and he shook his head. "No, dammit!" He looked up to the sky and breathed deeply. "I knew she was playing with fire. I just — oh, Angie." He closed his eyes. He pulled Abby into a hug and she clung on to him.

Carina cleared her throat and Steve let Abby go, but held her to his side. He glared at Will and Carina. "I went to the police on Saturday. I knew no one believed me. Is it true? Is Angie really dead?"

His tone was full of anger and accusation. Carina wondered where it was coming from. One minute he sounded like he was concerned talking to Abby, the next ticked-off. Anyone who could flip a switch that fast had anger close to the surface.

They showed their IDs. "Steve Thomas?" Will asked. "Did you try to file a missing person's report on Saturday?"

"Not that anyone would listen to me. I knew something was wrong, but because she hadn't been missing long enough, the cop said he couldn't do anything." He let out a deep breath. "I'm sorry. What happened? Are you sure it's Angie?"

"Do you have a few minutes to talk?" Will

asked without answering Thomas's questions.

He looked like he was going to refuse, then gave a curt nod.

Carina said, "Let's go to the student union, Mr. Thomas. Unless you would prefer to talk downtown."

"Fine," Thomas said through clenched teeth.

After taking down Abby's contact information, they let her go. Carina planned to talk to her again. Abby knew something.

Now, however, they were faced with a suspect. The overwhelming majority of the time, when a woman was killed it was by her husband, boyfriend, or an ex.

Will led them to a relatively quiet table on the far side of the student union, though with the lunch crowd coming in it was rapidly filling up.

"What happened to Angie?" was Thomas's first question.

"We're waiting for a positive identification of her body, but —"

"So it might not be her!" He started to rise, but Will motioned for him to sit.

"We're certain it's her," said Will. "The rest is just a formality."

Thomas sank back into his chair, his military-straight posture caving. Was his hope that she was alive an act? He sounded genuine, but killers were liars. They could con anyone, often keeping their crimes from their loved ones. Lying to the police was second nature to criminals.

"Where were you Friday night?"

He tensed, sitting up straight. Grief, if that's what it was, turned to hot anger. "I don't fucking *believe* this. I'm the one who told you guys something was wrong!"

Thomas was an explosive pendulum of emotions. Almost as soon as he finished his outburst, he took another deep breath and apologized.

"I'm sorry, I just — I thought I was doing the right thing going to the police, but now you're here talking to me rather than looking for whoever killed Angie."

"Mr. Thomas," Carina said, "I can assure you that regardless of your actions on Saturday, we would have been talking to you eventually. You're Angie's ex-boyfriend and she filed a restraining order against you."

"That was —"

Will interrupted. "Where were you Friday night?"

"When?" Thomas asked through gritted teeth.

"Let's start at dinner and work from there."

"I had dinner with a friend at a Mexican restaurant downtown."

"Does your friend have a name?"

"Yes."

"And?"

"It doesn't have anything to do with Angie's disappearance."

"It would establish an alibi."

"I can't believe this!" he repeated. "I didn't have anything to do with what happened to Angie."

"Did you see Angie Friday night?"

"I saw her at the Sand Shack when she got off work. Around ten. I offered to take her home. She declined. I left."

"You offered to take her home when she has a restraining order against you?" Carina looked at her notes. "According to the order, you are not allowed within a hundred yards of Angie unless you're in class."

"You don't understand."

"Enlighten us."

Thomas didn't say anything for nearly a minute. Trying to think up a lie? Concoct an alibi? Carina sensed that something was off, but she couldn't put her finger on it. "Angie and I broke up over two months ago. We parted friends — ask anyone. Ask Abby. But Angie — She started getting into the party scene. She started seeing this asshole

53

Doug Masterson. I swear, Angie never took drugs until Doug gave her some coke. I confronted Angie, warned her, we got into an argument and, well, I said some things I shouldn't have. Her friend Kayla convinced her to get the restraining order."

"Did you threaten her?"

"No."

"Then why was she scared of you?"

Steve clenched his fists. "She wasn't scared of *me,* she was scared of what I *said.* She just took it out on me."

"What did you say that scared her?"

He paused, looked at his hands, which were clasped tightly in front of him. "It sounds bad, but I wanted her to see that her actions have consequences."

"What did you say?" Carina repeated.

His face reddened as he stared at Carina. Anger? Guilt? Fear? His voice was low. "I told her if she didn't watch herself she'd end up dead."

FOUR

The Sand Shack was across the highway from the beach. A cross between a Hawaiian luau and surfer haven, the outside eating area was larger than the indoor, and there were racks for surfboards, towels, and backpacks. Several people were eating monster-size hamburgers wearing nothing but bathing suits and flip-flops. A half-dozen Web hookups along one wall allowed patrons to surf the Internet after surfing the waves.

When Carina was in college, the Sand Shack had been called Big John's and was one of the last fifties-style soda shops, less casual, but still a hangout for students. She'd have loved a place like the Shack, though she missed the old-fashioned soda fountain and jukebox that only played fifties and sixties bubble-gum rock.

She and Will approached one of the waitstaff, who wore a "uniform" of jeans and red T-shirt with "The Sand Shack" in white across the back. "We need to speak to the owner or manager."

"Sure." He scurried off.

Moments later a man approached. "I'm the manager. Kyle Burns. Can I help you?"

Burns was in his mid-to-late twenties with short sandy brown hair, inquisitive blue eyes, and the body of a weight lifter.

They identified themselves and Will said, "Do you have an office or somewhere private we can talk?"

He frowned, opened his mouth, then closed it and led the way to the back of the restaurant. A small alcove off the large, spotless stainless-steel kitchen served as an office.

Burns glanced at his watch and Carina asked, "Are we keeping you?"

"No, it's okay. I have a class at three. I just came in for the lunchtime rush because my assistant manager didn't show up."

He pulled a sliding pocket door from the jamb and closed them into the office, then sat on the corner of the organized desk. It was a tight fit for the three of them, and Will leaned in a deceptively casual stance against the narrow wall.

"What can I help you with?" Burns asked.

"When was the last time you saw Angela

Vance?" Will asked.

Burns looked from Will to Carina and back to Will. "She's my assistant who didn't show up. Did something happen? Is she okay?"

"Did you see her this weekend?"

Burns's jaw tightened, as if he didn't like that Will hadn't answered his questions. "She worked Friday night and I haven't seen her since."

"Do you have her schedule handy?"

The manager reached over to a swinging file system on the corner of the desk and pulled a folder from near the back. "Here."

Will looked through it while Carina asked, "Do you know if Angie was dating someone? Who her close friends were? If anyone has been giving her problems here at work?"

"She's been seeing this guy Doug Masterson. I told her to watch out for him after I had to kick him out for trying to sell drugs on the premises. I told her he wasn't welcome, and if I found out she let him come in when I was off, I'd fire her. I didn't want to, but this is a clean place. I want to keep it that way." He paused and asked in a voice tinged with worry, "What happened? You wouldn't be here unless something happened to Angie."

Carina answered. "Angie's body was

found on the beach early this morning."

"Her body? You mean she's dead?"

Burns seemed genuinely surprised and hurt by the news. But, as Carina thought while interviewing Steve Thomas, killers were skilled in deception.

"Angie worked Friday night," Will said. "Were you here?"

He nodded. "I close on the weekends. It's busy and I don't like the girls handling the cash at night. I know, that sounds sexist, and I've had more than one girl give me a hard time about it, but I'd rather do the bank drops, you know what I mean?"

"The streets are dangerous," Will agreed, glancing down at the schedule. "It says Angie worked from four to ten."

"Yeah, but she was hanging out with some friends until much later."

"Until when?"

"I'm not sure, but at least midnight. That's when her ex-boyfriend came in and I had to escort him out." He shook his head. "Angie really knows how to pick them. Dammit, I should have talked to her, done something to, hell, I don't know."

A knock on the door interrupted Carina's next question.

Burns leaned over and slid open the door. "What's up?"

A tall, clean-cut teen, probably a college student like most of the employees at the Shack, looked at Carina and Will curiously. "Uh, Kyle, the Pepsi guy's here. He wants you to sign off on the new order."

"Tell him I'll be out in five minutes. Go ahead and put the stock away, I trust you'll make sure everything's there."

The kid nodded, hesitating as if he were going to ask something, then slid the door closed.

"Anything else?" Burns asked.

"You said you escorted Angie's ex-boyfriend out. Do you know his name?"

"Steve Thomas. A couple weeks ago he came in when Angie was on duty and they got into a huge fight, both of them yelling. The next day, Angie tells me she filed a restraining order against him."

"Do you remember what the argument was about?"

"I'm not sure, but the rumors going around were that Steve still had the hots for Angie and lectured her about Masterson. Angie doesn't like being told what to do and who to date, but Steve was right on the money about that low-life Masterson." He sighed and suddenly looked older than what Carina had pegged as twenty-five. "I liked Angie, but the men she dated were all too

59

old for her. Steve has to be nearly forty. Masterson is over thirty. There were at least four or five other guys Angie brought in since she started working here last summer, all of them over thirty." He shook his head, frowning.

"On Friday," Carina asked, "what time did Angie leave?"

"I'm not sure. Probably shortly after I escorted Steve out, which was just after midnight. He wasn't happy, but he didn't give me a bad time."

"What did he say?"

Burns paused, thinking. "I think he said, 'Tell Angie to be careful.' "

Outside, Carina and Will called into dispatch to update the patrol watching Steve's apartment. Carina turned to Will. "Steve Thomas flat-out lied to us. He said ten, Burns says midnight."

"And just put himself at the top of the suspect list."

Maybe he was being paranoid, but he went home during lunch to double check that there was nothing of Angie's left in his room.

There was a smell, something that hadn't been there before. He went to the bathroom, pulled a can of Lysol disinfectant from under the sink, and sprayed it in the bathroom, bedroom, and then everywhere else. Just in case.

He'd made his bed with fresh linens before he left. Now he sat down and looked around. Everything was neat, organized, as it should be.

He reached into his nightstand drawer and pulled out a metal box, about the size of a shoe box, and ran his fingers over the combination lock until it sprang open.

Inside were pictures, a couple small jars, a knife, a few other items that held special importance for him.

And a faded birthday card from his father, still in the envelope postmarked Corcoran Prison.

He didn't look at the card, which was underneath everything else. Instead, he picked up the newest addition to the box, Angie's navel ring.

The first time he'd seen the navel ring he'd been at the Sand Shack and she'd walked in, off-duty, wearing a bikini top and short-shorts. He stared, he couldn't help it. It was like a light was shining on her, a bright light, and everything became clear.

He knew Angie. She and his online fantasy were one and the same.

He didn't need to confirm it, but he did.

Right there. He couldn't wait until he went home. He logged onto a computer — the Shack had several hookups — and went to MyJournal.com. Click, click, click.

There.

The navel ring, one of the "A for Anonymous" pictures, right there next to the journal entry where she described what it was like to give a guy a blow job.

Half the college girls had navel rings, but Angie's was unique. A gold hoop with three hanging charms — a seashell, a leaf, and a rose.

The same as the picture.

But if that wasn't enough to convince him that he *knew* his fantasy girl, she also sported the same rose tattoo on her breast, revealed by her bikini.

Angie was the slut.

He went home, read Angie's online diary again. His fantasies, which had been only that, untouchable, were now in clear focus.

She was meant to be his. It was as if some god had thrown all the pieces to the puzzle in his lap and he'd finally put it together.

Angie was a whore, a slut. Cut from the same cloth as the whore who'd lied about his father. On the surface, Angie was nice, sweet, polite. Almost demure. But in private she revealed her true self, talking about her sexual relations with nearly a dozen men over the last six months.

Fucking hypocrite whore.

And she walked right into his trap. It was obviously meant to be, everything. His plan worked, from setup to execution.

She had walked right up to him, smiled. "I came as soon as I could."

He'd driven to his place. She hadn't even thought to question it. The lie he'd told her was so believable she didn't doubt his sincerity for a minute.

It wasn't until they were inside that he saw a brief look of panic. He gave her a Coke.

Twenty minutes later she was unconscious. When she woke up, she was tied to his bed, her mouth glued shut, naked. His penis grew hard from the vision of Angie so vulnerable, shivering and trying to scream.

He shook his head, clearing the memories. He was going to be late for class. He locked up his treasures and rushed out.

He'd let himself fully remember Angie and his methodical breaking of her spirit later. Tonight. When he could enjoy it.

FIVE

Will and Carina were fifteen minutes late for Angie Vance's autopsy, and Chen had gone ahead and prepped the body.

"What did we miss?" Carina pulled on a smock and latex gloves, though she had no intention of touching the body.

"The next of kin left thirty minutes ago, so you haven't missed much. I just started."

"That was fast," Carina said to Will. "She must have come down right after we left her."

"Wouldn't you?" Will asked her.

Carina hated facing death, but she would want to know with every certainty. She'd need to see the truth with her own eyes.

Chen motioned for them to approach the table. "Something interesting I noticed as soon as I started the visual examination. Someone washed her body before she died." Chen stood at Angie's feet, a laser pen in hand.

"Why?"

"That's your job, not mine. There was soap residue under her arms and in her hair. I sent samples to the lab. But the body was cleaned, no doubt in my mind. From the moisture in her skin I'd say she was wrapped in the bags shortly after the bath."

"Why would he clean the body?" Carina asked, almost to herself. "To get rid of evidence?"

"Very likely," Will said, though Carina's question had been more rhetorical.

"Creepy," she said. "And planned. He held her captive, raped her, kept her under his control for forty-eight hours, then he releases her to wash her before killing? Why not kill her, *then* wash her body? It would be easier. She wouldn't be able to fight back."

"She may have been too weak to fight," Will offered, "or drugged."

Chen said, "We've sent blood samples to the lab and will collect tissue and stomach contents during the exam." He pointed the laser pen at her ankles and then her wrists. "She was restrained with rope, you can see the rope burns on her limbs. I was able to find a couple fibers embedded in her skin that hadn't been washed away. Probably nylon or a cotton fiber, not hemp."

Carina had been avoiding Angie's face, but now that Chen had turned his attention to her mouth, she had to look.

The bandanna had been removed, though threads of it still clung to her lips, which were grotesque, purple and red pulp. Her neck was bruised as well, though it didn't look like hand or finger marks, which would be one sign of possible strangulation. Her open eyes showed burst blood vessels. Not all suffocation deaths showed reticular hemorrhaging, which was why many nursing home or infant murders were deemed natural causes attributed to old age or sudden infant death syndrome. But Angie's death was not peaceful. She had fought for every breath, the evidence of her failure still in her eyes.

"The glue was an industrial-strength superglue of some sort. I've never seen this before in my career. Because the skin is a porous surface, glue would be absorbed in the skin and wouldn't hold its strength for an extended period of time. Because the skin is constantly losing cells, eventually the glue would flake off. But the addition of the bandanna gave the glue something to adhere to."

He directed their attention to the victim's overall appearance. "She hadn't been fed or given fluid in at least forty-eight hours. She has obvious signs of dehydration." The signs weren't obvious to Carina, but she took Chen's word for it. "I'm certain when we get inside I can confirm that. But there're two things that are odd."

Odd? This could get weirder?

Chen directed the laser to her stomach. "Bruising takes several minutes to hours to form depending on the trauma. Bruising is a constantly changing process, the color and size and depth of the injury growing, then shrinking and fading. Her stomach and upper chest appear to have the beginning signs of bruising. Very faint."

"Faint?" Will said. "I can't see anything."

Carina focused on the areas Chen indicated. She'd never have noticed anything unusual until he pointed out the very slight discoloration. "What can cause that?" she asked.

"Any number of things. And it happened around the time of death. Bruising stops after the heart stops beating. Something heavy was placed on her, perhaps to facilitate her death or to keep her body from convulsing."

A horrific thought came to Carina. "Could the killer have laid on top of her?"

"Yes," Chen said, a rare sigh coming from

67

deep in his chest. "It's cases like this that make me think about early retirement," he said quietly, looking at Angie's face.

"What's the second odd thing?"

He pointed the laser at her navel. "She recently had a navel ring ripped out. It had begun to heal, so I'd guess it was removed twenty-four to forty-eight hours before her death."

He turned his attention from the tear in the navel to the two detectives on the other side of the table. "Ready?"

No, Carina thought, but nodded along with Will. They silently observed Chen's meticulous internal examination, his assistant following orders expeditiously.

By the end of the autopsy, they had learned and confirmed several important facts:

Angela Vance had been raped multiple times. There was extensive tearing and deep tissue damage in both orifices, indicating that a sharp, foreign object had penetrated. There was no biological evidence. The killer could have used a condom. If he didn't, that evidence had probably been destroyed or contaminated when he cleaned the body.

Chen collected possible trace evidence, tissue samples, and additional blood samples to send to the lab. He confirmed that she hadn't eaten in at least twelve hours because her stomach was void of food.

Jim Gage joined them halfway through the autopsy and confirmed that Angie had suffocated in the bag. While the tox screen was clean, the additional tissue and blood samples would be sent to the county lab, which could test for a broader array of drugs. Jim also collected hair samples to test for cocaine to determine whether Steve Thomas's accusation that Masterson was feeding her the drug had merit. If she took cocaine more than a week earlier, it wouldn't show up in her blood, but it would show up in her hair follicles.

Not that drug use would prove Masterson was responsible for her death, but they never knew what information was important or incidental until they closed the case.

Time of death was fixed at approximately one a.m. Monday, with an hour window on either side.

"Fucking bastard," Will mumbled as they left the morgue, the bright afternoon sunlight assaulting them when they stepped outside the cool building.

"You can say that again." Jim Gage joined them on the walk back to the police station, though his laboratory was around the corner in the opposite direction.

"By the way," Carina asked Jim, "did you find a navel ring in the evidence collected at the beach? It might look like a regular earring."

"We found no jewelry whatsoever."

"I wonder if the killer kept it," Carina speculated.

"Or it was pulled out in a struggle," Jim suggested. "Dr. Chen is sending over the evidence priority and I'll rush it as best I can. It would help if you get a suspect in custody; my unit has sixteen cases up for trial in the next two months that I need to prioritize."

"We have a suspect," Carina said.

"Come by later, I'll try to give you a better time line."

"Sure."

She thought Jim's comment was odd, since she was always coming by the lab for reports on her cases, but she realized how strange when Jim added, "If you come by after five, maybe we can go out for drinks later."

"Um, okay."

They were outside the main police doors when Jim turned and walked back down the block to the forensics lab. Come by after five? For drinks? Did that mean what she thought it meant? She shook her head. No, they were over the relation-ship thing. They'd broken up nearly two years ago. And he'd never asked her out for drinks or anything social in all that time.

"He wants you back," Will said.

Carina laughed, dismissing Will's com-ment. How did her partner always seem to know what she was thinking?

"No word on Thomas?"

"The patrol says he hasn't come back. I have a BOLO on his car. We'll have another shot at him." A "be on the lookout" was standard procedure when they wanted to talk to a person but not bring them down to the station or into custody.

"Let's find Doug Masterson."

Minor drug offenses and a six-month stint at Descanso for possession of cocaine with intent to sell filled Masterson's rap sheet. He'd been clean — at least, he hadn't been caught — for the last two years.

They had his photo, description, and age — thirty-four.

After checking out his apartment, his place of work, and known hangouts, they came up empty. No one admitted to seeing him since Sunday afternoon, but his neigh-bor, a retiree, said he had taken "his girl" up to the mountains for skiing on Sunday

71

and he didn't expect him back for a couple days.

Carina had showed a picture of Angie to the neighbor. "Is this Masterson's girl?"

"One of them. Not the one he took skiing, though. Don't know her name, she's a new one. He goes through those pretty little things like candy." He grinned, revealing crooked teeth. The smell of cheap alcohol wafted toward the officers. "Yep, Doug has the lookers all over him."

In the car, Carina frowned, made notes. "He could have dumped Angie's body late Sunday night and then left town. But if the neighbor's right, Masterson couldn't have killed Angie."

"Did you smell the booze? I doubt he knows what day of the week it is, let alone what time Masterson left yesterday. *If* it was yesterday." Will picked up the radio and put a BOLO on Masterson.

Carina's money was on Thomas. Means, opportunity, motive. The means was a little difficult right now — where would he have kept her? — but he had no alibi for the time she disappeared, and she had dumped him for another loser. More damning was the fact that he'd lied to them.

"Let's talk to Abby Ivers again," she said. She filled Will in on her theory that Abby was hiding something. "We need to be let in on her little secret, or maybe the phrase *obstruction of justice* will mean something to her."

They found Abby at the apartment she shared with Jodi. The girls had another friend, Kayla Nichols, with them. The three of them had obviously been crying.

Carina wasn't going to leave the room without knowing what Abby had hinted at earlier. But after fifteen minutes of the run-around with all three girls — Abby, Jodi, and wannabe lawyer Kayla — first denying, then saying it wasn't important, then saying Angie would roll over in her grave if she knew they'd told, Carina lost her temper.

She looked each of them in the eye in turn, then focused her steely-eyed gaze on the weakest link, Abby.

"Okay, girls, let me explain something to you. Angie was raped. Then she was suffocated in a garbage bag. *Murdered.* She's dead, and if you don't spill this secret right now, I'm taking you all to jail. You can spend the night in a cold cell and maybe then you'll try to help, not hinder, our investigation."

Kayla jumped up. "We have rights, too!"

"Sit down, Kayla," Carina said. "I can and will arrest you for obstruction of justice.

You will be taken into court tomorrow and the judge will make you tell or you'll be in contempt of court."

Abby interjected, "No one can know."

"If it goes to court, it will damn well be public information," Carina said. "You tell me now, and I promise I will do everything in my power to keep the information private." Carina hoped she could. If it was material to the prosecution, all bets were off. She didn't like to deceive the girls, but finding Angie's killer was more important.

Abby and Jodi looked at each other. Abby burst into tears. Carina rubbed her forehead. She was getting a headache.

Jodi spoke. "Angie, um, she sort of had a double life kind of thing."

Double life kind of thing? Carina and Will exchanged glances.

"Angie dated a lot of guys," Jodi continued. "Some not really publicly. But she journaled about it."

"Journaled? Did she keep the journal at her house? In her purse?" Two officers had been to Angie's house to search her personal effects, but her purse was missing.

Jodi bit her lip. "No, an online journal. You know, MyJournal dotcom. But," she continued quickly, "she was anonymous. *No one* knew about it. I mean, no one would

74

even think that she did the things she wrote about. She's really sweet."

"You mean she made them up?"

Jodi shook her head profusely. "Oh no, it's all true. Well, most of it. I mean, I doubt she ever lied, but I guess she could have sort of exaggerated."

"Anonymous. How did *you* know?"

Abby glanced down sheepishly. "One day she borrowed my computer and after she left I looked at the Web page history because I needed something. There it was. I read the entries and knew it was Angie because she talked about us, but not our real names. Only our first initials. I asked her about it, and she told us everything, swore us to secrecy. It's, um, sort of a sex diary. Her profile was 'A for Anonymous.' "

"Anonymous online," Will said, his voice flat. "Where everyone in the world can read it."

"But no one knew it was her!" Abby exclaimed.

"You're positive she told no one else? What about one of her ex-boyfriends?"

"Oh no, especially not them," Jodi said. "They would have been pissed off. She detailed some of their, um, sexual failings." The three girls giggled, then abruptly stopped as the magnitude of the situation hit them.

Carina lost it. Even after being a cop for eleven years, she'd never be so cavalier about murder.

"Give me the Web page. And I'm putting you all on notice, right now. If my partner or I have any other questions, you will answer them. Got it?"

They sobered completely during Carina's lecture, and Jodi and Abby in particular looked guilty over their behavior. As Abby scribbled something on notebook paper, Jodi said, "I didn't mean to be disrespectful. I loved Angie, like a sister. I guess . . . I can't believe she's *gone.*"

Carina forgave the girls their behavior. They were eighteen and facing the brutal death of a friend. It was going to hit them hard over the next day or two, and grief would set in.

Abby handed Carina the paper: Journalme.iloverealmen.com.

"Two more questions. Do you know Steve Thomas?"

They all nodded.

"Why did Angie get a restraining order against him?"

It was Kayla who spoke up. "He threatened her."

"How?"

"He told her she'd be killed."

"He threatened to kill her?"

Pause. "Not exactly."

"*What* exactly?"

"He said she was being stupid and would get herself killed if she didn't watch her back. But he was so mean about it, and Steve isn't normally a mean guy, so we all figured he was jealous about Doug, and when guys get jealous they do stupid things. So Angie got scared and got the restraining order."

Stupid things? Carina had a few *stupid things* she'd like to point out to the girls, but she refrained. "Tell me about Doug Masterson."

Abby said, "He's hot. And he treats Angie like a princess. At least he used to." She glanced at Jodi.

"Were they still seeing each other?" Carina asked.

"Angie thought he had another girlfriend and planned to confront him, but I don't know if she talked to him or not," Jodi said.

"I don't think she cared all that much, though," Abby said. "I think she was looking seriously at someone else."

"Someone else? Who?"

"I don't know, she never told me. It was just a feeling I had. I mean, I've known her forever. I just sensed it."

Over twelve hours on-duty had taken its toll. Carina was exhausted. But they had one more stop to make: the patrol watching Thomas's apartment radioed that he'd just arrived home.

Will drove and she called the e-crimes unit. Patrick, her little brother, was on-call. Though he was only eleven months younger than Carina, she'd always thought of him as her "little" brother. He was a late bloomer, and her five-foot-eight-inch frame had towered over him until he turned eighteen. In three years he'd grown seven inches and now topped six feet.

He'd always be her little brother, though.

"Hey, Patrick, can you check out an on-line journaling website for me?"

"Shoot." She gave him the information. He whistled softly. "Haven for perverts."

"Sex offenders?"

"I'd bet half the people who hit the My-Journal pages are sex offenders or would-be sex offenders. The other half are naive teenagers and college kids who have no idea who's watching them."

Carina quickly filled him in on her case. "I'll call the mother and tell her someone will be by to pick up the vic's computer."

"I'll send someone out," Patrick said.

"While you're at it, put Steven Thomas on your list, too." She gave him Thomas's address. "I'm going to ask nicely that he hand over his computer. Otherwise, we'll get a warrant. Between the restraining order and not coming clean about his whereabouts Friday night, I think we can get it tonight."

"I'll be waiting for your call. In the meantime, I'll check out — holy shit."

"What?"

"You haven't checked out the victim's journal yet, have you?"

"No."

"Anonymous, sure. But I'd bet my pension that every perv out there was trying to discover her identity. And believe me, it's not as hard as people think."

Six

Steven Thomas didn't look like a killer, but most criminals didn't have "murderer" tattooed across their forehead.

Carina and Will wanted to postpone bringing Thomas formally to the station. Right now, he appeared willing to cooperate. With an easy rapport, they might just give him enough rope to hang himself.

The three of them sat in Thomas's tidy apartment. Had he glued Angie's mouth shut to prevent her from making noise? Kept her here in his bedroom? Hoped to make her see the error of her ways in dating the drug dealer Doug Masterson? Maybe things got out of hand. Maybe she said something that made him angry and that's when he glued her mouth and gagged her. Raped her out of anger and frustration. Rage. Maybe he didn't mean to. Then afterward, he knew he had to kill her.

Murder by suffocation was a step removed, almost impersonal. Most crimes of passion were violent, hands-on affairs done in the heat of the moment. Lots of evidence, blood. Strangulation, stabbings, shootings. Quick and effective. But Angie's killer had imprisoned and tortured her, then put her in a garbage bag and let her die on her own. *Watched* her die as opposed to actively participating in it. If Carina was correct, he'd laid on top of her while she died in the garbage bag. Just one more strange detail in a long list of oddities surrounding this case.

Why hadn't Dillon returned her call yet? Carina was confident he'd have additional insight. Getting into the mind of a killer was his specialty.

"Why did you lie to us about what time you were at the Sand Shack?" she asked Thomas.

"I didn't really *lie*," he said. "I really did go there at ten when she got off to talk to her." He paused. "I just didn't mention that I came back."

"Why?"

"It didn't seem important."

"The manager says that he had to escort you from the premises because of the restraining order."

"I told you I followed Angie." He ran a hand through his short-cropped dark blond

81

hair. "I was worried about her. I told you that," he repeated.

"You followed her when she left the club," Will said.

"Yes, yes, I told you that!" Thomas jumped off the couch and both Carina and Will had their hands on the butts of their firearms. She didn't need to draw, Thomas simply paced. Agitated. Out of guilt? Remorse? Fear?

"Where?"

"I told you. I followed her home. I wanted to make sure she was safe."

A tiny tickle about Angie's mother hearing her late Friday night disturbed Carina. She asked, "Okay, so she got home safe. What time?"

"Nearly one in the morning."

"Then what happened?"

"I left."

"That's it?"

"That's what I said."

"You left, but no one has seen Angie alive since."

"That's why I went to the police on Saturday. But the cop wouldn't do anything about it!"

"We still don't understand why you came in on Saturday — less than twenty-four hours after you allegedly watched Angie walk safely into her house when you weren't supposed to be anywhere near her."

"Because Angie posts to her journal every single day. Two, three times. She never went online Saturday. I was worried, so I went by her house. Her grandmother said she wasn't there."

"You knew about her online journal."

Thomas had no comment.

"Mr. Thomas, we can get a warrant to seize your computer and ISP records. It would benefit you to tell us the truth."

He leaned against the counter that separated the living area from the kitchen. "Yes, I knew about her journal. That's the real reason she got the restraining order," he admitted.

"Why?"

"She was afraid I'd be mad at her. Look, have you seen it? She's calling attention to herself. I found out about it by accident. She was posting something at the college library and I walked up behind her. She flipped out, first scared and then angry. That's what we'd been fighting about when that little bitch Kayla convinced her I was a threat. I wasn't a threat to Angie. I care about her. A lot. I never wanted anything bad to happen to her, but she was playing with fire. First Doug, then the journal."

"Was there anything embarrassing about your relationship with her in the journal?"

He paused, averted his eyes. "I don't know. I didn't read everything."

Lying again. Now Carina really wanted to read the journal.

"Would you object to a crime technician searching your apartment and borrowing your computer?"

"I'm a suspect." He said it flatly.

Carina was treading on dangerous territory. She couldn't admit he was a suspect without Mirandizing him. She didn't want to go there, not yet. They wanted his cooperation first.

Then she'd nail him to the wall.

"All we want is to verify your story," Will said. "If you're not lying to us, we have no reason to suspect you. Do we?"

"Fine. Whatever you want. I didn't kill Angie. You should be out there doing your job, finding Angie's killer, not wasting time with me."

He stared at Angie's picture, his fingers caressing the screen. So beautiful . . .

Like all beautiful girls, she knew how to play the game, made all the right noises. But in the end, she was like all of them, nothing but a liar.

Angie was beautiful, but she was a fucking liar and she deserved everything she'd gotten. *Everything.*

He missed her. She'd been nice to him, sometimes. But other times she had shown her true self, just like every whore out there.

He could still hear his mother.

"My poor baby."

He was far from a baby, but he could never contradict his mother.

Her speech had always been the same. "I know how hard it is for young men these days. Girls showing their tits to everyone, getting you all hard and aching and there's nothing you can do. They do it on purpose, you know. To get you to do something stupid. They spread their legs and tell you to fuck them. Then they start crying and scream rape. Don't fall into their trap. Don't listen to their lies."

"I don't, Mama," he always said. "I don't even look."

"Don't lie to me. Men look. All of 'em want to fuck every bitch that crosses their path. Isn't that why your daddy got into so much trouble? The whores. He was weak. He fell under their spell. Like those women of myth. What are they called?"

"The Sirens."

"Exactly! Sexpots, luring men. Sirens."

She seemed proud of him somehow, in a way he never understood. "You're a smart one, aren't you? Smart enough to stay away from the Sirens. If only your father had listened to me."

He ached. He wanted to talk to his father so bad. Dad would understand. The feelings. The darkness.

His father had been a great man. Great but weak, Mama said.

"Don't you be a weak man. Don't give in to those harlots. They only want to torment you with their titties and their twats. Don't touch or they'll cry rape so fast you'll be in prison before you know it. Sluts, all of them."

He would never be weak.

And when he touched them, they would never cry rape.

Angie would never say another word.

He locked the door, slid the deadbolt. Closed all the curtains. Double checked the doors and windows and curtains. Better safe. And then, only when he was certain no one could walk in, he brought the box of tapes to his bedroom. Shut and locked that door, too.

The tapes had been his father's. He'd seen his father with them before, though he'd not known what was on them until after his father disappeared. Left without a good-bye. He'd only been a kid then, and he'd had a lot of time to think about it.

The Sirens.

They'd lured him away, made him desert his family, his sons.

He used to sit in his daddy's closet just to smell him. Remember him and wish for something . . . more. He never knew exactly what, but he knew if his dad would come back everything would be different, better. Over time the Dad scent faded. Then they moved, and everything about his father was gone. He'd grown up and the memories became fuzzy, so he thought hard, trying to bring them back. He wasn't certain all his memories were true, but they comforted him, so he kept them close.

The tapes had been in his daddy's closet. Five of them in a shoe box, far in the corner, buried under boxes his mother had packed when his father hadn't returned.

Each tape was fifteen to twenty minutes long. Dark and fuzzy, old, colorless. But he knew what was going on. He knew what the faceless man in the picture was doing.

Head buzzing, he turned off all the lights except the desk lamp, which cast long shadows across his immaculate room. Took off all his clothes. He was hard with anticipation, his penis quivering. He stared at himself, picturing how he'd looked in the mirror at the head of his bed when he slid into Angie's body.

He'd come immediately, the excitement overtaking him.

The second time he'd forced himself in her he couldn't come. Angry, he didn't know why. But it wasn't the same. So he took a beer bottle and shoved it up her cunt. Her body arched; her vocal cords strained in her neck. He watched her neck, enthralled, the faint scream deep in her chest turning him on like fucking her hadn't.

He came.

Licking his lips, sweating, he slid the tape into the VCR.

The woman was naked on a bare dirty mattress. Because the film was black and white, he didn't know if the stains were dirt, urine, or blood. Her hands tied to the headboard. Tears on her face. Her mouth opened.

He heard no scream because the tape was soundless, but he saw her body jerk, fighting the restraints, her throat tense, revealing the bones in her slender neck.

A man came partially into view, his face obscured by the shadows. He might have been thirty, a little older. He wore a dark

T-shirt, no pants. His penis stood out in front of him. He fucked her. His hands went around her neck.

Fixated on the tape, he pulled at his own penis harder. Harder, to the point of pain, and still he couldn't climax. It used to be so easy, but after having Angie all to himself, after watching her die, reality was so much better than the old, worn tape.

Next time he'd fuck her with his hands on her neck. Maybe then it would last longer. He'd already bought the plastic wrap, a thin layer of protection.

He reached over to the computer and started a slide show he'd made with his digital camera and downloaded onto his hard drive. Pictures of Angie on his bed. No sound necessary because her face of fear was all he needed. Her eyes. Her body straining. The vocal cords on her neck stretched taut.

Just like the tape.

But his masterpiece was better, much better, than the cheap, grainy, black-and-white film — everything he wanted to see in vivid color. The fear, the blood, the sweat on her face. Each still shot gave him what he needed. The slide show he'd created went faster and faster until the best part, when his back was in view, and his dick stuck out, and he slid the condom on and fucked her. Just like the movie. At last, he came.

He closed his eyes, panting. His hands reached for the navel ring in his own abdomen. The thrill that he had something of Angie's in him began to diminish. Tears fell, but he didn't feel them.

Why didn't you kill her, Daddy? If you'd killed the bitch, she wouldn't have called the cops and had you taken away.

Five years had seemed like forever, but it really wasn't.

Only death was forever.

SEVEN

Nick Thomas sat uncomfortably in his wooden desk chair, rubbing his sore knee. He slipped on reading glasses and read the reports stacked precariously high on his desk.

He'd never before let the paperwork get this far out of hand. What a difference a year makes.

He watched the deputies outside his office window as shifts changed. The casual glances in his direction. The concerned look on the faces of some; the wariness on the faces of others. He'd been back on the job seven months, but no one had forgotten what had happened last May. Nick found himself glancing at the calendar more often now, as the anniversary of the Butcher's last hunt approached.

The Butcher wasn't the only reason he kept looking at the calendar. Three weeks from tomorrow was the deadline to file for reelection, and he still hadn't made his decision.

Frankly, he had no right to be sheriff. He should have resigned after he screwed up and lived to talk about it.

He didn't think he could do it. Not again. He'd screwed up, and his error of judgment had not only almost cost him his life, but the lives of citizens he had been sworn to protect.

At the same time, he'd learned about both himself and the nature of violence in a way that could only benefit him as a sworn officer. He was torn. Though none of his relatives had ever been in law enforcement, being a cop seemed to be ingrained in him. He didn't know how to do anything else.

Pulling his hand from his aching knee, he picked up a pen and signed reports, barely giving them the attention they deserved. Damn knee. He'd tossed out the painkillers as soon as he'd left the hospital last year, hating the ethereal feeling the medication gave him. He dealt with the pain. To remember? As punishment? Whatever, he preferred the pain to the vagueness that came over him when on medication.

One day at a time.

His phone rang, startling him. It was his private line. Few people called on it. Glancing at the clock, he saw that more than an hour had passed since he'd sat down. Had he really been staring at the same piece of paper for an hour? What was wrong with him?

He grabbed the receiver. "Sheriff Thomas."

"Nicky, it's Steve."

His brother. He hadn't talked to Steve in months. The last time they had had a real conversation had been just after Nick had been released from the hospital last summer. Nick had swallowed his pride and asked Steve if he had a couple weeks to come up and help. Steve had declined. He was taking summer classes at the university. When he offered to come up for a weekend, Nick said no. He hadn't wanted to entertain his brother, he had wanted someone to talk to.

He'd ended up dealing with the aftermath of the Bozeman Butcher alone, and maybe that had been for the best.

"Nick? You there?"

"Yeah. What's up?"

"Well, I need some help."

Steve? The Desert Storm war hero and savior of an entire school of Kuwaiti children asking for help? Steve, his brother who never asked for anything since he could do everything himself?

"You need *my* help?"

"The police have been here. They think I killed someone."

Nick didn't say anything, couldn't say anything. Steve? A murderer? Impossible.

"Nick?"

"What happened?" Nick asked.

"My ex-girlfriend was murdered. The police talked to me twice already, and they're coming tomorrow to take my computer and search my apartment."

"Do they have a warrant?"

"I didn't do it! I told them to take anything they want. If it helps them to find Angie's killer —"

"What did your attorney say?"

"Didn't you hear me? I said I'm innocent. I don't have an attorney. I don't need an attorney."

Nick closed his eyes. "Steve, call an attorney. Have someone present when the police arrive tomorrow to take possession of your computer. It's your right."

"I did call someone. I called you."

"I'm not a lawyer, Steve."

"I need your help. Please. The cops think I did it. They haven't arrested me, they don't have anything on me, but I can tell by the way they look at me that they think I killed Angie."

Nick rested his forehead on his palm, unsuccessfully trying to squeeze the tension from his growing headache. If the police thought Steve was guilty, there had to be some evidence to back it up.

Dammit, Steve, what have you gotten yourself into?

"Where are you now?"

"My apartment."

"Get an attorney."

"If I get an attorney, they'll think I'm guilty."

Nick said slowly, "They think you're guilty now."

Silence. Then, "Nicky, I really need your help."

"What aren't you telling me?"

Steve didn't say anything for a long minute, then: "Angie had a restraining order against me. It didn't mean anything," Steve continued quickly. "Really, she was just mad at me because I told her to be careful because she was hanging out with the wrong people, putting too much personal information online."

"I don't understand. People don't get restraining orders for no reason."

"Look, I just need you, okay? If you can't help me, I don't know who to go to. Please come. I don't have anyone else."

Nick found himself listening to a dial tone.

Slowly, he replaced the receiver. Steve suspected of murder. It didn't make sense. Nick couldn't see Steve killing a woman because she jilted him.

Nothing that Steve had said made much sense to Nick. His ex-girlfriend got a restraining order against him, then ends up dead. Yeah, if he were investigating the case, Steve would be at the top of the list of suspects. Maybe that's all this was, the detectives looking at the most likely suspect — ex-boyfriend. As soon as they cleared him, they could track down other ex-boyfriends, friends, colleagues.

Still, Nick really had no choice but to go to San Diego and do everything he could to help Steve. Isn't that what brothers do? Stand by each other?

These last few years they'd grown apart, living more than a thousand miles from each other, but now Steve had asked for help, and Nick would do anything he could.

He called in Deputy Lance Booker. Last year, during the Butcher investigation, Booker had been an overeager rookie. Today he was a solid cop. Violence and murder did that to you. Proved what you were made of. Or proved what you lacked.

"I have a family emergency," he told Booker. "I'm authorizing you to take over as acting sheriff until I return."

Booker looked surprised, but didn't say anything. Nick was breaking protocol, though he hardly cared at this point.

"If Sam Harris gives you shit, don't take it. I'm telling everyone you're in charge. You have my cell phone and pager if you need me."

"Yes, sir."

Though as undersheriff, Sam Harris was second in command, the sheriff had the authority to appoint *any* deputy as acting sheriff in his absence. Harris had taken over when Nick disappeared last year and had played the press and the politicians into thinking that he'd single-handedly stopped the Butcher instead of jeopardizing the investigation.

Nick wasn't about to give him that control again.

Nine months ago he'd faced a serial killer and lived, no thanks to Sam Harris.

For thirteen years, a killer had terrorized the college town of Bozeman, Montana. The Bozeman Butcher — as the press had dubbed him — kidnapped, raped, and tortured college women. But if that wasn't enough, he released them naked in the woods to hunt them down like animals. Twenty-two women, dead.

Last year after the Butcher struck again, Nick called in the FBI and together they worked the case, getting closer to identifying the Butcher. But Nick couldn't claim credit for ending the Butcher's reign of terror. Instead, he'd made a huge error in judgment and ended up being held captive. He'd needed to be rescued instead of doing the rescuing.

That was all water under the bridge, of course. The Butcher was dead, his victims avenged, and Montana State University, where the depraved killer had found most of his victims, was back to normal. But Nick's concussion and subsequent infection from being held captive had weakened him to the point where he wondered if he could ever again be an effective cop.

The doctors said it was his joints — the ligaments swelled with use and put pressure on the joints that had been ravaged by infection. A type of arthritis. Surgery might help. Nick had an operation three months after the attack, yet he still wasn't the man he'd been nine months ago.

Nick didn't see any other option but going through surgery and rigorous physical therapy again, even against the odds. He couldn't live like this forever. But his doctor, whom he trusted, insisted that he had to wait at least another month before repeating the surgery. Usually, patience was Nick's strong suit. Not now, not with the chance of regaining full mobility within reach.

"There are no guarantees, Sheriff," his doctor had told him during his last check-up.

"There never are," he'd replied.

But if he wasn't able to regain his strength, could he hand the reins of the sheriff's department to a man who had so blatantly abused his power? Harris was dangerous and the last person Nick wanted to see as sheriff, but Nick wasn't sure he was up for an election battle.

Not only wasn't he confident of victory, he didn't know if he wanted to win.

EIGHT

"Let's check out that journal site Abby gave us."

It was almost noon. Carina and Will had spent the entire morning talking again to Angie's mother and grandmother, then hitting the university and speaking with her academic advisor, stopping by the Sand Shack to interview employees about Angie and her relationship with both Steve Thomas and Doug Masterson, then finally spending two hours unsuccessfully trying to track down Masterson's current whereabouts.

They learned Angie had a 4.0 GPA, everyone liked her, she worked hard at the Shack, no one had seen her use drugs, and no one admitted knowing about her online journal.

Steve Thomas was seen as a "nice guy." Doug Masterson elicited stronger reactions. People either liked him a lot, or thought he was creepy.

Now they finally had time to read Angie's online journal while waiting until Patrick Kincaid in e-crimes and Jim Gage in forensics were able to break free and join them at Steve Thomas's apartment.

Thomas's cooperation was definitely a plus at this point, which made Carina wonder if he was really innocent or just playing them. She opted for playing them. If he had killed Angie, it hadn't been in his apartment. Otherwise he'd never let them inside. If he'd tracked her online, it hadn't been on his computer, or he wouldn't be so free to give them access to it. Unless of course he was a total idiot, which Carina didn't rule out. Many criminals thought the police wouldn't figure it out. Fortunately, the cops were usually smarter than the criminals. It was just a matter of time, patience, and asking the right questions.

Will sat on the edge of Carina's desk while she logged onto the Internet and brought up Angie's MyJournal page.

At first, nothing jumped out at them. On the right was an avatar, a photo icon of something brownish that Carina couldn't make out. She leaned closer.

"Will, tell me I'm wrong."

"You're not."

"Damn." The avatar, which was Angie's personal calling card in cyberspace, was a close-up of a nipple.

"Think it's hers?"

"Read the text."

They stared at the computer. Carina didn't consider herself a prude, but the sexual content in Angie's journal was detailed enough to make a sailor blush. And glancing at Will, she saw that he was equally uncomfortable.

The last entry was dated February 10, the day before she disappeared.

> This morning I woke up horny. You know how it is, you have this great sexy dream with a couple guys and then the damn alarm rings and you just know the vibrator isn't going to satisfy. So I went over to T.S. He's on my way to class, he always wakes up with a rock-hard dick, and he never says no.

She went on to describe exactly what "T.S." did to her in great detail.

"Holy shit," Will muttered. "What was she thinking?"

Carina shook her head.

They skimmed the journal entries. Every entry had dozens, even hundreds of comments. Most from men posting lewd pictures of themselves.

> You're so hot, come over to my place.
> I'll show you what rock hard really means.
> I'll fuck you like you've never been fucked before.

"Winners, all of them," Carina said irritably. "And she thought this was fun?"

"Young and stupid," Will said.

Angie Vance, straight-A student, had been playing a dangerous game that may have gotten her killed. Any number of sexual deviants could have been after her, men who thought she'd be into whatever sick fantasy they had. What if one of these men had tracked her down? What if she'd said no? Would that have set him off, knowing she'd slept with all these other guys, why not him? Would he then have stalked her, kidnapped her, killed her?

They skimmed the entries for any comments related to Steve Thomas or Doug Masterson. They found several entries they believed referred to each of them.

On Monday, she wrote:

> D.M. is cheating on me. I suppose it

shouldn't bother me, but I've been faithful to him since we started sleeping together. How do I know? The smell of sex. I know what D.M.'s bed smells like after I've fucked him. I went over last night without calling and the scent wasn't mine.

Was that why my mother kicked my father out of the house? She came home and smelled another woman?

Well, all bets are off. If he can screw around, so can I. I sometimes wish things didn't end the way they had with S.T. because he's exactly what I need right now. D.M. was rough and tumble, a hard, fast fuck that made me scream. S.T. was slow and easy, patient, like a tightening spiral until I quietly exploded.

Sometimes a girl needs to be fucked. Sometimes a girl needs to be loved.

"Sometimes," Carina mumbled, "a girl needs a good shrink."

Will looked at his notes. "Mrs. Vance said Angie's father left them when she was a toddler. Think she's looking for a surrogate daddy?"

"Hell if I know, but I have friends without a dad in their lives, and they don't sleep with multiple partners twice their age."

Farther down the journal they found this

interesting entry:

January 19. Okay you jerks out there.
You know who you are. Let me tell you
what it is. If you think you can scare me
into needing your protection, you have
another think coming. S.T. this means
YOU. I don't need you and I don't want
you. Stay away from me because it's all in
your head, got it?

The restraining order was dated January
20.

"It sounds like she knew Steve was reading her journal, presuming he's 'S.T.,' "
Carina said.

Will pointed to the screen. *Photos.* "Click
there, Carina."

She did and immediately thought they'd
accidentally hit a porn website.

Under the heading "Dicks I've Loved"
were close-up pictures of male genitals in
various states of arousal.

Under the heading "Me, Myself, and I"
were close-up pictures of the female
anatomy. No face shots, but there was no
doubt as to what the pictures were.

One picture stood out. Angie's breasts,
pushed close together by her hands. The
red rose tattoo on the top of the left breast

matched the tattoo on her dead body.

Carina turned away, surprised at her anger and deep sadness. She wanted to throttle Angie, yell at her, ask her what in the world was she thinking? But Angie was dead at eighteen with no chance of learning from her mistakes.

"Excuse me, Detectives."

Carina faced Sergeant Fields.

Sergeant Fields glanced at the screen and paled. He had a sixteen-year-old daughter. "The vic?"

"Yeah."

"Shit, my daughter has a MyJournal page. Just for her friends, but . . . I think I need to have a talk with her. Make sure she's being safe."

"Talk to Patrick and you'll learn there's no way to be a hundred percent safe," Carina said.

"No way to be safe in anything these days," Fields said. "I just don't understand why a smart, pretty girl like the vic would put stuff like that out for every scumbag to see."

"They think it's a joke, or fun," Carina said, still unnerved by what they'd discovered. It wasn't that she was naive, she knew what people did online, in chat rooms, the child predators, the pornography. It was making the connection between Angie Vance, dead; Angie Vance, alive; and Angie Vance's wild and reckless lifestyle. Her supposedly *secret* lifestyle.

Carina's thoughts instantly brought down a veil of guilt. Angie hadn't deserved what happened to her. Irresponsible, yes; but she was practically a kid, dammit, and she shouldn't have had to suffer violence any more than any other woman who walked the streets of San Diego, saint or sinner.

"What's up, Sarge?" she asked Fields.

He flipped open his notepad. "Daniels called to say that Thomas arrived home a few minutes ago. Diaz reported that he talked to Masterson's employer and he took a week's vacation at the last minute. Called in Sunday saying he needed the time. Guy's ready to fire him, he does this all the time. And for Hooper," he handed over a note, "Deputy District Attorney Chandler said your presence will be required in court — that would be the San Francisco Appeals Court — Friday eight a.m."

"Aw, shit," Will muttered. "Sorry, Kincaid. It's that damn Theodore Glenn appeal. I swear, that guy should have been put out of my misery years ago."

Theodore Glenn had killed four female strippers six years ago, before Carina and

Will had been partners.

"I'll be fine for the day," Carina said.

"You can have Diaz if you need him," the Sarge offered.

"Thanks, I might take you up on that."

Nick arrived in San Diego after the lunch hour and rented a car. He hadn't visited Steve in years, since before he was elected sheriff nearly four years ago, but remembered the location of his beachfront apartment.

A crime scene van was parked in front of the building, plus two marked cars and a sedan Nick pegged as unmarked police issue. Detectives.

He didn't feel comfortable going into an unknown situation, but knowing Steve, he hadn't called an attorney. Why is it that the innocent think they don't need a lawyer? Truth is, even those with nothing to hide need someone to protect their rights.

His right knee protested when he stepped out of the car, but he hadn't been on his feet much today so his joints weren't unbearably sore. He leaned back into the car to retrieve his Stetson and put it on his head, then walked up the single flight of stairs to Steve's apartment.

The door was open and Nick stopped just

across the threshold.

An attractive female plainclothes cop approached him. Five-foot-eight, one-forty, muscle where there should be muscle, and softness where there should be softness. She carried her primary gun in a side holster, but a slight bulge at her back showed a secondary firearm. Nick liked women who knew how to pack.

Her dark, sun-streaked hair was pulled into a loose French braid, and fathomless brown eyes sized him up quickly. Nick could tell she was a cop by her eyes — they took in everything about him all at once, just like he did her.

"Can I help you?" Her tone was polite, her body alert.

"Yes, ma'am. Steve Thomas, please." He took his hat off and held it at his side.

"Your business with him?"

"Personal."

The subtle change from professional curiosity to frustration on the pretty detective's face would have intrigued Nick if he weren't concerned about Steve.

"Can I see your ID, please?"

"My ID?" He raised an eyebrow, reaching for his wallet.

Her eyes instantly darted to his waist and he realized just a second too late that he should have identified himself as a cop immediately.

"Put your hands up." Her gun was out. Fast. He would have been impressed if he weren't so irritated at having a gun aimed at his chest. "Hooper," she called without taking her eyes off his.

"Hey!"

Nick recognized Steve's voice. He emerged from the bedroom. "Stand back, Mr. Thomas," the detective said without looking at Steve.

"He's my brother. He's a cop."

Cautious belief crossed her face, and her partner, Hooper, approached.

"Left back pocket," Nick told him, his hands still up.

"You're a cop?" Hooper asked as he disarmed him and pulled his identification.

"Yes."

Hooper opened his identification. "Nicholas P. Thomas, Sheriff, Gallatin County, Montana."

The female detective holstered her weapon. "Next time identify yourself," she snapped.

Hooper returned his gun and ID, extended his hand, and smiled amicably. "Will Hooper, Homicide. Quick-draw McGraw is my partner, Carina Kincaid. You'll have to excuse her temper — she has both Irish and Cuban blood in her veins."

Nick grinned as he shook Hooper's hand. "Nick Thomas."

Carina Kincaid glared at him. "Montana? San Diego is a wee bit out of your jurisdiction, isn't it?"

"A bit," he said.

"Care to share your interest in our investigation?" she asked pointedly.

"You know, Ms. Kincaid," Nick said with his best Montana drawl, "my mama always said you catch more flies with honey." He winked. For a second he thought she was going to throw a fit, then she relaxed, a half-smile turning up her lips.

Steve came over, clapped him on the back. "It's good to see you, bro."

"Let's talk outside." Nick motioned to the landing. He turned back to Carina. "If that's all right with you, ma'am."

She waved him off, shaking her head. But she wasn't stupid. He saw her motion to one of the uniforms to keep an eye on Steve.

He walked Steve down to the far end of the landing to prevent the police from eavesdropping, intentionally or otherwise. The uniform tasked with babysitting stood outside the door, within eyesight, but not earshot.

"Thanks for coming, Nick, really. I owe you big-time."

"You don't owe me anything." Nick had a million questions for his brother, but he started broad. "Tell me everything you know."

"Not much." Steve looked out onto the beachfront highway.

"Do they have a warrant?"

"No, I told them they could come in and look."

"Just look? I saw a crime tech packing up your computer."

"I'm innocent. I told them they could have anything they needed. Once they stop looking at me, they'll start looking for the real killer."

"You let them in without a warrant? They haven't arrested you, correct?"

"No, because they don't have anything on me. I didn't kill Angie, Nick. I swear. I wouldn't hurt her."

"Why do they suspect you?"

"I dated her. She got a stupid idea in her head and got this restraining order against me. It looks bad, but it really wasn't."

"People don't file for restraining orders for no reason, Steve."

"She was mad at me after we had an argument."

Nick frowned. Steve sounded like a petulant kid, not a grown man. "What kind of argument?"

Steve didn't say anything for a long minute. Nick found himself studying Steve as if he were a perp. He shifted uncomfortably, not enjoying the position of thinking his brother, his older brother, his sainted brother, was a possible murderer. Steve wasn't capable of it.

Was he?

Nick had a flash of a memory, the kind that comes and goes quickly but where you remember every detail. Steve had been eleven, he'd been eight. They'd been coming home in the rain late one afternoon, certain their mom would skin them alive. She'd warned them about the weather, said it would rain, but they'd believed the blue skies — what they saw with their eyes — instead of the four decades of wisdom packaged in their mom.

Nick could almost feel the cold rain on his face.

A car skidded around the corner, splashing them. Steve swore, using words only their father said in frustration or anger. If Mom was around, she would have washed his mouth out with soap.

Nick had said the f-word once. One taste

of Ivory soap cured him forever. To this day, he'd never bought Ivory soap — he still smelled it, tasted it.

They started jogging as their wet clothes made them shiver.

A movement in the bushes as they rounded the corner had made Nick stop.

"What?" Steve asked.

"What was that?"

"I didn't see anything."

Nick looked around carefully. He had seen . . . something. What was it? A cat? A squirrel?

"Nick, it's cold and Mom is going to go through the roof when she sees us. Let's get home."

Nick didn't say anything. He approached the roadside shrubbery cautiously. Parted the branches.

It was Belle. Belle the Beagle, Mrs. Racine's dog. Mrs. Racine lived on the corner, down the street from the Thomas house. She'd never have let Belle out in the front yard, but the dog was notorious for digging under his pen. Nick and Steve had brought her home on many occasions. Twice the dog had followed them to school. She was annoying in her eagerness to please everyone.

Now, Belle lay on the side of the road, dying.

For a minute, Nick and Steve stood there stunned. Stared at the bloodied animal. One leg was completely smashed. The other obscenely crooked. Her pant was rapid and shallow, her little tongue hanging out. She only had one working eye; the other was so covered in blood and dirt that Nick wasn't sure it was even there.

The brothers knelt in the mud and Steve gathered Belle into his arms.

"We need to take her to the vet," Nick said, his voice shaking with barely restrained sobs.

"She's not going to live, Nick." Steve looked at him, his own eyes bright with tears. "Who would do this to her? How could somebody be so cruel?"

Though Nick was the younger brother, he found himself consoling Steve. They sat on the ground, their jeans soaked with mud and water and now the blood of a little dog who had never hurt anyone but lay dying in their laps. Silently, they petted the animal. It seemed like forever, but only minutes passed before Belle succumbed to her injuries.

Steve carried Belle the two blocks to Mrs. Racine's house. Tears sliding down their cheeks, they silently handed the dead dog to the old woman. She broke down sobbing.

"Nick? Earth to Nick?"

Nick shook his head, looked at his brother, saw the pain of a young boy who comforted a broken dog until she died. The Steve Nick had known could never have killed a woman. He couldn't picture it, couldn't even think it.

But was his judgment impaired? Did he see only the good in Steve? Was there a streak of evil, of vengeance, of anger? Hidden until something set him off? Would he recognize a killer in his own brother?

"You didn't hear a word I said." Steve was irritated.

Nick pulled up the words he'd heard in the back of his mind. "You argued with Angie about a guy she was dating."

"A *drug dealer* she was dating."

"You think her murder is related to this guy?"

"*Masterson,*" Steve spit out. "I don't know. I can't imagine who would hurt Angie."

"But the police think you did it."

Nick could see why. Ex-boyfriend, restraining order, claimed to be home — alone — at the time of the murder. Oh, yeah, Nick would be all over Steve, too.

"How was she killed?" he asked.

"I don't exactly know. The police didn't say much, and the newspaper was short on

116

details — she was apparently suffocated."

"Suffocated?" Nick glanced at the door of Steve's apartment and saw Carina Kincaid standing next to the uniform, her face blank, her eyes watchful. "Let me see what I can find out. Why don't you go for a walk? Give me a few minutes with the detectives."

Steve noticeably relaxed. "Thanks, Nick. Really, I appreciate your coming down here and helping." He paused. "You up for it?"

Steve was referring to his health. "I'm fine," he said automatically.

Out of the corner of his eye, he watched the detective follow Steve's path down the stairs and around the apartment building until she could no longer see him. Her eyes then fixed on him. He approached her; she met him halfway.

"Detective Kincaid," he said with a nod, extending his hand.

"Sheriff." She shook his offered hand firmly, her skin soft except for pronounced calluses on her fingers — from time at the gun range. Her sharp, dark eyes didn't miss anything.

"Call me Nick."

"Thanks. I'm Carina. Sorry about what happened in the apartment."

"You followed your instincts."

"You didn't look like a threat. I just saw

117

the gun and . . ." She shrugged and gave him a self-deprecating grin, making what could have been an awkward situation comfortable.

"What are you looking for?" He nodded toward the apartment.

"Your brother offered to let us come in and check out his computer."

"You didn't answer my question."

"Your brother made some statements about how much time he spent reading the victim's online journal. We want to verify the information."

"What happened?"

"What did your brother tell you?"

"That his ex-girlfriend was murdered — suffocated — and she had filed a restraining order against him a few weeks ago because they'd had an argument."

Carina nodded. "A restraining order that your brother repeatedly violated, including the night Angie Vance disappeared."

"What about her current boyfriend?" asked Nick.

"He's out of town and we have a BOLO on him."

Nick raised his eyebrow. "Her current boyfriend has conveniently left town? Before or after the murder?"

"I can't discuss the details of the investigation with you, Sheriff. I'm talking to you as a law enforcement courtesy, but you have no authority here." While her tone was cordial, she was trying to shut the investigative door in his face.

Okay, play nice and she'll give up more, Nick thought. "What happened to the victim? Steve didn't know the details."

Carina mumbled something, sounded like a sarcastic *that's what he says* in Spanish, but she spoke so fast Nick wasn't quite sure he caught every word. But the tone and attitude were clear: she believed his brother was guilty.

"The victim was raped and suffocated in a triple layering of garbage bags, then left on a public beach. She was found early yesterday morning."

Raped.

Nick pushed back the memories that threatened to return. They usually stayed at bay until he was alone, but the faint echo of a scream reverberated in his head. He was acutely aware of Carina watching him. He swallowed and said, "Any similar crimes?"

She stared at him. "I know how to do my job, Sheriff."

"I wasn't implying that you didn't. I was just asking a question."

She paused, assessing him. Whatever she

saw, she must have deemed him trustworthy enough to share some tidbits. "Nothing in the area, but we've tapped into the FBI database to see if there's a hit. I'm covering all the bases. I'm going to catch Angie's killer."

"Was there any unusual damage to the victim's body? Something not related to her manner of death or rape? Something that might point to a repeat offender?"

"You're suggesting serial killer."

He gave a short nod.

She looked like she wanted to say more but stopped herself. "We're looking into all possibilities, like I said."

So there *was* something else. Probably a very specific mutilation, perhaps a message on or near the body. Something that only the killer would know about.

Nick assessed Carina Kincaid as a competent, focused detective who wanted to catch the killer because that was her job. Maybe if he understood her better, learned why she'd become a cop, if he could get her to trust him. Perhaps they could find a way to work together.

Some cops did it for the job, some for the power, but more often than not, Nick had learned that most people became cops for one of two reasons: family on the job, or because they had a personal reason for seeking justice.

Carina's partner exited Steve's apartment and walked over to them.

"We got what we need?" Carina asked.

"More or less," Hooper said. "Patrick's in there writing out a tag so we can take the computer."

Nick's instincts buzzed. "Why?"

"We need to spend more time on the machine. To verify your brother's statement."

They wouldn't take the machine unless they'd found something either incriminating or that contradicted what Steve had told them earlier.

"You don't have a warrant," Nick said cautiously. The best avenue would be to befriend the detectives; barring that, he had to protect his brother.

But so help him, if Steve was guilty . . . no. He wasn't a rapist. Not the kid who cried over a dying dog. Not the man who earned two congressional medals during Desert Storm. His brother, who'd always been there for Nick growing up, protected him against bullies because he'd been a runt until he hit puberty.

"Are you going to make this difficult? We can get a warrant," Carina said. "Your

121

brother is cooperating because he says he wants to help."

"I want information."

"You are not only out of your jurisdiction, you are related to our prime —" she caught herself, "a potential witness."

"I have experience in these types of cases," Nick said.

"What type would that be?"

"Serial killers."

Hooper interjected, "I think it's in the best interest of your brother that we do everything by the book."

"It's in the best interest of justice to do everything to stop this killer," Nick said. "I know my brother and he's not a rapist."

They assessed him, skeptical. Neither trusted him, but what did he expect?

"If Steve is guilty," he said, "I'll be the one to throw away the key. Blood is thick, but not thick enough to protect a killer."

Carina said, "I'd suggest that you find out *exactly* what your brother was doing every minute of Friday night and early Saturday morning, and find out exactly what he read on Angie's Vance's not-so-anonymous on-line journal. Maybe if we get the truth, we can stop wasting time looking at him.

"But," she continued, "your brother hasn't been completely honest with us, and that only adds to our suspicions."

"I'll find the truth."

"And if you don't like it?"

"You can arrest him."

NINE

Nick found Steve sitting on the beach watching the waves come in.

It was late afternoon, but it was still warm enough that they didn't need jackets. Unlike Montana in February, Nick thought. There was snow on the ground, and when he'd left this morning it had been clear and forty degrees, though they were expecting another storm to hit by tomorrow.

Steve had told Nick he hated the snow and rain. He'd settled in San Diego when he went on disability because of the weather and the proximity to other veterans — San Diego County had one of the largest veteran communities in the country. Steve felt more at home here than anywhere else.

There was something sad about that. Nick and Steve had each settled in a *place* they felt was home, but without a family to *make* it home.

They sat side by side without talking as

the minutes ticked by. Nick hadn't been to the coast since the last time he'd visited Steve. He found the rhythm of the ocean soothing, comforting. The anger he had walked across the sand with — anger at his brother for the situation and at himself for considering that Steve might be guilty — dissipated.

"What'd they take?"

"Your computer."

"They were there a long time."

"You told them they could search your apartment."

"And see? They didn't find anything because I'm innocent."

Steve jumped up and started walking down the beach. Nick followed him.

"She was raped," he said.

"Shit." Steve paused in stride. "I didn't do it, Nick. You have to believe me."

"I want to help you, Steve. But you need to be completely honest with me."

"What do you want from me, Nick? I told you everything I know. *I didn't kill Angie.*" Steve stomped off again, and Nick trailed at a distance to give his brother time to cool off and think about the situation.

The differences between Nick and his brother didn't elude him. Steve thrived here among the hordes of people, on the edge of a major city, where he couldn't possibly know even a small fraction of the population by name. So anonymous, it made Nick uneasy, coming from a town where he could engage in a conversation with a stranger and learn that they had more than one mutual acquaintance.

Even now, in the middle of a murder investigation where he was a suspect, Steve waved to people he recognized, smiled, acknowledged peers. Like he was on stage, always on show. It was the old Steve coupled with a Steve he didn't really know, and that bothered Nick.

Just how much had Steve changed since he left Montana?

Nick caught up with Steve and asked, "What do they want with your computer?"

"I don't know. I guess to see where I've been, what I've done online. It's actually really easy to track e-mail and Internet traffic. It should be a piece of cake for the police."

"Why?"

"Why what?"

"Why do they want to know where you've been online, what e-mails you sent? Why is *your* computer important to them?"

Steve paused. "Angie had an anonymous online journal. It was . . . irresponsible. I told her to tone it down, but she didn't listen. I know that journal had something to do with her murder. I guess the police just want to make sure I didn't say something incriminating online or threaten her or something. Or maybe they are looking for something like that to pin Angie's murder on me, but *I didn't do it.* And they're not going to find anything that said I did."

Steve sounded defiant, and Nick's uneasiness grew. The police had mentioned the website. Nothing in detail. "I need to look at this journal."

Steve shook his head. "There's no reason for you to."

"Dammit Steve!" Nick stopped walking. His brother turned around and glared at him. "You have to take this seriously," Nick said. "Your ex-girlfriend was murdered. The police are looking at *you.* You have motive and no real alibi."

"I had no motive to kill Angie! Whose side are you on?"

"I want to be on your side. I really do. But look at the facts. Angie was eighteen years old. You're old enough to be her father. That's —" Nick cut off what he was about to say, something that would be impossible to take back.

Instead, he softened his tone. "What's going on with you, Steve? You're not working, you've been going to school long enough to earn three degrees, and you're dating college girls. You're just shy of forty and your girlfriends can't even legally drink!"

"Why are you judging me? Don't you trust me? Don't you *know* me?"

"I thought I did." Nick hated the direction this conversation had taken, but he had no choice. The truth demanded that he push Steve.

"I don't make it a habit dating girls at the college. Angie was the only one. It — I understand what you're saying. Really. And you didn't know Angie. She was different. She needed me. We hit it off."

Nick wasn't certain he fully believed Steve, but why would he lie?

"Is there anything you're not telling me?"

Steve clenched his fists. "Do you think I did that to Angie?"

"No." But Nick had waited a beat before answering, and Steve seized on it, his jaw tight but his eyes filled with hurt.

"You think I'm capable of that type of cruelty? That I could *rape* a woman? You think that of me? You really don't know me." Steve stared at the ocean, his eyes watery. "You don't know me at all."

"That's not what I said —" Nick began, but Steve cut him off.

"I thought you were here to help me, Nick. I was wrong. I didn't think I had to prove to my own brother that I'm innocent. Maybe you're right, maybe I do need a lawyer. Because if my own flesh and blood believes me capable of murder, it's no wonder the fucking police are trying to hang me."

"That's not how it works —"

Steve shook his head, waved his arm toward his apartment building up the beach. "Why don't you go join your buddies who turned my apartment upside down? Skewer me because I'm the easiest to blame. And let Angie's killer walk the streets free. Because the truth doesn't mean anything, does it? As long as you guys have someone to throw in jail, the truth doesn't matter."

Steve turned and walked up the beach, back toward the apartment. Nick watched him, perplexed. What was that about? He replayed the conversation and didn't see what he'd said to set off his brother. But the pressure of a police investigation, the stress of being a suspect, of having the police in your home, asking personal, em-barrassing questions . . . maybe it had just gotten to Steve.

Steve had asked Nick for help and the only way Nick could do that was if he knew all the facts.

Nick understood why the police suspected his brother. Older man, much younger woman dumps him. Restraining order. There was more to that story than Steve let on. And Nick had to see Angie's website to know exactly what the police had on his brother. And hope that Steve trusted him enough to be completely honest once his temper cooled down.

Steve jumped into a small, sporty car and drove off. Nick started back up the beach, noticed that the police vehicles were gone. He hoped the apartment door was unlocked. If not, he knew a few tricks. Hunger and weariness ate at him. It had been a long day and he needed to get off his feet. Or rather his knees. Walking on the beach had not been a wise move. He wanted his pain pills, but refused to give in to the need.

Nick slowly crossed the beach and opened the rental car, unzipped his shaving kit, and poured two prescription-strength Motrin into his hand. He swallowed them with the now cold coffee he'd picked up at the airport after he'd flown in, hours before, wincing at the foul taste.

Grabbing his bag, he started toward Steve's apartment again. Grinding pain in his knees and ankles forced him to walk slowly.

He counted twenty-four stairs. There were twenty-two stairs in his house in Bozeman. He could have moved his bedroom downstairs to the guest room, but he had refused. It would have meant he'd been defeated by the pain, defeated by his mistakes, defeated by a killer.

He could do this.

One.

He put his right foot on the first stair, and pulled his left foot to stair two. Okay. The pain was minimal, but he had known it would be. His right knee hadn't been as damaged as his left.

Bracing for the electric jolt he knew would come, he pulled his right leg up to the second stair.

His vision blurred and he took a deep breath.

He did four more stairs in the same fashion, trying to pick up the pace, until it became obvious that he wouldn't make it, not like this. He swung the bag in his right hand to build momentum, then tossed it up the stairs, praying it would make it to the landing and not roll all the way down. It made it, barely.

He grabbed both railings and used them

as crutches, putting more pressure on his right knee than he should, but relieving his left leg. He reached the top and sank down on the landing to catch his breath and wonder again what he was doing. Could he even catch the bad guys anymore?

Inevitably when he was in pain, self-pity took hold.

That's it, Sheriff. Get off your ass.

Nick hauled himself up and shuffled across the balcony to Steve's apartment. The door was locked, but not bolted, and Nick easily popped the old lock.

When Nick opened the door, he was surrounded by a bright, orange glow. It took a moment to realize the light came from the setting sun shining through the large, sliding-glass windows that made up the back wall of the apartment. The sun rested on the ocean in front of him, bleeding into the sea, the water sparkling like bursts of firecrackers.

Spectacular.

For a brief moment Nick forgot everything that troubled him. Before him the vast ocean unrolled endlessly, the sun illuminating everything in sight. The orange turned red as the sun rapidly sank lower, with finally just the tip visible on the calm water.

For a minute, a far too short time, Nick

felt as peaceful as the glassy sea.

The sun disappeared. And while the colors were still vibrant, Nick saw that the ocean wasn't as calm as he'd thought. Its waves crashed on the shore, the night claiming its time.

The mess of the police investigation brought home the reason he was here in the first place. He reluctantly turned from the view and dropped his bag by the door.

On the wall next to the door was a framed photograph of a former president of the United States handing a much younger Steve a commendation. Nick remembered that day nearly fifteen years ago. It had been before their parents died, shortly after he'd joined the police academy. Nick was idealistic and eager, and still thought he could convince his dad that he was just as heroic as Steve. That he, too, would have risked his life and saved those kids.

But Paul Thomas had only had faith in one of his sons, something Nick had never understood, and with his father ten years in the grave, he would never get the answers.

The one thing Nick could figure was that Steve had followed in their father's footsteps. That he joined the army and moved up in the ranks. That he, too, had earned a Purple Heart. They had war stories to share, political discussions, a love of history.

Nick simply had a driving urge to right wrongs, and becoming a lawyer had seemed the perfect answer, until that day he knew he was destined to be a cop.

Some cops became cops because of tragedy, but Nick became a cop because of hope. He'd been at the police academy for a workshop on juvenile crime and gangs. One of the speakers was a kid, Jesse Souter, who'd grown up with a drug-addict mother and a petty thief of a father. Jesse's time spent in and out of foster homes coincided with his parents' prison stints. It was no wonder the kid had turned to crime.

But one day a Missoula beat cop had arrested Jesse for shoplifting a six-pack of beer and beef jerky. The five-dollar crime was a turning point. The cop befriended and guided Jesse, and showed him his own potential. Jesse grew up and became a cop himself.

He could have so easily gone the other way.

It was the hope that these kids could be helped, that all they needed was guidance and an example, that changed Nick's career choice. He enrolled in the police academy the next day and never looked back, never doubted his decision. He couldn't point to

134

a Jesse during his tenure as a cop, but he knew he'd helped a few lost sheep find the right path. And that had been enough.

Looking around Steve's apartment and the general mess left by the police, he thought that maybe he *should* have become a lawyer instead. Right now Steve needed a lawyer more than another cop.

Steve's natural tidiness was still evident through the disturbance. Steve used the dining area as his office, and the empty place where his computer had sat looked particularly barren.

Along the walls of both the dining area and adjacent living room were framed articles. Dozens of them. Nick limped along, glancing at the headlines. *Local soldier saves three dozen children. Sergeant Thomas brings fellow soldier to safety. Two presidential commendations for Thomas. Congressional Medal of Honor for saving schoolchildren.*

And more. All the articles had pictures of Steve in uniform, all taken more than a dozen years ago.

Staring at the history of Steve lining the walls, he couldn't help but wonder what Steve had really been doing for the past fourteen years since he left the military. He had no real job but collected a decent pension. He'd been going to college part-time for nearly ten years, dating a girl half his age, and getting wrapped up in a murder investigation.

The thought of Steve raping a woman made Nick physically ill. He wanted to stand by his brother, but if it were true Nick would walk away. He wouldn't be able to look at the brother he'd long admired, long respected, and see in his face a rapist. A man no better than the Butcher.

Nick had told the two detectives the truth: if Steve was guilty, he would turn him in himself.

As Nick looked at the framed awards, the commendations under a spotlight, the newspaper articles and photographs, Nick wondered if he really knew his brother.

Every answer came back no.

TEN

Elizabeth Rimes was the most beautiful creature on the planet. It was a shame she lived three thousand miles away.

She went to Atlanta Tech, which he'd discovered through a small picture on her online journal. She would never have expected anyone to research the statue in her photo's background, discovering its history and location on the Atlanta Tech campus.

She lived in an apartment near the campus ("I bike to school every day. It's a nice ride, not too far. But when it rains I take the bus.") He figured out which Starbucks she frequented ("I sat and drank my latte and looked at the small lake. It's peaceful here, I come by almost every day.") Her favorite singer was Enya, her favorite color sky blue, her favorite movie *Sleepless in Seattle.*

He hadn't seen *Sleepless in Seattle* until he read her journal, then he bought it. It was fate, an omen. The movie was about a long-distance relationship. A woman who was in love with a man she'd never met but felt she knew with all her heart and soul.

Just like he did about Elizabeth.

He had some money saved. He had it all planned. He'd register for classes at Atlanta Tech. Elizabeth had announced that she would be the teaching assistant for a computer design class in the fall. He would be in that class. Find an apartment near hers. Run into her at the Starbucks. Befriend her. Ask her out.

Kiss her. Touch her. Make love to her.

So beautiful. Long, long, soft blond hair. Sweet.

He'd been talking with her through her journal page for months. They'd become friendly and she had given him more details about her life, details that would help him track her down. He knew she had two cats. He pretended to have a cat, even took pictures of the neighbor's cat to send to her, but truth was he hated them. Dirty animals who licked their butts and ate rotten food. Disgusting.

But Elizabeth loved cats, and so he pretended to. He looked at the picture of Elizabeth with her cats on her journal page and grimaced. One of them had its filthy tongue out and was about to lick her cheek.

When he arrived in Atlanta, the cats were the first thing that had to go. He'd taken care of the beasts before, he would happily do it again. She would never know what happened to them.

He clicked on the message icon for Elizabeth and wrote a message. It was perfect, and he knew she would respond.

Hi Elizabeth. I'm sorry I haven't been around for the last couple days, but I had some sad news. Remember I told you about my cat Felix? I sent you his picture last month, he's black and white and very friendly. Well, he was hit by a car Sunday and I took him to the vet but they couldn't do anything. He died this morning.

I miss him already. The car didn't even stop.

I wanted to share with someone. My roommate never liked Felix and doesn't care that he's gone.

I knew you would understand. How are Scooter and Belle? I hope they're doing well.

By the way, I'm thinking of transferring to Atlanta Tech in the fall. I applied in the computer engineering department and my professor here gave me a terrific letter of recommendation. Do you know anything about AT? If you don't, that's okay.

Talk to you later, I'm going to take Felix's food and toys to the SPCA, maybe they can use them. Maybe I'll come back with another cat, though I don't think anyone can replace Felix.

Your friend.

He signed off with his auto-signature and the avatar of a bouncing smiley face.

If this didn't work, there would soon be a time when she would let him know everything. He'd make certain of that.

Angie had told him things because he was safe. She trusted him. And she betrayed him by whoring around.

Slut.

He glanced up, wondering if he'd spoken out loud. But no one looked at him. The library was quiet, everyone studying. Normally he wouldn't go to the library to go online — he didn't have to, he had a great setup at home — but there was a pretty girl he liked to look at. She worked part-time Tuesday and Thursday nights.

Becca. Not as pretty a name, not as pretty a girl, as Elizabeth, but she was close. So he came to the library when she worked just to look, to hold her image close to him so when he went home he could picture her.

Her wide mouth, red lips, sweet smile. He wanted to kiss her, but he never approached her. Twice, she'd come to him to gather books off the table. She smiled at him, murmured hello, complimented his shirt.

When he first met Angie, she was also nice to him. She talked to him, actually seemed interested in what he had to say.

She was a liar. When he'd found her My-Journal page the fantasy that was sweet Angie vanished. He was devastated, livid. She was a whore, a slut, just like the woman who'd turned against his father.

They were all better off dead.

His laptop computer beeped that an e-mail had arrived. *Elizabeth.*

Heart pounding, he turned his gaze from Becca working the desk and opened the message. It wasn't from Elizabeth. It was an automatic e-mail alert.

MyJournal tracker has found a recent update on your track list. Click the link below to be taken directly to the updated content.
MyJournal.iloverealmen.com

Angie's journal.

For a brief moment, a split second, he felt every eye in the library looking at him.

Of course they weren't. They didn't know what he'd done, they didn't know who he was. Becca didn't even know his real name.

He almost clicked on the link. But he didn't. Couldn't. Instead he packed up his laptop, avoiding eye contact with anyone. He rushed out, heard Becca ask behind him, "Is something wrong?" He just shook his head at her and left the building. Ran to his car, heart pounding. Drove home. Fast. Too fast.

Slow down. Slow down or you'll get a ticket.

He eased up on the accelerator a bit, but his head ran through every possible scenario.

That Angie wasn't dead, that she was alive and the police would be waiting for him at home.

That she was dead and writing from Hell.

That she was alive but didn't remember anything.

You're dead! You're dead!

In the glare of headlights, he saw her ghostly body, her bloody mouth open, accusing him. *You raped me.*

You're dead. You can't tell anyone what happened. You can't say a word. You're dead, you slut!

His heart continued to vibrate between

his ears, a loud ringing, and he couldn't hear anything but his internal organs working, working. Heart pumping blood through his veins, his head swelling, filling with certain knowledge that he would be discovered.

He escaped home. Locked, bolted the door. Ran into his bedroom, slammed the door as he tossed his laptop onto his bed. Angie's soundless scream vibrated in his head and he sank to the floor.

You're dead. You're dead.

Several minutes later, he rose unsteady and walked to his desktop computer. Booted the hard drive. The ritual of the computer checking files, the fast *zip-zip* of the hard drive spinning, soothed him. A few deep breaths later and he almost stopped shaking.

He logged onto his e-mail and clicked on the MyJournal link.

Tribute to our friend Mirage.

Angie's page, Angie's online name. But not Angie. A sigh of relief whistled through his lips, and he focused on the "Tribute." He quickly realized that the author of the journal entry was one or more of Angie's friends.

I remember a day last month when Mirage went to work. I stopped by to visit, even though it was raining hard. It rarely rains here, but that day it poured.

He thought. That was . . . late January. Had to be. There were only a couple days last month that it rained.

Mirage got off early because it was so slow, and we sat in the corner talking about our first time . . . you know, the first time we had sex.

Eager and anxious and horrified, he read on.

I was a late bloomer. My first time was only three months ago, shortly after I started classes at the same university where Mirage and our other friends go. His name was, oops! Can't say his name. Okay, his "name" was S. and he's a junior. Plays water polo. Fabulous body.

The first time was icky, but S. told me the second would be better. It was . . . Mirage promised me my first "real" orgasm would be wonderful (you know, the kind that isn't self-induced) and she was right. S. went down and licked me until I orgasmed and I swear I saw fireworks. . . .

Fists clenched, he read on. Each of Angie's friends wrote about their first time, and as the stories went on they became more lewd and detailed, just like Angie used to write.

I broke up with S. when I started seeing S. . . . whoops! Same initials, different guys, hahaha. S2 was really experienced. You know, an older man. And he did things to me that made my head spin. . . .
One night on the beach behind his apartment we made love in a sleeping bag. The possibility of being caught in the act was such a turn-on. I never thought having a guy suck my tits would be so sexy, but when S2 did it I felt hot from the inside out. . . .

At the end, he had the three whores figured out.

Abby wrote about her first time, first and only boyfriend. She was in high school, it was in the back of his car, and she was still dating him though he went to college out of state.

Kayla was a dyke. Well, "bisexual" was probably the politically correct term, since she screwed both men *and* women. Whore.

It was Jodi he was shocked about. Jodi who had dated the two S's. Jodi who he'd

145

thought was the nicest of Angie's three friends. The one he least expected this bad behavior from.

He knew it was her because of the last line she wrote.

> Mirage was the best friend I could ever have. She convinced me to cut my hair, which I had barely even trimmed in forever. I cut it to my shoulders, added some highlights, and haven't been without a date since. She brought out the best in me, inside and outside, and I'll miss her forever.

He remembered the exact day Jodi had cut her hair. At the time, he didn't think she was flirting, just proud of her pretty style, but now he knew better. Now he knew the truth.

Fucking whore.

He closed down the browser, unable to read the journal anymore, though he knew he'd be back online later. To read it again, to see the truth about the girl he never expected to kiss and tell.

So, she likes her tits sucked? Maybe she'd like them sucked right off her fucking body.

Pulse racing, he slammed a tape into the VCR. It was by far the most vicious of the five, and usually he couldn't watch it. He didn't like the blood. But this time he needed it, this time he would force himself to watch the whole thing.

The slut was thrown onto the cement floor. Fucked in the ass while her head banged against the wall. Blood, black in the grainy, colorless film, trickled from her mouth. Then, chained against the wall, arms and legs spread wide. Discoloration covered her body. He watched her mouth open, her vocal cords stretch. A whip came out, the dark stripes dripped down, down.

She stayed like that for a minute, crying, hanging against the wall. She was taken again, by a different man. Then another. Three men. They shared.

Disgusting. He would never share.

Then the worst part. Except for the first time, he always turned off the tape after the third guy screwed her.

But not now. Both repelled and fascinated, he forced himself to watch.

The first man came back, and he could see his profile. *Hard.* He brought the woman down off the wall and threw her on a mattress in the corner. The angle of the camera changed. A close-up of him pinning her down with his body. Entering her.

Then the knife. It came out fast, from

under the mattress. He pulled her head back by her hair and with one swift, deep stroke across her neck blood sprayed everywhere. The walls. The mattress. All over the killer as he arched his back and orgasmed.

His stomach churned at the sight, but still he watched as the woman bucked in her last response to inevitable death; as the blood spurted, a drop fell across the video camera's lens.

Drip, drip, drip.

Blackness.

He wiped his face, surprised that sweat poured off his skin. His body shook and he looked down, saw that he had come in his pants.

He hid the films, went to the bathroom, and showered in icy water. Soon, his blood cooled, his heart slowed, his body returned to normal.

And he came up with a plan to deal with whores who kiss and tell.

ELEVEN

Carina arrived at the station early Wednesday morning, having barely slept the night before. Every time she dozed off she pictured Angie dead on the beach, wrapped in three garbage bags. The longer this case went unsolved, the edgier she got. Though it had only been forty-eight hours, she kept waiting for something to break.

It was the manner of death. Restraining the victim. Gluing on a gag. Raping her. Washing her body, then suffocating her. Definitely weird. And for all the lack of evidence, the ritualistic act, it still seemed sloppy. Did Angie's killer put her body on the beach for a specific reason? Or out of convenience? Why so public? Because he didn't fear discovery, or because he was thumbing his nose at the police? Or some bizarre reason only the killer would know?

Her few sleeping hours were dominated by disturbing dreams about Angie; in her waking hours she thought about her conversation with Nick Thomas.

Would she turn in her own brother?

First, she couldn't imagine any of her four brothers raping and killing a woman. Nick seemed certain Steve Thomas was innocent. Wouldn't she immediately defend her brothers, *then* ask them what happened? She couldn't blame Nick for his loyalty.

Besides, though nearly everything Carina knew about the case pointed to Steve Thomas, Masterson and his disappearing act definitely cast doubt on her initial suspicion that Thomas was guilty. But Thomas had repeatedly lied, not only about what time he went to the Shack, but about how much time he'd spent reading Angie's not-so-anonymous online journal.

The cursory examination from Patrick the day before showed that Thomas had spent forty-one hours on the MyJournal website in the last month, averaging more than an hour a day, but Patrick needed more time to extract exactly what he'd been reading. As he pointed out, a good defense attorney could argue that while the window browser may have been up, there's no proof Thomas was sitting at the computer. They needed to make a correlation between the time his browser was open to a MyJournal page and any e-mails or interaction between Thomas and other MyJournal members.

In addition, Patrick was investigating every individual who commented on Angie's journal, which amounted to hundreds of online identities to match with real people, determine who was a potential threat, and uncover their physical location. Thomas's online identity was SThomasSgt, which was his name and rank in the military. But if he had been harassing Angie, he may have used another login, so Patrick had to verify every one.

And if Thomas really was innocent, Angie's killer might be one of the other MyJournal members.

Already, Carina was developing a headache.

Will came over and rubbed her shoulders. "Not enough coffee or too much?" he asked.

"Ugh," she answered and held out her mug. He grinned and poured her more inky-black coffee from the pot against the wall of the bullpen.

"Did Dillon ever call back?"

"Yes. Finally. You'd think he was this hotshot or something." Which he was, and Carina was proud of him. Though he didn't work directly for the San Diego Police Department, he was often retained on criminal cases to interview suspects in custody and present a psychiatric report to the court. She didn't always agree with his assessments — the cop in her said killers should go to prison for hard time, not to a padded jail cell in the desert — but Dillon backed up his recommendations with facts and solid analysis.

"And?" Will asked.

"He's meeting us for lunch at Bob's." Bob's Burgers was across from the police station and a regular hangout for Homicide. If Carina didn't get a Bob's Ultimate Cheeseburger at least once a week, she became irritable. Will insisted the fries there cured any foul mood.

"So we have a couple hours. Any word on Masterson?"

"Nothing," she said.

"By the way, I did a little research last night on Sheriff Nick Thomas."

She raised an eyebrow. "And?"

"Do you remember hearing about the Bozeman Butcher?"

"Who hasn't? The sick bastard was responsible for more than a dozen murders up in Montana." Her eyes widened. "And Bozeman is in Gallatin County." She hit her head. "Why didn't I make the connection last night?"

"We were preoccupied. It's been a couple long days."

"So Nick Thomas was responsible for taking the killer down?"

"In part. But what wasn't widely reported was that Thomas was held captive by the Butcher, and afterward was hospitalized for more than a week."

Carina nodded. "I thought he was walking a little stiffly yesterday when he followed his brother down to the beach."

"If anyone knows about serial killers, it would be Sheriff Thomas. He'd been building the case against the Butcher for years. Maybe we should talk to him and get his perspective, see if he thinks we have a serial killer here."

"You're right, he has the experience, but he's the brother of our primary suspect. And besides," argued Carina, "the definition of a serial killer is three or more like crimes with an established MO and —"

Will interrupted. "Don't tell me you haven't seen signs in Angie's murder that point to something more than a crime of passion."

She couldn't argue with him. She'd been wrestling with it all night. "Point taken. But what if it is Steve Thomas? What if he's the killer?"

"Then having Nick Thomas on our side might help stop another murder."

"Has anything come back from the feds' database on like crimes?"

Will shook his head. "The system is haphazard at best. And I read an article last year that serial killers often change and refine their method of killing. So our killer might have started with a different MO. In another state, maybe he strangled previous victims, or stabbed them —"

"Or maybe Angie is the first. Something about her set him off."

"Like her sex diary."

Carina's phone rang. "Kincaid," she answered.

"It's Jim. I've typed the glue."

"And?"

"Commonly used industrial-strength adhesive, available at most major hardware stores."

"Match anything we found at Thomas's apartment?"

"Sorry."

"Thanks."

Will was on the phone when she got off, so Carina cleared paperwork from her desk, her least favorite part of the job, until he hung up.

"Patrick has a printout of all of Thomas's

e-mails, Internet travels, and chat room logs for us," Will told her. "He skimmed them, didn't find anything big, but they're worth a closer look. He has to run some computer program," he waved his hand in the air, "to decipher exactly how many times Thomas went to the site and get an approximate amount of time he spent there. Since we haven't arrested the guy yet, and Patrick's preparing for a trial next week, he doesn't have the time to thoroughly go through the reports, but he thinks by early next week he'll have answers."

"Such is our lives." Carina frowned. "Will, why do I feel like this isn't a priority to the department?"

"I don't understand."

"We have a dead girl. Eighteen years old. We have a suspect. True, only circumstantial evidence, but damn good circumstantial evidence. But Jim has priorities, Patrick has priorities, and this case isn't it. I don't like it. It makes me feel like Angie's death has been relegated to the bottom of the list. That because she was a promiscuous young woman who posed in pornographic positions on her Web page, no one cares what happened to her."

"That's not true, Carina. You know that."

But she was fired up. "Really? I know

what? You heard the guys around the bullpen when they saw her MyJournal page. Reading her descriptions of having sex and masturbating. And the pictures! I have four brothers. I know what guys think about nudie shots.

"She's dead. Just because a woman has sex with a lot of guys doesn't mean she deserves to be raped and murdered. Suffocated. She was terrified when she died. She was tortured. It's not fair that no one cares!"

Will pushed Carina back down in her chair and leaned over her. "Listen here, Detective Kincaid. Don't *ever* imply that I don't care about a victim, or that I think anyone deserves to be raped and murdered. You're walking a thin line here. Angie Vance deserves justice as much as any other victim in the city, and I'll do everything I can to bring her some. So get off your high horse and let's do the job right. Get some evidence against Thomas — or anyone else who might want her dead. Hell, we have at least nine other men she kissed and blabbed about on the Internet who could have been embarrassed enough to kill."

Carina took a deep breath. "I'm sorry. I wasn't aiming that at you, Will. I guess . . . I don't know. I'm just frustrated."

He gave her a curt nod and leaned back against her desk, arms crossed. "We thought we had an easy case, open and shut, and it's turned out to be anything but."

Carina felt sheepish. Will cared as much about the victims as she did. She had to remember that he was not only her partner but her best friend. "Did Patrick say he had anything from Angie's computer?" she asked, changing the subject.

"Oh, yeah. We have our work cut out for us. A lot of legwork, but maybe we'll get a break."

Will's phone rang and he reached across Carina's desk to answer it.

"Will Hooper."

"It's Patrick. Are you at your computer?"

"Two feet away."

"Log on to Angie's MyJournal page ASAP. Seems Angie's friends have paid a tribute to their dead friend, and you're not going to like it. I'm on hold with MyJournal security because Angie's journal needs to be taken down. Immediately."

He walked down the street, around the corner, and down two blocks to the Quik-Stop. He bought a newspaper, a thirty-two-ounce Coke, and a breakfast burrito, using the store's microwave to heat it.

He sat at a picnic table at the park across the street, eating as he turned to the obituaries.

There it was. Angie's memorial service: *Thursday. Six p.m.*

He'd learned a lot from his mistakes with Angie. She was the first, and of course it wasn't perfect. That's why the end wasn't satisfying. He'd kept her too long, for one. The excitement of that first night gave way to fear of being caught, an urgency that he couldn't fulfill.

Last year he'd made a mistake, and it had taken him a full year to plan and gather the courage to go through with his idea.

He should have killed Randi, but he'd been too nervous to go through with it. Fortunately, he'd scared her into silence, and she'd since moved away.

He'd taken Randi to dinner and a movie. She was perfect. Shy, quiet, timid. All he wanted was to fuck her. They'd been dating for several months and it had been time.

They'd eaten dinner at a nice restaurant, seen a movie, did all the things they usually did on a date. Then he took her to a wooded park up in the San Diego hills with a distant view of the ocean and kissed her. She let him, her mouth soft and warm, tentative. They'd kissed before, but he wanted more.

158

Needed more.

At first she gave him what he sought. Her breasts. Her neck. She let him touch her through her pants, but when he unzipped them she grabbed his wrist. "I'm not ready."

She was out of breath.

"We both want this. You know it."

"I thought . . . but no. I can't. Just kiss me. I like that."

So he kissed her and heated up. Kissed her and wanted more. He pinned her down in the dirt with his body — he was bigger than she — and she protested again. This time, he didn't stop. He unzipped her shorts and she began to squirm and cry.

"Please, stop! I don't want to do this."

"I want to."

And shouldn't that have been enough? She was here, she liked him, she kissed him, and she wouldn't let him fuck her? There was something very wrong with that, and he wasn't going to let her get away with it.

He held her down, his body rigid, and she screamed. She screamed so loud he thought every person in town could hear. They would come and take him away.

It stunned him into stopping.

Randi was sobbing and he rolled off her. They were both covered in dirt and leaves.

"Don't tell anyone," he warned her. "If

you tell anyone, I'll kill you."

"I won't," she whispered. "No one."

He took her home in silence. They never spoke about that night, never spoke again for that matter. She transferred to another school two weeks later.

After she found her dog dead.

Still, he'd been nervous for months. But his fears gradually began to subside. Randi hadn't told anyone what happened that night. And besides, what *had* happened? It was all a misunderstanding.

But he'd never let another woman scream.

What he'd learned from Randi he'd applied to Angie. What he'd learned with Angie, he would apply to the next whore.

Jodi.

He had lots of planning to do before Angie's funeral, and he couldn't afford to miss class today even though listening to a boring lecture was the last thing he wanted to do. But missing class would be a *mistake* and he didn't make mistakes. Not anymore.

He definitely wouldn't make any mistakes with Jodi.

TWELVE

Nick pulled his laptop computer from the bottom of his overnight bag. He wasn't a computer expert by any stretch, but it was the twenty-first century and he'd broken down and bought one a couple years ago.

He glanced at Steve's closed bedroom door. His brother had come in late the night before while Nick tried to sleep on the couch. He didn't let on that he was awake, and Steve quietly went into the bedroom and shut the door. It sounded like he was still asleep, which was good. Nick wanted to do this alone.

He set up his laptop on Steve's desk and hooked in the Internet connection.

There was a family picture on the desk. Nick, Steve, their parents. Paul Thomas had his arm around Steve's shoulders, Miriam Thomas had her arm around Nick's. That's how Nick always remembered the family. Nick was the outsider to his father. It must

161

have been evident from the day he was born because his mother overcompensated when his father left for his monthly reserve duty.

But when Dad was around, the world revolved around Steve, and Nick was a distant star falling deep in Steve's shadow. It had bothered him a lot when he was a kid. Except that Steve had always been good to him.

Nick poured coffee he'd brewed earlier, then opened the sliding glass door to let in the ocean breeze. He breathed in the unfamiliar salty air and listened to the squawk of the seagulls. They were loud scavengers, but they never pretended to be anything but.

The rhythmic ebb and flow of the waves rolling over the sand and even the annoying birds were somehow relaxing, so he left the door open and sat at his laptop. He didn't have Angie's Web address, but he knew it was part of the MyJournal community, so he started there.

After a half-dozen searches he found it. An entry dated today popped up and he frowned at the "Tribute." The more he read the more uncomfortable he became. He wondered if the detectives had seen this.

He also wondered if one of the "S's" was Steve. The older man. Coincidence? Maybe. But if the entry really was written by the victim's friends, they would be here in San Diego. Nick didn't believe it was a coincidence.

"I don't make it a habit dating girls at the college. Angie was the only one."

Nick's heart sank as he realized Steve had probably lied to him. He hadn't fully believed him at the time because Steve hadn't looked him in the eye, but the evidence in front of him was still a blow.

Nick read as much of Angie's journal as he could stomach, skimming most of it, until he found a few paragraphs in the middle of a long commentary about a variety of subjects. His heart twisted at the anguish in the few short lines.

I just received my first quarter report card. 4.0. That's perfect. No one is surprised because I've always been a straight-A student. I couldn't be anything but, right? I mean, people see what they want and we give them what they want to see.

Sometimes I want people to see the real me, to hear what I really say. But they don't. This journal is a perfect example. Is this me? No, it's not. It's what you think I am, so I give it to you.

I don't know me. I don't think I ever have.

Hopeless. She sounded desperate and begging for something that even she couldn't name. Her friends hadn't seen it, and the men who lusted after her sexy writing certainly didn't see it. Had Steve? Or had he been as blind as everyone else?

Nick focused next on the comments left by visitors to her site. Steve believed Angie's killer had frequented her Web page. If that were the case, would he have commented? Positive or negative? There were several men who wanted her phone number. Some who wrote lewd descriptions of what they wanted to do with her. And many were downright mean.

Repent now, sinner, or you're going to Hell.
I used to be addicted to sex. You can be cured.
Fucking whore.

Nick frowned at that last comment. He clicked on the ID and su went blank.

404. Page not found.

He surfed around a bit, was able to view other pages, but Angie's was gone.

The police must have worked with the

MyJournal company to take down her journal. It was both a relief and frustrating to Nick. After reading the Butcher's personal journals — handwritten, not online — he'd developed a feeling for how these sick predators thought. How they communicated. He'd hoped to read more of the comments and come up with something solid to take to Detectives Kincaid and Hooper. A profile of sorts, proof his brother was innocent. If he could use his experience with serial killers to narrow down the suspects, maybe they could get ahead of the game.

Hell, he would have given his right arm for something solid on the Butcher before twenty-two women had died.

Nick poured another cup of coffee, then sat back down at the computer to download a map to the police station. He was here to help Steve, but he felt for Angie Vance. She'd been confused, desperate, and very sad. No one in her life had seen that she needed help, maybe because she was so good at hiding her pain. But wasn't that why he'd become a cop? To help young people straighten out their lives before it was too late?

It was too late for Angie, but he could damn well do something to help find her killer.

165

Behind him, a woman cleared her throat.

Nick stood slowly and turned. A tall, slender girl holding her own steaming mug leaned against the door. She had straight golden-blond hair that touched her waist, and worry lines creased her pretty face.

"How did you get up here?"

"I live next door." She gestured to the half-railing that separated Steve's apartment from his neighbor's. "What happened to Steve? There's a rumor around campus that the police were here searching his apartment. That they think he killed Angie."

"And you are?"

"Ava James. You're his brother, Nick, aren't you?"

Nick nodded.

"Steve talks about you all the time."

Nick hid his surprise.

"Where's Steve?" she asked.

"Inside."

"Poor guy. I can't believe the police would ever think he's capable of killing anyone."

"Did you know Angie?"

She squinched up her nose as she sat on one of two Adirondack chairs Steve had positioned to view the ocean. "Yeah."

"How long were she and Steve involved?" Nick asked, stepping onto the deck.

"A couple weeks. It didn't mean anything

to her, but Steve always falls quick." Panic hit her face. "I shouldn't say that to the police, should I?"

"Ava, you need to tell the police the truth. Lying will not help Steve."

"It just looks bad, but it's not bad," she said quickly. "Steve got over her when she broke up with him, like he always does."

Nick froze. "Always does?"

"Yeah. Jodi, then Katrina, then Deena, then whoever. Since I moved in eighteen months ago he's fallen in love at least a dozen times."

"Are they all from the college?"

"Of course. That's where we hang out. There or at the Sand Shack or a couple other places. Deena works at the Starbucks next to the college. I liked her the best because I think she really cared about Steve, not like Jodi and Angie and the others, who just wanted to screw around with an older man."

"What about you?"

She blushed, glanced down. "Steve and I are just friends."

"Friends." Nick felt ill again. If Ava was twenty-one, Nick would eat his Stetson. And all the other girls . . . how old were they? College age? Twenty? Eighteen like Angie?

Steve had told him Angie was the only one. That he didn't make a habit of dating college girls. His brother had lied to him. He *was* the other "S" on the "Tribute" entry, no doubt about it now. Nick hadn't realized that he'd harbored faint hope that his instincts were wrong.

What else had Steve lied about? And if he lied to him, his own brother, he had probably lied to the police.

Dammit! Why lie? Criminals think they can outsmart the cops, but the truth is that lies are uncovered each and every time. Especially verifiable information like who Steve publicly dated.

Criminal. He'd just thought of his brother not only as a criminal, but capable of rape and murder.

"What's wrong?" Ava asked.

"Nothing," he said. Reaching into his pocket, he pulled out a card. "Here's my cell phone number. Please call me if you have any information about Steve, Angie, or anyone who didn't like Angie. Or someone who gave her undue attention. Do you know her current boyfriend?"

Ava took the card and shook her head. "No, except what Steve has told me. The guy's into drugs and a bad scene. Real ego trip. But Steve also thought Angie was about to break up with him."

"Why's that?"

"Because of something he read on her journal. You've seen it, right?"

He nodded and wished he'd read the entries more carefully.

Ava blushed, averted her eyes. "It's pretty risqué."

Steve walked onto the deck shirtless, wearing only sweatpants. He yawned and sipped coffee. "Thanks for making a pot." His face lit up when he saw Ava. "Hi, sweetheart!" He draped an arm over her shoulders, gave a squeeze, and kissed her cheek.

"You okay?" she asked, concern on her face. *She's half in love with him,* Nick realized.

"I'll be fine," Steve said. "Nick came down to help. Once the police stop looking at me, they'll focus their search on finding the real killer."

Nick was disturbed by his brother's casual comments. He wanted to confront him about the lies, but right now he needed more information. "We'll talk later. I have to go."

"Go where?"

"Out." Nick left Steve and Ava on the deck, not trusting himself to control his temper.

He grabbed his gun, holstered it, pulled on his jean jacket and hat, and left.

Carina paced, not from nervous energy but because she was so mad at the three girls who sat in front of her that she wanted to throttle them.

"What were you thinking?" she repeated for the umpteenth time.

All three had the sense to look ashamed.

She and Will had pulled the girls from their classes and they now sat in the dean's office, evicting him for the joint interview. In passing, Carina noticed the numerous degrees, awards, and photographs — reminiscent of Steven Thomas's apartment but more appropriate in the large, opulent, and brightly lit office.

She was scared for these girls. They hadn't seen Angie's body. They didn't know what had been done to her. "Don't you know there's a killer out there? Do you want to be his next victim?"

"Detective," Will warned quietly, and Carina turned around and took a deep breath. *More flies with honey.* She heard Nick Thomas's deep, sexy voice in her head. Where had that come from?

"Abby." Will sat across from the scared girls, his calm, firm demeanor a better fit in this situation. Carina's half-Cuban/half-Irish temper sometimes helped, sometimes hindered. "We're simply concerned about your safety. Putting sexually suggestive photographs of yourselves for the whole world to see was not smart."

"I'm sorry," Jodi said. "We're all sorry. It seemed like a good idea at the time." She was blushing and didn't look Will in the eye.

Carina sighed and said, "The fact remains that we haven't arrested Angie's murderer and we don't know if you've all put yourselves in danger."

Will nodded. "We don't want to be investigating another murder. These cases can take a long time to build. This isn't television. Smoking guns are rare. That means that we need to go through all the evidence carefully, investigate alibis and backgrounds, interview witnesses. We put all the information we gather together and see if it points to a suspect. If it does, then we dig deeper and make an arrest. Finally, it's up to the District Attorney's Office to decide if there is enough evidence to warrant prosecution.

"Sometimes," he continued, "we're confident we know who the killer is, but we don't have enough evidence to arrest him. Sometimes it takes years to build a case."

"And sometimes the killer is never

171

caught," Carina said.

The girls looked contrite. "We're sorry," Abby said. "Really. We'll take down the page," she quickly added.

"We've already had it removed, your entry and Angie's entire journal." Before the girls' "Tribute," Patrick had suggested they keep the site up in case the killer wanted to go online and gloat, or taunt the police or someone else. Now they couldn't without risking Abby, Jodi, and Kayla. Though they hadn't given their identities, if the killer knew Angie, he would be able to figure out who her friends were. At least that had been their theory an hour ago.

"Each one of you needs to be careful," Carina said sternly. She glanced at Will, who nodded. "Abby, Kayla, you may go. Jodi, we'd like to talk to you alone for a minute."

"Am I in trouble?"

"No, we just have some questions."

"Can't we stay? For moral support?" Abby said.

Will shook his head. "We need to talk to Jodi alone. But we may be talking to each of you later. Stay safe, okay? If you get any weird vibes, like anyone is watching you or you meet someone who gives you that funny feeling, call me. Anytime, no matter how minor you think it is."

172

Kayla and Abby reluctantly left. Jodi bit her thumbnail. "I'm sorry," she muttered. "You're not going to tell my parents, are you?"

"You're over eighteen," Will said. "We have no reason to speak with your parents."

She noticeably relaxed. "You didn't know Angie. You only saw her journal. I know it looks bad, but it really wasn't as bad as it looks. She was a great person." Tears sprang to her eyes.

Carina squeezed her hand. "Jodi, no one deserves what happened to Angie. You don't need to convince me that she was a good person. I'm not judging her, or you, or your friends. Finding her killer is my only priority. Okay?"

Jodi's lip quivered, but she nodded.

"Jodi, we need to know if S-two on your post was Steve Thomas."

Jodi's eyes widened with surprise. "How'd you know that was me? I didn't use my name!"

Carina reached out and touched the ends of her hair. "Hair."

"Oh."

"Jodi, this is important," Will said. "Was he Steve Thomas?"

"Y-Yes."

"When were you involved with him?"

"Before Angie started seeing him. In November."

"For how long?"

"Umm, just a couple weeks. Angie hooked up with him after."

"Who broke it off?"

"It was mutual."

"Jodi."

She glanced down. "He did."

"What did he say?"

"That he cared about me and I deserved someone better than him." She bit her thumbnail again.

"Were you upset that Angie and Steve were together?"

"No."

She was lying, but Carina didn't think she could press out the truth, and what would it accomplish if she did? "Why do you think Angie got a restraining order against Steve?"

She looked them in the eye. "She was scared."

"Of Steve?"

"I don't know. He scared her, something he said, and she didn't want to talk about it. I don't think it was just because of Steve."

"Why do you think she was scared?"

"I don't know. Really, it's something Abby and I were talking about last night. Just a feeling. But it was also around the time she found out Doug was two-timing her, and that really upset her. So maybe we're just trying to read something into it because of what happened." She took a deep breath. "She did start getting some weirder than normal comments on her posts."

"Anything specific?"

"I never saw them. She deleted a bunch of them. But they made her nervous, and then with Steve hounding her all the time to stop writing the journal, she wondered if he was the one posting the comments. You know, to scare her into not posting her sex diary."

Carina glanced at Will and saw that he was thinking the same thing she was.

"Thank you, Jodi," Will said. "Please be careful, okay? Don't go anywhere alone, at least for the time being. Be aware of your surroundings. We're concerned about your safety."

"It was a dumb thing to do. We were drinking and one thing led to another . . ." Tears welled in her eyes. "Will you find out who killed her? Can you stop him?"

"We will," Carina said. She hoped.

Carina and Will thanked the dean for the use of his office and walked back to their car. Carina called her brother Patrick.

"Patrick, it's your big sister."

"What do you want?"

"Do I always want something?"

"Yes."

She grinned. "We might have a break." She filled him in on the deleted messages. "Do you think you can retrieve them?"

A long silence. "Don't think so, Cara."

"Why not? I know those undelete programs the department got from the FBI e-crimes division are the best."

"True, but those comments would have been saved on the external server, not the victim's own hard drive. Unless she copied them for some reason and saved them, you'll need a warrant to access the MyJournal server, and then if they were deleted before a backup was complete, I doubt there'll be any record of them."

"Dammit, Patrick, that wasn't what I wanted to hear."

"But," he continued, "I can find out if any of the comments were posted by your suspect. And there'll be a log on Angie's computer as to when the comments were deleted. Maybe she e-mailed them to someone, maybe she saved them. I'll look, sis, but I can't promise I'll have the answers you want."

"Thanks." She hung up and relayed the conversation to Will. "We need to get back downtown ASAP. Dillon's probably already waiting for us."

"I hope he can help with a profile," Will said.

"Dillon is unusually good at getting into the mind of murderers," Carina said. "If anyone can help, it's him."

Nick arrived at the police station just before the lunch hour, hoping he could convince detectives Kincaid and Hooper to accept his assistance with the investigation.

If they didn't want his help, he'd work it alone. But he hoped it wouldn't come to that.

"May I help you?" the desk sergeant asked.

Nick showed his badge, knowing it was the fastest way to get information. "Sheriff Thomas, from out of state. I'm looking for Detectives Kincaid and Hooper about a case they're working."

"They just left." He glanced at a sheet in front of them. "Signed out for lunch. I can page them for you."

Nick hesitated. He'd rather talk to them in person, especially with what he wanted to discuss. "When will they return?"

The sergeant sized him up, approved. "They went across the street. To Bob's

Burgers. They left five minutes ago."

Nick smiled, put his hat back on. "Thanks, Sergeant."

"Anytime, Sheriff."

THIRTEEN

Carina greeted her brother with a hug, then sat down across from him in the booth. "Sorry we're late," she said.

He waved off the apology. "I only just got here myself."

"We really appreciate you doing this off the clock." Though Dillon was a freelance forensic consultant for the District Attorney's Office and often worked with the police department on complex cases, he was rarely called in before a suspect was in custody. He also maintained a private practice.

Dillon looked more like their Irish-American dad than any of the seven Kincaid children. While Carina shared the darker complexion of her Cuban-born mother, Dillon had the fair skin and red-brown hair of their father. He was built more like a lean football player than a shrink, which made sense since he'd played college ball and had intended to go into sports medicine before being diverted into criminal psychiatry.

Carina let her partner fill Dillon in on the details of Angie's life, as they knew it, and her death. Dillon looked through the crime file while Will spoke.

"The DA doesn't think we have enough to prosecute Thomas," Will said. "That's why we came to you. Carina and I are leaning toward him as the killer, but there's no hard evidence. It's all circumstantial."

"And you think he's guilty because she put a restraining order on him."

"That and she ridiculed him in public," Will said. "Through the online journal. He lied to us at least twice."

"In addition to Thomas, we have a missing boyfriend, a small-time drug dealer named Doug Masterson," Carina added.

"Are you certain the killer is somehow connected to her sex journal?" Dillon asked.

Carina glanced at Will. "We're not certain about anything at this point. But because the murder was sexual and her body defaced with profanity, it was the logical place to start."

Dillon agreed. "After reviewing the autopsy report Will sent over, I think it's personal as well. She knew her killer."

That had been Carina's gut reaction as well. "Someone like Steve Thomas. Exboyfriend." Carina stopped speaking when she sensed someone watching them.

Sheriff Nick Thomas crossed the length of the burger joint, hat in hand. He wasn't rushed, but ambled over with a steadfast stride. She was struck again by his quiet confidence. He didn't exude arrogance like so many cops she worked with. Instead, Nick Thomas had an aura that bespoke competence, intelligence, focus.

And he was nice on the eyes. *Very* nice on the eyes.

"My Mama always said you can catch more flies with honey."

One conversation with Sheriff Thomas the day before and she was already eager to listen to him again. His voice was even sexier than his firm body. She picked up her iced tea and sipped. The temperature in the room felt like it had risen at least ten degrees.

"I'm sorry to bother you at lunch," Nick Thomas said matter-of-factly, "but I was hoping you might have a few moments to discuss the Vance case."

Carina's first instinct was to dismiss him. Set up something for later. He was the brother of a suspect. But Nick knew about serial killers, had caught one in his own jurisdiction. And he was a cop first, she had known that the minute she had laid eyes on him yesterday.

She glanced at Will and he gave her a half shrug. *Her call.* She nodded, and Will said, "Sheriff, we're talking about the case now. Your input may prove valuable, in light of your knowledge about your brother and your experience with sexual predators."

Carina watched something intense flash behind Nick's blue eyes, then disappear. He didn't so much as move a muscle, but his entire body gave off a warning vibe.

"But," Will continued, "how do we know you won't take something from our conversation and screw with our investigation?"

Slowly he said, "You only have my word."

No one said anything for a long minute. Carina was still torn — she didn't want to jeopardize a conviction for anything. But what Nick had said yesterday had stayed with her. *If Steve is guilty, I'll be the one to throw away the key.*

"All right," Carina said. "Your word is good with us."

Nick slid into the booth, extending his hand to Dillon as Carina introduced them. "Dr. Dillon Kincaid — yes, he's my brother — is a forensic psychiatrist. We're talking informally right now, trying to get a handle on the situation."

She filled Nick in on the manner of Angie's murder. When she was done, Nick said, "You think you have a serial killer on your hands."

"We don't know enough of anything," Will said, "except that the crime seems both ritualistic, like a serial killer, and personal, like she knew her attacker."

"It doesn't sound like a crime of passion," Nick said carefully. "Too carefully planned. Premeditated. Generally crimes of passion are sudden, unplanned attacks fueled by some perceived wrong."

Dillon leaned forward, nodding. "I agree."

"Doesn't mean it wasn't an elaborate setup. To make the murder look like something it's not," Will said.

"Anything's possible these days. But I'm just saying, in my experience, Angie's killer enjoyed it."

"This is unofficial, right?" Dillon asked, looking at Carina.

"Completely off the record," she said, realizing that Nick was right. Whether the killer had attacked Angie for lust or anger or power, he'd enjoyed it. And when he stopped having his fun, he killed her.

"We need a little direction," Will said. "If

there's a better than fifty-fifty chance that the killer is our suspect, we'll work hard to find the evidence to prove it. If we're barking up the wrong tree, we need to learn the identity of each and every man the victim wrote about on her website, then everyone who posted comments. That'll take weeks, months, and I don't see the chief giving us any more help on this one."

Carina concurred. She hated it, but that was the politics of working in a big-city police department. Angie's murder wasn't high-profile enough.

"Your chief will give you the resources when the killer strikes again," Nick said.

Dillon concurred. "Nick's right."

Carina's stomach sank. "That's what I'm afraid of."

"A crime of passion might have some elaborate cover-up to make it look like something else," Dillon explained, "but I don't see that here. The killer glued her mouth shut before he killed her, and according to Dr. Chen, before he raped her. You might think it's a variation on a gag, but it's more than that. A gag can be removed. Glue might be seen as a permanent seal. The killer was essentially telling her to be quiet forever. He didn't want to hear anything she might have to say."

"Could that be some sort of grotesque punishment for what she wrote online?" Will asked.

"Possibly. Something she wrote may have set him off."

"So we're looking for someone she wrote about. That's one of at least eight men, all of whom are identified only by their initials."

Carina commented, "Her friends might be able to identify some of them. We know of Steve Thomas and Doug Masterson. There must be others they've met." She jotted down a note to remind herself.

Dillon put up his hand. "While it may be someone she was intimate with, I'm more inclined to think it was a lurker, someone reading her journal, becoming excited by her comments, and hating himself for it. If he already has an unhealthy fantasy life, her blatant sexuality may have spurred him to action.

"But I'm undecided on that point," he continued. "I've read the coroner's report in detail. Because she was repeatedly raped with foreign objects, including a capped beer bottle, the damage to her body was extensive. However, piecing together the evidence, Dr. Chen believes she was initially raped by the killer, then he used a beer bottle and other devices on her."

"Why?" Will asked. "Isn't rape about power? Isn't the ultimate power for these sick bastards to dominate?"

"Having forcible sex with her wasn't enough of a high for him," Nick said quietly.

Dillon stared at Nick. "Exactly," he said. "After he raped her he didn't obtain the satisfaction he thought he would. It angered him and he blamed her. So he tried other means of bringing on the reaction he wanted."

"Each weapon he used on her," Carina said, "was a common household item. Nothing that had to be specially purchased."

"Yes and no," Dillon said. "Rope and glue? I'd say he planned to kidnap her and rape her. Maybe he didn't plan on killing her, or hadn't thought it out completely. But once she was captive, he knew he was going to kill her. He had to. She wasn't blindfolded, and unless he had a mask on the whole time, she'd be able to identify him."

"The question remains *how* he kidnapped her," Will said. "She came home late Friday night, but disappeared before her mother woke up Saturday morning. She wouldn't have left the house voluntarily with a stranger."

"She knew her attacker," said Carina.

"Yes. Someone she trusted or had no reason to fear."

Nick played devil's advocate. "If she was scared of Steve, why would she go off voluntarily with him?"

"Maybe she was drugged," Carina countered. "Forensics is running additional tests."

"Let's consider another possibility," Dillon interrupted. "For the sake of argument, put aside the restraining order for a moment. The manner of death is particular. The glue. The journal is anonymous, but you and I both know how easy it is to learn the real identity of the posters."

Carina nodded. "Patrick explained it to us."

"There was a case I consulted on last year where a girl in Poway had one of those journaling Web pages. A sexual predator tracked her down, lured her out by convincing her he was a high school senior at a neighboring school, then raped and killed her. Her content was all very innocent, and her parents had helped her set it up according to all the safety rules — no personal information, no identifying comments. One of her friends had a picture of her on *their* journal page and identified her by her login name; another friend on the list mentioned some geographical information; another friend talked about losing a big game on Saturday night and named teams. The killer put all the information together, tracked her down, lured her out, and killed her."

"So even being anonymous doesn't help," Nick said.

Dillon shook his head. "Unfortunately, it's a false sense of security. Getting back to this killer, I think you need to look at the manner of her murder.

"Using industrial-strength glue to seal her mouth may have been personal, but I think it's simpler than that. He didn't want to hear her cry; he didn't want her to say anything. Maybe he feared he could be talked out of it, maybe he was in a location where someone might hear her. With the glue, the victim would be in extreme pain if she tried to move her mouth. She would be focusing on breathing through her nose and not choking. But there's something about her mouth and her voice that sets him off.

"The other thing that really stands out to me is that he didn't kill her with his own hands. He put her in garbage bags, bound them, and she suffocated to death. This might indicate that he's removed from the killing, that he feels it has to be done but *he* doesn't want to do it."

"So this isn't some elaborate setup?" Will asked.

"Setup?"

"Like some guy wanting payback for the victim talking about him online. Rapes her, hurts her, kills her, but then trying to make it look like some psychotic asshole."

Dillon looked at him. "Anyone capable of a murder like this is a sociopath."

"May I look at the report?" Nick asked.

Carina hesitated, then handed him Dillon's copy. "It stays here," she said.

"Of course."

Dillon continued. "Your killer is very immature. The crude manner of the rape, the awkwardness of the way she was bound, writing across her breasts in marker — it all points to someone who isn't a seasoned killer. The supplies he used were common household supplies, as you already noticed."

"Why is writing in marker a sign of immaturity?" Will asked.

"Virtually every similar case I've investigated, a killer marks a body by carving into it or taking something away like hair or an appendage. Writing on the body with a marker or pen or paint seems almost like an afterthought. Not so much branding the victim, but sending a message as to what he thought she was in case anyone missed it. It

189

wasn't for him so much as for anyone who might find her."

Carina said, "Dr. Chen's report indicated that the marker had been applied after she'd been washed."

"And then there's how he disposed of the body," Dillon said.

"Killers often leave their victims in plain sight," Carina said, "as a way to taunt police. To show us they're 'smarter.' "

"I'm looking at the big picture," Dillon explained. "The common restraints. Not wanting to hear her talk or cry or scream. Putting her in garbage bags to *die on her own* without any help from him."

"He put her in them!" Will exclaimed.

"Yes, but he's a step removed, he's watching her die as opposed to being an active participant in her death." Dillon had a rare look of frustration on his face. "I guess what I'm trying to say is that each step he took — restraining her, sealing her mouth, washing her body, suffocating her, dumping her body — fits together if you look at it from the killer's point of view."

"She's dead, she's nothing, he throws her out like garbage," Nick said.

"Right. She holds no more allure for him. Dead, she's an annoyance, a chore that needs to be done. Like taking out the trash.

Now, there's one more thing that's important."

"He cleaned the body," Nick said.

Dillon smiled as if Nick was his star pupil. "Exactly. Notice he washed her *before* he killed her. Before he put her in the garbage bags."

"Some sort of ritual for him?" Carina suggested. "Maybe he thinks sex is dirty and therefore needs to be washed away?"

"That's a good analysis," Dillon said, "and I think it's partially true. He grew up in a house where sex was considered dirty or forbidden or otherwise unhealthy. Puberty is a dangerous time for sociopaths. Hormones, unhealthy fantasies, and no outlet. Either they have no one to talk to about their feelings and how to deal with anger and their sexuality, or their fantasies have been reinforced through sexual abuse or indifference or observation."

"So it's the parents' fault," Will said derisively.

"No, I'm just saying it's one factor. Put it all together. You have a child with sociopathic tendencies — and researchers have shown that you can see these tendencies as young as the age of four."

"Four?" Carina couldn't imagine being able to pinpoint a killer as a toddler.

191

"Remember, Cara, not all sociopaths kill. They are identified through lack of empathy, ease of lying, lack of remorse for bad behavior, among other things. But they don't all grow up to become serial killers. I believe other factors, environment in particular, twists these kids. An abusive mother or father, usually a one-parent household or a stepparent in the picture. Not always, of course — if we knew the formula that created monsters we could put an end to them."

Dillon continued. "You asked for my professional opinion, and based on what we know about the victim and the manner of her death, I believe that the secondary reason he cleaned her body was because of a deep-grained feeling that sex is dirty. It could have been developed by a mother who punished him for wet dreams, or something more sinister."

"Secondary?" Carina asked.

Nick was the one who spoke. "He washed her body to get rid of evidence."

No one said anything for a long minute. "You're not suggesting that he's a cop or someone with forensic knowledge?" Carina asked.

"Everyone these days is a forensic expert," Nick said. "Look at the popularity of crime shows on television. I recently read a report about a killer who disposed of a body by feeding it to his neighbor's pigs. Why? Because he saw it on television."

"And the husband who put his dead wife in a drum of lye and buried it in the back-yard," Dillon added.

"Today's criminals know what we look for, and they are doing everything they can to cover their tracks," Nick said. "It makes our job a hell of a lot more difficult."

"So who are we looking for?" Carina finally asked. "You said he was immature, but he has the wherewithal to clean up after himself."

Dillon explained. "Immature in that he's not a seasoned, practiced killer. He will get more proficient."

"He's going to do it again," she said flatly.

Dillon and Nick both nodded. "How old do you think he is?" Nick asked Dillon.

"Under thirty. There're no definitive stud-ies on the subject, but there's evidence that most serial killers begin killing in their twen-ties. Killing is the first end point in a series of escalations, usually started during pu-berty, and sometimes younger, with bed-wetting, killing animals, and setting fires. It sounds cliché, but studies have shown that these three acts are identifiable in known serial killers."

"If he's under thirty, he may be new to this," Carina said.

"Exactly. Angie may be his first, or he may have another under his belt. Or perhaps a failed attempt."

Dillon said. "He also has a strong sense of survival. He's abnormally neat in appearance and environment. His house will be immaculate. He'll have no tolerance for dirt. You won't see him working in construction, for example, because he can't stand the thought of getting that dirty. He most likely lives alone. He may date, but he can't maintain a long-term relationship. He'll appear safe, innocuous, pleasant, polite. He will not seem like a threat, but he has a vicious temper. He has it under control, but when it gets away from him he can't easily regain control. Very likely a student or a college dropout. Above-average intelligence, but an underachiever. He won't take criticism well, probably because he's so involved in his fantasies that he doesn't pay enough attention to anything that he doesn't think is important."

Nick interrupted and tapped the coroner's report. "Dr. Kincaid, what do you make of the subdermal bruising on her torso? The coroner indicated that the marks came minutes before death."

"You noticed that, too? What's your guess?"

Nick shifted uneasily in his chair. "I hope I'm wrong, but I don't think so. He laid on top of her while she died."

Dillon nodded soberly. "I concur."

Carina stared at the ceiling, anger and frustration building. They had more to go on, but with every comment Dillon and Nick shared, her suspect seemed less and less guilty. "God, why would he do that?"

"It's part of the fantasy. He wanted to feel her life fade away."

They parted company with Dillon on the street. He left in a black Lexus, and Nick walked with Carina and Will to the police station. He surmised that their silence was because of the intense, disturbing conversation they'd had at the restaurant, not because they were still uneasy around him as a relative of a suspect.

"I have a proposition," he said.

Carina stopped outside the main doors of the station and leaned against the base of a statue. Nick couldn't help but notice her lips. A hint of shiny gloss highlighted full, kissable lips. The rest of her long, lean body and her probing eyes said *cop, stand back,* but her lips spoke loud and clear: *kiss me.*

Her brow furrowed. Nick realized he'd been staring at her lips a beat too long. "What?" she prompted.

"I'll bring Steve down to the police station, with a lawyer present, and you ask him anything. I'll make sure he answers. I think with the right questions maybe he has some answers we need to find this killer."

"We?"

"I want to be part of your investigation."

"Why? Let's say we clear your brother. He won't need you here, you can go back to your own job."

Returning to Montana was the last thing Nick wanted to do. He wasn't ready to make the decision that would change his life, no matter what choice he made.

But more than his personal problems, Angie had gotten to him. He couldn't get her out of his mind. "I went to Angie's journal," he said tightly, unable to keep the emotion out of his voice. "I read between the lines. She was crying out for help and none of her friends knew or understood. I just — I want to find her killer. She deserves justice, and you know as well as I do that once the press figures out what's going on, they'll destroy this girl's reputation. She doesn't deserve that, and her grieving family doesn't deserve it."

"And if your brother says something you don't like?"

"I've already answered that," he said, angry. "My credentials are solid."

He stared at Carina, trying to read her mind. She stared back, her face blank as she considered his suggestion. Without taking her eyes from his, she asked her partner, "Will, do you have a problem with it?"

"No."

She nodded curtly. "You're in. But we play by my rules."

"Yes, ma'am," Nick said, surprised that he was relieved that it hadn't been more difficult. He smiled. "My mama told me women are always right."

Carina watched, surprised into silence, as Nick followed Will up the stairs. *Women are always right?*

After the intense meeting with Dillon, and Nick's sharp analysis — he'd certainly impressed Dillon, not an easy feat — she knew the easygoing country sheriff act was just that, an act. Nick Thomas wasn't an ordinary country cop. In fact, he was extraordinary. There was far more depth to Nick Thomas than he wanted anyone to see.

Good thing Carina liked digging.

FOURTEEN

As soon as he arrived back at his brother's apartment, Nick confronted Steve. "You lied to me."

Steve frowned, rubbed his chin. "I've never lied to you, Nick."

"Bullshit." Nick had been harboring anger for the entire drive back from the police station. Partly because of the unnerving information he'd learned about Angie's torture and death, and partly because his brother wasn't the man he'd always believed him to be.

"You lied to me about Angie being the only college girl you dated."

"I think you have it wrong." But Steve averted his eyes. *Lying.*

Nick sat down. This wasn't going like he had planned. He tried to remain as calm as possible. "Steve, sit down. Please."

Steve stiffly sat in the chair across from Nick. Nick saw the lines framing his brother's eyes, his tanned skin looking dry and leathery. Too much fun in the sun. Steve still had a full head of hair, but it was starting to recede at the temple, a few silvery strands mixed into the sandy blond.

"Steve, I want to help you. That's why you asked me to come down here."

"Not to accuse me of lying."

"It's not an accusation, Steve. You did lie to me. You said Angie Vance was the only girl at the college you had a relationship with. I know for a fact that you also slept with Jodi Carmichael."

Steve shifted uncomfortably. "It was just once. Twice. I know I should have said no, but she'd just broken up with her boyfriend and I was consoling her and one thing led to another . . ."

Nick glanced around Steve's apartment, unable to look him in the eye. The medals, newspapers, commendations. Once upon a time Steve had been a hero, on top of the world. After being injured, what had happened to him?

"You haven't grown up," Nick said, surprising himself when he heard his voice. He hadn't meant to voice his fear. Fear that his brother was spiraling down into a fantasy life that only existed in his mind.

"I don't know what you're talking about."

"I'm talking about you, Steve." He waved at the walls. "You're living in the past. You're still savoring the best part of your life, a part that ended fifteen years ago. You were a hero — you still are a hero. But an *older* hero. You haven't lived since you've returned to the States. You haven't done anything with your life except wish you were still twenty-one years old. And that's what you've been acting like."

"How would you know? You don't know me."

"You're wrong, Steve. I know who you were, and I know who you are now. But you're not the same brother who left Montana twenty years ago."

"Everyone changes."

"True. They usually grow up."

"The Butcher really did a number on you, didn't he?" The abrupt change of subject startled Nick. He hadn't expected Steve to attack, and he was speechless.

"That's why you're ready to believe the worst of me," Steve continued, standing, pointing a finger at Nick. "You're the one with a problem. Just because you lost the only woman you ever loved doesn't mean I can't find someone to love."

"What does that have to do with anything?" Nick rose, slowly, his anger rising.

His own past relationships had nothing to do with his brother's current situation.

But Steve was on a roll. "That's what this is about. You're ticked off because I have meaningful relationships with women who care about me."

"*Meaningful?* How many of these *meaningful* relationships have you had in just the last six months?"

Steve continued as if Nick hadn't spoken. "And you're still pining after the woman who got away. Who's pathetic here, Nick? I have what I want, do you?"

Deep down Nick knew Steve had changed the subject to avoid talking about himself. Going on the attack was a standard ploy to keep the attention off him, but Steve's question startled Nick and he couldn't help but think about what he'd gained, and what he'd lost, after the Butcher investigation.

He pushed those thoughts aside. "Steve, you lied to me and you lied to the police. How can I trust you?"

"Maybe you never trusted me."

"Don't twist this around, Steve."

"I can't believe this," Steve said, avoiding the conversation once again.

Nick had just about had it with his brother. "Just tell me you didn't kill Angie."

Steve jerked his head back, staring wide-eyed at Nick. "You sound like you think I did it."

"I don't think you killed her, but I want you to look me in the eye and tell me the truth for once. Did you have anything to do with Angie's death?" Nick didn't believe his brother was guilty, especially after Dr. Kincaid's analysis, but Steve had goaded him, and Nick had reacted.

He also wanted to hear it from Steve's mouth, without excuses, without lies.

Steve started pacing. "You think . . . you think I could do something so cruel? That I would *rape* a woman?"

"You lied to the police about what time you were at the Sand Shack on Friday night."

"I forgot." Again, he was lying.

"Dammit, Steve!" He took two steps across the room and spun his brother to face him. He held him by the shoulders, forced him to look in his eyes. "How can I help you if you keep lying to me?"

"Whose side are you on?" Steve asked through clenched teeth.

"I *want* to be on yours. But do you know how bad it looks to the police if you lie to them?"

"It's not important."

"Hell yes it is!" Nick released Steve. "I

think you should get a lawyer and talk to the police. Tell them everything — *everything* — about your relationship with Angie, why you broke up, when you knew about her journal, how much time you spent there, what you know about deleted comments . . ."

"Deleted comments?"

"Yes. Everything. If you cooperate, maybe we can catch her killer."

"Cooperate! I've been cooperating from day one."

"You've been lying through your teeth so that you look like the hero you used to be, not the man you are today."

Nick wanted to take the words back. The shock, the hurt, on Steve's face hit Nick in the gut.

They stared at each other in silence. "I'll talk to them. Tomorrow morning. Set it up." Steve turned and walked toward his bedroom. Looking over his shoulder he said, "You might want to find another place to stay. My couch isn't very comfortable."

He slammed his bedroom door.

That certainly hadn't gone as Nick planned.

As he packed up his laptop, Nick realized Steve didn't think of himself as a thirty-eight-year-old man. He held close to the image that he was a young, twenty-one-year-old war hero who fit in at college. And in some ways he did, because he certainly acted like an irresponsible, immature kid. Dating college-aged girls was Steve's way of holding on to the illusion that he was young. Since he'd given up his own college years to the military, this was Steve's way of changing the past.

But fifteen years was a long time to grow up.

How could Nick help Steve see that he was living a lie? Maybe he couldn't. Maybe it would take a severe jolt to his ego to make him realize that he didn't fit with the college crowd, that he needed to grow up, get a job, do something other than go to school for the rest of his life.

Nick just didn't know how he could help.

As he walked out the door, Nick felt a deep chill penetrate his bones, and not from the late-afternoon breeze.

Steve had never answered his question about whether or not he'd killed Angie.

FIFTEEN

Will dropped the phone in the cradle and turned to Carina. "Masterson just got back to town. His neighbor called."

"Let's go." Carina shoved her notes in the drawer and jumped up.

They were heading out the door when Nick Thomas walked in, looking a little worse for wear. "What's wrong?" she asked.

He didn't answer her question. "I set up the meeting. Steve will give a formal statement tomorrow morning and answer any questions."

"You didn't have to come all the way back downtown," said Carina. "You could have called."

"I didn't have a choice. My brother kicked me out of his apartment. Know a decent hotel in the area?"

There was more to it than that, but Nick was a man of few words and Carina didn't press.

Will spoke up. "Why don't you ride with us? Masterson just got home. I'd sure like to know what he's been doing since Friday night."

"I appreciate it."

The afternoon commute had just started and it took them thirty minutes to get out to the San Diego coastal community of La Jolla. Masterson lived in a small, poorly maintained house near the campus, about a mile from Steve, though he wasn't a student.

"Easier to sell drugs if you're close to the buyers," Will mumbled.

Carina filled Nick in on Masterson's criminal history as they approached his door. "He seemed to have skipped town with a girl Sunday night. Considering he's Angie's last-known boyfriend, his behavior raises serious questions."

Carina fidgeted as Masterson took his sweet time answering the door. Will acted his usual casual self, though looks were deceptive: his hand was only inches from his gun. And Nick looked all cop, standing tall, face blank, a Stetson on his head. Must be part of the uniform in Montana.

She'd never realized a cop in a hat could look so sexy. She needed to get out of the city more.

Carina shook the errant thought from her

mind and focused on the door.

Will rapped again. "Doug Masterson, Detectives Hooper and Kincaid with the San Diego Police Department."

Finally, they heard a chain sliding open and Doug Masterson stood in the doorway, shirtless and in jeans, reeking of cigarette smoke. He was tall and lanky, with long blond hair and a deep dimple in his chin. He smiled when he saw Carina, sizing her up from head to toe, lingering too long at her breasts.

Jerk.

She flashed her badge. "Detective Kincaid with SDPD. Can we come in?"

She took his barely perceptible nod as a yes and walked through the door. Will and Nick followed.

The apartment was borderline filthy with overflowing ashtrays and dirty clothes tossed around. The fifty-inch flat-screen television took up half of one wall along with a deluxe stereo system that, if turned full-blast, Carina was certain she'd be able to hear down at the station.

The first thought that came to mind was that Masterson couldn't be Angie's murderer if Dillon's analysis of a "tidy, immaculate" killer was accurate.

"Hello, officers of the law," Masterson said

condescendingly. "To what do I owe this pleasure? May I get you coffee? Doughnuts?"

"Cabrón," Carina mumbled, then asked, "When was the last time you saw Angela Vance?"

He blinked, the question obviously startling him. Or he was a good liar. "Angie? Why?"

"She's dead," Carina said flatly.

Masterson sat heavily in a chair and ran both hands through his long hair. He stared at Carina, all flirtatious behavior gone. *"Angie?* Angie Vance?"

"Yes. Your eighteen-year-old girlfriend, Angie Vance."

He shook his head, mouth open. "Dead? How?"

"Let's start with Friday and work our way to today," Will said. "Where did you go Friday morning?"

"Friday. Um, I just hung out here most of the day. Went out about eight at night. Couple parties. Came back about four."

"Alone?"

"Alone?" he repeated.

"Did you bring someone home with you?" Carina repeated slowly.

"Friday night?"

"It can't be too hard to remember," Will

said. "Five days ago."

"No, I came home alone."

"When was the last time you saw Angie?"

Whether he seriously couldn't remember, or he was just trying to come up with a viable lie, Carina didn't know. "I think," he began slowly, "it was Thursday night. It might have been Friday. At the Sand Shack. It was toward the end of her shift."

That should be easy enough to verify, Carina thought.

"I really don't remember," he said. "Last time I saw her she gave me the cold shoulder."

"Did you know she suspected you were seeing another woman?"

This time, the surprise on his face was genuine. "Hell, no! I-I-I'm not seeing anyone else," he stammered.

"Your neighbor told us you went skiing in the mountains."

"Big Bear. My folks have a cabin up there."

"With whom?"

"Is that important?"

"Yes."

"Why?"

"To establish your alibi. With whom did you go to Big Bear?"

He glared at her. "Ellen."

"Ellen what?"

"I don't know her last name."

"When did you leave?"

"Sunday night."

"What time?"

"Ten, eleven. It was late."

"And you don't know her last name?"

He shrugged. "We met at a party Sunday, hit it off, and split."

"Why did Angie think you were seeing another woman *last* week?"

"I don't know. She's the jealous type."

"How so?"

"Look, she has this double standard. She's been with a lot of guys, but says she's loyal. I believed her, told her the same goes for me. Then she sees me talking — just *talking* — to my ex-girlfriend and she goes all frigid on me. So I think, okay, she's having a bad day. I go down to the Sand Shack when I know she's going to get off work, say hey, let's go see a movie or something, and she blows me off. So I went out and partied all weekend. Met up with Ellen, she didn't have those issues, and we had fun. I don't need the drama, you know what I mean?"

"Yeah," Carina said sarcastically, "relationships are hard work."

"Exactly," he said, oblivious to her jibe. "I'm sure you don't have any relationship problems." He licked his bottom lip and grinned at her.

She glared at him. A biting remark was on the tip of her tongue when Nick took a step forward.

"It's not very smart to piss off a lady with a gun," he said simply.

Nick's hardened expression belied his light words. Once again, Carina suspected there was far more beneath the surface than Nick Thomas showed the world.

"Hey, no offense!" Masterson put up his hands. "Look, what happened to Angie? I mean, I saw her on Friday, okay, but I didn't see her all weekend. Really, I didn't see her."

"Do you know where Ellen lives?" Nick asked.

Masterson rattled off the address where he'd dropped her off earlier.

"Be available for questions," Will said.

"What happened to Angie?" Masterson repeated.

Carina had no desire to give him any of the details. "Go buy a newspaper," she said and they left.

In the car, Will said, "I don't think he has the guts to kill anyone."

"*Huevon,*" Carina said. "Too stupid to cover up the crime. Did you see anything in his apartment that looked out of place?"

211

"I don't think he could find clean boxers, let alone glue."

"How far is Big Bear?" Nick asked.

"About two, two-and-a-half-hours."

"If his parents have a cabin up there, it would be a remote place where he could have kept Angie," the sheriff suggested.

Carina and Will glanced at each other. "Go on."

"He dumped the body Sunday night. Could he have dumped the body, then picked up this Ellen and taken her back there? Did anyone see him on Saturday?"

"We have a lot of work to do," Will said. He glanced at Ellen's address. "She's out in Carlsbad. Up for a nice coastal drive?" he asked Nick.

"I have no other plans."

Ellen Workman was a twenty-five-year-old college dropout who lived with her parents and worked part-time as a cocktail waitress. By the time they arrived in Carlsbad, she had already left for work. They stopped by her business and, while she was irritated at being pulled off the job, she was sharp and credible.

"Doug and I hung out from about three o'clock Sunday afternoon onward. When he suggested we go skiing, I was all for it, especially since he was paying. I work Wednesday through Saturday, so I told him I had to be back by five o'clock today. He brought me home, end of story."

"What time did you leave for Big Bear?"

"Eleven. I wanted to pick up my stuff, so we drove here."

Carina was confused. "You left La Jolla at eleven? I thought you said you were with him after three in the afternoon?"

She sighed heavily. "Okay, we met up at three at a friend's house. Had a few beers. Dinner. Then he wanted to go skiing, so we left La Jolla about ten at night for my place, I packed a bag, and we left for Big Bear at eleven. Okay?"

"Did Doug leave you at any time between three and ten that day?"

"Maybe to take a piss. Look, what's this about?"

"We're just verifying information that he told us."

"Whatever. Can I get back to work?"

Ellen walked away. Carina shook her head. "The time line doesn't work for Masterson to be the killer."

"Unless she's an accomplice," Nick said.

"Why would she?"

No one had an answer. Their one other lead had dried up. Masterson wasn't guilty,

213

and Carina looked at Nick. She saw in his eyes what she was thinking.

All eyes would now be on Steve.

With good reason. Police didn't like it when suspects lied.

Nick knew that as well as she did.

Her heart went out to him. He was going to have a rough time of it tomorrow if his brother incriminated himself. While Carina hoped Steve gave himself up so she could close the case, find justice for Angie's family, and stop another brutal murder, she couldn't help but feel for Nick and what he would go through knowing his brother was a murderer.

Rope. *Check.*

Glue. *Check.*

Plastic wrap. *Check.*

Garbage bags. *Check.*

He went through the supplies in his mind as he watched the webcam he'd set up earlier that day in Jodi's apartment.

It would be more difficult this time because he wouldn't be able to lure Jodi out like he'd done Angie. Angie knew him well, so she hadn't thought anything was wrong even when he tapped on her window in the middle of the night.

"Angie? Angie? Can we talk?"

She'd been so trusting. Came right out, got in his car, and *wham!* He had her.

Jodi knew him, of course, but not as well. And with Angie dead he wasn't so naive as to think Jodi wouldn't be at least somewhat on alert. It was better to assume than to screw up, right?

So he'd set up the webcam and drugged the two-liter bottle of diet Coke, the milk, the orange juice, the bottle of white wine. Every open container in the refrigerator. He'd watch the kitchen, see when she poured herself something to drink, and wait.

The anticipation was almost as good as the real thing. He wished he could have gone home to watch, but the library was only a couple blocks from Jodi's apartment, and he didn't want to risk taking too long or getting stuck in traffic before he was able to get to her apartment. And he had his own private nook here. No one could see what he was working on. He used his own laptop, not the library's computer, and he could see everything.

As soon as Jodi drank what he'd drugged, he'd leave. The few minutes it would take to get to her apartment would be just enough time for the sleeping pills to make her drowsy.

Abby had a late class every Wednesday. While she usually went out after her class, he couldn't count on it tonight. Not when Angie's funeral was tomorrow night and Jodi was home. Alone.

Come on, Jodi! Don't fuck this up. Don't mess with me. I'm going to have you no matter what.

Another lying bitch, acting like a sweet, nice girl and nothing but a slut like Angie.

Jodi came on-screen, the cheap webcam distorting her image. But he knew it was her. She opened the refrigerator and he held his breath.

She retrieved a bottle of beer, twisted off the cap.

No!

He couldn't drug the beer. It wasn't fair, it fucking wasn't fair. How dare she screw up his entire plan! He'd been waiting for tonight, planning for tonight, had everything ready.

He slammed down the top of his laptop.

"Is everything okay?"

He jumped, turned, and saw that Becca had walked over to him. He'd been so focused on watching Jodi that he hadn't noticed her standing right there, at the side of the table. Had she seen his screen? What if she knew what he had planned?

Her face didn't give anything away, but she was a liar. All women were liars. Her tits were right at eye level, her low-cut blouse hinting at the flesh beneath.

"Yes. I'm sorry." He glanced away from her, pulse racing.

"What's wrong?" She sat down in the chair next to him, put a hand on his arm. He looked at her small, slender fingers and the pink nail polish with tiny white flowers glued on. And he knew this was a sign, an omen. Becca didn't normally work on Wednesdays, but she was here tonight.

Becca was his.

He looked back up at her, his face long and sad. "It's my cat, Felix. He died today."

"Oh my God, I'm so sorry. How did he die? Was he old?"

He shook his head. "I found him on the front porch. He was bleeding."

"Hit by a car?"

He began to get into the story he was creating, based in part on a long-ago truth. "That's what I thought at first, then I took him to the vet. The vet said someone shot him with a BB gun. He found sixteen pellets in Felix." He looked at her with dry eyes. "How could someone do that?"

She hugged him. "I'm so sorry. Do you know who did it?"

"I can't prove it, but I think my brother did it. He always hated Felix." He didn't know why he said that, but it worked. She squeezed his arm, her eyes full of compassion. Her fingers were so soft . . .

The librarian motioned for Becca, and she stood. "I have to get back to work. Take care of yourself, okay? Losing an animal is hard. People don't realize how much we grow attached to our pets. And you should definitely talk to your brother. That was cruel." She gave him a spontaneous kiss on the cheek and went back to work.

Slowly, methodically, he packed up his laptop. He walked to his car, heart racing. If Becca worked her regular hours, she'd get off in less than an hour.

He would be here when she did.

Suddenly, losing his opportunity to take Jodi didn't anger him as much anymore. There was always tomorrow.

All Nick had asked for were directions to a halfway decent hotel; what he got was a ride to Carina's parents' house and his own private apartment above their garage.

"I really appreciate your hospitality," he said as he sat in Carina's car in front of a modest, two-story house. One of Carina's parents had a green thumb, as evidenced by the excessive flowers in the ground, in pots, and hanging on vines that covered four trellises lining the walk to the front door.

"Don't mention it." She didn't make any move to get out of the car, instead turned to face him. "I read a couple articles about the Bozeman Butcher."

Nick tensed. He didn't want to talk about it. "Water under the bridge."

"It was a tough case."

He didn't comment.

"I noticed you were limping after we drove back from Carlsbad. Are you okay?"

She sounded casually concerned, like any colleague would be. But beneath the easy tone there was something else . . . did she doubt he could do the job? Did she regret including him in the investigation?

"Why did you let me join you and Hooper?"

She didn't answer him for a long time. Finally, "I didn't want you working the case on your own. Secondary to that was your familiarity with sex-related murder. We felt your experience would be valuable." She looked at him. "And you more than proved yourself during our meeting with Dillon. I don't regret it. Do you?"

"No." He leaned back into the seat, closed his eyes. "Steve and I had an argument earlier today. We'd never gone that far before."

She was waiting for him to say more; what could he say? That Steve lived in his own fantasy world? That he had a dark side Nick was only beginning to discover? No, not yet. They had the interview in the morning and then . . . maybe then he and Steve could work to get back what they used to have.

But Nick wasn't holding his breath. He was a different man today than he was two decades ago. So was Steve. They had grown apart, and Nick didn't know how to bridge the divide. At this point it seemed wider and deeper than the Grand Canyon.

"I'm fine," he finally said. "My knee gets sore at the end of the day, especially after a lot of use. By tomorrow morning I'll be as good as new." He smiled, winked at her. "Nothing a good night's sleep won't cure."

He found Carina looking out the windshield, a thoughtful expression on her face. Her profile was unusually exquisite, elegant. It wasn't the first time since yesterday that he'd noticed how attractive Carina was, but it was the first time he'd had more than a moment to think about it.

She turned to look at him, her lips parted, and once again he noticed her sensuous mouth. It was a sin for a woman to have such kissable lips and not be kissed.

He looked away and said, "Maybe you should introduce me to your parents so they're not surprised to see a light on over their garage."

"I called them, they're expecting us. And Nick?"

"Yeah?" He looked at her again, this time focusing on her eyes, not her lips. He didn't particularly like the fact that he was attracted to the cop who believed his brother was capable of murder.

"I'm glad you're on board."

Becca was still unconscious.

He'd had to take her fast, because he didn't know who would be coming in and out of the library parking lot. He knew she drove the little sporty Toyota because he'd watched her before. If someone was around, he had planned to follow her home instead. But everything worked out for the best: she left alone, no one was in the parking lot, no one was walking on the street.

She was petite, and because she recognized him, she wasn't scared. She even smiled and waved as she approached her car — he was parked next to her, trunk up, pretending to look for something.

"See you later," she said.

He grabbed her and pushed her into the trunk, hit her once, twice to shock her, then quickly gagged her. The thrill of taking her in a public parking lot, without drugs, just by being smart and fast, excited him. He tied her hands behind her and slammed the trunk closed.

No one saw anything. Forty-five seconds had passed.

He drove off, heart racing, his prize in the trunk.

She was unconscious when he got home, which helped. No one would be able to hear her, and it was dark enough now that no one could see him carry her inside.

He stripped her naked and tied her to the bed. He removed the gag, then glued it on. She stirred a bit, but didn't open her eyes.

And then he watched.

"You're so beautiful, Becca," he said softly, almost reverently.

Becca and Angie were completely different. Angie had brown hair she'd dyed blond, big tits, and a tattoo. She was coarse and crude, and posted disgusting things online for everyone in the world to see that she was a slut.

Becca was pure, smooth, small breasts and a slender body. Sweet and kind, always smiled at him. He wondered how it would feel, how different than Angie. He would be gentle with Becca because she wasn't the slut Angie was. He would be kind and considerate. Like he would have been with Randi if she hadn't said no.

"They always say no."

The voice of his father echoed in his mind. His dad hadn't been talking to him. He'd been talking to his mother, but he'd been eavesdropping.

He'd been nine at the time and his father had just come home. He'd been in prison for rape. He hadn't known what that meant when his father first left, but over the next four years he'd learned exactly what it meant. It was all his mother ever talked about.

"Why don't you just pay a fucking whore?" his mother had shouted at his dad.

"I don't pay for it."

"You just paid four years for it!"

He was in the living room watching television, but he heard everything because his parents hadn't closed their bedroom door.

"You liked it last time. You love it when I tell you all about it."

"You're going to be thrown in jail again."

His father laughed, a loud bellow, and then there were other sounds. The bed creaking, slaps, moans. His parents were having sex. He listened to the sounds of sex outside the bedroom door.

"Do you want to watch next time?" his father asked.

He hadn't realized his father had seen him. He stood in the doorway, his jeans unbuttoned.

He shook his head but his father laughed and ruffled his head. "Sure you do, kid. You have to learn somehow."

And his dad walked out of the house.

His mother came out of the bedroom in a robe and kicked him. "Fucking pervert, just like your father. You're going to end up in prison, too, mark my words, unless you listen to me. Stay away from women who say they want it. They're lying, and they'll whip around and cry rape the minute your back is turned."

Not his women. His women couldn't cry rape even if they wanted to.

His women couldn't talk.

He stared at Becca. He'd already decided to only keep her for twenty-four hours. He'd kept Angie for too long and it had ruined his excitement. The clock was ticking. It was after midnight.

"Wake up." He tapped her. She moaned but didn't open her eyes.

He slapped her and her eyes opened. Like

a bug pinned to a board, she squirmed, realized she was trapped, and fought harder.

"It's time, Becca."

She tried to scream.

Sixteen

Carina and Nick arrived together at the police station early Thursday morning. They didn't talk much on the drive over. Carina was sure Nick was uncomfortable about having his brother brought in, even willingly, for questioning in a capital murder case.

Her? She didn't want to talk for fear of saying something stupid. Something like, "Why were you in my dreams last night?"

As soon as her head had hit the pillow, she'd been out. And dreaming about Nick Thomas, his hard body, his too-sexy-for-words cowboy hat. If Nick was an example of the type of men who lived in Montana, maybe she should put in for a transfer.

She'd woken up rested for the first time all week. She didn't remember every detail of her dream — probably good, lest she blush when she saw Nick — but in her dream she had kissed him and he had pulled her into his arms. Then the way dreams go, they were both naked in her bed and he was about to make love to her . . .

She cleared her mind, focused on the task at hand. "Ready?" she asked Nick.

"Yes."

She'd agreed to let Nick observe the interview, but suggested that he stand in the adjoining room where he could watch and listen unnoticed by his brother. He nodded a curt agreement, his face blank. She didn't know what he was thinking.

At least Steve had taken Nick's advice and retained a criminal defense attorney. Both were waiting in the interview room.

In the adjoining room, Dillon and Will joined Carina and Nick. "Are we ready?" Carina asked her brother and her partner. On the phone late last night they had decided that the primary purpose of the meeting was to push Steve Thomas to tell the truth about Friday night as well as his past arguments with Angie. Next, they would ascertain what, if anything, he knew about the deleted comments.

They entered the room, leaving Nick behind, introduced themselves, and set up a recorder.

"Let's start with how you met Angela Vance," Carina began.

They'd met last September at the beginning of the school year when he sat next to Angie in computer class.

"We became friends immediately." Steve sat military straight, hands clasped in front of him.

"When did you become romantically involved?" Carina asked.

"In December."

"How did it happen?"

Steve tensed. "Why does that matter?"

"Anything, no matter how small, could be relevant."

Steve glanced down at his hands and Carina couldn't help but wonder if he was trying to come up with a believable lie. "She asked if I wanted to get together one weekend. I said sure. I thought she meant go out for a date."

"What did she mean?"

He paused long enough for Carina to prompt him again.

"She wanted to be 'friends with benefits.' "

Carina had heard about such "special" friendships. Friends who had sex but no emotional or permanent attachment. An open relationship. Angie had written about several "friends with benefits" relationships in her journal, including hers with Steve. Carina would be a failure at that sort of arrangement. She loved sex, but it meant little without an emotional commitment. Maybe she was a romantic at heart, but the idea of an eighteen-year-old being so nonchalant about meaningful relationships made Carina sad.

"And what did you want?" she asked Steve.

"I wanted what Angie wanted."

Carina didn't believe him. "So you were okay with the relationship."

"More or less."

"I don't think you're telling us everything."

"It's not important."

"You don't know that."

"Yes I do!" he said, his fists clenching. "This isn't about me, it's about Angie. I didn't kill her. I keep saying it and you don't believe me."

Dillon interjected. "You and Angie had a sexual relationship that you wanted to be exclusive, but she didn't."

"But that makes it look wrong, or like I would want to hurt her because we didn't want the same thing."

Dillon continued. "Steve, what we want is the truth. Sometimes the truth shines a light on things that you know nothing about."

Steve didn't say anything for a long

minute. "Yes, I cared a lot about Angie and I didn't like having an open relationship. I was monogamous, but Angie wasn't comfortable with that. She thought we should both be seeing other people."

"And did you and Angie break up because you couldn't agree on the type of relationship you wanted?"

"Not exactly."

"Then why?"

"I discovered her journal and confronted her."

"What was her reaction?"

A faint tic pulsed in Steve's cheek. "She told me to lighten up."

"And then she broke up with you, correct?"

He nodded.

"Please answer for the tape, Mr. Thomas."

"Yes, she broke up with me the next day. But I understood. It hurt, but I understood."

"Understood what?" Carina asked.

"Angie needed attention from men. Her father skipped town when she was young. Used to promise to visit, never made it. The last time she saw him, she was thirteen. He didn't come to her, she ran away and tracked him down in San Francisco. With his new wife. He didn't want children, never

230

had, and told Angie that.

"She was devastated. She lost her virginity when she was fourteen to a nineteen-year-old high school senior and just fell into that cycle."

"So you think she slept with you because she wanted to sleep with her father?" Dillon asked.

"No! She slept with me — and others — because she wanted to feel love. She equated sex with love. And I —" he stopped.

"Go on," Dillon prompted. "What did you get from your friendship with Angie?"

"I thought I could help her."

"If you showed her love then maybe she wouldn't think it had to come with sex, too."

"Exactly!" Steve's face lit up. "We were making a lot of progress. Until the journal fiasco. I didn't handle that right at all. Maybe if I'd done something differently, said something more supportive, didn't argue with her — I don't know." He sank his face into his hands.

"What prompted Angie to get a restraining order against you?" Carina asked.

"I don't know why she did it, except she was scared. Not of me," he continued quickly, "but of other things going on."

"But she got the restraining order against *you*," Will interjected. "No one else. She

231

was scared of you."

"She wasn't scared of me," Steve insisted.

"You fought with Angie on January 19 at the Sand Shack in front of witnesses," Will said. "What was that argument about?"

"After I discovered her journal online, I was worried about her. I started monitoring the page and the comments because she was really going too far, even engaging in conversations with some of these guys. The night before our fight there was a comment that really disturbed her. She called me, accused me of posting it to scare her. I, of course, said I didn't. I'd never purposefully scare her."

This was the first they'd heard of Angie contacting Steve after the breakup. It would be easy enough to check through her phone records, which they already had a copy of.

"What did the comment say?"

"I don't know, she said she deleted it after she read it."

"And that was what day?"

"January eighteenth, I think."

"What disturbed her about that comment?" If it was worse than the comments she'd kept online it must have been violent or personal.

"He knew something about her. That's why she thought it was me."

"What did he know?"

"Where she worked."

Carina and Will glanced at each other. "He said that?"

"I didn't read it, but Angie basically accused me of trying to expose her and scare her. The next day I went to talk to her, to convince her it wasn't me, that I would never hurt her, and, well, it was a big fight. I told her to go to the police, give them the information about the person who scared her. She didn't want to tell anyone about her journal. I told her she was going to end up dead if she didn't watch herself. Her pal Kayla convinced her that *I* was the threat. It wasn't me. It was never me. That's why I started following her."

"You followed her on the Friday she disappeared. Why did you lie to us about going to the Shack twice that night?"

"I didn't want to admit that I had been following her. It looked bad. Believe me, I'm sorry. I didn't think you'd look at me as her murderer. I didn't want you to have a reason to, because I know I'm not guilty and if you looked at me, you wouldn't be looking for the real killer . . ." his voice trailed off. "I was stupid."

"You also lied about how much time you spent reading her journal," Carina said, putting her hands on the table and looking him in the eye. "You flat-out lied to us two days ago. We know you've spent more than forty hours on her journal."

"I told you, I was trying to protect her. She didn't want me around, so I had to watch her any way I could."

"Including stalking her."

Steve's attorney finally spoke up. "My client did not stalk the victim. He admitted to following her for her own protection, not stalking her."

Carina dipped her head. "You *followed* her home the night she disappeared. You were the last person to see her alive."

He swallowed and his brow began to sweat. "You don't know how sick I feel. You don't know how much I hate myself for assuming that she was safe in her own home. If I'd handled the entire situation differently, if I'd gone to the police myself . . . I don't know. I don't know what I could have done to stop Angie from self-destructing." He closed his eyes.

"Can you think of anything else about that posted comment that scared her?"

He shook his head, looked first at Carina, then the men. "She didn't give me any details except that the comment implied the location of her work. That it was on the beach. Not by name. But it freaked her out."

"Was that the only time she contacted you about being scared about a comment?"

"Yes."

Carina turned off the recorder. "You're free to go, Mr. Thomas, but I have to ask you not to leave town. We may have more questions."

He nodded. "Anything to find Angie's killer."

When Steve left with his attorney, Carina pulled out her cell phone and called Patrick. She filled him in on the deleted comments and asked, "Is there any way to work with the MyJournal people?"

"We're working on it right now," Patrick said, "but it's slow. However, she banned nineteen people from commenting on her journal. I have the list for you."

"Do you have any personal information?"

"No, but you might want to start by hitting their personal pages and see if there's anything that jumps out."

"Thanks, Patrick, we'll be right up."

Nick cornered Steve in the hall when he left the interview room. "Steve," he began.

"I had a feeling you were around. You heard everything." He sounded so bitter.

"Yes. I'm glad you told the truth."

"Are you?" he asked. "I told you the truth before and you didn't believe me."

"You told me a half-truth, Steve. You lied to me."

"I told you what was important. Instead, you pushed and pushed, just to humiliate me."

"That wasn't my intention."

"Funny, that's how I felt."

They stared at each other, at a standstill. Nick didn't know what to do to fix the broken relationship with his brother.

If Nick went back to Montana, when would he see his brother again? It would be much easier to just continue his life as if this had never happened.

Carina, Will, and Dillon walked out of the interview room. Steve looked at them, then Nick, then walked away without another word.

Nick let him go. He asked Dillon, "What's your take?"

"I'm ninety percent certain he's innocent." Will concurred.

Carina said. "We gave him enough opportunities to trip up. But at least we have something to follow up on."

"I'll run upstairs and get the list of screen names from Patrick," Will said and left.

"List?" Nick asked.

Carina said, "Patrick has a list of nineteen MyJournal members who Angie banned from commenting on her page."

"And you think the deleted comment that scared her came from one of those people?"

"Exactly. We'll see who she banned around January eighteenth and go from there. Maybe we'll get lucky and there will only be one."

"I think Mr. Thomas's assessment of Angie Vance is accurate," Dillon said, "at least from what I can tell without talking to her. She was seeking both validation and attention from men. Seeing from early on that she was receiving both when she had sex with them, she kept looking for someone to give her what she needed. Not finding it, she moved on."

"And that's why she dated older men?"

He nodded. "Boys her age didn't give her the approval or affection she needed. Not that she got it from older men, but they were more mature than eighteen-year-old college kids."

Carina's cell phone rang. "It's Will," she said as she answered it. "Any news?"

"We have three MyJournal members banned by Angie on either January eighteenth or nineteenth. Patrick is working with the company to get any information they have about them. Patrick is all over it, and we might have something tonight or tomorrow. He's also going to set up a way to track the three members online so if they post to any MyJournal page, we'll know instantly."

"Fabulous. Maybe we can find out who his next victim is before he gets to her."

SEVENTEEN

Because killers often attend or observe the memorial services of their victims, the chief gave Will and Carina additional resources to cover the event. It took them an hour to debrief the team and formulate a plan for Angie's memorial service. Then they went upstairs to talk to Patrick.

Carina introduced Nick to her brother. "The Kincaid family seems to run San Diego," Nick said with a smile.

"You haven't even met half of them," Carina said. "But Patrick's my favorite."

The young cop smirked. "She only says that when she wants something." He rolled his chair across his small office and picked up a printout. "But maybe I really will be your favorite now. I got details on all three banned members. I printed out their My-Journal pages. No personal information — they didn't use their real names. One has an e-mail address, and I ran it through the database and hit on a name and physical address." He handed them another page. "Damon Bader lives in Detroit, Michigan."

"What are the chances he came to San Diego to track down Angie and kill her?" Carina asked half-seriously.

"Next to none. I called the e-crimes unit and they did some preliminary work. The guy has a record, all misdemeanors, and works as a sanitation engineer. Twice divorced, two kids, and he's fifty-six."

Didn't fit the profile, but they had to cover their bases. "We should check the airlines just in case he's been out here recently," Carina said. "And talk to his employer about any recent time off."

"Consider it done," Patrick said.

"The other two?"

"The first has the screen name 'Bondage,' and I read some of his comments on other pages. Probably the world's biggest liar, but he claims to have done some wild stuff. If he's for real, he's a major contender for us. The other screen name is 'Scout.' Again, checked him out. Some heavy stuff, but nothing that popped as threatening. Both were banned on the eighteenth by Angie."

"This is great," Carina said, "but can't we find out where they live?"

Patrick shook his head. "MyJournal is a

free site. There's no verification process. Just create a login and password and you have a profile page. Bondage lists his hometown as USA, and Scout doesn't list a hometown. The only way I can narrow them down is to trace their comments through the MyJournal server to a local Internet service provider. Then, with a warrant, we can get the payment information from the ISP and locate them that way. But the MyJournal attornies are sticklers about privacy law. I've already put a call in to their security chief. It's going to take some time."

E-crimes were exploding, and the police department was still catching up with the twenty-first century. When they thought they'd gotten a handle on the casework, another cyberscam hit and they were scrambling for more computer resources.

"The answer is here somewhere." Carina flipped through the pages of printed material from the MyJournal site. "But we need a hundred people and a thousand hours to find it."

"Welcome to my life," Patrick said. "I have some other ideas I'm working on, but I'll talk to you about them tonight."

"Tonight?" Carina hit her forehead. "Lucy's birthday party!"

"You *have* to be there," Patrick said. "Or

she'll give you the cold shoulder for the rest of your life."

"I'll be there, but late. It's Angie's memorial service tonight."

Patrick nodded solemnly. "I'll cover for you. But I get your slice of cake."

"Deal."

They went back downstairs and while Will filled in the team covering the memorial service, Carina looked at Bondage's page on her computer and Nick looked at Scout's on Will's.

"Bondage says he's twenty-two," she said as she investigated the site. "This is awful. I don't believe in censorship, but I still don't think this stuff should be allowed. Hey, look at this."

Nick leaned over to see her screen. When his shoulder brushed hers, a jolt ran down her spine, leaving her with tingles and goose bumps. She licked her lips, then hoped Nick didn't notice.

"What?" he asked, his voice low as he looked at the screen. "White nylon rope."

On Bondage's main page was a picture of a partially clothed woman bound by white nylon rope around her wrists and ankles. The woman didn't look in distress; she was posed with her lips open and her tongue out, her face heavily made up.

The caption read: *I love a woman who likes to be tied up.*

"Same kind our killer used."

"It's common," Nick said, "but it's certainly damning. Any identifying information?"

Carina skimmed the personal profile. "Nothing about where he lives, what he does — wait. Here. 'I work at a coffeehouse in a college town and the girls here are wild.' "

"Did Angie frequent any coffeehouse?"

"I don't remember her friends talking about a specific place other than the Sand Shack. But I'll ask them tonight at the memorial service."

Nick said, "Steve's neighbor Ava said something about how a lot of their friends hung out at the Starbucks near campus."

"We'll check it out. We might have time before the service tonight."

Nick went back to his own screen and Carina felt distinctly colder with him several feet away. She glanced at his broad back, the muscles defined under his white polo shirt. He wore jeans, and wore them very well.

Her heart was beating too fast and she swallowed, turned back to her computer. It took her a moment to focus, all her senses attuned to Nick Thomas and his hot body, his low drawl, his piercing blue eyes.

Get over it, Kincaid. He's a cop. You don't date cops.

But he lives in Montana. He's going home. You know you want to see how he kisses.

Stop it! You don't do things like that. No one-night stands, remember?

But he's special.

Was he? Carina wondered as she debated silently with herself. She snuck another quick glance at him. Yeah, there was definitely something about Nick that had all her female hormones working overtime.

"Look at this." Nick scooted his chair to the side so she could bring hers over.

She read what was on the screen. "What?"

"This is old. He set it up nearly two years ago, but there's only this one post."

"So what does that mean?"

"I don't know. He obviously comments on other people's pages, but he doesn't draw people to his page."

Heads together, they read the sole post on Scout's MyJournal page.

Hello. I'm Scout. Why? Because I'm always looking around, you know, scouting things out. Ha.

I just got my own computer and the first

thing I did was set up this MyJournal account. Everyone talks about what a great place this is and I've already visited a lot of the people here and they're great.

About me? There's really not much to tell. My life is actually boring. Not much of a life, really. But I'm going to change that. My dad always told me if I wanted to make my mark on the world, I needed to be in control and not take shit from anyone. I know I'm destined to do great things. Everyone will know my name. I won't be a nobody forever.

"He sounds young," Nick said thoughtfully.

"Too young. Like he's in high school."

"He posted this two years ago. He may be in college now."

"Unfortunately, we can't do anything with this information," Carina said, discouraged. "I'd really hoped I'd see something like, 'I killed a woman last weekend and dumped her body on the beach.' "

"Too neat."

"You're telling me." She paused. "How long did it take you to catch the Bozeman Butcher?"

Nick tensed and she wished she hadn't asked. "He killed twenty-two women in

245

thirteen years. I was sheriff for the last three years of his reign. Under my watch, four women died."

"But you caught him."

"I didn't have much to do with his capture," he said cryptically.

"But —"

Will approached, interrupting the conversation. "Okay, I have eight guys in place as we discussed earlier, and two more checking everyone's names and ID when they enter. We'll have a list. Might not do us any good, but I'll never forget the Fremont case."

"What was that?" Nick asked.

"A year ago," Carina said, "a nurse was killed in the parking lot of the hospital. We caught the case — my first as detective — staked out the memorial service, which was in the hospital chapel. The killer was cocky enough to use a stolen hospital ID and sit right up in front. We had a team of men in the next room verifying every ID and we found him, arrested him as he left."

"Very neat and tidy."

"Wish this case was," Will said. He glanced at his watch. "We need to talk to the chief."

"I'll meet you outside," Nick said.

"Actually, we need you to be there,"

Carina said. "Will talked to Chief Causey earlier today and he wants to meet you and get a copy of your credentials."

"Sure," Nick said, sounding cautious. "Is there a problem?"

"No, but since the press has started making calls, Causey wants to make sure all *i*s are dotted and *t*s crossed. I'm also making another push for a task force, using Dillon's informal profile to back it up."

"Because he's going to kill again."

"Seems likely. But maybe if we get the manpower we need we can stop him before he becomes the textbook definition of a serial killer."

Soundlessly, she cried as he washed her body.

"I didn't mean to hurt you like that," he told Becca as he washed the streaks of blood from between her legs. The water was tepid, neither hot nor cold, but her body trembled, making the water ripple.

He stroked her hair, kissed her cheek, ran a hand over her breasts. Scrubbed her body with a rag and soap, lots of soap. Rinsed her well.

"You were very good. Not like the whore. You were sweet and fresh and new. All for me." When he'd penetrated her the first time he'd realized she was a virgin. He'd come instantly, the knowledge that he'd be the first and the last man to have her providing such intense excitement he didn't want to hold back.

She strained against the gag. "Don't do that. You'll make it hurt more. You can't tell anyone what happened."

She shook her head back and forth, her eyes wide. She tried to say something, guttural sounds rumbling in her throat. He didn't understand her, but he didn't have to. She'd just lie to him. All women, even beautiful virgins like Becca, lie. She'd say she wouldn't tell, but the first thing she would do is go to the police and tell them who he was.

Obviously, he couldn't allow that to happen.

He washed her hair and poured water over her head. She breathed heavily, tears running from her eyes.

"I'm sorry, it has to be done." He motioned for her to get up. "Walk back to the bed," he told her.

Her entire body shook, water dripping off her to the floor. He walked behind her with a towel, one he bought just for her. Brand-new, never been used.

Suddenly, she ran for the door.

"No!" He took three long strides, but she had the door open and ran down the hall.

He was faster. He caught her before she even touched the front door.

He threw her body down on the floor. Her head hit the coffee table and he saw blood on her scalp. He'd have to clean the table later.

She struggled as he picked her up and she scratched his neck. He held her tight, brought her back to his bed. She fought and cried as he tied her up, her hands above her head and her feet to the posts at the end of the bed.

His breathing was rapid, his face flushed with the exertion. And, if he thought about it, the excitement of chasing her. He'd been scared, very scared, for a minute, but he couldn't ignore the rush when he caught her, subdued her, brought her back to his bed, and tied her up.

He looked at the hand that had scratched him. He couldn't see anything under her nails, she had barely even broken his skin, but that didn't mean something wasn't there. He had to be careful. He took a sharp knife and cleaned under her fingernails. She bled. He then held her hand in a bowl of bleach. A guttural scream reverberated in her chest and he watched her vocal cords and the small, thin bones strain against her neck.

"I'm sorry," he said. He hadn't wanted to hurt her, but she *had* tried to escape.

He took the time to flush the bloody bleach down the toilet and carefully wash the bowl.

Then he returned to Becca, plastic wrap in hand.

He started at her feet. Slowly, carefully, wrapping Becca's body.

First one leg. Then the other. Her butt, everything but her vagina. Her waist. Around and around. Her breasts. Then each arm. And to be safe, he wrapped her again.

His entire body quivered with excitement.

He looked in her eyes and saw fear.

"Good night, Becca."

He rolled on a condom and pushed himself into her with one stroke. Her body jerked beneath him. He brought the plastic heavy-duty garbage bag from his nightstand, pulled it over her head, and tied it around her neck.

Then he laid on top of her as her body convulsed beneath him.

This time, he was done when she was.

EIGHTEEN

Angie's memorial service was held at a funeral home near the college in the middle of the business district. More than a hundred people crowded into the chapel waiting for the service to begin. To Carina, it was particularly depressing that so many in attendance were young. And at the front of the room poor Angie lay in her coffin.

Will touched Carina's arm. "I'm sorry I have to bail on you. My flight leaves in two hours. I'd better hightail it to the airport."

She squeezed his shoulder. "Keep that scumbag in prison where he belongs. That's part of our job, so don't worry about it." She glanced over to where Nick and his brother were in a quietly heated conversation. "Nick can fill in for you until you return."

"Hmmm."

She jerked her head back to Will and narrowed her eyes. "What's that supposed to mean?"

"What's what?" He was grinning.

"That *hmmm.*"

"You're reading way too much into my noncomment."

"We've been partners for over a year, friends for even longer. I know you."

"And I know you." Will looked over her shoulder at Nick. "I don't make it a habit to check out men, but he seems smart and reasonably good-looking. Not as handsome as yours truly, of course, but men of my attributes are rare."

She rolled her eyes. "Don't you have a plane to catch?"

Will laughed. "He's a good cop. The chief was impressed with his background. I like him, too."

"Ask him out on a date when you get back," she snapped.

"I think you're more his type."

"Go away."

"Going, going. Be careful, okay?"

"I promise."

Will left and Carina walked over to Nick and Steve.

"I don't like being treated like a suspect by my own brother," Carina overheard Steve say to Nick before he saw her. He glared at Carina. "Detective Kincaid," he snapped.

"I don't mean to interrupt, but Hooper left and I need to talk to you, Nick." She eyed Steve suspiciously. She flat-out didn't like him. Though he'd moved down on the suspect list, his attitude about his affair with Angie and the other college girls left her with a sour taste in her mouth. She certainly wouldn't want him anywhere around Lucy, though she suspected her sister had a good head on her shoulders and wouldn't be sweet-talked by a guy twice her age, regardless of how attractive or clean-cut.

Steve opened his mouth to speak, then shut it and walked away. Carina watched as he spotted Angie's friends Abby, Jodi, and Kayla. The foursome embraced.

Nick tensed beside her.

"I'm sorry," she began. "Will left and I wanted to point out the undercover team since you're not familiar with our people."

"I saw them."

She raised an eyebrow. "I guess we're not as discreet as I thought."

He grinned at her. "Maybe I'm just better than you thought."

She hadn't thought of Nick Thomas as much of a joker. She liked the lighter side of him.

But a memorial service was no place for lightness. His humor dissipated as he kept his eye on his brother.

"You know," she said, "he's not guilty."

"I know."

She watched Steve Thomas closely. Angie's friends certainly didn't look scared of him. Kayla was a bit standoffish, but that was her personality. Rough and prickly. Abby and Jodi, on the other hand, constantly touched his arm, his back. Jodi left her hand on his forearm, leaned over and whispered something in his ear, then kissed his cheek.

Dillon's explanation of why Angie was attracted to older men made sense, even if Carina herself couldn't relate to the girl. But Abby? Jodi? They were from traditional families, didn't seem to have the same dysfunctional issues that Angie had dealt with.

As she observed Steve, she realized that it was *him*. He didn't act like a man nearing forty. There was no difference in the way he acted and dressed than any of the other college guys who'd come to pay their respects. She remembered Dillon pointing out that he would have assumed, based on action and demeanor, that Nick was the older brother.

She'd thought he was, too.

The two brothers couldn't be more different. Steve was gregarious, friendly, talked to everyone, and fit in with the students, though he was substantially older than most of them.

The sheriff, on the other hand, was aloof. Serious. Focused on his task. Even now, he was scanning the room. Discreet. On the outside he appeared casual, but she felt his rigid posture, his intense, subtle perusal of each person who walked up to the casket.

Carina couldn't read Nick's expression, which bugged her. She prided herself on being able to read people. "I guess things are still strained between you and your brother."

"You could say that."

"Were you two close before . . . this?"

He shrugged. "Not as close as when we were kids."

"Why's that?"

"Living in different states."

"Why didn't he return to Montana when he was put on disability?"

"Why does this sound like an interrogation?"

"It's not. Just a conversation."

"Hmm."

He wasn't answering her questions so she

changed focus. She was curious about Nick Thomas, far more curious than simple professional interest. "How long have you been sheriff?"

"Nearly four years."

"Before that?"

"Deputy."

"For how long?"

"Eight years."

Getting Nick to answer questions was like pulling teeth. Either he really didn't want to talk, or he was truly a man of few words. She'd thought they'd broken through this reticence over the last few days they'd been on the same team.

"You?"

"Eleven years on the force, made detective fifteen months ago. I dropped out of college to join the police academy."

The corner of his mouth lifted. "I dropped out of law school for the same reason."

"Law school?" She looked at his profile. Ruggedly handsome, tan from spending a lot of time outdoors. "I don't picture you as a lawyer."

He shrugged. "I guess I didn't, either." Was that regret in his voice?

"What happened that you changed your mind?"

He didn't answer right away. Then, "I

didn't like the idea of sitting at a desk all day." He looked right at her and Carina swallowed. There was something very intense about Sheriff Nick Thomas. It wasn't the first time she'd felt the brunt of his scrutiny, and it was a little unnerving, a little heady. Sexy. "That, and I wanted to help troubled kids," he said. "You know the type, good kids in bad situations. One thing led to another and I joined the sheriff's department." He gave her a half-grin that made her insides melt. "What about you?" he asked. "Why'd you drop out of college?"

Her answer to that had always been flip: *to spend more time on the waves.* But the truth was that she'd spent more time in the ocean during her three years of college than the last eleven years on the police force.

"Someone I loved was murdered."

Nick inched closer to her. He didn't touch her, but she felt the caress in his voice more powerful than any physical connection. "I'm sorry. Violence changes lives. Everyone evil touches is affected."

She couldn't pull her eyes from his. The depth of compassion, of pain, of *understanding* . . . Outside of her family, she'd never found anyone who truly understood how she felt, why she'd needed to be a cop. Nick did.

"My nephew," she whispered. "He was seven."

Nick's jaw clenched. "Did they catch the bastard?"

Carina shook her head, turning away as unwanted tears sprang to her eyes.

Nick squeezed her shoulder, briefly, but with strength. She took a deep breath.

"What do you think of that guy over there?"

Nick didn't point, he barely gestured, but Carina read him like a lifelong partner.

A young man stood alone, separate from the crowd, half-obscured by a potted palm. Just shy of six feet tall, lanky, wearing slacks and a button-down.

As they watched, he approached Angie's mother, who sat looking shell-shocked in front of the closed casket. They'd spoken to Mrs. Vance earlier in the day, sharing the bare minimum information they could, while still honestly answering her many questions. The pain and anguish in Mrs. Vance's eyes, learning about her daughter's sexual activities, had broken Carina's heart. Already, the chief of police was fielding calls from the press, which had begun to sensationalize the case.

Carina would have given her right arm to protect the Vance family from the media onslaught, but there was nothing to be done. The media seemed to think freedom of the press meant freedom to be callous.

Angie's mother blinked, then jumped up and wrapped her arms around the man who'd approached.

"Friend, relative of the family?" Nick asked, almost to himself.

"Probably, but it was a good call; solitary male under thirty watching the crowd."

Carina's radio beeped and she spoke into it. "I need to check with the team outside. I'll be back in ten."

Nick watched Carina briskly exit the room. She was an interesting woman. Full of confidence, drive, intelligence. Driven by her nephew's death, though it didn't consume her. She had allowed his sympathy when offered, accepting it without bristling or complaint.

He admired that. It took a strong woman to accept sincere condolences and not go on the attack.

If he was in a better place in his life, if he knew where he was going, what he was doing with his career, Carina would be the type of woman he'd like to get to know. Intimately.

Lord knew he needed a woman who

didn't have baggage that weighed more than his.

Nick watched Steve's neighbor Ava enter the room, glance around, and make a bee-line toward Steve when she spotted him in the corner, surrounded by a large group of girls. Steve's face lit up when he saw her, and they hugged. Platonic? No. They may not have had sex, but there was an affair of the heart going on.

What did these girls see in Steve? Sure, he was attractive and in shape, he was obviously attentive and liked to have fun. But wouldn't they be more interested in boys their own age? Nick had been around college students most of his career and had never wanted to date any of them.

But he'd pretty much spent most of the last ten years in love with one woman. A woman who couldn't return his feelings. A woman he had voluntarily walked away from, hoping she'd follow him.

She hadn't.

He approached the group, standing aloof, not wanting to become involved, but Ava motioned for him to come over and made a space for him. "We were just talking about who could have done something like this to Angie."

"We *know* Steve didn't do it," one of the

girls said. "I can't *believe* the police even talked to him like he was a *criminal.*"

Another girl squeezed Steve's arm. "You're okay, right? They didn't hurt you, did they?"

"No, no, nothing like that. The police really want to find Angie's killer. Since I'm her ex-boyfriend, it's logical they would look at me first. I understand that. But now that they know I didn't do it, they can focus on finding the real killer."

Nick watched the interaction, his complex feelings about Steve and his behavior weighing heavily. Steve glared at him, the accusation of distrust in his expression hitting Nick hard.

He said "Excuse me" and went to find Carina.

He needed fresh air.

NINETEEN

Carina fidgeted as she drove with Nick from the police station to her parents' house twenty minutes east in an older, established San Diego neighborhood. It was nine o'clock, and the memorial service had been a bust — at least as far as learning anything about Angie's killer was concerned.

All the guests had arrived safely and left unharmed; between herself, Nick, and the undercover cops, they'd matched up every guest with a friend or relative in the room. No one looked out of place, no one lurked in the bushes, no one wrote slut on the bathroom wall.

She felt like it had been a complete waste of time. She slammed her fist against the steering wheel.

"What are you frustrated about?" Nick asked.

"Nothing happened!"

"You wanted someone to be abducted?"

"No. I just wanted him to show up so I could nail the bastard to the wall." She glanced at him, saw the bemused expression on his face, and lost some of her anger. "I'm good at that, you know. Apprehension."

"Yeah, women cops have all the tricks. They have no qualms about hitting low because they don't know how much it hurts."

"Oh yes we do. That's why it's so much fun."

"Our presence at Angie's funeral could have prevented an abduction."

"Yeah, but —"

"Seriously. He could have driven by, seen our people — even undercover. Killers have a sixth sense about cops, I'm convinced of it. And even if he only made one cop, he wouldn't be stupid enough to stay."

"Or made us and decided to stay and gloat."

"That's a possibility, too. If it's someone close to her."

"You don't think so?"

"I think he knew her, but wasn't close to her. I think he's going to attack again, when or where I have no idea. The Butcher only killed women in the spring. He sometimes waited two full years between kills."

263

"If you think I'm frustrated now, just watch me if I have to wait a year to get this guy. I don't like unsolved cases."

"You've never had one?"

"A couple. That's why I hate them."

"What about the Sand Shack?"

She frowned. "I don't understand what you mean."

"That deleted e-mail Angie mentioned to Steve. She thought the poster knew her identity because it implied that he knew where she worked."

"And you're thinking our perp could be someone connected to the Shack?"

"Connected, maybe, or a regular customer."

"That makes sense. What if he already knew Angie and then stumbled across her online diary? Because of something he knew about her personally, he was able to make the connection."

"It's plausible," Nick said. "But why kill her?"

"Maybe he hit on her and she rejected him. Because he thought she'd be easy, he had a fit and killed her."

"Possibly."

"You don't sound like you're buying it."

"I'm not discounting it as a theory. I agree with your brother Dillon. It was personal in some way, which means I think he knew her or saw her on a regular basis."

"I feel like we're working on borrowed time, but I have no idea where else to look." She stifled a yawn.

"I know that feeling," Nick said. "On the Butcher investigation, every time we thought we had a lead it was a dead end. We knew he would attack again, we even knew it would happen in the spring. But every time it still shocked the town, almost as if it were unexpected, and we scrambled, searching for a college girl who most certainly had a death sentence."

"That must have been Hell."

"I'm just relieved it's over." He paused. "What happened to your nephew?"

Justin. She'd adored her nephew. Who wouldn't have loved that little hellion? The first grandchild, the first nephew, the first of the next generation. With dimples like his mom and the statesmanship of his political dad, he would have been a heartbreaker, or president, when he grew up.

She missed him.

"I'm sorry I brought it up," Nick said. "I've upset you."

"I'm okay." She pulled the car into the Kincaid family driveway and turned off the ignition. "I just miss him. But my feelings are nothing like Nelia's, my sister. His mom. She was devastated, but she kept everything bottled up for so long. When she finally burst . . . it wasn't pretty. She and Andrew divorced, then she just left, moved to Idaho. More than anyone, my parents want her home so badly. They built the apartment you're staying in for her. But she won't come back. Maybe she can't. Maybe she just can't be anywhere near the family."

She looked up at him with tears in her eyes. "Justin was kidnapped when I was babysitting. Taken right from his bed in the middle of the night. I didn't hear a thing."

Nick touched her cheek and she found herself leaning into the light caress before realizing how inappropriate it was.

"It's not your fault," he said.

"I know that up here," she tapped her head, then put her hand over her heart, "but in here I can't help but blame myself."

He took her hand. "What happened?"

"Nelia worked as an attorney for a defense contractor. She was working late nights, and Andrew — her husband, who was a prosecutor — was in the middle of a big case. I was in college, I could give up a few nights, study at their house. I remember that day so clearly. I had two midterms and a swim meet. I was wiped out. My mom always watched Justin after school . . . he and Lucy were born a month apart. Justin loved to tease Lucy and call her 'Auntie Lu' though she was twenty-seven days younger than him." She smiled at the bittersweet memory. "My mom thought she was in menopause, and was shocked when she found out she was pregnant at the age of forty-five."

"Nice surprise, anyway."

"Yeah. Lucy can be a pain in the neck because she's a bit spoiled. But she's fun and I was really happy to have a baby sister."

She didn't say anything for a long minute, and Nick didn't interrupt. She entwined her fingers with his and it felt right to sit here with him, touching him, sharing her worst nightmare.

"So, anyway, I picked Justin up when I got out of class. My mom said he could spend the night at the house, but I knew she and dad were beat. I even offered to take Lucy with me." Her voice hitched. "But," she said, "it was a school night. So I took Justin over to his house. We ordered out for pizza. Together, Justin and I devoured an extra-large pizza with the works, minus mushrooms because I can't fathom eating anything that is grown in animal dung."

She remembered when her older brother

Connor used to chase her around the house with mushrooms her mom bought for the spaghetti sauce. *"It's alive! It's going to con-shroom you!"*

"We watched *Star Wars* together. Still the single best movie of the twentieth century. I let Justin stay up past his bedtime. I was studying, then Nelia called, said she was running later than she thought and why wasn't Andrew home? Hell if I knew, and I told her so. I never liked him, anyway. Still don't, even if he is a good DA.

"Then I fell asleep."

Why hadn't Justin screamed? Had the killer subdued him while he slept? There was no evidence of a struggle. Justin was just . . . gone. And the window to his bedroom was open. Had she forgotten to check it? Nelia was a stickler for always checking doors and windows. She had been sure she'd checked it . . .

"I woke up to Nelia screaming."

Carina! Where's Justin? Where's Justin?

"I didn't know what was going on. I looked at the clock. It was two in the morning.

"But Justin was missing. His bedroom window wide open. No sign of forced entry." Carina looked at Nick, saw the sympathy and understanding in his eyes.

"Nelia blamed me. For not locking the window. I thought I had, but I don't know anymore." She took a deep breath. "She hasn't spoken to me since."

Nick rubbed her neck. The gesture soothed her even more than their entwined fingers, made her say more than she'd intended. She had never told anyone the whole story, not like that. It was oddly cathartic. Even though she couldn't forgive herself completely, telling Nick had helped purge something that had been eating her inside.

"I'm sorry to dump all that on you. It's probably the last thing you wanted to hear."

"No." He cleared his throat. "I'm glad you told me. I wish I had answers. The only thing I've learned being a cop is that good people get hurt and bad people enjoy it. Our job isn't to stop the pain, but to prevent it in the future."

His hand cupped her cheek and this time she let herself relax, just for a minute, and savor the affection.

Suddenly the car started moving violently up and down.

"What the hell?" Carina exclaimed, reaching for her gun. She looked in the rearview mirror and saw her brothers Connor and Patrick pushing up and down on the trunk.

"You immature brats!" she yelled, biting back a smile. "I'll get you back!"

"Oh, we're so scared," Patrick laughed.

"Come on, you might as well meet the rest of the clan," she told Nick, reluctantly letting his hand go.

Maybe it was for the best. She'd been close to kissing him.

Everything had worked exactly like he'd planned.

After Becca died, he watched the webcam he'd planted in Jodi's apartment and saw Abby making two drinks with the spiked Coke. Then Jodi came in and made two more drinks. That was certainly enough to knock them out.

At midnight he left Becca in the library parking lot. It was fitting, really. He'd first met Angie on the beach, so he'd left her there. He met Becca at the library, so naturally he left her there. It seemed somehow complete, finished. A circle. He couldn't imagine doing it any other way.

Jodi was going to be more difficult. He didn't dare leave her where he'd first met her, but he had a couple of ideas that might work.

Getting into her apartment was easy enough — he'd unlocked Jodi's bedroom

270

window the day before when he'd planted the webcam.

At first he was scared — Jodi wasn't in her bed. He listened, fearing the drugs hadn't worked, that Abby and Jodi were awake and would scream as soon as they saw him. He listened carefully. In the apartment upstairs the drone of a late-night talk show. In the far distance, a siren. He listened until the siren stopped.

Nothing in the apartment stirred.

The kitchen light was on, casting an odd glow over the living room, which had only a dim, solitary lamp in the corner. Jodi was sleeping on the couch, her arm hanging over, her hair in her face.

Out cold.

Abby was in the chair, her head back, spittle dribbling out the corner of her open mouth.

He crossed the living room, unhooked the chain on the front door, and carefully opened the deadbolt. Neither girl stirred.

This was the dangerous part, but just like when he took Becca from the library parking lot, he felt an odd, rumbling thrill deep inside. He couldn't help but think he was smarter than most everyone out there. He'd broken into the apartment yesterday morning and no one had noticed. He'd drugged their drinks and they drank without thinking anything was strange.

There was no doubt in his mind that he could take Jodi and leave the apartment without being seen.

He picked her up and she gave a slight moan. He froze, watched her face, glanced at Abby. No movement. Good. With Jodi in his arms, he left the apartment as quickly as possible.

To his left, he heard a group of young men coming up the the street toward the apartment building. He was parked in the rear, in a vacant carport, and he now quickly turned to the right, going around the building. It was late and a weeknight, but being a building dominated by college students, there were a lot of lights still on.

But most of the blinds were drawn.

It took him forty-two seconds to get from Jodi's apartment to his car. He popped the trunk and put her in. He wanted to tie her hands, but heard the men laughing, getting closer. Where were they going?

He slid into the driver's seat and pulled out — slowly, so as not to draw suspicion. While he didn't see the noisy group, he knew it had been close.

He breathed easier once he got home and saw that Jodi was still unconscious in his trunk. His neighborhood was quieter than Jodi's, all houses pitch-black except for the old woman who lived on the corner. Her lights were always on; he wondered if she ever slept.

Jodi stirred when he carried her through the back door, down the hall, and into his bedroom.

"Where . . ." she began, her mouth thick. She didn't open her eyes and her head rolled back.

He put her on the bed and took off her clothes, then tied her wrists to the headboard. She squirmed again, opened her eyes, confused and disoriented.

"Stop, what are you doing?" She tried to sit up, realized she couldn't, and opened her mouth wide.

She was going to scream.

He clamped her mouth shut with his hand. Her legs bucked and kicked; he hadn't tied them down yet.

He gagged her, but she was still too loud. He didn't think anyone could hear, but he couldn't be certain. She kicked him in the chest as he tried to grab one of her ankles. He slapped her across the face.

"Don't," he commanded.

She didn't listen, fighting and trying to scream. But he was stronger. After some effort, he was able to restrain her. She fought against the binds, but they didn't budge. He panted heavily, catching his breath.

He had wanted time alone with just her body, without her pleas, without her lies. Just her beautiful, exquisite body. She'd ruined it by waking up too soon. It wasn't fair.

His fingers moved down her breast, delicately brushed against her darker nipple. Down her stomach to her cunt. He spread her legs, looked at her, trying to see it all. Pink and moist.

She jerked and moaned out a sob.

"Hi Jodi," he whispered. "Do you recognize me?"

She shook her head back and forth on the bed. Anger followed the stab of pain in his heart. She didn't know him. She'd seen him at least once a week for months, had said hello to him, had *smiled* every time she saw him. But she didn't *really* see him. She looked past him, through him, around him, never *at* him. The phony smile, the phony hello. She didn't care about him, she never really *talked* to him. She didn't know him and didn't know his name.

Phony bitch. At least Angie had known who he was. She knew who killed her.

He stared into Jodi's eyes, willed her to

remember him. He saw a spark, something . . . she *did* know him. Now she was trying to remember where. Where had she seen him . . . he could practically see her pathetic phony slut mind working, working on the puzzle.

He slid off her body and retrieved the glue from the locked drawer in his desk. He took off the lid. The smell reminded him of last time, and his penis twitched.

He walked over to her, took the large brush from the can. With one hand he removed the gag. She screamed and he slapped her. He painted glue on her mouth. She sputtered, gagged, tried and failed to scream as the glue clogged her throat. He tied the black bandanna tight around her mouth and held it there. It hardened with the glue. Her nostrils flared as she tried to draw a breath.

"Calm down. If you fight it you'll choke to death. And that wouldn't be any fun. Just calm down." He talked to her soothingly for several minutes, until he felt her pulse rate drop a bit, until her breathing became easier.

"My mother warned me about girls like you," he said after several minutes. "You tease men, lure them into your bed, fuck them, and then turn them in for rape. It happened to my father, you know. A woman, just like you, gave herself to him. He had sex with her and then she went to the police. Can you believe that? Lying bitch."

His dad had been in prison for four years and three months. And during that time his mother had brought other men into her bed. She was a liar as much as the woman who talked against his dad. Spreading her legs for men all the while telling him that sex was dirty and he'd get diseases and his dick would fall off.

He turned away from Jodi. He missed his dad. He'd only been out of prison for a few months before he disappeared. Late one night he'd walked out the door and never came back.

Mother chased him away. Daddy got mad at the way she treated him. Maybe he found out about all those men she let touch her. Why didn't you take me, Daddy? I wanted to go. I hated her, I wanted to be with you.

Then the police came a couple days later asking about his father. Where he was, when they'd last seen him. And that's when everything became clear.

Another woman had lied about Daddy and made him go away. He'd come back when it was safe.

A sound startled him and he looked

around his room. He almost didn't remember bringing Jodi home, but there she was. Everything came back. He glanced at the clock. He'd been sitting there over an hour.

He thought he'd have been excited to have Jodi with him, but right now he was sad. Thinking about his dad. Where was the thrill?

He knew how to bring it back. "Watch this, Jodi." He put a tape in the VCR and turned the television so Jodi could better see it.

It was his favorite tape, the one where the guy strangled the woman with his bare hands.

By the time it was over, the sadness was gone and he was ready. He turned to Jodi, not seeing the tears, her body shaking, not hearing the sobs deep in her chest.

He shoved a beer bottle up her cunt and watched as she tried to scream.

TWENTY

He wore nothing but his hat.

She wore nothing at all.

"Come here, Carina," Nick said in that slow, easy drawl that she now equated with rugged Montana.

She walked to him. His blue eyes darkened, and he focused on her with such intensity that every muscle melted in her body. She reached for his face, pulled him down to her, touched her lips to his. His hard, lean body hovered over her, teasing, tempting, and she arched to meet him. Suddenly they were one, moving together, his hands on her breasts, her waist, wrapping her with flexing muscles, getting closer, but not close enough.

"More," she whispered in his ear.

The phone jolted her from her erotic dream and Carina moaned.

"I hate my job," she muttered as she reached for the receiver next to her bed.

"Kincaid."

As she listened to dispatch she sat up, now fully alert. "La Jolla Main Library? I can get there in forty minutes."

Carina flipped the switch on her coffeepot, took a two-minute icy shower, and with two travel mugs of hot coffee drove the two short blocks to her parents' house and knocked on Nick's door. It was four in the morning. He opened it almost immediately, wearing boxers and nothing else.

Wow! Nick in person was even better than her interrupted dream. In an instant she took in his broad chest, flat stomach, narrow hips . . . and scars on both knees.

No time for questions about old injuries, no time to enjoy his near-nakedness. "We have another one."

"Who?"

Carina handed him one of the travel mugs of black coffee. "We don't have a positive ID. A body, female, approximately eighteen years of age, was found in the middle of the parking lot of La Jolla Public Library. A patrol found her, thought it was either a drunk or hit and run. Until he approached."

"Same MO?" Nick zipped up his jeans and pulled a black T-shirt over his head. Threaded his holster through his belt, secured his gun.

"Her head was covered by a garbage bag."

"Her head? Where's the rest of her body?"

She blinked, at first not understanding what he meant, then realizing he thought just her head was found. "It's all there, but her body was wrapped in plastic wrap."

"Mouth?"

"Don't know. The responding officer didn't remove the bag from her head. He checked her pulse and she was dead. He secured the scene, called it in. The crime techs are meeting us there."

Nick slid his feet into boots and picked up the coffee Carina had brought, took a sip. "Thanks for the coffee."

"I don't know about you," she said as she headed down the stairs to her car, "but three hours of sleep doesn't cut it for me anymore."

Since it was the middle of the night with no traffic, it took less than twenty minutes to reach the library. The crime scene van was already there, but they were still un-packing their equipment. Carina introduced Nick to Jim Gage and his assistant, Blair Duncan, who was fresh out of college. Jim pulled the case when he heard it might be related to the Vance homicide; Blair pulled the case because she had the misfortune of being the lowest man — or woman — on the totem pole and drew the graveyard shift.

Another car drove up and Jim said, "Did you know Dillon was coming?"

Carina glanced behind her. Dillon got out of his Lexus and walked over. "Yeah. He's been consulting informally, though now . . ." she didn't need to finish. Chief Causey had put together a small task force for Angie's funeral; Carina would demand that they expand it after this. Two girls brutally murdered in less than a week. Carina was certain she'd win the argument this time.

"I called Missing Persons on my way in," Dillon said. "A seventeen-year-old intern has been missing since Wednesday evening. She left the library at eight but never arrived home. Her car was found here, in this lot, the next morning."

"Do you have a name?" Carina asked.

"Becca Harrison."

Gage approached the victim first while his assistant photographed the scene. When she was done visually cataloging the body and immediate surroundings, she walked in a circle outward while Gage inspected the body.

"Carina, look at this," he said.

She approached. A plastic garbage bag had been tied with white nylon rope around the victim's neck. Her body had been wrapped with plastic wrap. Her hands were bound together by rope.

"Could it be a copycat?" she asked, her voice unusually quiet.

"One way to know for sure." The press had gotten wind of the garbage bags, but they'd never released information about the glued-on gag.

Gage carefully removed the rope and bagged it. Next, he gently pulled the bag from her head.

Her mouth was sealed with a black bandanna identical to the one found on Angie.

Carina turned to Nick. "Let's find out if she had a sex diary and if Bondage or Scout commented on her page. And I'm going to wake Patrick up. We need something more to go on than two unknown profiles in cyberspace." She motioned for Dillon to approach.

Her brother stared at the body, his face long. "She's so young."

"Do you have a description of Becca Harrison?"

"Long dark hair, blue eyes, five-foot-four, one hundred five pounds."

"It fits. Let's run her prints before we call the parents, just to be sure."

Dillon looked at her with compassion. Was he thinking about the day when the police came to the Kincaid house and told them that Justin's body had been found? Every time she had to talk to her parents, she thought about the anguished cry that came out of her sister's throat, a sound that could only be described as the voice of pain itself.

"I'm sorry," Dillon now said.

"I'll be okay." She would, that was her job. And doing the job helped make her okay.

"Look at her." Carina pointed toward the victim's body, harshly visible in the lights Gage had set up around the perimeter. "The MO changed. Why the plastic wrap?"

"The media has always jumped on the similarities between crimes, the so-called signature of a serial killer," Dillon said. "But in truth, killers are always trying to perfect their crime. With every kill they lose something, part of the fantasy. This is why they start killing in the first place — the mental fantasy is no longer enough to satisfy them. They escalate. Some might rape first, then rape and kill. But the kill itself, while it's a momentary high, leads to depression when it's over. So a killer will change things to keep the excitement high."

"But why plastic wrap?" Carina pushed. "Is this a way to keep evidence off the body?"

"I think that's one purpose, yes," Dillon said.

"And the other?"

This time Nick spoke. "He wanted to feel her die, be closer to her when she died. The plastic wrap is thinner than garbage bags. And look how carefully he wrapped her. Not bulky. He could feel her beneath the plastic while still keeping trace evidence — his hair and skin fibers — off her body." He looked from Carina to her brother. "I'm not a shrink, but I'd bet my pension that he had sex with her while she was dying."

Carina paled. "That's —" she was going to say *That's sick,* but the entire case sickened her. She pulled out her cell phone and woke Patrick up at home, told him about the murder. "Two hours, downtown."

Dawn had just crested by the time Carina and Nick entered police headquarters. The smallest interview room had been converted to the task force headquarters and Chief Causey had come in early so Carina and Nick could brief him privately, then he joined the task force meeting.

After Carina brought everyone up to date on the case, Patrick took the floor.

"I woke up the security chief at MyJournal as soon as Detective Kincaid called

284

about the Harrison homicide. I told him we had enough for a warrant but if he wanted to pull together the information now we would appreciate it."

The chief interrupted. "I talked to Stanton this morning. He's getting the warrant as we speak."

Patrick nodded. "The MyJournal people are pulling every comment both Bondage and Scout posted in the last three months, including the deleted comments that are maintained on the server for three months. Beyond that, everything is wiped unless archived on an individual MyJournal user page. There's no way to retrieve it, but three months should be enough to establish any pattern."

"But is one of these people the killer?" one of the cops in the room asked.

"We're not sure, but it's all we have to go on right now. One of the deleted comments scared the first victim enough that she believed someone dangerous knew where she worked," Carina interjected. "We're not only focusing on the first victim's online journal. We also have Becca Harrison. The fact that she disappeared from the library Wednesday night and her body was dumped there thirty hours later is significant. We're looking at any connection between Angie and Becca, but on the surface we haven't been able to find anything other than they both worked in La Jolla."

"Becca has no online diary that I could find, but that doesn't mean one doesn't exist," Patrick said. "Her parents have been notified, and I'm sending a team to retrieve her home computer this morning. I'll also check the library network. When I get the unique user identification code from My-Journal for the two people we're interested in, I can run it against any network and know whether they used the library to log on to the MyJournal site. I'll go first to the library, then Angie's place of employment, since they have a public network for patrons."

Chief Causey spoke. "I need something for the press. They've already sniffed out that these cases are connected." He looked pointedly at Carina.

"Sir, they showed up only thirty minutes after I did. The police scanner is not as secure as we would like."

"Point taken."

Office Diaz spoke up. "What happened with the evidence against Steven Thomas? Or the first vic's boyfriend, Masterson?"

"The evidence against Thomas was circumstantial at best, and we can't find anything to link him to the murder. Thomas has been cooperating, turned over all his computer equipment and came down for a formal interview," Carina said. "Masterson has a solid alibi for Angie's murder, but we're going to talk to him again to confirm his whereabouts on Wednesday between seven and nine, when Becca Harrison was kidnapped."

Chief Causey spoke, walking slowing around the desk to stand in front of his men and women. "Detective Patrick Kincaid is handling all computer-related aspects of the case, and Detective Carina Kincaid is heading the investigation. I've approved overtime on this case, so please give them as much time as you can.

"As you may have heard, Detective Hooper was called up to the appeals court to testify again in the Theodore Glenn case. If you haven't met Sheriff Nick Thomas from Montana, he's over there" — he pointed to Nick standing in the far corner — "and I've brought him in officially as a police consultant. We don't want the press or the defense attorney to have any reason to slam us when we nail this bastard. Sheriff Thomas has experience with serial killers, and he's already been an asset to our investigation."

Causey turned to Dillon and nodded.

Dillon spoke. "I've been working on this case with Detectives Kincaid and Hooper almost from the beginning. Angie Vance's murder was disturbing and showed immediately that we were up against a vicious predator. Now that we have two victims, the evidence is clear: he's not going to stop until we stop him.

"I'm working up a more formal profile, but Detective Kincaid knows what we're looking for. Going around now is a sheet of the basic characteristics of our killer, but remember: profiling is not a science. It's using what we know of human nature and previous crimes to make an educated guess about the individual capable of these atrocities.

"One thing I can guarantee: he will act again, and sooner rather than later. I suspect he already has his next victim in his sights."

Dillon nodded at Carina, who handed out assignments. Two officers added to e-crimes to help Patrick; one officer to canvas the university; two officers to interview Becca's friends and family; and two officers dedicated to reviewing like crimes and following up with outside jurisdictions.

"Chief Causey is also issuing a warning through the media for young women in the

La Jolla area to be cautious, not be out alone after dark for any reason, and to go through the standard safety checklist," Carina said. "Any questions?"

Finally, Chief Causey looked everyone in the eye. "Let's get this guy before he strikes again. Dismissed."

TWENTY-ONE

Nick walked with Carina to the coroner's office. "I'm glad Dr. Chen is willing to come in early and take care of Becca Harrison," Carina said. "You don't have to observe."

"I do," he said. Of course he would observe. Knowing the victim helped know the killer.

So far, law enforcement hadn't come up with any similar crimes. Nothing in California matched, and so far the FBI database had come up dry.

He couldn't help but think about the Butcher's first victim. If the investigators had followed up on every thread, talked with more people, did more legwork, maybe — maybe — the killer would have been stopped before claiming twenty-one additional lives. Because the Butcher's first kill had been personal. Something starts the chain reaction. Something leads to the first kill. Going back to the first kill of the

Butcher led them to the killer.

If Angie was, as Nick suspected, the first victim of this San Diego killer, it was personal. Something about Angie had specifically set him off. What was it? Her double life? Something else?

They walked into the overly air-conditioned laboratory and Jim Gage, who Nick had met at the crime scene the night before, approached.

"I'm assisting Dr. Chen on this one." He stared at Becca's prepped body on the cold stainless-steel table, his expression unusually grim.

"You okay?"

"Fine." He looked over her shoulder at Nick. "You were right."

"About?" Though he didn't need to ask.

"Her entire body is covered in plastic wrap except for her vagina. There's residue from a condom and spermicide. I've already sent it to the lab for identification."

"DNA?" Carina asked.

"Don't know yet."

"Was her body washed?"

"Yes. But he was rushed this time. There's a lot of soap residue. And get this: there was a head injury."

"Maybe he hit her when he abducted her," Nick said. "The Butcher lured his victims

291

from their vehicles, then knocked them unconscious."

"Possibly, but —"

Chen interrupted. "Rather than speculate,
let's observe the body."

Carina gathered her professionalism and
looked at the victim as a puzzle, not a
person. Becca Harrison's autopsy was as
methodical as Angie's, but this time Carina
focused on similarities and differences.

Both victims had been sexually assaulted,
including raped with a closed beer bottle,
the marks on the inside of the vagina now
distinctive. Both had had their mouths
glued shut and secured with a black bandanna, and had been restrained with white
nylon rope. Both had been released from
their restraints and thoroughly washed
before being killed. Both victims had suffocated in a garbage bag. Both victims were
in their late teens. Both victims lived or
worked in La Jolla, the upscale community
in north San Diego but still within the city
limits. Both had been kidnapped after dark.

Angie had been raped both anally and
vaginally, Becca only vaginally. Angie had
been imprisoned for more than forty-eight
hours before being killed, Becca between
twenty-four and thirty. While both bodies
had been dumped, Becca had been returned

to the library where she was last seen.

Why had Angie been dumped on the beach? Had Angie gone to the beach after Steve had followed her home? If so, why? Or did the beach hold some significance for the killer?

Carina noted that the plastic wrap on Becca was a key difference. Dillon and Nick had agreed that the plastic wrap had allowed the killer to get physically closer to his victim while still giving him a level of protection against leaving evidence on her body. Gage was taking the plastic to the lab to see if he could collect any trace evidence, because plastic attracted hair and fibers.

"We might get lucky here," Gage said. "The plastic garbage bags don't hold fibers as well as plastic wrap. Different properties. And the contamination at the scene with the sand is making any evidence harder to find. I'm going to prioritize this."

"The killer has been so careful with the bodies and not leaving evidence, it seems odd that he'd change his MO to a less-safe method," Carina said.

"You have to think like the killer," Nick said. "It's not about protecting him, though he has taken a greater effort than many serial killers to foil forensics."

"If it's not about forensics, what's it

about?" Carina asked.

"His pleasure. His fantasy. It's all about him. On the surface, he gets what he wants — closer to the dying victim. Logically, he's thinking the plastic wrap will prevent evidence transfer. And if he'd dumped her body on the beach, the sand would contaminate any evidence. But a parking lot isn't the same, just like the properties of the plastic wrap and garbage bags aren't the same."

"So he made a mistake."

"He's going to realize it," Nick said.

"You think?"

"Eventually."

Jim Gage spoke. "He's taking such pains to stymie the forensics investigation it makes me think that he's in the system."

"We've run like crimes," Carina said, "and so far nothing. I have two dedicated officers on it now, so we're digging deeper."

Gage said, "Dr. Chen, you said there was another difference between the first and second victim."

He nodded and motioned them to a light box against the wall, flipping the switch while dimming the overhead lights at the same time.

"The second victim has two head wounds. The first is a faint subdermal bruising. Not fatal and likely caused by a hand — see, you can see distinct fingers. It's on the side of the head, as if he slapped her hard. The second is on the lower left quadrant of her skull. I don't see how he could have hit her there. He would have had to swing up with something sharp enough to leave this deep gash."

The wound was about two inches long, wider in the middle.

Gage nodded. "From the angle, I think she fell."

"How could she fall if she was restrained?" Carina asked.

Nick spoke up. "He untied her to wash her, probably in a bathtub. He wouldn't let her walk behind him, so she comes out first and makes a run for it. Maybe slams the bathroom door to delay him, throws something in his path. It had only been a day, she wasn't as weak as Angie, with a burst of adrenaline she runs."

"But he catches up with her," Gage said, nodding. "Maybe pushes her."

"Look here," Chen said. "This is another faint subdermal bruise, a minor wound, in the very back of her head, which might indicate that she was pushed against a wall. No broken skin."

"So," Nick used Carina to demonstrate,

295

taking her by the shoulders and gently pushing her against the wall. "Becca runs. He catches her and slams her against the wall."

Nick stood very close to Carina and she held her breath.

"He's angry. Furious that she tried to run. He wants her back in position so he can finish it. But he's mad, throws her down." Holding Carina by the arms, Nick pretended to throw her, going with the momentum to control it. "Maybe a coffee table, a cabinet, a chair — something with a sharp corner — is in the way and she hits it." Without letting Carina hit the ground, he pulled her up. She stumbled and he caught her, gave her a wry grin. "Sorry."

She swallowed, nodded, unable to talk. Few men made her feel small and feminine. Nick Thomas was definitely one of them.

Gage was nodding. "I can see it."

Chen concurred. "Holds with the evidence. There is no soap residue in the wound, which suggests it occurred after the washing."

"Anything else that's different about this crime scene?" Carina asked, finally finding her voice.

"Look at her right hand." Chen lifted the victim's hand, showing deep gashes under her nails.

"What did he do to her?" Carina asked.

"Cleaned her fingernails with a knife," Chen answered. "Then doused them in bleach."

"Why?" she asked.

Nick answered. "Remember that she ran. She's unrestrained and fighting back. What would you do?"

"Hit, kick, scratch —" she paused. "She scratched him. Were you able to get a sample of his skin?"

Jim shook his head. "Doubtful, though we're taking extensive samples from her fingers. The knife turned the ends of her fingers to pulp, the bleach messes with the tests."

"Anything else?" Nick asked.

"Becca Harrison had been a virgin."

"Well, that certainly shoots down the theory that she had an online sex diary," Carina said. "So where's the connection?"

"Let's go to the library," Nick said. "They should be open by now."

The library wasn't open to the public yet, but several people were inside. Carina knocked briskly on the glass double doors and flashed her badge when someone looked her way.

A petite silver-haired woman unlocked the

door, her eyes red-rimmed. She clutched a pile of damp tissue in one hand.

"Is this about Becca?"

"Yes, ma'am."

The woman's eyes teared again. She let Carina and Nick in, locked the doors behind them. "I can't believe it. I can't believe it."

"Are you the librarian?"

"The head librarian, yes. Marjorie Kimball."

Carina introduced herself and Nick, then asked, "Were you working Wednesday?"

"Yes." She rubbed the tissue against her eyes. "Please come in. I called the other staff and volunteers when Mr. Harrison told me Becca had been . . ." Her voice trailed off. "We were so worried yesterday, but thought for sure there was some logical explanation. At least we tried to tell each other that."

"Ms. Kimball, we'd like to speak with you first, then to the rest of the staff, in private. Is there a room we can use?"

"Um," she looked around as if she'd never seen the library before. "We have a meeting room in the back. Will that do?"

"Perfect."

Carina let the librarian lead the way. The La Jolla Public Library had been lovingly maintained and upgraded. It was multi-leveled, with skylights in the large reading room and work stations throughout. Far different from her small neighborhood library, which had been walking distance from the house her parents still lived in. But this library smelled the same, of books new and old, newspaper, and quiet.

Carina let Ms. Kimball give them Becca's schedule — Tuesday and Thursday from four in the afternoon until eight in the evening. Becca had been volunteering at the library for more than a year, since she turned sixteen. She'd been filling in for a friend on Wednesday.

After going through the preliminaries, Carina asked, "On Wednesday did Becca tell you she was planning on being picked up or meeting with anyone?"

Ms. Kimball shook her head. "No. She left promptly at eight."

"Has she talked about a boyfriend or special friend?"

Again, no. "She didn't date. She's shy around boys. A late bloomer."

"Do you know if she had a Web page or an online journal of some sort?"

"She never said."

"Did she ever tell you about someone who'd been harassing her or any fears that she was being followed?"

"No. She was always joyful. That's what I

think of when I think of Becca: joy. On Wednesday she was just as happy as ever."

This wasn't getting anywhere. "Did she talk to anyone here?"

"Patrons."

"Anyone who was new? A stranger? Someone who wasn't a regular patron?"

"I don't know. No one I noticed as strange. I don't know everyone who comes in here, but I recognize most of the faces of the regulars."

"Okay, think back to that night. Was there anyone who left either right before or right after Becca?"

"I wouldn't know. I was at my desk, which is in the back of the library. Midge, she's out in the annex waiting, was at the front desk. She would have a better view of everyone who enters."

Nick escorted Ms. Kimball out and brought in Midge. They went through the same questions. "Becca talked to everyone," Midge said. She was younger than Ms. Kimball by at least ten years, but seemed stodgier. "I had to constantly work on her to focus on her job, not chatting. But she's a volunteer," she said in a "what can you do" tone.

"And on Wednesday?"

"She talked to at least six people while

she was working. I can't imagine any of them hurting her."

"Can you describe any men she spoke with?"

"Mr. Sanders and his wife. They come in every Wednesday and Sunday to read newspapers."

"How old are they?"

"In their eighties."

Forget them, Carina thought.

"Who else?"

"The nice young man who lost his cat."

"Do you know his name?"

"No, he comes in a few times a month, in the evenings usually. Doesn't have a library card."

"And his cat ran away?"

She shook her head. "Becca said that someone shot the poor animal. Can you imagine? She was heartsick over it."

Carina glanced at Nick and he gave her a brief nod. "When did he leave?"

"Oh, early. Five, five-thirty. I don't really remember."

"What does he do when he's here?"

"Studies."

"He's in college?"

"I think so, I'm not sure. He brings in textbooks and his laptop."

"He doesn't use the library computers?"

"No. He prefers one of the laptop stations in the annex."

"Can you describe what he looks like?"

Her brow furrowed as she concentrated. "Nice-looking. Average. Tall, but not as tall as you." She pointed to Nick. "A little on the skinny side. But he's very nice, polite. Clean-cut. I think Becca had a crush on him, but she was too shy to ask him out and I think he was too shy to ask her out." She shook her head. "She was such a sweet girl."

"About how old would you say he was?"

"I don't know, maybe early twenties. Maybe younger. Kids look so much more mature these days."

"Do you remember his hair color?"

"Um, light."

"Blond or light brown?"

"I don't know. More on the brown side, I'm not really sure. You don't think . . . he's not . . . he can't be. He's just a young man."

As if being a young man meant you couldn't rape or murder. "We don't know right now, we're trying to talk to everyone who spoke to Becca the day she disappeared. We'd like to talk to him, maybe he saw something."

"Oh, right, that makes sense. I can get you the Sanders' information."

"Do you know if the young man Becca spoke with has a car?"

"No."

"But you're certain he left during the five-o'clock hour."

"Yes. I left at six and he'd gone before then."

"Do you remember if he looked at any specific book while he was here?"

"No, he came in about four, just before Becca came in, and sat at the table near the front of the annex like he always does. He worked on his laptop the whole time, at least from what I saw. I didn't have to clean up his workstation like I do *some* people."

Carina thanked Midge for her time and continued with the interviews. When they were done speaking with everyone who'd been working Wednesday night, no one else remembered the light-haired "young man." They asked Midge to call them if he came in again, and then they looked at the table she'd indicated that he always used.

It was a small, flat maple table, no drawers. Immaculate. A power outlet was within arm's reach. The man could see the entire library, but no one could see his computer screen. Not that that meant anything; Carina herself never sat with her back to a room or door. Most civilians didn't have that phobia.

"I need to put an undercover in here in the evenings," Carina said almost to herself. "I'm getting a feeling about this."

"It's our only solid lead right now," Nick agreed, "until Gage brings us some physical evidence."

"You think he'll come back if he's guilty?"

"He might think that's the way to not attract attention. Keep up the same routine."

They left the library and Carina called in her request to Chief Causey, who agreed to put an undercover officer at the library from four to eight every evening.

Carina had just pulled away from the curb when her radio beeped. She picked up the receiver. "Unit Charles-One-Four-Four here. Over."

"Charles-One-Four-Four, missing person reported at two-four-zero Beach Boulevard, apartment one-one-six. The caller asked for you specifically."

Carina looked at Nick. "That's Abby and Jodi's apartment."

TWENTY-TWO

Abby and Jodi shared what was considered a "garden" apartment, a small two-bedroom unit on the ground floor of a large U-shaped complex near the university. Carina would bet that ninety percent of the residents were college students.

They lived in a corner unit. The front door opened into a small living/dining/kitchen area. Three doors on the south wall led to what Carina presumed were two bedrooms and the bath. A police officer, Mimi Danvers, was sitting with a hysterical Abby.

"She's gone!" Abby wailed when she saw Carina. "Please please find her. Something awful has happened."

"Calm down and tell me everything you remember." Carina sat on the other side.

Abby took several deep breaths and said, "Last night, after the memorial service, we went to the Sand Shack. It was closed, just open for friends of Angie. So we could talk about what we love and miss about her." She drew in a shaky breath. "But Jodi and I weren't into it. After what you said, we were kind of scared. We didn't know who'd hurt Angie, and so we left and came here. We drank some rum and Cokes, but we were so tired. I-I fell asleep in the living room. I woke up late this morning — I swear, I didn't get that drunk, it was just the stress — and I'd already missed all my morning classes. Not that I cared, not after Angie." She took another deep, shaking breath.

"What time did you wake up?"

"Ten-thirty. And I went into Jodi's room to wake her up . . . and she wasn't there. So I thought she already went to class. I showered and dressed and tried her cell phone at eleven because I knew she'd be between classes. I heard it ring in the apartment. That's when I saw her purse." She pointed to an overstuffed desk in the small eating area that separated the kitchen from the living room. "She'd never go out without her purse, and her car is in the carport — so I called nine-one-one, then I called the number you gave me."

Officer Danvers squeezed Abby's hand. Nick slid on gloves and went to the front door. "It's not forced." He turned to Abby. "Which room is Jodi's?"

She pointed to the door on the left. Carina followed Nick. He looked at the window. "It's unlocked. And look —" He pointed to the windowsill. "Dirt on the ledge."

"I'll call the crime techs and get them down here ASAP."

While they waited for the crime techs, Carina had Abby call every one of Jodi's friends to find out the last time they had spoken with her. No one had seen or talked to her after they left the Sand Shack at ten the night before.

Jim Gage arrived with his team only thirty minutes after being called. He looked as tired as Carina felt. It had been a long morning.

Carina explained what they knew so far, then left Jim to do his job.

She spoke to Officer Danvers. "Don't let Abby out of your sight. I'll clear it with the chief. I'm putting her and Kayla under twenty-four/seven protection until we find this guy."

Abby heard her. "It's him? Angie's killer has Jodi?"

"We don't know for certain," Carina said carefully, "but we need to proceed with caution until we know exactly what's happened."

Carina ordered two more uniforms to

canvas the apartment building first, then every adjacent structure. "Anything, no matter how minor, I want to know about."

On the way out she called Chief Causey and had a squad car sent over to Kayla's dorm room at the college. "I didn't think they were in danger. I asked the chief early on for extra protection, and he approved additional patrols in the neighborhood, but I should have pushed for more. I told them to be careful, but I really didn't think he'd go after any of them. It's my fault."

"It's not your fault."

"Yes, it is." She slammed her fist on the steering wheel as Nick slid into the passenger seat. "I should have had Angie's journal taken offline immediately. Then they never would have been able to post those stories about themselves and draw the attention of the killer."

"First," Nick said, "you had no reason to think they would do something like that."

"But —"

"It was Angie's journal, you kept it online for a valid reason. Her killer could have wanted to gloat, he could have posted a confession for all we know."

"Yes, but —"

"And you took it down as soon as you discovered what the girls had done."

"Yes, but —"

"Your boss told you no extra protection beyond patrols. He takes the heat, not you. I should know."

She turned to him. "That sounds personal."

"The buck stops at the top, Carina. That's the way it is. And you know what? I don't think in a city of one point three million that I would have put twenty-four/seven protection on three college girls who had not been threatened. The killer never contacted them, none of them felt they were being stalked. What could you have done? Can you protect everyone in the city at all times? No. We do what we can. We work overtime, we're watching everyone, everything around us even when we're off-duty. Because you know it's true: cops are never truly off the job."

Carina stared at Nick. She couldn't remember him sounding so impassioned. His blue eyes had darkened, his feelings on the surface instead of buried deep inside.

"Do you have regrets from the Butcher investigation?" she asked quietly.

He drew in a breath. "Many. But I don't know if it's from playing Monday-morning quarterback or because I really made the wrong decision. All we can do is use the information we have coupled with our experience and make a decision. Everything comes down to choices. I made decisions based on what was best for my county and my people. They were right then. The only time I made the wrong choice —" He stopped.

Nick had replayed the entire Butcher investigation over and over in his mind, from the beginning thirteen years ago when he'd first met Miranda Moore, the only survivor of the Butcher, who ran miles through treacherous terrain only to almost die when she jumped into the Gallatin River to escape her attacker.

That case had still been active when he became sheriff nine years later.

"Nick?" Carina asked quietly.

"I made the wrong decision once. Almost got me killed." He didn't want to tell her about it, not now. Maybe not ever. It was one of the few things he honestly regretted in his life, and showing his weakness to a woman he admired and respected made him uncomfortable.

He'd learned from his mistake.

"Where to now?" he asked, changing the focus back to the current investigation. "The Sand Shack?"

"We need to trace Jodi's steps from when

she and Abby left the Shack last night until they came home." She pulled out her notepad. "The manager, Kyle Burns, had classes all morning. He should be there by now."

She started the engine but before she could drive away, Jim Gage ran up to her car. She rolled down the window. "What?"

"Two preliminary findings. The first: Abby and Jodi were drugged. There are trace narcotics in the two-liter soda bottles, the orange juice, and an opened bottle of wine."

"He was in their apartment," she said flatly.

"We're dusting the entire place, including everything in the refrigerator. I have my assistant taking blood from Abby to confirm that she was also drugged. They were drinking rum and Coke last night. The alcohol coupled with the narcotics would have knocked them both out."

"Which is why she didn't wake up until late this morning."

Gage nodded. "And we found something else. A small hole in the kitchen cabinet."

"Why is that important?"

"Because there was also a small motion-activated webcam attached. It runs on a battery. I've bagged it for Patrick. I don't know enough about the electronics to tell you the range, but I'm sending my assistant downtown to get it analyzed ASAP."

"Thanks, Jim."

"He was watching them," Nick said.

"Why the kitchen?" Carina asked. "Why not the bedrooms?"

"Because he wanted to know when they were drugged," Nick said. "So he could come in and kidnap Jodi without commotion."

"Why Jodi?" Jim asked. "Why not Abby? Or both of them?"

"Like Angie, Jodi slept with my brother," Nick said quietly.

"Becca had no relationship with Steve," Carina said.

"Coincidence?"

They looked at each other and Carina started the car. "It warrants a conversation with him. Maybe there's something else going on here."

They found Steve at his apartment drinking iced coffee on his deck with Ava.

"Jodi is missing," Nick told Steve.

Ava exclaimed, "Oh my God. It's not the same guy, right?"

"We don't know for sure what happened," Carina said cautiously, "but I need to ask you, Mr. Thomas, where you were from four p.m. Wednesday afternoon until now."

"You want me to recount the last nearly forty-eight hours?"

"Yes, sir," said Carina.

Steve faced Nick. "So you're on staff with the San Diego Police Department now?"

"Please answer the question, Steve," Nick said.

"I don't have to. Isn't that what you told me? Get a lawyer to protect myself? I just didn't think I would need to protect myself from my own brother."

"I don't think you killed Angie or kidnapped Jodi. What I think is that it's a coincidence that one woman you slept with is dead and another is missing. Maybe you know something you don't think is important, something that can lead us to Jodi before she's killed."

Ava put her hand on Steve's shoulder. "Steve, you need to help."

Steve glanced over his shoulder at Ava, then pulled her to his side. "I had a class Wednesday afternoon. I left campus at five-thirty. Picked Ava up and we went to dinner. Came back here about eight. Watched a movie."

"What time did you go home, Ava?" Carina asked.

She cleared her throat. "I didn't."

"Do you know Becca Harrison of La Jolla?"

He shook his head.

"She works at the La Jolla Library," Carina prompted.

"I don't think I've ever been in there," Steve said. "I don't know a Becca, at least that I can remember. If I need to go to the library, I use the one on campus."

"Ava?" Nick turned to her. "Do you know Becca Harrison?"

"No, I don't."

Nick looked at his brother again. Steve was still angry at him for the interview at the station. Would they ever get beyond it? "Steve, can you think of anyone who would want to hurt you?"

"Me?" His eyes widened. "I don't have any enemies."

"No threats? Have you felt like you're being watched, especially when you're on a date?"

Steve shook his head. "No. And no one knew about my relationship with Jodi. It was . . . brief."

"No one knew about it until Jodi posted it online," Carina said. "But she didn't identify you, Steve. We were able to pick up on it because of the connection to Angie."

"Coincidence?" Nick wasn't sure he

bought it.

"Sometimes coincidences are real," Carina said. "Rare, but possible." She faced Ava and Steve and said, "Be careful. Don't go anywhere alone, especially at night. The killer has been targeting specific women — it doesn't seem random — but we can't discount that it may indirectly have something to do with your relationship with Jodi and Angie."

Steve nodded. "If I can do anything, *anything,* to help, please let me know."

Nick motioned for Steve to come into the apartment. Alone, he said, "Steve, I'm sorry. I should never have pushed you the other day."

Steve looked like he wasn't going to forgive him, but then he sighed and gave Nick a tight hug. "You're right about something."

"I am?"

"I haven't done anything with my life." He glanced through the sliding glass door at Ava. "I really care about Ava. And I can't provide for her. I don't have a job. I can support myself but a wife? A family? I didn't think I wanted one, but . . ." he shrugged.

"What are you going to do about it?"

"I'm going to talk to a career counselor at the university next week. See what they recommend for a disabled veteran with three degrees." He gave Nick a self-deprecating grin.

Nick's conscience felt lighter. He clapped Steve on the shoulder. "I'm glad. You let me know how I can help, okay?"

"You hanging around San Diego?"

"For a while. I need to finish out this case."

"What about your job? You're a sheriff in Montana, Nick. Not like you can just walk away from it."

"I know." He glanced at Carina. He wasn't ready to go home yet. "But for now, I need to find this killer."

"Are you okay?" Carina asked Nick when they were back in the car heading to the Shack. She wanted to talk to the manager, Kyle Burns, about the closed party the night before.

"Yeah. I think Steve and I came to an understanding." Nick had been worried he'd gone too far the other day with Steve, telling him to grow up. But it seemed to have done some good. He couldn't say that he approved of Steve's relationship with Ava, but she was more mature than many of her college-aged counterparts, and maybe there was some balance there. Nick suspected Ava had more to do with Steve thinking about the future than he did.

"Becca's body was discovered at the library at four this morning," Carina said, recounting the time line, "but she died between eight and ten the night before."

"He had her for twenty-four hours before he killed her. That gives us a few more hours for Jodi. If his MO holds this time."

"I don't like the changes," Carina mumbled. "Why can't killers be logical?"

"They are. In their own heads. Everything he does has a purpose. We might not be able to see it, but it's there."

"You sound like Dillon."

"I'll take that as a compliment."

"You should. I think he's the smartest guy on the planet. Next to my dad, of course."

She pulled into the Shack parking lot and said, "So he kills Becca. Watches the web-cam to see when Jodi drinks the Coke. Sees it, dumps Becca's body on his way to kidnap Jodi. Brazen, arrogant."

"He's ultraconfident right now. He's gotten away with two murders. He thinks he's invincible."

"Becca lived and worked across town," Carina said. "There doesn't appear to be any connection between her and Angie or Jodi."

"There is a connection between her and the killer, though. He didn't pick her randomly. He knew her schedule, when she would be leaving the library. He was waiting for her."

"Yes, but she didn't regularly work on Wednesdays. She came in because they were short-handed." Carina frowned.

"But Midge said the young man Becca spoke to looked familiar, that he'd been in before," Nick reminded her. "Maybe Becca had told him she'd be working Wednesday night. For all we know, she'd made arrangements to meet with him."

"So we're looking for someone who knew Angie — knew her well enough to identify her from information on her journal. And who knew Becca, most likely through the library."

"Steve said he used the library on campus," Nick said. "That makes sense. If the killer goes to the university, why would he go to a public library? Why not the campus library?"

"He could live near there," Carina said. "It's convenient for him."

"Or he doesn't go to that college."

"Then how would he be connected to Angie?"

"This place." He motioned to the Shack.

"Her work. Which connects to her feeling that someone who commented on her journal knew where she worked."

The lunch crowd filled the tables in the Sand Shack. Carina saw Kyle behind the back counter. She waited until he was done with a customer before approaching him.

"Mr. Burns, you had a private party here last night, correct?"

"Yes, after Angie's memorial service."

"What time did you close up?"

"What's this about?"

"Jodi Carmichael is missing. She was a friend of Angie's. We're hoping you know what time she left the Shack, who she left with, if anyone was watching her or asking about her."

He looked confused at first. "Jodi? Um, the one with the short light-brown hair?"

"Yes."

"She was here last night with her friends, after the memorial service. I don't know when they left. But she wasn't here when we closed up, which was about eleven."

"Do you have a guest list?"

"Mrs. Vance asked people to sign in at the door. I don't know that everyone did, but the hostess — Maggie last night — was greeting people."

"Where's the book now?"

"Mrs. Vance took it with her."

Carina made a note.

Burns added, "Masterson showed up. Late. He didn't go to the memorial service, at least I didn't see him. I left early to set up the restaurant. But he showed up around ten-thirty and Steve Thomas had it out with him. I told them to take it outside. Thomas came back in fifteen minutes later."

"And Steve Thomas was here the whole night?" Carina asked.

"Yes, he helped clean up. I know he drove Mrs. Vance and her mother home. He and some girl I didn't recognize."

"But you didn't see Jodi leave."

He shook his head. "By eleven almost everyone was gone and I know I didn't have to ask her to leave like I did a couple other people."

"Have you seen a solitary man hanging out over the past few weeks? Perhaps using the computers here?"

He gave her an incredulous look. "We have a lot of people who come in here alone. To eat, surf the Internet. Can you be more specific?"

"Around twenty, possibly a student, blond or light brown hair, six feet tall, slender."

"That describes about twenty percent of my clientele," Burns said. "I want to help, but you're going to have to give me a little more."

"Would you object to a detective from e-crimes coming down and checking the histories and hard drives of your public computers?"

Burns frowned. "I'll have to clear it with the owner, but I don't think it's a problem. Can we do it after hours?"

Carina handed him Patrick's card and wrote his direct number on it. "Call the detective and set it up."

"Will it help?"

"At this point, we need to cover every base." Carina turned to leave, then looked back at Burns. "By the way, have you ever been to the La Jolla Public Library?"

"Never. I always go to the library on campus. Anything else? I really need to get back to work."

"We'd like to talk to your employees again. We can come by when it's quieter, later this afternoon?"

"Fine. Anytime after two."

They left and Nick asked her, "You suspect Burns?"

"I don't know, I just thought it was a shot with the library."

"He's a little older than twenty, but Midge at the library wasn't certain about the age.

He has light brown hair and is about six feet tall."

Carina said, "We ran all Shack employees, and other than one who was arrested for misdemeanor drug possession a year ago, they were all clean, including Burns. But I'll put someone on it. Pull his DMV photo and show it to Midge."

"It's worth a shot," Nick said.

He didn't have a lot of time, just enough time to bathe her and finish her. He'd been dreaming about it all day. Still on the high from Becca, he expected to maintain it with Jodi.

The first thing he noticed was the smell. Putrid. She'd shit in the bed, just like that whore Angie. He'd punish her for that before killing her.

She was asleep, in the same position he'd left her in.

"Wake up, I need to clean you up." He looked at her carefully. She appeared . . . odd. "Come on, don't be that way." He sat on the edge of the bed. She didn't move.

He slapped her hard and she didn't wake up. Then he noticed something different about Jodi. Her skin was a strange color. Sort of blue. He slapped her again. Her flesh felt thick, pasty, cold.

What was wrong? What had happened?

He pulled back her eyelids. Her eyes had a weird glassy look to them. And he knew.

She was dead.

"No! *NO!* That's not fair!"

He shook her, but her body felt hard, unreal. He punched her in the chest with both fists. "Stupid slut! How dare you die on me! It's my choice, not yours! You bitch!"

He punched her again, and again, an unfamiliar rage building. He tried to control himself, but it was like he was watching from the outside, from high above, seeing himself hitting Jodi's lifeless body.

Her eyes were half-open, looking at him through slit lashes. Did the dead see? No, that was his imagination, his mind playing tricks.

He'd come home, risked everything, to finish it. He only needed an hour. And she ruined it. How could she *die* on him? Before he was done with her? It wasn't fair!

He was breathing fast, too fast.

Calm down. Think.

He turned away from her body, looked at his hands. The skin across his knuckles was red and broken. Had he hit her that hard? Why didn't he remember?

Think.

He had to get rid of her. As soon as possible. But not stupidly, he couldn't be stupid about it. He was smart, he could think this through.

He had planned on dropping her someplace near her apartment after work tonight. But he had to get rid of her *now*. The thought of her, dead, in his bed until tonight made him ill. She had died without anything to stop her body from spreading its sick germs and fluids all over his stuff. The smell was awful, her urine and shit. Seeping into his mattress.

Damn bitch. She stole what was rightfully his — her life!

He had to wash the body, but it was getting late. Did he chance dumping her without a proper cleansing?

No, no, that would be dumb. He had to do it.

Jodi was heavy and he struggled. Sweat poured from his body, dripped onto hers. He was panicking, he felt it, knew it, could do nothing about it.

He ran the water over her body and left the bathroom to collect his thoughts.

Sitting heavily in his chair, he looked around. Okay, maybe things weren't as bad as he feared. It was just the sheets he'd bought for her. His mattress, maybe he could buy a new one. Tomorrow morning, first thing. Burn this one. Yes, that was right, burn it. Good, good.

He collected all of Jodi's clothing and bundled it in a garbage bag with the sheets and soiled blankets.

Deep breath. Calm. It hadn't gone according to plan, but he was smart. He could improvise. As he worked through the new plan, his breathing evened out. He deliberately took time washing her body. Made sure anything that connected to him was gone. He used antibiotic ointment on his knuckles. He hoped no one noticed, but if they did he would have an excuse. Something believable.

He dried her off and branded her. *Slut.* Right across her breasts. Just like Angie.

Her body was stiff, hard to bend — it took some effort to force it into the bags. Tied them with rope. He was taking a chance driving her during the day, but he had to. The garage was behind the house, and trees partially obscured the yard from nosy neighbors. The old biddy with the cat on the right might be home, but she wouldn't be able to see anything. On the left, the guy would have a view of the side garage door if he was at his kitchen window and looked way over to the left. But it didn't look like he was home.

It was a risk. But it was *always* a risk. His heart beat mostly from exertion as he picked up Jodi's body. Angie had been lighter, but he thought maybe because she'd only been dead for a few minutes when he'd put her in his trunk. Jodi's body didn't bend or move as easily, and he did contortions getting her out the back door and into the garage.

Inside, he took a minute to catch his breath. Okay, okay. Everything was fine. No one had seen him.

He put her in the trunk and left. He only had ten minutes to get to work, and he was going to be a little late.

He didn't think anyone would notice.

TWENTY-THREE

Patrick called Carina with an update on his efforts to locate Bondage and Scout through the MyJournal corporation. "We're running in circles right now, but we're getting somewhere. MyJournal dumped all the data on us — millions of bytes of data — and we're going through it. We're running a program that compares the data with the IP prefixes of the Shack's network and the La Jolla library."

"You're talking nerd again," Carina teased.

"Essentially, every computer connection has a unique IP number. Like a home address for computers — anyone in the country can find it. An ISP — Internet service provider — has a set of IP numbers that it assigns to its subscribers. The Shack and the library have one prefix, like an area code, and every connection in their network has a unique number. Individual computers, like Thomas's, have a unique number assigned by their ISP. An ISP may have multiple prefixes, but no other ISP will share a prefix. For example, one company might have eight unique prefixes. No other company will have those prefixes."

"I think I get it. So you're telling me that you're comparing the data and at some point you'll get a match and know who sent Angie that message she deleted?"

He laughed. "I wish it were that easy! If we get a match to one of the Shack's computer connections, for example, we'll know which computer sent the message to Angie. If we get a match to the library, we'll know that someone at the library sent the message. If someone logged onto the library's network, we'll be able to see that."

"But we won't know who."

"True. But we have one more program running. We're running the Bondage and Scout messages against all assigned IP addresses in Southern California. If we get a hit there, we can get a warrant and obtain the personal data for that specific IP connection."

"And that'll lead us to his house?"

"If it's a private account, like you have at your house, where you pay a fee to access the Internet. If it's a public account, like the library, then you'll be led to the library."

"You're giving me a headache."

"I can find out where they sent the message from. Then it's up to you."

"Thanks, Patrick. Did Kyle Burns contact you about the Shack's computers?"

"Yes, I'm good to go with them. When I finish setting up the programs to run I'm going to take my team and go on-site."

"Great."

"One more thing."

"Yeah?"

"I inspected the webcam Gage found at Jodi Carmichael's apartment."

"And?"

"It has a wireless connection. The end user would be able to log onto the frequency and see whatever it was aimed at. Gage thought it was motion activated, but it's not. It's always on."

"Can you trace it?"

"I wish. If he was logged onto the frequency, I could trace it. But it's like a one-way street — he knows the access codes and can view the stream. The stream isn't being sent anywhere. The battery has a seventy-two-hour life. I tested it and there's about twenty hours of juice left."

Carina thought back. "Which means he was in Jodi's apartment sometime on Wednesday."

"Yes."

"Can you put it back?"

"You think he's going to go for Abby?"

"I don't know, but maybe next time he logs onto the computer his computer will try to access the stream or something."

"I think that's unlikely, but I can put it back."

"No prints?"

"None. And there's nothing unique about it. He could have bought it anywhere. There's a serial number and we're tracing it, but all it'll tell us is what distributor had the unit."

"Dammit."

"Be careful, Carina. I'll call you when I know anything."

Carina and Nick never made it back to the Sand Shack during the day, but Patrick called to say that he was on-scene so she was heading back there when her cell phone rang.

"Kincaid."

"It's Jim. We found Jodi."

"And?"

"She's dead."

Carina's jaw clenched. "Where?"

"Her apartment. In the carport."

Carina made a U-turn and headed back

to Jodi's apartment. The entire carport area was sealed off, and several dozen onlookers stood behind bright yellow crime scene tape.

She and Nick put on gloves and shoe protectors and went into the crime scene.

"How did the killer get here unseen?" she asked the two cops who had spent all day in the area interviewing residents.

"We were across the street at the other building. We've talked to eighty-one people, and no one saw anything last night that seemed out of the ordinary."

You're too late.

They were in the carport of Abby and Jodi's apartment building. Jodi's body was next to her car, discovered by a resident at nine p.m.

"Go back and get a time line. She couldn't have been here long."

Jim Gage was already processing the scene, barking orders to his staff, his normally calm, methodical demeanor frazzled by the brazen disposal of Jodi's body by her killer. His team finished setting up perimeter lights, and he began to inspect her body under the artificial brightness.

Jodi had been tied in the garbage bags, but during transport they had loosened and her arm had fallen out. The responding officer had partially removed the garbage bag, revealing her face and the telltale black bandanna glued to her mouth.

Her nose was broken, twisted at an odd angle, surrounded with dark blood. Jim carefully unwrapped the body, bagging and preserving evidence as he went. The process was laborious, but necessary.

Jodi's wrists and ankles still had ropes attached, cut with a sharp, nonserrated knife. Her legs were streaked in dried blood, *slut* was scrawled across her chest in black marker, but what really drew Carina's attention and horror was Jodi's stomach. It looked like pulp underneath blue skin. Her skin was also red and splotchy in places, like a bad sunburn.

"He beat her up?" she asked Jim.

"It's postmortem. In fact, all the injuries except gluing her mouth shut and the sexual assault were made postmortem." Jim looked up. "She's been dead for over twelve hours."

"Since this morning?" Carina asked, incredulous.

"I'm guessing between seven and nine. The postmortem damage happened several hours after her death, three to six. Her muscles had already started to stiffen, but not enough for full rigor, which occurs at eight to twelve hours." Jim looked from Carina to Nick. "Want to know my guess?"

Nick said, "She died on him and when he found her, he was angry."

Jim looked surprised. "Exactly."

"How'd she die?" Nick asked. "Shock?"

"She choked to death or suffocated. Dr. Chen will know for sure. I have her medical records, and she has a history of allergies to latex, and mild asthma. But shock or stress may have triggered an asthma attack, and she couldn't breathe."

Jim shook his head. "But," he continued, "see the discoloration of her skin? It looks like hives. She may have died from anaphylactic shock. Maybe he wore latex gloves when he assaulted her, and she had an allergic reaction."

"She could die from that?" Nick asked.

"Absolutely. You've heard of people dying from bee stings and peanuts, right? It can take a few hours, but repeated exposure can increase the reaction. I had a case where a guy died ten minutes after a wasp sting. He couldn't find his epi pen." Jim looked at them. "Jodi had an epi pen in her purse, which was left in her bedroom when the killer abducted her."

"Not that she would have been able to tell him with her mouth glued shut." Nick's voice was laced with anger and frustration.

"There is good news," Jim said.

"Tell me there are hidden security cameras."

"Can't do that. But by these wounds I think he beat her up with his hands. There is likely biological evidence on her from the killer."

"DNA." It was their first real hope at solid evidence.

"And here —" he pointed to the ropes.

"What?"

"There's some fabric attached to the rope. Possibly a cotton sheet, but we can test it."

"Did he wash her body, too?"

"Yes, but not as thoroughly as the others. There's more blood here than with the first two victims. She was dead, heavy, awkward to move around."

"But the killer is strong," Nick said.

"To carry a dead body? Absolutely. Someone who works out and is physically fit."

"Unless there are two of them," said Nick.

"Two killers?" Jim asked, uncertain.

Carina thought about Nick's comment. "It's possible. We can't rule anything out yet, but Dillon didn't mention the possibility of a killing team."

"Just an idea. I'm not even sold on it, but I wanted to mention it."

Carina turned to Jim. "How fast can you get DNA?"

"DNA takes months, Carina. You know that."

"I also know that this is a priority case."

"I can't even get a sample until the autopsy and we sift through the trace evidence. She's been washed, he may have cleaned off any evidence. It'll take a couple days. Then, if I rush it and have no court-mandated tests, I can do it in two to three days."

"We can send it out."

"Private lab?" Jim frowned. "Yeah, but Causey has to sign off on it."

"I'll worry about the chief."

San Diego County had its own DNA laboratory, a onetime purchase by the board of supervisors. The city shared it with the sheriff's forensic department, but they were backlogged, as usual. Too many crimes, not enough resources. When a case was particularly high-profile, they could sometimes get approval to hire an outside lab for DNA testing.

"I'll see what I can do," Jim said, "but it'll still take at least thirty-six hours for the autopsy, collection of evidence, and preparing the chain-of-evidence paperwork. Maybe I can clear a machine in the lab and work it myself. If there's even any DNA to analyze."

"I'd appreciate it."

"I know." Jim stared at Jodi's body. "I'll

be at the autopsy in the morning."

"Saturday?"

"I talked to Dr. Chen on the way over here. He's taken this case personally. He wants the killer as much as we do."

The dinner hour long past, Carina and Nick ate cold pizza late Friday night in the SDPD conference room while running through their notes. Patrick and Dillon came in with a stack of papers. Both looked as tired as Carina felt. Even Dillon, the clean-cut, immaculately dressed doctor, had the sleeves of his button-down shirt rolled up, and the waves he tamed every morning with gel now fell loose across his forehead.

"Both these guys are winners," Patrick said as he dropped the papers on the conference table.

"I'm tired," Carina said. "What guys?"

"Bondage and Scout," Patrick said.

Nick pulled the top sheet. "These look like comments off MyJournal pages."

"Bingo," Patrick said, sitting down backward in a chair and grabbing a slice of cold pizza. "This is part of the huge info dump we got from the MyJournal corporate office. Every archived comment made by Bondage and Scout."

Dillon interjected, "I think we need

to focus on Scout. Both may be dangerous, and we're going to continue to look
into Bondage for possible underage solic-
itation issues, but I think Scout killed Angie."

"Based on what?" Carina asked, looking
at the comments herself. They weren't
exclusively posted on Angie's Web page, but
a variety of MyJournal pages.

One comment from Scout on a page
dedicated to cats: *My cat Felix died last week.
Someone hit him with a baseball bat. He died
in my arms.*

"You think being upset about a cat dying
makes Scout the killer?"

"Scout posted seventeen different times
over the last two years that his cat Felix
died. Hit by a car, hit with a baseball bat,
drowned by his neighbor. All to women who
then started an e-mail relationship with
him. Interesting, none appear to still be talking to him."

Carina sat up and grabbed one of the
pages. "The cat. Midge at the library said
that the man Becca was talking to the night
she disappeared told her his cat had been
shot to death."

"That's a better connection than I have,"
Dillon said.

"What do you mean?"

"It's not the cat that tipped me off, though it's suspicious. Read this."

Dillon handed both Nick and Carina copies of key comments. Carina frowned as she read them.

Women are beautiful. Soft. Delicate. I'm careful with women, because I don't want them to break. You can't put them back together.

My girl isn't broken and I'm being careful. Very careful. When we make love, it's beautiful. I made love to her three times tonight. She likes it when I use a dildo. Because deep down all women are sluts. I wonder what they think about when men shove their dicks in them. How it feels. What they really want. Why they lie all the time, saying one thing and doing another. Doing one thing, then lying about it. Why can't people just tell me the truth? Why does everyone have to lie?

I'm the best liar out there. It takes one to know one, know what I mean? I can lie and no one knows. Even people who know me can't figure it out.

The next was just as disturbing.

All women lie. Even the ones who are

338

nice to your face, they lie behind your back.

You're all sluts.

In a response to a guy who'd posted a journal entry about how he learned his girlfriend was cheating on him and how he wanted to strangle her, Scout wrote:

All women are cheating cunts who need to be shut up. Whores. Bitches. Sluts. Lying whores should be thrown out with the trash.

Kill your bitch.

"There's a lot more like this," Dillon said. "But read this one dated Sunday late afternoon."

"Angie was still missing but alive."

"But Scout had time to go online and write this."

I'll be bathing my girlfriend soon, cleansing all the impurities from her body so we can unite as one. It'll be like her first time, and her last time.

Nick said, "Why won't the MyJournal people do anything? This is obviously threatening."

"Misogynistic, true, but not threatening to any specific woman. No one with a My-Journal account has filed a report against Scout for any threatening posts or e-mails," Patrick said. "Even Angie. She banned him, but didn't use the MyJournal service, which allows members to file complaints."

"What can we do? Can we find him now? Do you have an address?"

"Slow down. This is a huge leap forward, but we still only have his public persona. No IP, no home address."

"The key here," Dillon said, "is that we can focus our resources on finding Scout instead of wasting time chasing other people down."

"You're that certain," Nick said.

"You have doubts?"

Nick was silent for a good minute, looking over the comments. "No, I think you're right."

"We have our work cut out for us," Carina said, "but we're getting closer. I can feel it."

Twenty-Four

Shortly after Dillon and Patrick left — telling Carina to go home and sleep a couple hours — Carina took Nick back to her parents' house. She glanced at the dashboard clock: 1:13 a.m. The lights were off, except for the front security lights. One in the morning was too late for her parents.

She shut off the car, turned to Nick. The entire drive over she couldn't get him out of her mind.

Maybe it was because they'd just been at a crime scene and she wanted to rid her mind of the images so she could sleep tonight. Or maybe it was because Nick Thomas was so damn sexy she'd been having erotic dreams about him for the past two nights.

But, if she wanted to be honest with herself, it was two reasons. First, Nick *was* sexy and he didn't know it. He didn't flirt, he didn't try to be anything he wasn't. The

341

raw realism that what you see is what you get with Sheriff Thomas attracted her like little else. She didn't date much because she didn't want to sort through truth and lies to figure out if her date was someone she wanted to explore a relationship with. And, frankly, her job kept her so damn busy she didn't want to spend that much time separating the wheat from the chaff.

And second, well, this was a little too close for comfort, but Carina knew herself well: she'd always been attracted to guys who didn't flirt, the hard-to-get type. Since she turned fifteen, grew breasts, and developed a curvy figure, she'd had guys hitting on her wherever she went. While she didn't particularly like it, she expected it, so when it didn't happen, she looked twice at the guy.

Certainly Nick found her attractive. He wasn't married — no ring, no phone calls to or from a spouse or girlfriend. At least in her presence, and they'd been together virtually every waking hour since he'd come to town. Maybe he was discreet, professional. Called late at night.

There was one surefire way to find out.

She turned to Nick, taking in his rugged sexiness that had been the subject of her hot dreams. His square jaw, piercing blue eyes, the scent of soap and sweat and nothing else. She licked her lips. His eyes dropped to her mouth.

Carina reached over with her right arm and grabbed Nick's neck. She pulled herself to him, her lips to his, and kissed him. No tentative kiss, no wimpy damsel. A full-frontal, openmouthed assault on the mouth of the man who had captivated her for three days.

There was no turning back now. His mouth was heavenly, hot and sensuous and far better than any dream.

Nick knew Carina was going to kiss him the second before she latched her lips onto his. It took him a moment to adjust — no woman had ever initiated physical contact, not like this.

But Carina Kincaid was not like other women. Self-confident, in both her career and her body, she had a sensual self-awareness that enticed him.

He didn't wait long to return her embrace.

As soon as he responded, she wrapped both arms around his neck, her fingers running through his short hair, massaging his head as she reached deeper into him with her mouth.

He wanted her.

Nick reached for her face, her soft skin silky against his rough hands. He pulled his mouth from hers, kissed her jaw, her long, sleek neck. She moaned into his ear, her reaction to his attention giving him the confidence to explore further. To touch her breasts, rub his thumb over her hard nipples. She gasped, clutched at his neck, kissed his ear, her hot breath sending shivers down his spine until all he wanted was to strip her naked and make love to her.

They'd become twisted in the front seat. Contrary to what teenagers thought, cars were not made for sex. Carina whispered in his ear, "Take me upstairs."

At the same time her hand moved from his thigh to his knee. A jolt of fiery pain shot through his nerves. Damn, why now? Why couldn't he have one night the way *he* wanted it?

He pulled away from her, hating to let her go. He swallowed back the pain that ran from his knees through his entire body.

"That's probably not a good idea." Nick turned his head, unable to look Carina in the eye. She was a woman who demanded honesty, and he couldn't lie to her face. "I'm sorry, I shouldn't have let that happen."

"Did I hurt you? I'm sorry." She looked at his knees and he felt uncomfortable but not surprised. She was a cop, trained to observe. He didn't want her to know how much pain he was in, didn't want her to think that it impacted his job. By tomorrow morning after a few Motrin he'd be good as new. He just overdid it today. He wasn't used to twenty-hour days anymore.

"I'm fine," he said, too sharply. To compensate, he reached over and kissed her lightly on the lips. Damn, she tasted so good. He kissed her again.

He touched her beautiful face, the slender lines and thick lips, naturally red from their hot kisses. He wanted her. But not now, not like this. Not in a car, not when he couldn't carry her up the stairs.

"Good night, Carina."

It took every ounce of strength to get out of the car without his knees buckling and crumbling to the driveway. He stood next to the car, unable to walk away.

Carina stared at him through the windshield, thinking. *Don't think too hard, Carina.* He didn't want her pity, he didn't want her sympathy. He just wanted her to leave so he could take care of himself, so he'd be ready tomorrow morning for the autopsy of another young woman who didn't deserve her fate.

Finally, she started the engine and backed up. She stopped the car, rolled down the window. "Dream of me tonight, Nick."

She drove off. He watched the car until it reached the end of the tree-lined street. He expected it to turn the corner; instead, she pulled into the driveway of the corner house. The garage door went up and she pulled in.

She lived really close to her parents.

The garage door closed behind the car and Nick released his breath, not realizing he'd been holding it.

Damn. Even now, nearly a year later, the Butcher had left a permanent mark on Nick.

His knees were so shot he didn't think he'd make it up the stairs. He almost hadn't made it out of Carina's car, and he was grateful she hadn't said anything.

He'd taken the ibuprofen back at Jodi's apartment, but it had done nothing to help the pain. Worse, he'd forced himself to stand longer than he should, not wanting to show any weakness in front of the San Diego Police Department or Carina. Especially Carina.

He dry-swallowed two more pills and shuffled over to the stairs leading to the apartment, then sat on the bottom step. A light above the apartment door illuminated the stairs.

Something about Carina . . . it drew him

in like no woman had done before. She intrigued him. Pretty, certainly, and sexy, but it was more than her looks: there was a sharp brain and deep confidence. Like so many people in the world, she'd suffered tragedy, but her strength and natural optimism gave her the ability to persevere and create something much, much better with her life. Her drive to be a good cop, a great cop, was alluring. Almost as sexy as the way she put her hand on her hip, subtly, unconsciously, drawing attention to her oh-so-feminine curves.

He closed his eyes and wondered what would happen between him and Carina if he didn't have so much baggage. He liked the way she thought, the way she looked, the way she loved her parents and respected her family. She'd kissed him, not a tentative, uncertain kiss, but a fierce and confident embrace that told him she wouldn't be a shrinking violet in bed. She would give as good as she got.

He wanted her in his bed. Her bed. He would have taken her in the car, and knew she'd be more than willing if, perhaps, they weren't sitting in her parents' driveway.

More than anything, he appreciated her straightforward manner, the fact that she said what she thought and didn't agonize over every decision she made.

He realized that's exactly what he'd been doing back home in Montana. Agonizing over whether to be sheriff or give it up. Not because he wasn't a good cop, but because he didn't know if he wanted it anymore. The only person his bad decision had affected last year in the Butcher investigation was himself. It could have been worse. Someone could have been killed because he'd acted the maverick.

Still, being here, working this case, showed him he still had a sharp mind. Maybe sharper now for what he'd gone through in the past. If only his body would cooperate, he'd be at the top of his game.

Carina was a physically active, intelligent woman. Could he keep up with her? He wanted to. But look at him now, sitting on the stairs, unable to walk to the apartment above. Was it even fair to her?

"Beautiful night."

Nick tensed until he recognized Colonel Pat Kincaid's deep voice.

"Yes, sir," he said, opening his eyes. By the colonel's expression, he didn't know if he'd witnessed Nick's make-out session in the car with his daughter. "You snuck up on me."

The colonel grinned, leaned against the

348

stair railing. "I'm light on my feet."

Nick knew he should stand, but if he tried he'd fail. Embarrassment warred with his predicament. He needed help; he didn't want to ask.

"Carina has been working long hours on this case," the colonel said.

"Yes, sir."

"You can drop the 'sir.' I'm retired. Makes me feel old. And on duty."

Nick couldn't help but grin. He remembered telling his favorite deputy, Lance Booker, virtually the same thing. *Can the "sir."* But old habits die hard. He'd always said "Yes, sir" to his father. His father demanded the respect.

Already, Nick had more respect for Pat Kincaid than he had for his own father, and that thought unsettled him. The respect for Colonel Kincaid came from the results of his parentage, and one night of good conversation. He loved his family, showed it. Not only in the way he spoke of them, but in the way his children spoke of him.

"Carina is a good cop," Nick said, feeling like he had to say something. He didn't do well with small talk.

"That she is. Driven. You know about my grandson."

"Yes, I'm sorry."

The colonel took a deep breath. "It was the worst day of my life." He paused. "When Nelia came home from law school and said she was pregnant, Rosa and I were shocked." He grunted. "We shouldn't have been. Kids have sex. They get pregnant. It happens all the time, but . . . we thought we'd raised a nun." He looked pointedly at Nick. "Nelia was our first — first daughter, first child. We shouldn't have been surprised. She was twenty-three. Not a young kid. And Andrew was willing to do the right thing. Marry her."

They were silent for several minutes. The colonel wanted to talk, but Nick didn't rush him. He understood the need to collect thoughts, try to make sense of the insensible.

"Rosa and I are from the old school. The right school, in our minds, even now. Men did the right thing in our day. You got a girl pregnant, you married her. Everything worked out, more or less.

"But maybe, sometimes, marriage isn't always the right thing."

The colonel paused again. "A lot of women are capable of raising kids on their own. Especially with family," he said, more to himself than to Nick.

"Nelia and Andrew, they never argued.

They never disagreed. They were always respectful, always polite. I should have seen it sooner."

When the colonel didn't say anything, Nick asked, "Seen what?"

"That they didn't love each other."

"But that certainly didn't have anything to do with Justin's murder."

"No, it didn't. But it's never just one thing, is it? Wrong place, wrong time . . . or maybe a gradual layering of choices? First, having sex. Then getting married. Moving here, or there. Taking this job, or that one. Every decision, every choice, changes the path we're on.

"Nelia and Andrew didn't love each other, but they are both good people and they loved Justin. They did the wrong thing for the right reasons. If they had really loved each other, they wouldn't have spent so much time apart."

"But that has nothing to do with Justin's murder." Nick didn't see where the colonel was going with the conversation. Maybe he was too tired, or in too much pain. But there seemed to be a disconnect that Nick just wasn't getting.

"Have you ever been in love, Sheriff?" the colonel asked.

Nick's jaw clenched. "Yes."

"Did you want to spend your free time with her? Did you think about her when you were apart? I mean, not all the time. There're other things, like the job, the World Series, but work and sports aside, didn't you just want to be with her?"

Nick thought about Miranda. He would have given his life for her. He'd wanted to marry her. He'd loved her. She hadn't loved him. He'd known it from the beginning, thought he could change her, convince her that he was the right man for her. That he could protect her, take care of her, keep her demons at bay.

But he couldn't do anything she didn't want him to do, and it took another man to fix Miranda's wounded soul. He'd finally accepted that, moved on.

The colonel continued. "Andrew and Nelia, separate, are incredible people. Wonderful. I admire both of them. Separately, they made great parents. They loved Justin. They would have done anything for him." He paused, eyes glistening with unshed tears. "Together? They *respected* each other. And as the farce of a marriage continued, they spent more time apart."

Nick could picture the relationship perfectly. Two people who stayed together, without anger or love, because of a child.

"So when Justin died, they had nothing left," Nick said quietly.

"Not even each other," the colonel said equally quietly.

He sat down on the stair next to Nick.

"Carina said his murderer was never found."

"True. Nelia left, she couldn't stay here with the memories. I haven't seen her in years. Rosa, she talks to her once a week. Every Sunday. But no one else. Nelia is grieving alone, and to me, that's the saddest thing. It's been eleven years."

They sat a long moment in silence.

"I heard about the third murder," the colonel said. "That the girl was kidnapped from her apartment."

"Yes."

"How did Cara handle it?"

"Like a professional."

Nick remembered the pain in her eyes, pain and anger, and a hint of doubt. But she still did the job, not letting her personal feelings interfere with her duty.

Nick knew how difficult it could be to push down personal feelings to do what was right. He'd had to do it repeatedly on the Butcher investigation. When he was involved with Miranda, he had to keep reminding himself that she didn't want his protection, or his help. He had never wanted to bring FBI agent Quinn Peterson back to town, knowing that he still loved Miranda, but Nick had had to, to find the Butcher.

In a perfect world, there'd be no sick men torturing and hunting down women in the wilderness, or gluing their mouths shut and raping them while they suffocated. And in a perfect world, feelings wouldn't hurt. Failure wouldn't be a word. Mistakes wouldn't happen.

"That's my girl," the colonel said with pride. "Professional, focused, determined. I just — I can't help but worry. She took Justin's death personally."

"I know."

Carina's dad looked at him, surprised. "She told you?"

"That she was babysitting? That she was never allowed to watch Lucy again? Yeah. She told me." Nick was surprised that it bothered him, that he felt closer to Carina because of the quiet, unconscious distrust of her family, even though her family loved her.

Neither man spoke for a long while. "It wasn't intentional. I didn't even think about it for the longest time. It wasn't, well, it wasn't until Carina said something last year that made me realize what Rosa and I had

354

unintentionally done."

"What did she say?"

"It was just before Lucy's seventeenth birthday. She wanted to go to the mall to buy these shoes she had to have, but we don't allow her to go alone or just to hang out with friends. Kids get in trouble that way. It was Rosa's Ladies Guild night at the church, and I was getting over a cold. Carina offered to take her, and I said great.

"Carina turned to Lucy and said, 'This will be fun. The first time us girls get a girls' night out.' "

"After they left, Rosa and I talked and re-alized we'd never let Carina take Lucy anywhere, just the two of them. Both of us remembered many times where we'd volun-teer to join them, or one of the boys would be in the house and would tag along. I think all of us went into protective mode."

"It hurt Carina."

"I see it now, but she'd never said any-thing. Not to me or her mother, at any rate." He looked at Nick, cleared his throat. "I saw you get out of the car when Carina dropped you off."

Nick tensed. Had the colonel been able to see him practically having sex with his daughter in his driveway? Nick was usually discreet about his relationships. Not that he and Carina had a relationship, especially now after he'd pushed her away.

"Dream of me tonight," she'd said. And he definitely would.

"Bum knee?"

"You could say that."

"Let me help you up the stairs."

"I don't need help."

The colonel stood, extended his hand. "It's not a sin to accept help once in a while."

Damn. Nick would make it up the stairs alone. Struggling the entire way. Making the situation worse, which would mean paying for it in the morning.

"Thanks," he managed to grunt out, taking the old man's hand.

Wrapping an arm around the colonel's shoulders while the colonel supported his back, Nick made it up the stairs without incident. He unlocked the door with the key he'd been given, and faced the colonel, embarrassed.

"Thank you," he said clearly.

"Anytime, son." He clapped Nick on the back.

Son.

His own father had rarely called him son. For the second time in as many days, he'd felt more affection from a man he'd just met than he'd felt in a lifetime with his father.

TWENTY-FIVE

The brisk knocking on the door woke Nick from a deep sleep. He sat up, trying to get his bearings. The Kincaid apartment. Right. Carina's father had helped him up the stairs after their conversation.

He ran a hand through his damp hair. He'd slept rough, the memories and nightmares weaving in and out, deserting him finally to give him two hours of heavy sleep. The clock read 8:30. He never slept that late. But after the colonel helped him up the stairs, they'd shared a couple shots of good whiskey, talked some more. Nick didn't know if it was the colonel's way of sizing him up for his daughter, or just because he was a guest at their house. But he'd enjoyed the company.

Expecting to find Carina on the doorstep, he couldn't hide his surprise when Dillon Kincaid stood outside with two tall mugs of coffee. He handed one to Nick. "Can I come in?"

"Sure." Nick stepped aside, sipped the coffee. "I guess I slept in. Did we have a meeting scheduled?"

"No."

"Any word from Patrick about the My-Journal information?"

"Not that I know."

"You know he's going to kill again." Nick pulled on a T-shirt and sat on a chair at the small table. He sipped the coffee; it was rich and spicy, and hit the spot.

"If we don't find him. Third time's the charm — separates the standard killer from the serial killer. Angie, Becca, Jodi. I wish we had more evidence, but it looks like you and the rest of the team have been working virtually around the clock." Dillon sat down across from him, sipped his own coffee.

"I'd say yes, except you caught me sleeping in." Nick played with the mug. "Why Becca?" he asked. "She doesn't fit the profile."

"There's definitely a connection, even if she doesn't fit what we think is the profile. Becca didn't have a MyJournal page, didn't spend any time online that wasn't related to school or e-mailing friends. But there *is* a connection between Becca and the killer, probably through the library. My biggest question right now is, why? Why did he go after Becca *now?* When we knew he had targeted Jodi."

"I've been thinking about that," Nick said.

"You have a theory?"

Nick paused to put together his thoughts. "You heard about the webcam in Jodi's apartment, right?"

Dillon nodded.

"Patrick said it was installed Wednesday, late morning or afternoon. Which makes sense because we determined that the girls were out of the apartment at that time. Jodi's window was unlocked. Whether she did it or the killer did it, we don't know."

"Becca was abducted Wednesday night, not Jodi."

"Right. Why?"

Dillon thought, then shook his head. "I don't know. Maybe he couldn't get to Jodi."

"Exactly. Because she didn't drink the right beverage. He drugged every *open* container. There were a couple of beer bottles and water bottles in the refrigerator, too. Untampered. Because if you pull out a beer bottle, open it, and it doesn't make that *whoosh* sound of carbonation being released, you think there's something wrong with it and you toss it, right?"

"Sounds logical."

Nick leaned forward, on a roll. "So what if he's watching her, sees that she takes the wrong drink? What's his reaction?"

"Anger. Frustration. She's not playing along."

"Right. His first instinct?"

"To prove he's still in control."

"Which means that he takes the first girl he sees, someone he's familiar with, at least on the surface."

"That's reckless, and he's been anything but reckless."

"Yes, but remember what you said the other day?" Nick asked. "That the killer was young? *Immature* was your exact word. When someone acts immaturely, they're reckless. Make mistakes. Lash out. He's an amateur. So he's mad that Jodi didn't drink a tainted beverage, and he looks up and sees Becca. He *tells her about his dead cat.*"

"Matching the MO of Scout online."

"Exactly. Scout was at the library Wednesday night and because Jodi didn't do what she was supposed to do, he took the first woman he could."

"Becca Harrison."

"The librarian said she'd been talking to him, friendly. He tells her about the cat, she feels sorry for him. Maybe looks at him and smiles, further egging him on. She doesn't

361

know it, she thinks she's being nice and sympathetic. He leaves first, waits for her."

"But any number of things could have happened. Someone could have walked out with her. The library is on a busy street, anyone could have walked past."

"Yes, but Becca was in the parking lot in the back. More secluded. And if she wasn't alone, he could have followed her, learned where she lived."

"Abducted her from her home, just like he did Angie and Jodi." Dillon nodded. "I see what you're getting at."

"Crime of opportunity."

"But why watch the webcam from the library? That's more dangerous than going home."

"I don't know. Maybe the thrill of being in public. Maybe he was working or going to work or school —"

"And couldn't get home between wherever he was and where he had to be," Dillon suggested.

"Any number of reasons."

"So, Jodi didn't work out, and he kidnapped Becca instead."

"And he escalated, brought her closer to him so he could feel her die."

"And kidnapped Jodi at the first opportunity."

"Because she was his first choice."

Dillon and Nick realized they'd hit on something important, the reason Becca didn't fit the victim profile. She was a spontaneous abduction.

"Who's next?" Nick asked.

"I should be asking you. You could do my job."

"I don't envy you. I had enough of serial killers in Montana to last a lifetime. We should bring Carina in, tell her our theory. We need to get back to the library, track down everyone who was there Wednesday night, or any other night Scout was there. Maybe between all the potential witnesses we can get a good physical description."

Dillon nodded. "I agree, but I didn't come up here to talk about the case."

Nick raised an eyebrow. "Oh?"

"I had breakfast with my dad. He said your knee is giving you some trouble."

Embarrassment and a touch of anger washed over Nick. He didn't like talking about his physical problems, and he hadn't expected the colonel to talk about them, either.

Dillon went on. "What happened?"

"It's nothing. I have medication, but I don't like to take it."

"Medication is to mask the pain, not fix

the problem."

"The problem isn't fixable."

"I find that hard to believe."

"I didn't know shrinks were also sur-
geons." Damn, he sounded defensive. He
didn't mean to, he just didn't feel comfortable talking to Carina's brother about his
limitations.

"I was in sports medicine before Justin
was murdered. I'd already finished med
school at the time, so yeah, I guess you
could say I have some experience with
injuries, especially joints and muscles."

Nick didn't say anything for a long
minute. "I had surgery. It didn't work the
first time. I'm scheduled to go back next
month, but I'm not holding out hope that
it'll work."

Dillon looked at his knees, nodded. Nick
resisted the urge to cover his scars. And
while he'd done everything he could to
regain the weight he'd lost the past year, he
was still twenty pounds short of his goal.
His legs looked too skinny and damaged.

"Surgery on both knees. I can see they
went in aggressively."

"I had an infection, among other things,
that weakened my joints. I now have septic
arthritis." He tried to laugh and make a
joke. "Thought arthritis was only for old

people."

"Septic arthritis is usually caused by physical damage that results in severely reduced blood flow for an extended period of time." He paused. "Do you want to talk about it?"

"No."

Dillon nodded. "Well, if you ever want me to take a look, I'm still up to speed on sports injuries. Patrick played ball in college and considered me his personal physician."

"It's not a sports injury."

"Same joints, same muscles. And you *are* human."

"That I'm well aware of." Nick shifted in his seat. "Thank you for the offer. I probably won't be around long enough, but I'll let you know how the surgery goes."

Dillon stood, looked at him. "I hope you'll keep in touch when this is all over." He nodded at Nick's empty mug. "My mom cooked enough to feed an army. I think she's expecting you."

"I don't want to put her out."

"She'd probably be more upset if you *didn't* show up. Wouldn't want her to think you didn't like her cooking."

Dillon left and Nick buried his face in his hands. The upcoming surgery worried him. He wanted it to be a success, but the doctor had told him not to get his hopes up, that there was no guarantee his knees would ever get better.

"Just do it, Doc. The earliest you can."

"March is the soonest. Don't expect a miracle."

"It can't get any worse."

"Don't be so sure, Sheriff."

March first was two weeks away, the week before the filing deadline. He wanted to know the outcome of the surgery before he made a decision on running for sheriff again.

It wasn't fair to the people of Gallatin County if he couldn't do the job.

Jim woke Carina Saturday morning with a phone call. "Dr. Chen is coming in to handle Jodi Carmichael's autopsy at eleven. Can you make it?"

"Absolutely."

"Bringing the country sheriff with you?"

"You have a problem with Nick?" She slid out of bed and went into the kitchen to start coffee.

"No." He paused. "He's out of his jurisdiction. Don't you think that's a problem?"

"He's a sworn officer of the court, Jim. Why's it a problem if he wants to spend his vacation helping us on this case? We have three dead girls, and he has experience with these types of cases."

"I know. I did a little research on him last night."

That irritated Carina. "What? You did a background check on him?"

"Nothing that intensive. And I'm surprised you didn't."

"I did check into him." While her coffee brewed, she opened the French doors that led to her wrap-around deck.

"How deep?"

"I know about the serial killer in Bozeman. My partner and I discussed this already and decided to use Sheriff Thomas's help. Why do you care? I'm not compromising the investigation."

"But what do you really know about him?"

"He's a good cop who caught a serial killer."

"Well, the FBI caught the serial killer. Your sheriff was kidnapped by him. Doesn't sound like a competent cop to me."

"You don't know what happened."

"It was all over the papers, Carina. Read between the lines."

"I don't need to. I know what I need to know. Thanks for the heads-up on the autopsy. I'll be there." She hung up, frowning.

She didn't want to listen to Jim. She knew what she needed to know about Nick Thomas, and she was confident in her judgment. A little tickle in the back of her mind: why was Nick still here? His brother had been cleared of Angie's murder; there was really no reason for him to stay.

Except that the case had gotten to him. Just like it had her.

But eventually, sooner rather than later, he'd be going back to Montana. She just didn't want to think about it. She liked him, liked having him around, liked working with him.

She went back inside, poured herself a cup of coffee, and took it with her to the shower.

If she'd had her way, Nick would be in the shower with her right now. What had gone wrong last night?

She had felt how much he'd wanted her. Maybe she'd pushed too much. And his knees — he'd been in pain half the night and hadn't said anything. Why hadn't she thought about that when she'd been thinking about taking him to bed?

Nick was also a gentleman, and she had suggested they go upstairs. Above her parents' house. *Not smart, Kincaid.*

She'd never once asked any man to bed under her parents' roof. In fact, when she'd lived in the apartment above the garage she'd never had a man over. It felt wrong, somehow. But that had completely slipped her mind when she'd been kissing Nick in the car. All she'd thought about was *him,* how much she wanted to make love to him. Common sense had disappeared.

What was she doing even thinking about becoming involved with a man who wouldn't be around? He would go back to Montana in a few days, maybe a week. Could she do that to herself? She'd never been able to have sex with someone and just walk away as if it meant nothing. She'd never wanted to have sex with a man she didn't feel something special for.

She shivered. The thought of Nick leaving made her uncomfortable. But wouldn't that be best? Have a great, sexy affair, no strings attached?

Was that what she wanted?

She turned the shower off and grabbed her towel. She didn't know *what* she wanted anymore, except somehow Nick had become involved in her life and she didn't want to extract him. One day at a time. Close this case, have sex with Nick, then maybe she'd figure it all out.

She wrapped the towel around her body and walked toward her bedroom.

"Hey, sis."

She jumped, holding her towel tight, and twirled around. Her brother was standing in the kitchen, looking straight down the hall toward her. "Dillon Kincaid, you're lucky I don't have my gun."

"And you're lucky I'm not an intruder. Taking a shower with the door unlocked?"

She ignored the jibe. She'd forgotten to lock it when she came in from the porch. "Give me five minutes."

She dressed in jeans and a white T-shirt with "Beach Bum" stenciled in blue across the front. She wasn't on duty and had already logged all the overtime hours she was going to get for the week, but since she was going down to the station to put in time on the three homicides and observe another autopsy, she holstered her gun and tossed a blazer over her shoulder.

She went into the kitchen for a second cup of coffee and to find out why Dillon had stopped by.

"You make great coffee, sis," Dillon said, taking a sip. "Too bad it doesn't extend to your cooking."

"*Tirón,*" she mumbled. *Jerk.*

Dillon grinned.

"Did you stop by just to annoy me?"

"I had breakfast with Mom and Dad and

thought I'd stop by and tell you Andrew and I are petitioning Judge DuBois at noon to obtain a warrant for IP addresses that match the ones on the MyJournal list."

"DuBois? That's good. She'll give it to you — wait! Are you saying Patrick had a breakthrough? Why didn't he call me?"

"Not yet, but he's close and didn't want to have to drag a judge out in the middle of the night. He called me because I'm going at it from a psychiatric angle — that the killer is going to strike again based on what we know, and that obtaining the private information of citizens who may not be involved in order to learn the identity of the killer is essential to protecting the public, yada yada. DuBois will give it to us, but we have to jump through the right hoops. If we get the warrant thrown out after an arrest, I don't have to tell you how screwed we are. We'll get the warrant, then it's all up to Patrick."

"I owe him one. He's been pulling all-nighters for me."

Dillon drained his coffee and put the mug in the sink. "I saw Sheriff Thomas over at the house. I'm surprised he's stayed on."

"Why?"

"He's a sheriff, for one. He has a busy job."

What was she supposed to say? She'd been wondering about the same thing just this morning.

"Have you noticed any physical limitations?"

"You mean his knees."

Dillon nodded. "You know he had surgery."

"He told me."

"Be careful. He's not Will."

"What's that supposed to mean?"

"Will has your back, and he's capable of covering it. Sheriff Thomas isn't even officially involved in the case, and he's not your partner."

"I think you're worrying about nothing."

"I hope."

"What's all this dumping on Nick?" She put her own mug in the sink. "I get a call from Jim and he's all uppity about him."

"Jim's jealous."

"He has nothing to be jealous about. We broke up over a year ago."

"It's a guy thing."

"Guy thing. Right." She took a brush from her purse and pulled it through her hair. "Nick has been an asset on this case. You said so yourself."

"I agree. He has a sharp mind. He has a theory about the killer that I think is right on the money."

"Why'd he share it with you and not me?"

"Because I was there and we were bouncing ideas back and forth. I hadn't intended to talk about the case. He thinks the killer planned to kidnap Jodi on Wednesday night, after he planted the webcam in her kitchen, but she didn't drink the drugged beverages. He grew angry and grabbed someone else."

"Becca. Wrong place wrong time?"

"More like he knew her or had seen her and she was easy to subdue."

"But that makes a connection between him and Becca, if they were in proximity."

"Exactly. The library. And thinking about it, I think Nick is right."

"Why?" But already Carina was putting together the pieces.

"Because the killer is immature. He was angry that Jodi messed up his plan. Ruined his fantasy. He had to take a woman that night. He had it all thought out. Probably had all the supplies on hand. Becca was there, she was nice to him, he waited for her."

"It makes sense. Doesn't help with figuring out who's next."

"Chief Causey said you have a twenty-four/seven watch on Abby and Kayla."

"If his plan was Jodi all along, and Becca

was just convenient, then Abby and Kayla could very well be in danger."

"I agree. I also think he has other women he's stalking. Probably connected with where he goes to school or where he works."

"I have an undercover cop at the library during the hours he is most likely to be there, but now I'll put one on-site full-time."

"Good."

Carina glanced at her watch. "Jodi Carmichael's autopsy is in an hour. I have to pick up Nick and head over there. Do you want to observe?"

"At the beginning, then I need to meet Andrew at the courthouse. By the way, I like him," said Dillon.

"Him who? *Andrew?*" She scrunched up her nose. Though she respected her former brother-in-law as the district attorney, she and her brothers had never liked him.

"The sheriff."

"You were just lecturing me about what he was doing hanging around the case."

"Hmm, not quite. I was just curious, mostly."

Carina playfully hit him.

"Seriously, I like him. He's one of the good guys."

Carina shook her head. "Get out of here

so I can lock up. I'll meet you at the morgue." She didn't know what to make of Dillon's pronouncement, but decided not to look too deeply at it. It made her feel, well, like a teenager again when Dillon put his stamp of approval on her boyfriends.

But she was secretly pleased. Dillon's instincts about the men in her life were usually accurate.

It took less than two minutes to back out of her garage and drive the block to her parents' house. She ran up the stairs to the garage apartment and pounded on the door. "Hey Nick! You decent?"

No answer.

She ran back down the stairs and through the side door into the kitchen. Nick was standing at the sink rinsing dishes and loading the dishwasher. Nick was a big guy, broader than her dad, built more like her brother Connor, the PI. He looked strange in her mother's kitchen, but at the same time oddly domestic, almost like he fit.

She shook her head. It was all Dillon's fault, coming into her house telling her he liked Nick. What was with that? She knew better than to get involved with cops. No matter how sexy they looked doing dishes. Especially since he would be going back to Montana, and that would be that.

But it wasn't like he worked in the San Diego Police Department, so technically he wasn't a colleague, so she wouldn't be breaking her rule.

That's it. She had to do *something* to stop thinking about Nick carnally. Right now she was thinking about him doing the dishes *naked.* Now that was sexy. A man doing the dishes was one thing, doing them sans clothing was just plain fun.

She *really* needed to get him out of her system.

"Cara, darling." Her mom came out of the walk-in pantry, a smile on her round face. "Let me get the fruit salad from the refrigerator. Do you want some toast?"

Carina jumped, blushed. Had she ever blushed before? She didn't think so. But her mom had caught her thinking about sex, and Carina was positive her mother could read minds.

"No, Mama, I'm fine. Really."

Her mother stared at her closely, eyes narrow. Carina put on a blank face and pushed all thoughts of Nick's naked body from her mind. "What did you eat this morning? You don't eat breakfast, so don't lie to me."

Food. Her mom's favorite pastime was feeding her, so maybe she hadn't seen the lust on her face. "I had coffee."

"Pshaw! Coffee!"

She opened the refrigerator. Carina glanced at Nick, who'd finished with the dishes. He was grinning, trying to suppress a laugh. For the first time, she saw him relaxed. She wasn't surprised; her mother had that effect on people.

She caught Nick's eye, wrinkled her nose at him.

"Mama, we have to go. Duty calls."

"How can you do anything on an empty stomach?"

"I promise, I'll have a good lunch."

"No come bien, míja. Solamente trabája, trabája, trabája. ¡Madre de Dios! ¿Como te ayuda?"

"Mama, stop that." Carina turned to Nick. "She said I never eat."

"I know."

"You speak Spanish?"

"Some. Enough to get by."

Her mother smiled broadly. "I knew I liked Nicholas the moment he walked into my home."

"Mama, we have work."

She glared at Carina. "Work, always work. It's Saturday." She shook her head. "I raised a house of workaholics. Even Lucy is upstairs doing homework!"

"I don't believe it," Carina laughed.

"Homework on a Saturday morning?"

"She's on that computer Papa bought her last year. She never gets off."

Carina glanced at Nick, his expression turning as serious as hers. She'd never really talked to Lucy about the dangers of being online. Even though Lucy was a smart kid, online predators were viciously smart. Street smart. She needed to talk to Lucy about being safe, but she'd have to do it later.

Her mom smiled widely at Nick. "You've been very helpful, Nicholas." She surveyed the dishwasher, closed it. "My sons tend to be rough with my dishes. You have good hands."

"Thank you, ma'am."

"Rosa."

"Mama, we really have to go," Carina said. She glanced at Nick. "Autopsy," she mouthed.

"I'm ready," Nick said. "Thank you for a delicious breakfast, Mrs. Kincaid. Unlike some people," he glanced at Carina with a half-smile, "I appreciate a good morning meal."

"Kiss-ass," she said.

"Carina Maria!"

She cringed, gave her mom a hug. "See you later, Mama."

"Don't know where you learned that language," her mother said as they walked out.

In the car, Nick said, "Your mom is a great lady."

"You are *such* a kiss-ass, Nick Thomas."

She thought he'd smile, joke back with her, but instead he grew serious.

"Is something wrong?"

"I like your mom. And your dad. They're really genuine people."

If there was one thing that endeared someone to Carina, it was appreciating her parents, quirks and all. Her heart warmed and she pictured Nick in her mom's kitchen. He fit in well.

She was in serious trouble. "I like them, too," she said, trying to keep the conversation light. "What about your parents?"

Nick didn't say anything for several minutes. Carina itched to ask a follow-up question, anything to get the conversation moving. She hated the silence.

Finally, he said, "We had what I thought was a normal family. My dad was in the military, like yours, but not career. He had two years in Vietnam, when Steve was a baby. I was born nine months after his discharge."

Carina was about to make a joke, but a

quick glance at Nick's face as she turned the corner to the main road told her this wasn't funny, not to him.

"Dad joined the reserves because he missed the military, was gone one weekend a month minimum, volunteered for everything. I don't think my parents loved each other, not like yours. But they had, I don't know, something. It was Steve and me, though, all the time. I followed him around everywhere. I wanted to be more like him, I guess. Confident and outgoing."

"I like you just fine the way you turned out," she said.

"I don't have many complaints. I had a good life for the most part. Normal. But after my father died, my mother didn't really have the heart to keep going. She died a couple years later."

I'm sorry seemed so inadequate. "I'm lucky, I know," Carina said instead. "We had some rough spots over the years — I was an army brat until I was sixteen. We moved all over the country. I hated it. When my dad retired here, it wasn't soon enough for me. But even with all the moves, the new schools, making new friends, my family was always there."

"Yes, you're very lucky," Nick agreed.

Twenty-Six

When Carina and Nick arrived at the coroner's laboratory, Jim was already there. "You didn't tell me you were coming in today."

"I have no life outside work anymore," he said pointedly.

"You didn't ever have a life outside work," Carina retorted.

"Ouch."

"Children," Chen said as he walked into the room.

Carina sobered up as Chen's assistant wheeled the gurney into the autopsy room with the prepped body of Jodi Carmichael. They were in the main room, which Carina appreciated. The smaller room had a lower ceiling and was a third the size, putting Carina closer to the proceedings. Here, she could stand back and look at other things — cabinets, tools, lights — if she couldn't stomach the autopsy. And three in one week? It had to be a record for her.

Dillon walked in and Chen said warmly, "To what do I owe this pleasure?"

"If you don't mind I'd like to observe."

"By all means, Dr. Kincaid. Glad to have you."

"I need to leave early, but I wanted to get a sense of the killer's mind-set. The body looks abused."

"Yes. However, most of it occurred post-mortem. She had been dead several hours."

Dillon frowned. "She was sexually assaulted, correct?"

He nodded. "After Dr. Gage told me she had been drugged, I took the liberty of running a tox screen last night. A near-lethal dose of Rohypnol was in her system."

Rohypnol, the so-called date-rape drug, was too often deadly. Some jerks gave it to their girlfriends thinking they'd become more compliant in bed. Others drugged their dates in order to get past first base. But sexual predators used it to knock out their victims. The women didn't pass out immediately. Some became more susceptible to suggestions, others fell asleep, others acted like themselves but didn't remember anything while on the drug.

And many died.

"Did the drugs kill her?" Carina asked.

"I don't know yet, Detective," Chen said.

"From the levels in her system, I don't think so, but I'll know more when I inspect her organs. It may have been a contributing cause."

He continued. "I have the victim's medical records, which indicate that she had a history of asthma and was allergic to latex." Chen continued his visual inspection of the body, documenting each external wound. While he did that, Nick said to Dillon, "No plastic wrap. Why?"

"She died on him. He didn't have time."

"There was no postmortem sexual assault," Jim interjected. "He didn't need the plastic to keep evidence off her body."

"He gets his thrill from killing her during the rape," Dillon said. "After she's dead he doesn't want to have anything to do with her. Gets rid of the body as quickly as possible."

"Like a snuff film," Nick said, and everyone grew silent.

"Yes," Dillon said finally. "The suspect Scout's profile says he's studying computer science and photography."

"I'll pull Vice into the equation to watch and see if any films or photographs of the murders start showing up."

"He's not going to want to share," Nick said.

"Why?" Dillon asked, curious.

"It's just my gut feeling. I don't have anything to base it on. I just think these are his women, he wants to keep them for himself. He might have pictures, or maybe even filmed the murder, but it will be for his eyes only. For his pleasure, no one else's."

Chen cleared his throat to indicate that he was getting started, then he cut open her chest.

Carina never felt the need to "be strong" and watch something that thoroughly disturbed her, so she turned her head and took a deep breath. The smell she could handle. She'd smelled far worse — her second homicide was a week-dead decomposing prostitute in a Dumpster in the heart of the Gaslight area. In general she could handle dead bodies in various states of murder.

But watching an autopsy seemed too clinical. Scientists dispassionately documenting injuries, weighing organs, as if the human body was a thing. It made her feel vulnerable, mortal. She didn't want to think about what would happen to her own body after she died.

Jim walked over to the table. "Just what I suspected."

"What?" Carina couldn't help but ask,

turning her attention back to the autopsy.

"Asphyxiation," Jim said, "from anaphylactic shock."

"Why didn't Angie die the same way?"

"She wasn't allergic to latex," Jim explained. "In this victim, her airways became clogged with hives. With no medication to reduce the swelling, she suffocated."

Carina pictured Jodi tied to a bed, struggling for her last breath, alone and scared. Her stomach flipped and she turned away from the dead girl's corpse.

Nick touched her lightly on the small of her back, cleared his throat. "He came in and found her dead. Became enraged and punched her."

"Repeatedly," Chen said. "Two broken ribs, the nose, severe postmortem damage."

"Her abdomen looks like pulp," Jim said, disgusted. "She'd been dead about four to five hours before he found her."

"Did he use his bare hands?" Carina asked.

"Absolutely. He may have had on gloves of some sort, but I don't see any latex or fiber residue under the microscope. And if he'd used a hammer or another object the wounds would have a smaller center. These are fist-size impressions."

"But if he didn't use latex gloves, how

could she have died from a latex allergy?"

"Some glues have latex in them. I'm going to check for latex on the glue samples when I get back to the lab."

"His hands would be damaged, wouldn't you say?" Carina asked. She couldn't rid her mind of the image of Jodi fighting for breath as her body swelled up.

"Very likely. Bruised. Possibly split, especially on the knuckles."

"He's like a kid with a bug jar," Nick said.

"Excuse me?" Jim looked over his shoulder. Nick had even attracted Chen's attention.

"Essentially, he has a woman in a jar. She's restrained, trapped. He can watch her if he wants. Prod her. Attack her. He touches her to see how she reacts. Rapes her for the sensation, then uses convenient items so he can watch. Like pulling the wings off a fly. It can't go anywhere, can't escape. When the bug finally dies, sometimes a kid gets mad. How dare the bug die on him. Stomps on it. Shows it how powerful he really is, though he really feels small and helpless because he couldn't keep the bug alive long enough to do everything he wanted."

No one said anything for a long minute.

"Sheriff, I think you're right," Dillon said. "She died before he wanted her dead. She shattered his fantasy. The ultimate high for him is sex and death."

Dillon looked at everyone in the room. "He's going to act again, and soon. Jodi cheated him and he's angry. But because he's angry, he has a greater chance of slipping up."

Carina prayed they caught a break before another woman died.

His skin prickled, as if a spider were crawling on him. He batted it away, and it was replaced by another phantom spider.

It was Jodi's fault. She'd ruined everything. She wasn't supposed to just *die* like that. She wasn't playing her part. In the back of his mind he kept thinking that somehow he'd forgotten something, that maybe he'd made a mistake. So he kept replaying everything in his mind. From going in through her window — he'd worn gloves — to putting her in the trunk — no one had seen him — to cleaning her body. He'd covered all bases.

So why did he feel so odd?

The high he'd had after Becca plummeted, and he didn't know what to do. He watched his special tapes over and over. They didn't help.

He watched the slide shows he'd made of

Angie and Becca. That was a little better, but then the show he had of Jodi reminded him of his failure.

When his father disappeared, he knew it was his mother's fault. She was loud and disrespectful, and she slept with other men. Even then as a child, he'd known it. He'd seen it. For years he'd blamed his mother and wished he had the courage to kill her with his bare hands, watching her eyes bulge, squeezing her throat until every bone in her neck broke.

But it was his fault, too. His failure as a son. If only he'd been older, smarter. If he'd followed his father and begged him to take him, too.

For a long time he'd thought his father was back in prison, but his mother denied it. Said he wasn't coming back and to forget him. How could he do that? How could he forget his own father?

His dad would understand the feelings. The pictures that popped into his mind all the time.

When he looked in the car next to him and saw a pretty woman, he could imagine her naked and bloody beneath him — a vision so vivid he believed he could touch her and feel warm blood on his fingers.

Or when his mother was around and he

dreamed so distinctly of going into her bedroom and cutting her throat. He'd wake up after that smelling blood, certain he'd done it, needing to check that he hadn't somehow killed his mother in his sleep.

He never had.

Or when he saw his brother and wondered if he had the same feelings, that maybe if he talked to him and explained everything clearly, he would have a partner. Someone to help. Someone who understood.

But he didn't dare go after his mother, and didn't dare tell his brother. It was just him, alone. He had to figure everything out.

He stopped the slide show and stared at a picture of Becca dressed in plastic wrap. She wasn't dead, but waiting. Becca had been the best. Why? Why had he felt complete with Becca and not Angie or Jodi?

Because she wasn't a slut. She wasn't like them. She was pure and beautiful and whole.

He needed to find another girl like Becca. Elizabeth Rimes, his MyJournal penpal in Georgia, would be perfect, but she was too far away.

He needed someone here in San Diego.

But soon he'd go to Elizabeth. And they'd have a real relationship, date, see each other like boyfriend and girlfriend. He'd be ready for her then, because he'd have gotten all these strange needs out of his system.

So if he couldn't have Elizabeth tonight, he knew exactly who could replace her.

Already, he felt better.

TWENTY-SEVEN

It was a beautiful Saturday afternoon, but Carina and Nick were sitting in the windowless task force room painstakingly reviewing all three autopsy reports for any odd detail or stray piece of evidence that might offer them another direction in which to look.

But there didn't appear to be anything other than the differences they'd already noted. Until Carina saw something odd in the personal effects record.

"It says that only one earring was found with both Becca and Jodi."

"Is that unusual?"

"I can see how an earring might fall out, especially with a body that has been manhandled, but *one* earring in *both* victims? Angie had six ear piercings, three on each side, and she still had six posts in her ears when she was found."

"Maybe the killer kept an earring as a souvenir," Nick guessed.

"It's the only thing that makes sense."

"It's good news. It connects him with his victims."

Patrick walked into the room. "What does?" he asked.

"Angie was missing a navel ring. Becca and Jodi were each missing one earring."

"That's creepy," Patrick said.

"You can say that again. So what brings you down here?"

"Good news, bad news," Patrick said.

"What else is new," Carina grumbled. "Give me the good news first."

"I have proof that Scout used a Sand Shack public computer."

Carina grinned. "Really? When?"

"Several times over the last three months, usually in the late afternoon during the week."

"Only three months?"

"That's all MyJournal has archived."

"But the time frame suggests that he's a college student," Nick said. "He comes by in the late afternoon."

"Nothing he said using the Shack computer system was incriminating. Most of it was viewing MyJournal pages and surfing the Internet. But I have every private message or public post he made through that server on a grid to see if we can find a pattern or anything that identifies him."

"We need to talk to the employees again," Carina said. "Someone might recognize a general description. What about the library?"

"I went there, showed the librarian Kyle Burns's photo like you asked, and she put on thick glasses and was noncommittal. The woman can't see more than two feet in front of her is my guess."

Patrick sat down and slid the files across to Carina. "You think it might be the manager?"

"I don't know. He loosely fits Dillon's profile. Under thirty, college student, underachiever."

"How is he an underachiever? He works full-time and goes to school."

Carina rifled through papers until she pulled Kyle Burns's transcript. "I had one of the uniforms pull his transcript. He was in and out of college for three years. His grades are good, not great. His advisor put a note in his file that he aspired to do great things with his life, but didn't have the focus to stick with any one thing. His strength is management because he's neat, organized, and disciplined."

Nick nodded. "Our killer is organized, but I wouldn't call him disciplined."

"Still, Burns fits. He lives alone in a small duplex near the university. He has the light brown hair the half-blind librarian noticed. He has access to the Shack public computers. I think we need to interview all the employees again while Burns is off-site."

"He doesn't work Sundays," Nick said.

"So we go there and talk to the employees, then track everyone else down at their homes. I have the files here. We were focusing on friends of Angie, so we only talked to the employees who regularly worked the same shifts as Angie. Now we need to dig deeper. We have a connection with the Shack and the killer — assuming Dillon is right and Scout is who we're looking for. We focus there."

"One more thing popped," Patrick said. He put a printout in front of him. "This is a private message to an Elizabeth Rimes that he sent through the MyJournal server using the library Internet connection. He talks about his cat Felix being hit by a car."

"And he told Becca that someone shot his cat."

"When we pulled down messages from the Shack from the last three months, and reviewed all public comments posted by Scout that are stored indefinitely, he's told several female MyJournal members over the last year that his cat had been killed. Died of cancer, hit by a car, drowned by his roommate."

"For sympathy," Nick said.

Patrick concurred. "Women are suckers for a good cat sob story."

"Oh, stop that," Carina said. "They sympathized because they didn't think anyone would lie about something like that. It's the old 'help me find my lost puppy' trick that pedophiles use to lure kids away."

"Now where?" Nick asked. "Do we have an ISP?"

Patrick sighed, sat down. "Not yet. We know that Scout was in both the Shack and the library. We can get a warrant to search a house or business if we can get a name that goes with the profile — Dillon already convinced the DA of his reasoning, and he's ready to take the stand on it if questioned. But because the MyJournal site is a free Web page, no one has to give truthful information. We have an e-mail address and it goes to a free e-mail account that is open, but it's been inactive since Scout registered with MyJournal two years ago."

Carina stood and walked over to the map. Red pins showed where the victims were abducted, blue pins where their bodies were found. "Angie was last seen more than ten miles from where her body was found, but Jodi and Becca's bodies were found where they were last seen. Why?"

"He's taunting us?" Patrick suggested. "He doesn't care that they're found."

"Maybe it's convenience," Nick said. "Or he has a personal connection to the places."

"We know he's been to the Sand Shack, which is less than a mile from where Angie was found." Carina placed a green pin on the Shack. "And the library." She put a pin at the library, right next to the blue and red pins where Becca was abducted and found. "Nick, what's Kyle's address?"

He read from the report. "45670 Rupert Street."

She found it on the map, put a yellow pin there. "Burns lives smack dab in the middle."

"There were no drugs in Angie's system, which suggests that she trusted whoever kidnapped her. She didn't make a fuss, she seemed to voluntarily leave her house," Nick said.

"And Becca he physically subdued. She was petite, much easier to control than Angie," Carina said. "Do you think we have enough to ask for a warrant?"

"On Burns? Nowhere near enough," Patrick said.

"But it makes sense, right?" Carina frowned at the map.

"Logically it makes sense, but you're making a lot of leaps in reasoning and filling in blanks with theories, not evidence. We need something solid to tie Burns to the crimes."

Carina knew Patrick was right. "I can still get the tail. Watch him until we gather enough evidence. And tomorrow, when he's home, maybe we can stop by for another talk. See if he lets us come in, take a look around."

"If he lets you in, you're good to go. What does Jim have right now?"

"Nothing yet, but he's working on it," Carina said.

They sat in silence, reviewing the logs, when Patrick suddenly exclaimed, "I have an idea!"

"Give it to me," Carina said. "I'll take anything at this point."

"What if we set Scout up?"

"How?"

"He has an e-mail alert through the My-Journal system that let's him know whenever certain Web pages are updated. One page is that Elizabeth Rimes I told you about. We send an e-mail ostensibly from her to Scout with a redirect to my account."

"For what purpose?"

"To get him into a chat room. To keep him in one place until we can locate him. If he's logged on as Scout, I can find him within an hour."

"I like it. I really like it."

"Thank you, sis. I aim to please."

"How long to set it up?" Nick asked.

"A couple hours, maybe less. I want to make sure we protect Elizabeth Rimes, alert the Atlanta police to keep an eye on her. We know Scout is in San Diego, but on the off-chance that he slips through."

"I agree. I don't want to jeopardize a civilian."

"And I need to set up the technical end. I'm going to ask Dillon to chat with him online — he's good at pulling people into conversations and he'll know what to say."

"Perfect. Thanks, Patrick."

"I'm going to get started on it," Patrick said, standing. "Sorry to leave you with all this paperwork."

"I live for paperwork," she said sarcastically.

Carina and Nick ordered dinner in. The task force room looked like a war zone, and they had come to the conclusion that until forensics came up with evidence they could use, or Patrick got a hit on his trap, they had nowhere else to look.

Carina was about to call it quits for the night. It was Saturday and there was little they could do until they had something to work with.

Then Jim Gage rushed into the room. "Good, you're still here."

"Like I'm going anywhere in this lifetime," Carina said. "What is it?"

He waved a paper around. "I got a hit."

"DNA match?"

"Almost as good. I have a match to a relative."

"Explain," Carina said.

"Mitchell Joseph Burns."

"Burns," Carina said. "You matched DNA to this Mitchell Burns? Is he a relation to Kyle Burns?"

"I don't know at this point." Jim pulled out a chair and sat. "Nearly eight years ago Mitchell Burns raped a woman in West Los Angeles. He used a condom, but either there was a tear in it or he wasn't careful. Semen was found around the toilet bowl in the woman's apartment."

"And it matched Mitchell Burns? Was he already in the system?"

"He's a repeat offender. Served four years for two counts of forcible rape."

"Is he still in prison?"

"No, I'm getting to that," he said impatiently. "He served his time, then a series of rapes popped up in West LA. When the investigators ran the DNA from the vic's toilet, it hit on Burns. They went to arrest him, but his wife said he walked out one day and never came home.

"Ironically, the same day he raped the West LA woman."

Jim let that sink in before continuing. "So when I ran the DNA we extracted from Becca —"

"Wait," Carina said, "I thought you said you didn't have anything from Becca."

"I should have told you, but I was swamped running DNA myself. I don't have to tell you how short-handed we are right now."

"I'm sorry, it wasn't an accusation —"

"No, I should have said something. Anyway, I found a hair with a follicle in one of the layers of plastic wrap. One hair, that's it. There's some other trace evidence — wool from a blanket, some cotton fibers — but this was the only DNA evidence. So I ran it against the database and it popped up Mitchell Burns. But there's something else."

"What?"

"Another commonality to our current murders."

"Glue?"

"No, but close. Burns gagged his victims with a black bandanna and tied them to the bedposts with white nylon rope."

"White rope is common," Nick said.

"But black bandannas aren't," Carina added. "So he broke into their house to rape them?" Carina wasn't surprised. It was common, but her fear that no one was safe even in their own homes was deep-seated.

"Yes. Ground-level apartments in low-security buildings. He was a repeat offender, and had used the bandannas in his previous crimes as well."

"Any particular reason?"

"None that was in the file."

"But you said he's not in prison."

"He's still missing. LAPD watched his house for a while, but he never returned."

"Maybe he realized he'd made a mistake and ran," Nick said.

"That was my thought."

"Eight years is a long time to disappear," Nick said. "Especially a wanted man and repeat offender."

Carina wrapped her mind around the information Jim had given her. "So the DNA matched a known rapist who has been missing for eight years?"

"No," Jim said. "Mitchell Burns didn't

rape our three victims. But a close relative did. A brother, first cousin, uncle, son."

"Son."

"He has two. According to the police reports, he had two minor sons at the time of his first arrest twelve years ago, twelve and five."

"That would make them about twenty-four and seventeen," Carina said. "Names?"

"They're not in the record, but get this. Burns's wife moved to San Diego six years ago." Jim handed her another sheet of paper.

"Here's the address of Regina Burns. She lives in University City." University City was between downtown San Diego and La Jolla to the north.

Carina gathered the information and checked her weapon. "Who wants to take a bet that Kyle Burns is the rapist's son?"

No one took the bet.

"Do you want backup?" Jim asked Carina.

"We're just going to talk to Kyle Burns first, then Mitchell Burns's wife," Carina said. "If Regina Burns confirms what we think we know, we need to put twenty-four/seven surveillance on Kyle Burns and fight for a warrant."

"It's going to be next to impossible to get Kyle Burns in with what we have. No attorney will allow him to submit to a DNA test."

"Then we'll have to find other evidence to give us probable cause for an arrest. Then we can get his DNA."

"Don't you need a warrant for DNA?" Nick asked.

"In California all you need is probable cause for an arrest. Everyone arrested for a felony in California is subject to DNA testing."

With a solid lead at last, Carina rushed from the room, and Nick followed.

TWENTY-EIGHT

Hi Scout:

I'm so sorry about Felix. How awful! If anything happened to my kitties, I would be so upset.

I've been visiting my mother for the last week and haven't had time to e-mail you. My mom's been sick and we've had a hard time with it. I just hope she gets better. The doctors are afraid the cancer has come back, but I'm praying it's not that again.

If you want to talk about Felix, go ahead.

By the way, I'm really struggling in one of my classes. You really helped me with my midterms last semester, in calculus, remember? Do you think you have time today to help with another problem? I'll hang out in the private chat area. I have Room 303 reserved and open on my computer. I'll be studying here

all day, so if you can help just pop in.
Elizabeth.

Dillon composed the e-mail from "Elizabeth Rimes" and sent it off to Scout's public e-mail account through the MyJournal server.

"Smart kid," Patrick said.

"Smart enough to not use her real name and to realize Scout was obsessing over her."

Dillon had spoken to Elizabeth — real name Bethany Eggers — over the phone, and she had told him she'd stopped responding to Scout's e-mails when she found out he'd lied about his cat dying. She'd found three other messages on the MyJournal board from him talking about "Felix" dying. "It was downright creepy," she said. "When you're done with my account, just close it down."

Because Elizabeth had never responded to the cat message, Dillon composed it in a way to encourage interaction. He had the chat room window open, and Patrick had a mirror of the site on his computer screen.

"Now what?" Dillon asked.

"We wait."

"How long?"

"As long as it takes."

Dillon let out a sigh. "I'm a patient man,

Patrick, but this tests even my resolve."

"I'm going to call Carina and tell her we've set the trap and to be on alert."

"Tell her to be careful, too."

"I always do."

Carina and Nick arrived at the Sand Shack after the dinner rush. Kyle Burns didn't look particularly pleased to see them, but he approached and said, "What can I help you with, Detectives?"

"We'd like to talk to you about your father."

Carina gauged his reaction, surprised at the intense anger that flashed across his face.

"I don't want to talk about him." Burns realized he'd spoken too loudly and looked around. Several of the waitstaff looked away. "Let's go to my office," he said through clenched teeth.

Carina and Nick followed him back. She assessed the situation. Kyle didn't appear to be armed, but she wasn't going to be crammed into that little office of his where he might be able to turn the tables on them.

"Mr. Burns —" Carina began.

"I don't want to talk about my father," he said again. "I have nothing to do with him."

"Well then, maybe you'll listen. We know

that Mitchell Burns was a convicted rapist who disappeared eight years ago while under suspicion for rape. Have you seen or heard from him since?"

"No."

"What about your mother?"

He gave a half-laugh. "She can have him. She's no better than he is."

"Are you saying that your mother may have had contact with her husband?"

Kyle rubbed both hands over his face. "No, he never contacted her."

"How can you be so sure?"

"She would have told me."

"You're close?"

"No, but if she saw Mitch she would have told me."

"What about your brother?"

"What about him?"

"Do you think he may have had contact with Mitch Burns?"

"No, never."

"You sound certain."

"Brandon would have told me." Kyle shook his head. "Ask him yourself. He's busing tables right now."

Carina was surprised. "You didn't give us any employee records about your brother."

"He just helps out sometimes after school and on the weekends." He sighed. "Look, I pay him under the table, okay? Is that a crime?"

"Actually, yes."

Kyle frowned. "It's just that —"

Carina put her hand up. "I'm not going to arrest you for IRS problems. But I'd like to talk to your brother. Maybe your father has contacted him."

"You don't understand what it was like. I was twelve when he went to jail. I sat in the courtroom during the trial and listened to what he'd done. Listened to my own mother lie for him." Kyle grimaced. "And then the prosecutor didn't go after her for perjury because he felt sorry for her. What a joke. She was pathetic. We were all better off without him."

The amiable man they'd interviewed earlier in the week was gone, replaced by a bitter, angry son.

"But he was released."

"Four years. Only four years for raping two women. He probably raped more, but they didn't come forward. Why?" He looked at Carina. "Why don't they come forward? He would have gotten more time."

Carina said, "They're scared. They don't think the police will believe them. They think it's their fault. There are lots of reasons."

Kyle's face fell. "All stupid reasons."

"What happened when your father was released?"

"My mother took him back. Can you believe it?"

Carina had seen it many times. Either the women were blind or stupid, scared or complicit. Or all of the above.

"The police said he disappeared. According to the interview with Regina Burns, he left after dinner on April eight, eight years ago, and never returned."

"That's true."

"That was the same night as the last rape."

"I don't know if I knew that at the time. When the police came, my mother sent us out of the room. I was eavesdropping but didn't catch everything. And my mother never said anything when I asked."

"Your brother was there as well?"

"Yeah. He's now in high school. Amazing considering he still lives with that woman."

"That woman?"

"Our mother."

"Do you own a computer?" Carina asked, changing the subject.

"Yeah, why?"

"Would you object to having someone from the department come down and look at it?"

He tensed. "Why?"

"We believe Angie's killer frequented her online journal several times before her murder."

"I didn't even know she had one . . . wait. You don't think I —"

Kyle jumped up, irate. "Just because my father was a damn rapist, you think I could have done that?"

"Calm down —"

"I've lived with the guilt of what my father did for years! I hated him. I'm glad he's gone. I hope he's in Hell where he belongs."

He stormed out of the kitchen.

"Well, that certainly was interesting," Carina said.

"Maybe it's in the blood," Nick said. "Shall we go talk to Mrs. Regina Burns?"

"Absolutely. She sounds like a real winner. But you know what? I think I'd like to wait until Brandon Burns gets off work, chat him up a bit."

"He's seventeen."

"If he says he doesn't want to talk, I won't push it. Maybe we'll see him later tonight when we talk to his mother. I'd just like to get a read on him before then."

Nick frowned. "Burns didn't give us permission to search his computer."

"I noticed. I'm going to make sure the

twenty-four/seven surveillance on Burns has been approved while we wait for Little Brother to leave."

Brandon Burns walked out of the Sand Shack alone shortly after nine-thirty that night. Carina recalled seeing him the first time she visited the Shack with Will. Brandon was tall and skinny, still growing into his awkward height. He was pleasant-looking, if a bit nondescript, and well-groomed with short brown hair and pressed clothes. Carina and Nick approached and showed their police identification.

"Do you have a couple minutes to talk?" Nick asked.

"Um, sure, I guess. Do you want to go inside?"

Carina didn't want Kyle to interrupt her conversation with Brandon. "Here's fine. It won't take long."

"Okay." He looked from Nick to Carina. "You've been here a couple times this week."

Carina nodded. "Yes, we're talking to everyone who worked with Angie. Did you know her?"

"A little." Brandon played with the change and keys in his pocket.

"When was the last time you saw her?"

"I don't know. Last week sometime, I guess. I think we both worked on Wednesday and I worked Friday to set up for dinner, but Kyle doesn't want me working more than four hours a day."

"That makes sense, since you're in high school. Don't want your grades to slip," Carina said. "Do you like working for your brother?"

He nodded vigorously. "Yeah. He's really great."

"Do you know if your father has been in contact with your brother?"

He stared at them wide-eyed. "My dad? Do you know where he is?"

Nick's heart went out to the kid. His father, a convicted rapist. What must it be like growing up with the weight of that on your young shoulders? He'd just been a little kid when his father was in prison, then nine or ten when he disappeared.

"No, we don't," Carina said. "But we're trying to find him. Has he contacted you at all in the eight years since he disappeared?"

"Me? Why?" A hint of wariness, uncertainty.

"We'd just like to talk to him."

The kid bit his thumbnail. "I haven't talked to him since I was nine. He stopped coming home one day. I didn't want to

412

move here because how could he find us? But my mother said we had to."

"Do you think your mother has talked to him?"

He shook his head. "No. She's probably the one who chased him off, always yelling at him. Stupid this, dumbass that, pathetic fool. That's what she called him and he didn't like it. She's the reason he left."

"What about your brother? Do you think Kyle has kept in contact with him?"

No comment.

"Brandon?"

His face turned red with barely restrained anger.

"Kyle doesn't like him."

"Why's that?"

"I don't know."

Whether Brandon really didn't know about his father's history, or was lying, Nick couldn't tell. He did sense that Brandon was embarrassed, which suggested that he might have an idea of what had happened years ago, but maybe his brother or mother had tried to protect him.

Nick spoke up. "Brandon, do you know why your father went to prison?"

He stuck his lip out. "Yes."

"Was Kyle angry with your father because he was in prison?"

Brandon shook his head. "Kyle was angry all the time when he got out of prison. He didn't want him to come home."

Carina handed Brandon her card. "I want you to call me anytime, day or night, if you hear from or see your father."

"Why?"

"We really can't say."

Brandon's face lit up with hope. "Do you think he's here? In San Diego?"

"Brandon," Nick said, "call if you hear from him, okay? Or if he contacts your mother or brother."

The teen nodded absently, and Nick wondered if he'd even heard what Nick had told him.

They left to track down Regina Burns at her house in University City.

"What do you think?" Carina asked.

"I think he misses his dad and either doesn't know why he went to prison or doesn't care."

"He was just a kid." Carina frowned. "He's the same age as Lucy. I can't imagine what she would have felt if she found out someone she loved had done something like Brandon's father did."

"He may be a kid, but . . ." Nick paused.

"What?"

"Never mind."

"I want to know what you're thinking."

He didn't know if he could trust his instincts, but the last time he'd had a hunch and didn't tell anyone, he'd almost been killed.

"Brandon's reaction was odd."

"To what?"

"To the idea that his father might be in town."

Carina pondered that. "If you were a seventeen-year-old kid who hadn't seen his father in eight years, forgetting that his father is a criminal, wouldn't you be excited? Hopeful?" She paused. "I regret giving him false hopes, though. If Mitch Burns *is* in town, if he has anything to do with these murders, it means he'll be going back to prison. But I don't think he's around. I'd guess he got himself a false identity and moved out of state."

"Brandon has probably worked up some fantasies about his father. Made him into a hero, not a villain."

"You sound just like Dillon, and I think you're right. Brandon said that his brother was angry when their father was released. Because he thought he should stay in prison?"

"Do you know many kids who have that strong a sense of right and wrong? That they'd *want* their father in prison for rape?"

"Most would probably act like Brandon, put their criminal father up on a pedestal."

"There may be something else going on here."

"Like what?"

"We have a similar but not identical MO to Mitch Burns. We have DNA of a male relative of Burns. What if one or both of the brothers are involved?"

"A killing pair?"

"Kyle is a strong-willed, dominant older brother with a hair-trigger temper and huge chip on his shoulder about his father," Nick said. "Brandon is quieter, reticent, looks up to his brother and worships a nonexistent father. He'd be very susceptible to outside influences."

"There's no evidence. I can't just walk in and take Brandon's computer without cause. He's a minor. But maybe his mother will let us have the computer. At least we can rule him out if nothing else."

It was after ten Saturday night by the time Carina and Nick arrived at Regina Burns's house in University City, roughly halfway between downtown San Diego and La Jolla.

Mrs. Burns lived in a small, post–World War II cinder-block house in a quiet neighborhood. By the looks of the automobiles and neatly trimmed lawns, most of the houses' owners were original, and were now well past retirement age. The houses that had changed hands were split between would-be mechanics with multiple cars in various states of assembly in oil-stained driveways, and young families with kids' toys as lawn art behind chain-link fences.

Carina looked at the DMV report she'd run while driving to the University City home. "Regina Burns has two cars registered in her name, a 1996 Camaro and a 1990 Taurus."

The house was dark and there were no cars in the driveway.

"What about Brandon Burns?"

"I'm waiting for a call back to see if there is another licensed driver at this address," Carina said. "The registration database is separate from the licensed driver database."

A sense of déjà vu filled Nick. The last time he'd gone up to a house where he hadn't expected to find anything, he'd been attacked. He glanced at Carina, fearing he was growing paranoid. She looked alert, but calm. The events last year might be clouding his judgment, and he didn't want to make another mistake. The thought of risking Carina's life through his missteps was foolish, he knew: she was a trained cop, she knew what she was doing. Still, he couldn't shake the feeling that something was about to go wrong.

They approached the house cautiously. Carina knocked on the door, then took a step back. No movement in the house. No sound whatsoever.

"Let's talk to the neighbors," Carina said finally. "Maybe someone knows when Regina Burns is expected home, or something about her kids."

The house to the right of the Burns residence was brightly lit, the television loud enough to wake the dead. Carina rapped loudly on the door. No answer. She peered through the window, then used the doorbell multiple times.

A full minute later, the television went from ear-shattering to loud, and the door flew open. Instinctively, Nick's hand rested on his gun. Towering over both of them was a sixty-something bald man with a large beer belly, to match his breath.

"What?"

Carina identified herself and Nick, learned the neighbor was Ray Grimski, then asked, "We're looking for Regina Burns, your neighbor."

The man narrowed his eyes, took a step

out onto the small porch, shaking his head. "Don't know where that bitch is. Probably working."

"When was the last time you saw Mrs. Burns?"

He shrugged. "Whenever. Last week, maybe. I don't know. She left Friday or Saturday. She works for a cruise line. Don't know what she does for them and I don't care. But she's gone a week or more at a time, which is fine by me."

"You don't get along with her?"

"Hell no."

"How long have you been neighbors?"

"Ever since she moved in six or seven years ago. Old-man Krauss croaked and his kids put the old woman in a nursing home, sold the house, and split the money, the fucking brats. She died there, don't think those girls ever even visited."

Carina and Nick glanced at each other. Sometimes, values weren't evidenced by appearance.

"What about Regina Burns's sons?"

"Sons? Oh, right, she has an older son. Don't know his name. He goes to that college on the coast, I think. Works at a restaurant. Temper. Never comes by when she's around. Sometimes he comes over to pick up the kid, Brandon. Last time I saw him with his mother was over a year ago. Maybe longer. They got in a huge shouting match. Thought he'd strangle her. The kid came out, everything sort of stopped, and the older kid took off."

"Do you remember what the argument was about?"

Grimski shrugged, scratched his hefty stomach. "That was ages ago. But that woman has a temper, too."

"Does she abuse her son?"

"Don't know. Never saw anything like that."

"You talk a lot to the younger boy? Brandon?"

"I hired him to fix my back fence. He's pretty handy. I've paid him for odd jobs, though he doesn't seem to have time anymore. He took a regular job working for his brother. Why? He's not in trouble, is he?"

"Not that we know of," Carina said carefully.

"Then why all the questions?"

"He worked with a woman who was recently murdered. We're talking to all of her colleagues."

Grimski frowned. "Brandon's a good kid. A little weird, but with that bitch for a mother who wouldn't be?"

"Weird how?"

"I dunno. When my son was in high school, this place was Grand-fucking-Central. I was glad. It kept him out of trouble if he brought his friends here. But no one visits next door. The bitch probably doesn't allow it."

"Have you ever seen Mrs. Burns's husband?"

"Husband? Someone married her?" He barked out a laugh. "Never seen anyone else around. I can't blame the guy for leaving that woman. I almost sold the house a year after they moved in, but the market wasn't hot enough, and where would I go? I've been here forty years, since my wife and I bought the place, rest her soul."

"What happened that prompted you to consider moving?"

Grimski's face grew hard, though his eyes started to water. "My Peg was a sweetheart. She died two years ago this May, of cancer. But this was when she was still healthy. She was beautiful. Fifty-five years old and still looked terrific in a bikini." He grew wistful for a moment, then scowled. "My Peg was sunbathing in our backyard. Our property! In a bikini. That bitch next door yelled at her over the fence. Called her a whore and a slut and a slew of other indecent words. Peg tried to laugh it off, but she never went outside in a bikini again."

Carina thanked Grimski. She and Nick went back to the car, but didn't get in.

"What do you think?" she asked Nick.

Nick could too easily picture Mrs. Regina Burns and the sad homelife Kyle and Brandon Burns must have had. And, unfortunately, he could picture either of them as killers. Kyle with his anger problems; Brandon, an antisocial kid living under the overpowering presence of a woman who hated other women.

"I think we need to have another talk with Kyle Burns," he said. "And Brandon Burns as well. Maybe watch their dynamic together."

"We have two suspects."

"They could be working together. A teenager might be susceptible to the influence of an older, forceful brother, especially since his father is out of the picture."

"Or maybe the father came back, instigated the murders." But even as Carina said it, it didn't feel right. Rapists often escalate to murder, but she didn't think they'd be dormant for eight years. "We need to check unsolved rapes cross-country," Carina said. She almost laughed. There were likely thousands of such cases. "We were only looking into rape-murders."

"But if Mitchell Burns was continuing his pattern, he may not have killed."

"Before now." She frowned. "Except we have no evidence that Mitchell Burns is in San Diego."

In the car, Carina called the officers she had tailing Kyle Burns.

"Where's Burns?"

"He went home with a waitress from the Shack."

Carina tensed. "Did she look like she was in any distress?"

"No, but we're sitting outside her apartment now."

"Stay there. Watch his car. Don't let him leave. I'm on my way."

Then she called for backup.

When they arrived, Carina talked to the officers sitting outside the woman's apartment.

"Where's the suspect?"

"Still inside."

"Do we have an ID on the woman?"

He nodded, flipped open his notepad. "Maggie Peterson, twenty-two, senior at the university and has worked for the Sand Shack for the last year."

"Good stuff."

"I went to talk to the manager. She lives

with her younger sister, Leah Peterson, nineteen."

"Do you know if she's home?"

"No confirmation either way."

Carina told her backup that there was one, possibly two potential hostages inside the apartment. "We'll try to do this the easy way. Knock on the door and ask Kyle Burns to come down to the station for questioning." She turned to Nick. "We should have done it earlier."

"We didn't have enough earlier. We need a warrant."

"I know," said Carina. "I'm going to try to convince him to come down and answer questions. We might be able to get his DNA that way." There was a trick often used by law enforcement. If a suspect took a drink from the police and left the drinking container behind, they could collect it as evidence and have it DNA tested. Same principle if the suspect smoked and tossed his cigarette butt on the street. Evidence.

But if Burns didn't voluntarily come down to the station they had no reason to hold him. They had no DNA to compare to the DNA found on Becca. And without evidence, they couldn't get his DNA.

She looked at Nick. "Ready?"

Nick should have said no. They had been

going all day and his knees were on the verge of giving out. But he'd popped extra ibuprofen and no longer felt the intense pain.

"Ready," he said.

Maggie Peterson lived on the second floor of the four-story apartment structure. Carina directed two officers to stay with Burns's car, and two to stake out the back and front entrance of the building. Carina rapped on the door.

No answer.

She knocked again. "Maggie Peterson? Detective Carina Kincaid with the San Diego Police Department. I need to talk to you again."

She heard something in the back of the apartment, then nothing. She was considering ramming the door when she heard the rattle of the security chain sliding open.

"What's wrong?" the woman asked. She was dressed in a robe.

"We're looking for Kyle Burns."

"Kyle? Why?"

"We know he's here. We'd like to talk to him."

The bedroom door opened and Kyle Burns walked out, buttoning his shirt, his face a hard mask. "I can't believe you followed me here."

"We have some more questions for you, Mr. Burns."

"It's nearly midnight. This can't wait?"

"No, it really can't."

"I don't believe you."

Carina tamped down her own anger. It wouldn't do her any good dealing with Burns. "Maybe you'd like to come down to the police station with us."

"Are you arresting me?"

"No."

"Then ask your questions here." Kyle reached over and took Maggie's hand.

Carina had hoped that Burns wouldn't want to answer questions around his girlfriend, that he'd voluntarily come to the police station.

"Tell us about your father," Nick said.

"Hell, no. I'm not talking about him. He's long gone."

Just the mention of Mitch Burns set Kyle off.

"It sounds like you don't like him much."

"Are you insane? Who would like him? The man was a bastard."

"What was it like growing up with him? Did you know he was a rapist when you were younger?"

"What are you, a shrink?"

Kyle's rage was building. Carina wondered

if someone who had so little control over their temper could plan and execute such a meticulous crime.

The killer is immature. Carina remembered Dillon's profile, and lack of temper control was a sign of immaturity. She just needed to play it all the way through. Make him lose his temper and tell her the truth.

"Would you like to talk to a psychiatrist?" she asked.

He didn't say anything. He stared straight ahead, not looking at Nick or Carina.

Nick took over. "I understand exactly how you feel, Kyle," he said.

"Bullshit," Kyle muttered without looking at him.

"You hate your father for what he did. To your family, to you, to those women. And when you were just a kid, you couldn't do anything about it. The anger and humiliation."

Kyle didn't talk.

"You probably wanted to kill him, didn't you?" Nick said softly.

Something in Kyle's eyes flickered.

Carina watched Kyle closely as Nick continued the questioning.

"The trial humiliated you, but your father was in prison. Away. Your mother lied, right? You told us earlier that she'd lied to give him an alibi. Yet you still had to live with her. That must have been Hell."

"You don't know the half of it," Kyle said, looking at his hands.

"You wanted to protect your little brother, didn't you? He was just a little guy, what, five years old? He didn't know what was going on, and you didn't want him to find out. So you took everything on your shoulders, tried to protect him."

"You don't know anything," Kyle said.

"I know that you were angry when your father went to prison and were still angry when he got out of prison."

"He should have been put away for life."

"You're right." Nick paused, then asked, "Has he contacted you since he disappeared that night?"

Kyle shook his head.

"What about your mother? Your brother?"

"No! You don't get it. He's never coming back!"

"Why?" Nick quietly asked.

"He's just not," said Kyle.

Maggie spoke up for the first time, putting her arms around Kyle. "Why all these questions? Just because you can't find out who killed Angie you're coming after Kyle?" She stood straight and looked Carina in the eye. "Kyle was with me all last weekend, from when our shift ended at eleven Saturday night until we went to classes Monday morning at eight."

Burns wasn't talking anymore, so they left the apartment. Carina said to Nick, "Do you think she's lying."

"Maybe," Nick said.

"Her alibi for Burns is too convenient."

"I agree, but that doesn't mean she's lying. We never asked Kyle Burns for an alibi before."

"Kyle's reaction to his father is plain weird. Something's going on there." She glanced at her watch. "It's after midnight. No way we can do anything more tonight."

"Stop beating yourself up. We've done all we can."

"Have we?" Carina rubbed her eyes and suppressed a yawn. "We're close, but our hands are tied. No evidence, no arrest."

"Do you want me to drive back?" Nick asked.

"Actually, that'd be great."

TWENTY-NINE

Nick pulled into Carina's driveway and turned off the engine. She'd fallen asleep, her head on his shoulder. He looked down at her, his heart doing a little leap as he realized she'd become so important to him in such a short time.

For years, he'd believed Miranda was the only woman for him. Though they'd split up several years ago, in the back of his mind Nick had thought he'd never find another woman who had that special spark, that indefinable something, that appealed to him.

He was wrong. Watching Carina sleep, Nick felt as if he'd known her his entire life.

"Wake up, princess," he said quietly.

"Hmmm?" She sat up slowly, stretched. "We're here already?"

"You fell asleep."

"Did not." She grinned at him. "Maybe for a minute. Why don't you come in?"

"Do you think that's a good idea?"

She didn't miss his meaning. Leaning over, she kissed him lightly on the lips. "Did you dream of me last night?"

He took her face in his hands. "Last night and all day."

Her lips parted and he kissed her, the playfulness leaving as he sank into her warm mouth. His hands spread on the back of her head, holding her to him, their kiss deepening until he found himself pushing her back into the seat.

He pulled back. Her eyes were closed, a smile on her lips. "You can kiss me anytime," she said, her voice low and sultry.

"I hope to do more than kiss you."

Her eyes opened wide. "Come with me."

She jumped out of the car. Nick followed, slower. His knees weren't as bad as the other day, but he wouldn't be running any marathons.

She stopped at her door, frowned at him. "Are you okay?"

"I will be."

"I have something for you."

He grinned. "That's what I was hoping for."

She laughed. A warm, deep, infectious rumble that warmed his blood.

"Well, I was thinking of something for

your joints."

"I don't want to think about them." He made it up the three steps to her porch without falling. "I just want to lie down." He touched her face again. He couldn't *not* touch her. "In your bed."

Her eyes darkened and she didn't move. "Who's seducing who?" she asked quietly.

"Does it matter?" he asked.

She shook her head, took his hand, and led him inside. He put his hat on the small entry table and pulled her into his arms.

"Hold that thought," she said and reached into her purse. She held up a small bottle of what looked like lotion. "How would you like a massage?"

He swallowed. It was her tone more than the words that turned him on. "Can I be naked?" he asked.

Carina licked her lips. "That's a requirement."

She took his hand and led him down the short hall to her bedroom. She couldn't help but smile, seeing the big cowboy standing in the middle of her ultrafeminine bedroom.

"Wait here," she said suddenly and ran down the hall.

Nick looked around the bedroom. It was mostly white, a little frilly. And there was a worn, stuffed bear against the multitude of colorful throw pillows against the distressed white iron headboard. Three true crime books sat on her nightstand, which fit what he knew of Carina more than the rest of her house. He was still trying to reconcile the fluffy room with Carina's lean and sexy exterior when she popped back into the room with his hat.

"What's that for?" he asked.

"Me," she said with a smile.

"Carina, are you sure?"

"Yes, I'm sure." She turned off the overhead light, leaving on a small table light next to her bed. "Take off your pants."

He raised an eyebrow and grinned. "Isn't that kind of forward, ma'am?"

"Do you want that massage?"

"I might even want more, ma'am," Nick drawled.

"That little catnap in the car gave me my second wind," she said. "I'm wide awake."

"So am I." He dropped his pants.

"Lie down."

"You're getting kind of demanding," Nick teased.

"What, you don't like strong women?"

"Strong women are the only kind I like." He lay down.

Carina took the bottle of lotion and

started working on his calves. "I have a confession."

"Anything."

"Dillon gave me this lotion. It's really an ointment for your joints. I hope you don't mind."

It surprised Nick that he didn't mind. In fact, the ointment plus Carina's strong hands were doing wonders for his muscles and his libido.

"Thank you for caring."

"I hated seeing you in pain."

"I wasn't."

"You hid it well. But . . ." Carina didn't finish her sentence.

By the time she reached his thighs, Nick was entirely turned on. Her fingers, her warm breath on his bare legs, her occasional kiss on his thigh . . . it was unexpected, but definitely wanted.

"How are you feeling?" she asked, her voice heavy.

"Incredible," he sighed.

She stood up and looked into his eyes. She took off her blazer, then her shoulder holster, putting her gun on her nightstand. She pulled her T-shirt over her head, revealing an incredibly sexy lace bra barely restraining her full breasts. He swallowed.

"Your bra's red," he said, his voice husky.

"You like red bras?"

"I sure do now." He couldn't help but smile. Carina's confidence was as sexy as her bra.

She smiled back, slowly unzipping and sliding out of her jeans. Her panties matched her bra. What little of them there were. His mouth went dry.

She turned around slowly, revealing a perfect heart-shaped ass, before facing him again.

Nick couldn't remember a time when a woman tried to seduce him. Not a woman he wanted. And he wanted *this* woman now.

She leaned over him and kissed him full and hard on the mouth. His hand went up to hold her face to his, but he didn't have to worry about her getting away. She wanted him as much as he wanted her, and that knowledge made Nick feel heady and turned on all at once.

He pulled her into his lap, and she straddled him, her barely clothed body rubbing against his hard dick. He held her close, tight, his hands finding her hair, so soft, so silky. He kissed her jawline, her neck, breathed in the floral scent of her dark, luscious hair. Breathed into her ear, and felt her shiver in his arms.

"Nick," she whispered, her voice husky, sexy.

He laid her down on the bed, his body half on top of hers, his hands unable to stop touching her, every inch of her tan skin. He could have easily made love to her right then, but he wanted to wait, prolong the pleasure of discovery, the increasing spiral of tension building in both their bodies.

Carina's arms wrapped around his neck, her hands trailing up and down his back. Squeezing, massaging, holding on to him. Her quiet moans spurred him on, telling him where she liked to be touched, how she liked to be kissed. She was giving herself so freely, without reservation, without holding anything back, that Nick fell half in love with her right then.

He'd never had a woman give herself to him so enthusiastically, so fully.

Carina sighed as Nick kissed every inch of her neck, not leaving one spot unloved. Her ears . . . since when had her ears become such an erogenous zone? His tongue licked one lobe and she gasped.

"Nick," Carina murmured, her hands running up and down his lean, rock-hard body. She'd never felt small and petite before, but in Nick's arms she felt protected and desired. Feminine, all woman.

His mouth skimmed along her chest, heading toward the right place, but slowly, much too slowly. She arched her back, egging him on. His tongue played with her breast along the edge of her bra, darting in and out, mimicking a French kiss.

She reached down and grabbed his T-shirt in her hands. "Off," she ordered.

Nick leaned up and she pulled the shirt roughly over his head. He then lay back on top of her, his chest hot against her skin. His mouth found hers as his hands reached under her bra and rubbed both her breasts simultaneously. She wriggled beneath him, trying to find relief, but only increasing her desire for him.

"Take it off," she said, passively waiting, and Nick removed her bra.

He looked down at her in the dim light, his face mirroring her desire. "You're so beautiful, Cara." He kissed her softly, gently. But she didn't want soft and gentle. She wanted to make love now, hot and furious. She pushed down his boxers as far as she could, and he removed them the rest of the way.

"Is your knee okay?" she asked quietly, not wanting to break the mood, but not wanting to hurt him, either.

"What knee?" he said and kissed her again.

"Make love to me, Nick. *Now.*"

He slid his mouth down her body until his teeth grabbed her thong. He pulled it down her legs. Her body quivered in anticipation. He kissed her toes and she moaned. Everywhere he touched ignited her nerves, sending bolts of electricity through her body, pooling in the one place he had yet to touch . . .

Seeing Carina's naked body on the bed next to him was enough for Nick. He could now die happy. Her chest rose and fell, her body shivering with anticipation. Every touch brought a reaction, every breath on her skin raised a moan from her throat. She wanted him as much as he wanted her, and her willingness to give herself over to him freely, happily, wantonly, brought him intense joy and deep arousal.

Slowly, he spread her legs. Touched her wetness and she shook beneath his fingers. He laid fully on top of her and she opened her eyes and smiled so seductively that he couldn't help but stare at her beauty.

"Here." She reached over the side of the bed, picked up his hat, and placed it on his head.

"I thought that was for you," he whispered.

"It is, Nick, all for me." She didn't close

her eyes; they stayed locked on to his. "I'm more than ready for you, cowboy."

He entered her slowly, slow to keep control, slow to give her as much pleasure as possible before he completely lost it. Her eyes drooped, but didn't close, never left his gaze.

"Cara," he whispered onto her lips. He kissed her lightly, trying to hold himself under control.

She arched beneath him, sheathing herself fully onto him, startling both of them. Her eyes wide and full of lust and affection, she moved to a tempo that pleased her, and Nick joined, his hands finding hers and holding tight.

Their rhythm quickened together, faster and harder, sweat covering Nick's body as he held himself back without giving up the fierceness of their lovemaking. He almost couldn't watch Carina, the deep pleasure infused in her expression almost setting him off. Then her eyes fluttered closed and she gasped, a high-pitched feminine and almost feline purr. Nick let himself go with a growl of his own, and they rocked together, hot, sweaty, and completely satiated.

Carina had never been so swept away by desire. She held on to Nick, catching her breath. He kissed her neck, found her lips.

"Carina, that was . . ." he sighed.

"Me too."

"You like the hat?"

She smiled. "Very much."

"I want you to wear it next time." He looked down at her, his expression serious but his eyes sparkling.

She took the hat off his head, pushed him to the side, and put the hat on her own head.

"Okay," she said and kissed him hard and long, until they were both breathless again. "If you insist."

When he figured out that an unmarked police car was watching Maggie's apartment, he got worried. *Very* worried.

Then he realized they didn't have anything on him. If the police *knew* he'd killed Angie and the others, they would have arrested him. That knowledge gave him confidence.

He drove right on past the car without another thought.

Besides, he didn't want to kill Maggie. Not yet, anyway. It was her younger sister, Leah, who reminded him of Becca. Her smile, her soft dark hair, her translucent skin. If he wanted to feel the intensity he had with Becca, he had to find another woman like Becca. That's where he'd gone wrong. Jodi was like Angie, and while at the beginning it was good, it ended all wrong.

But Becca had been perfect, from beginning to end.

And Leah would be, too.

He waited outside her boyfriend's apartment and frowned. The windows were dark. What were they doing in there? Why wasn't Leah going home? Her car was out front, right there on the street. She should be leaving. Going home. Not staying here with *him.*

The idea that Leah was having sex with another man greatly disturbed him. That put her right there with Angie and Jodi, a slut.

He wanted, needed, Leah to be pure. She looked innocent, acted sweet.

Women are liars.

He stared at the window, pictured Leah spreading her legs for a man. Imagined her asking him to fuck her, *liking* it, wanting it, just like a common whore.

Had she slept with other men? Did she have boyfriends all over town, just like Angie? Maybe she posted pictures of herself online for every man to see, to jerk off to, to lust after.

It was her fault. She deserved everything he was going to do to her.

And more.

Three in the morning. She didn't come

out of the apartment. His hand clutched the door handle.

Wait, his inner voice commanded.

He didn't know if he could wait for her to come out on her own. He didn't know if he *wanted* to wait. But he didn't know the layout of the apartment, how to get in, how to dispose of her boyfriend.

He wanted to kill the bastard for fucking Leah. That's exactly what they were doing. It was three-oh-six in the morning. What else could they be doing? Watching cartoons?

So he waited. And watched.

Leah Peterson would eventually leave. And then she would be his.

THIRTY

Carina woke to a low moan next to her in the bed. Instantly she was on alert, then remembered that Nick Thomas had slept in her bed last night. Slept, among other very wonderful things.

She glanced at the clock. Four fifty-five. She closed her eyes again. Three hours sleep was not enough. It was Sunday. She deserved to sleep until the sun came up.

"Leave her alone."

Nick's voice was as clear as day and Carina rolled over to face him. "Go back to sleep," she said.

"Stop. Don't touch her."

She realized Nick was talking in his sleep. Talking and moving restlessly, which is what had woken her up in the first place. He moaned, a mournful, guttural cry that tore at her heart.

"Nick," she said softly, touching his face.

His eyes shot open and he grabbed her

hand. She didn't move.

"Nick, it's me."

His eyes came into focus and he saw her. "Carina."

"You were having a bad dream."

He shook his head.

"Yes, you were. You were talking in your sleep."

"It wasn't a dream," he said, his voice thick. "It was a memory."

"Do you want to talk about it?"

"No."

"All right," she said. "Go back to sleep." She rolled over, trying not to be upset with him. She wasn't going to force him to relive a memory that gave him nightmares.

He rolled over and spooned himself around her bare back. Touched her loose hair, breathed into her neck.

"You know about the Butcher," he said finally.

"What I read in the papers."

"You know he held me captive."

"Yes."

"The papers never reported that he raped one of his victims while I was chained in the corner."

"Oh Nick." Carina tried to turn to face him, but he held her close against him, her back against his chest.

"He trussed me up like an animal so that any movement tightened the binds. I heard every scream, every assault. It was a living Hell and I wanted to die. I wanted to die because I couldn't stop it. I was trapped and forced to listen."

"How did you escape?"

"I didn't. Search and rescue found us. I didn't do a damn thing, I couldn't."

Nick had never told anyone what had happened in the shack. Not the shrink his doctor sent into his hospital room, not FBI agent Quinn Peterson, not even Miranda. They knew — the evidence spoke for itself — but he'd never talked about it.

Until now. He felt it was important for Carina to know what had happened, to understand how much those days had changed him.

"The Bozeman Butcher killed twenty-two women over a thirteen-year period," Nick began. He focused on the facts, even though she knew some of them. "My first murder investigation was the Bozeman Butcher's third victim, though we didn't know it at the time.

"When I became sheriff, I made it a priority to solve what seemed like an unsolvable case. I brought in the FBI. That didn't make

445

me popular with everyone, but it had to be done. They'd helped with the original investigation, when we had a survivor, but nothing came of it. No suspects, no evidence. Dead end."

He'd felt helpless to stop the Butcher, who seemed to kill and disappear at will.

"He usually killed and moved on, to return one or two years later to claim a couple more victims before disappearing again. But the last time, something spurred him on and he kidnapped a coed named Ashley van Auden less than a week after killing Rebecca Douglas. We had evidence from Rebecca's murder we'd never had before that helped us narrow down previous suspects and revisit the old cases with new insights.

"I had a hunch. It wasn't based on anything, really, except my knowledge of southwest Montana. I didn't tell anyone where I was going. I didn't think it would lead anywhere. And if I was wrong, and I was partly wrong, I didn't want good people to be damaged by the hint of suspicion in a brutal murder.

"I was attacked from behind and woke up hours later, bound, with Ashley chained to the floor next to me. And there was not a damn thing I could do to help her."

"Nick."

"You read the articles. You know what the Butcher did to those women."

"Cruel. Sadistic. But you're not responsible for his actions, and you certainly weren't responsible for his victims."

"When you're neck-deep in an investigation, you're responsible for everything."

Carina's heart broke at the strain in Nick's voice — he had been living with the guilt for so long, he'd somehow become convinced that what happened to that poor girl was somehow his fault.

"Nick, the Butcher kidnapped Ashley. He tortured her, not you. It happened before he knocked you out. You can't blame yourself."

"I know in my head that I'm not responsible for what happened to her, just like you know that you're not responsible for what happened to your nephew."

She tensed, and Nick said, "Honey, you do know it's not your fault."

"Like you said, in my head I know, but in my heart . . ." She took a deep breath. "In my heart I live with the painful void where Justin used to be."

He kissed her cheek. He'd never talked to anyone about what had happened when he was held captive, but Carina understood.

Maybe she was the only one who really could.

"I used to have nightmares about Justin," she said softly. "I'd wake up and start looking for him. He'd be on my mind for days, I'd replay that night over and over, trying to remember something I know I never heard or saw. I slept through his abduction and I'll have to live with that for the rest of my life."

She rolled over and he let her hold on to him. Touch him. He responded by feathering light kisses over her shoulder, her arm.

"The nightmares are few and far between," she told him. "Just sometimes . . ."

"Sometimes they come back with a vengeance." He kissed her lips.

"Yeah."

She settled into the crook of his arm and in minutes she was fast asleep.

Nick watched her sleeping for the second time and couldn't imagine holding any other woman in his arms.

Soon he fell back into a deep sleep, this time devoid of bad memories.

He stared at Leah tied naked to his bed, the black bandanna glued to her mouth.

"I never wanted to hurt you, Leah."

Sound came from her mouth, but no words.

Leah had left her boyfriend's apartment at dawn. He was waiting. He was patient. And patience was rewarded.

He'd called out to her and she'd turned, smiled even though she'd been surprised to see him there.

"I've been looking for you. Maggie's in the hospital. I'll take you."

She believed him. They always believed him because he looked honest and trust-worthy.

When you're a pathological liar, looking like an honest man truly helps.

He'd drugged the coffee he'd had waiting for her in the car. She didn't like that it was cool, but she drank enough anyway. Yawning, she fell asleep and didn't wake up until he'd already glued her mouth shut.

The thought of fucking her didn't appeal to him like he'd thought it would, and he frowned, wondering again why he couldn't regain the thrill he'd had with Becca, the excitement with Angie. What was wrong?

But when he thought about slowly squeez-ing the life out of Leah, his blood stirred and his penis twitched. Forget the other stuff, what was important was the finale. He would bathe her and wrap her in plastic

449

wrap. He had latex gloves. Forget the garbage bag. This time he wanted to look her in the eyes, watch her life drain away.

His body responded to the fantasy. No playing around. It had been fun playing with Angie, trying different things to see what would happen. The games now held no more allure. Staring at Leah, all he wanted was to feel her die in his hands.

Controlling life and death was the ultimate discipline. And isn't that what he did? He controlled his own universe, the people around him, with a focused restraint that few people had. No one knew, no one even suspected, what he'd done. It wasn't about the sex, it wasn't about women, it was about *victory.* The powerful surge he felt when he killed.

It was indescribable. Irreplaceable. Nothing came close to it. Watching the women trapped, squirming, wanting to scream but unable to say a word — all that was part of the delicious package. But the reward was their death.

Anticipation wasn't watching them fight the pain. Anticipation was the hunt, choosing his next prey. Now that he'd picked Leah, the next thing was her death.

He left the room to start the water. When he returned, he accidentally bumped his computer desk. The mouse moved, and the screen came to life.

Curious, he glanced to see if he had any messages.

1 message.

He clicked on it.

Your MyJournal tracker has logged a message from Elizabeth_Rimes at 8:44 p.m. Click here to read.

Elizabeth. He'd been worried about her, then angry. She had no right to neglect him, to stop e-mailing him. They were *friends*. That's what she'd told him.

He logged onto MyJournal, then read the message Elizabeth sent last night. That explained it; her mother was sick. And she needed his help again! Chat room 303. He hoped she was still there.

He almost logged onto the chat area right then.

But he had something else to do first.

"Let's take a bath," he said to Leah and untied the ropes.

He looked her in the eye.

"If you even think of running, I'll hurt you so bad you'll wish you could beg me to kill you."

She shook her head rapidly back and forth.

"Good. You understand me."

He carried her into the bathroom.

"Got him!"

Patrick shook Dillon awake, shoving a cup of coffee on the desk in front of him.

"He's in the chat room?" Dillon yawned and stretched, the aroma of bad coffee assaulting his senses.

"Not yet, he just read our message." Patrick stared at the screen as if to will the killer to respond.

"Come on, Scout. Take the bait!"

THIRTY-ONE

Carina woke to a terrific smell. Had to be a dream. Nothing that came from her kitchen smelled that good.

She grabbed Nick's T-shirt, pulled it over her naked body, and followed her nose.

Nick stood in front of her stove in his boxers and nothing else. His muscular build took her breath away. He glanced over his shoulder when she entered the room. "Good morning, Sleeping Beauty."

"You must be Merlin," she said, wrapping her arms around him from behind. "Conjuring up food out of nothing."

"I found the linguica in your freezer. Canned tomatoes and olives. I threw away the green cheese, but fortunately the eggs were fresh."

She remembered buying a dozen eggs the last time she went shopping because one of the few things she could make in the kitchen was chocolate chip cookies. But she hadn't had time since Angie's murder to even think about baking.

She kissed his bare shoulder. "Great in bed *and* in the kitchen. I think I'll have you stick around awhile." Though she was being flirty and flip, her heart twisted as she realized Nick would be returning to Montana in short order. She admired that he'd stayed on the case even after his brother had been cleared. Nick's dedication to the job and his desire to seek justice for the victims was as sexy as his physique. But he couldn't take an indefinite amount of time off, could he? He had responsibilities, more than just to her or this investigation.

A deep sadness shot through Carina. She dropped her arms and poured herself a cup of hot coffee. Nick was a keeper. But she'd thought Jim was a keeper, too, and look what had happened there.

Nick was like Jim in that he didn't like to talk about himself or his feelings. But when she prodded a bit, Nick opened up. She liked that he wasn't afraid to share what disturbed him, that he was willing to let her see inside, even when things weren't perfect.

She couldn't remember a time when she'd really pushed Jim to talk. If she had, maybe things would have been different. But maybe she hadn't cared as much as she'd thought she had.

And if things were different, Nick Thomas wouldn't be half-naked in her kitchen cooking her breakfast.

"Sit," he said, dishing up something that smelled far too good to come from her stove.

Her stomach growled as Nick served her a plate of scrambled eggs with linguica sausage, olives, tomatoes, and green chiles — hot sauce on the side.

"I'm in heaven," she said, pouring hot sauce liberally over her food.

"Heaven was last night," Nick said, sitting across from her and taking her hand. He kissed her fingers, taking a moment to plant a seductive kiss on the tip of her index finger. Hot chills raced down her spine.

"If you keep doing that I'm going to forget breakfast and take you back to bed," she said.

He smiled, licked her finger, then dropped her hand when the phone rang.

"Hello," she answered.

"It's Patrick. He took our bait."

"He's in the chat room?"

"Not yet, but he read the message we sent from 'Elizabeth.' "

"Great. I'm going to jump in the shower, then meet you at the station."

"Shower, but wait for my call. As soon as he goes into chat it won't take me long to get his ISP, and the DA came through with the warrant. I just have to fill in the provider."

"I'll be waiting."

She filled Nick in on her conversation with Patrick.

"I haven't showered yet."

"Neither have I."

"It would be a shame to waste water."

"Yes, it would."

"Eat."

"Fast."

They ate only half the food in front of them before Carina dropped her fork. "I can't wait." She grabbed Nick's hand, pulled him out of his chair, and led him down the hall to the shower. She turned on the shower, then pulled off her shirt, leaving her completely naked. She smiled and pushed Nick against the door, seeking his mouth with hers.

"You taste good," Nick mumbled as he nibbled her lip. His hands were on her bare ass, holding her tight against him.

When had she felt so right, so comfortable with a man so quickly? Never. It was as if she and Nick had been friends and lovers for years.

"We have to do this fast," she said, her breath quickening.

Nick gathered her tight into his arms, kissed her, water running over them. "Fast now, slow tonight. Very slow."

He bathed Leah, but couldn't stop thinking about Elizabeth. She'd asked for his help.

He itched to get back to his computer.

He could drown Leah. That would be fast. Just hold her underwater a couple of minutes and that would be it.

But that didn't do it for him. He wouldn't have the connection with her. He wouldn't get the same high.

He began to understand now what he'd been doing wrong. The watching, the waiting, that was the anticipation. That's what he needed more of. He was patient, he needed to be more patient. He'd been a little reckless, he could admit that now that it was all becoming clearer. He should have waited longer before taking Jodi. And Leah.

After this, he'd take some time off. Months. Plan the next one more carefully. Find someone innocent, unused. Like Becca.

It was the watching that turned him on. Then the killing that completed it. The games in between were fun, but they didn't give him that intense rush.

That's why Becca worked. He'd been watching her for a long time and he must have sensed her freshness. Though he hadn't planned to kill her until Jodi screwed everything up, it had all worked out in the end. He had killed her quick, felt her die, his body one with hers.

He wasn't going to drown Leah. He was going to regain that oneness he had had with Becca.

Leah whimpered.

"Shhh, Leah. It'll all be over really soon."

"What's taking him so long?" Patrick asked, slamming his coffee mug on his desk. Cold coffee sloshed over the sides.

"He might be upset that it took her a while to respond to him," Dillon said. "Give him time. He'll definitely go into the chat room. He won't be able to stop himself."

"I hope you're right. We're pinning everything on this trap working."

"I'm right. Just wait."

Carina's cell phone rang as soon as she stepped out of the shower. The after-sex glow disappeared as soon as she listened to the distraught voice on the phone.

"What happened?" Nick asked when she

hung up.

"That was Maggie Peterson. She said her sister, Leah, never came home last night and when she called Leah's boyfriend, he said she'd left at five this morning because she wanted to go home to change before work."

"Maybe she went straight to work."

"Her car is still at her boyfriend's."

"You think it's our guy."

"If it's not, it's a huge coincidence."

"Where's Kyle Burns?"

"With Maggie. She said he was there all night."

He tied Leah back on the bed, on the sheets he'd bought just for her, and dried her off. Touching her made him feel good. Her breasts were small and soft. Her stomach flat, smooth, so fair. A navel ring protruded from her stomach. He frowned. Why hadn't he noticed it before? He'd been too preoccupied thinking about Elizabeth.

He hooked the ring with his finger and ripped it out.

Leah's back arched and a scream vibrated in her chest. Tears rolled down her face.

"Sorry," he said, though he didn't mean it.

Becca and Jodi didn't have navel rings, but he'd kept one of their earrings. He looked at his own navel. Three hoops, two gold and one silver with charms, protruded from his stomach.

He reached into his desk and took out the piercing gun. The first time he'd had it done professionally, then he'd swiped the hand-held device.

He pierced himself and put Leah's ring in the hole. He wiped the small drip of blood off his stomach.

This was no good. He couldn't get his blood on Leah.

He went to the bathroom and bandaged the spot. Washed his hands. Much better.

Now he could get started. He took out the plastic wrap and started unrolling it on one of Leah's legs. With every turn of the wrap he grew antsy with anticipation.

Maybe this was going to be better than he had thought.

He glanced at the computer screen. Elizabeth's message was still up there. She'd been waiting for his response.

He bit his lip. He wanted to help her, but he had to take care of Leah first.

Just one quick message.

"He responded by e-mail," Patrick said, disappointed.

Dillon looked over Patrick's shoulder.

Hi Elizabeth. I'm in the middle of some-thing important, but I'll go to the chat room as soon as I'm done. It won't be too long.

"What is he doing?"

"He could be doing anything," Dillon said, "but he's obsessed with Elizabeth. I don't see him making her wait."

"What should we do?"

"Try to get him to respond faster." Dillon typed out a message.

Hi Scout, I'm so glad you can help me. You're so smart in math. I'm really desper-ate. I need to leave in ten minutes, though, and I don't know when I'll be back. I'll wait for you in the chat room as long as I can, but if you're too busy I understand. Don't worry about me. I'll find someone else to help.

"I think that'll do it," Dillon said.

"I hope so. I'm getting a bad feeling about this."

"So am I."

He finished wrapping Leah's body. Just like Becca. He unzipped his pants. He was semi-hard. Not good enough.

He went to launch the slide show on his

computer that he'd made from pictures of Becca. He turned the screen at an angle so he could watch her die again as he strangled Leah.

Another message. He clicked on it. *Elizabeth.*

He read her note and frowned. She could only wait for him *ten minutes!* What did she have to do that was so important? Certainly nothing as important as what he was doing!

He angrily replied.

Okay, I'll come by but I don't have a lot of time. Why do you have to do this now? Do you have a date or something?

He hit send before he really thought about it. It sounded mean. He didn't want to scare her off. He instantly logged into the chat room.

Hi, Elizabeth, I'm here. What do you need?

He heard the side door slam shut and froze. Who was here?

He listened carefully, swallowing faint panic. *Thump, thump.* "Dammit! Brandon Henry Burns! Where are you?"

Mother. She's going to ruin everything.

She wasn't supposed to be back until tomorrow. She worked ten days on, five days off for the cruise line. Like clockwork. But there was no mistaking her smoky cackle.

Hatred grew hot, and he clenched his fists. If it weren't for her, his father would still be here. He wasn't going to let the bitch ruin his chance to finally find his dad.

He zipped up his pants and pulled open his nightstand drawer. His fingers wrapped around his knife.

Dillon read Scout's message. He waited a full minute, then responded.

> Hi Scout, I'm so glad you're here. You're so smart in math. It's my basic calculus class again. You probably think I'm really dumb, but I'm having a problem demonstrating a proof of the fundamental theorem of calculus. Can you help?

He waited a minute. "He's not responding."

"That's okay, he's still logged in. The trace is working And . . . yes! I have his IP address. I'm going to run it through the ISP lists we got with the warrant. Ten minutes and we'll have a provider. And let's hope they don't make us jump through hoops before giving us his name and address."

Carina and Nick arrived at Maggie Peterson's apartment twenty minutes after she called, breaking all speed records to get to La Jolla from San Diego proper.

Maggie was a wreck, and Kyle was trying to console her.

"What happened to my sister?" Maggie cried. "Where is she?"

Carina had two cops talking to Leah's boyfriend, and so far his story held. He had a roommate who saw him kiss Leah goodbye, but not follow her out.

"Has your sister complained about being followed? Any strange feelings?"

"She was worried after Angie was killed. Leah works part-time at the Shack, so she knew Angie. Why didn't Tommy walk her to her car? This would never have happened!"

Carina had also asked the officers watching Kyle if he'd left at all during the night. They assured her that he hadn't budged.

It was ten in the morning and Leah had been missing five hours. She was supposed to be at work at eight, but hadn't shown up.

"Maggie, stay here by the phone. Wait for Leah to call. We'll put an APB out on her. We'll find her."

"What if that guy has her? Angie's killer?"

"Don't borrow trouble," Carina said. She looked at Kyle. "Where's your brother?"

Kyle blinked. "Home, I guess. He's just a kid."

"He's nearly eighteen." If Brandon and Kyle were working together, this ploy was brilliant. Kyle had the best alibi — spending all night with the victim's sister.

She hoped she was wrong.

Her cell phone rang. "Kincaid."

"It's Dillon. We have a location on Scout. It's Regina Burns's house in University City."

"I'm on my way." She slammed the phone.

"I heard that," Kyle said, and Carina mentally hit herself for not taking the call in another room. Cell phones were notoriously easy to eavesdrop on. "What's with my mother?"

"We've been tracking Angie Vance's online stalker. And we just tracked him all the way to your brother."

Kyle shook his head as he paled. "No. I don't believe it."

"Believe it." She turned to leave.

"Let me come with you."

"Absolutely not."

"Please, he's my brother. He'll listen to me. I-I don't want anything to happen to him."

"You sit in the cage," Carina said, referring to the back of her police sedan. "One false move and I'll nail you. Do what I say and nothing else."

"I will, please."

"Let's go."

THIRTY-TWO

His mother called his name. She was in the kitchen.

"Brandon, dammit, where are you?"

He waited, playing with the knife. Leah whimpered behind him.

"You parked in my spot, you idiot. I've been working all week catering to rich bitches and I can't even park in my own garage!"

Brandon waited.

"What have you been doing while I've been gone?"

She was getting closer.

"Brandon! Damn you, open this door! If you have a slut in your bed I'm going to cut off your dick and shove it down her throat!"

She pounded on his bedroom door. He opened it wide and stood there, his hands at his sides.

"Hello," he said.

Her face was red with anger as she began

to berate him. Then she saw.

He stepped aside and let her see Leah tied and wrapped on his bed. "She's like a present, isn't she?" he said.

"What?" Her voice didn't sound right. "What have you done?"

"You're early." He grabbed her wrist. His whole hand fit around it. He squeezed.

Regina stared at him, stunned into silence. Fear clouded her eyes. Good. She should be scared. He hoped she shit herself she was so scared.

It wouldn't come close to the terror he'd felt growing up. But he was in charge now. He was no longer scared.

"You let strangers into the house while Dad was in prison. Men who fucked you and gave you money. You're the whore, Mama."

She tried to slap him with her free hand, but he caught her other wrist easily.

"I don't know what you're talking about, Brandon."

"You betrayed Daddy."

"I loved your father. You know that! I was the only one who defended him. Let me go!"

He shook his head slowly, back and forth. "You lied about the whores. You lied about Daddy. You're just like them. You're a slut and you're going to get what's coming to you."

The fear and knowledge grew in her eyes. She rushed at him and fought him, but he was stronger.

She sucked in a breath to scream.

His hands came around her neck and he slammed her body into the wall. She couldn't move. She clawed at him with her hands. He squeezed. Tighter. Harder. She kicked, trying to catch her breath. She couldn't scream, couldn't talk. Her head grew light, her eyes saw nothing but darkness. Her lungs shrank, failing to draw in air.

Brandon tightened the hold on his mother, watching her face turn bluish, as her arms and legs stopped moving. A bone cracked beneath his hands.

"One. Two. Three. Four." He counted. How long would it take for the old bitch to die?

It took just over three minutes. It didn't seem very long, so Brandon held on another minute, just in case.

When he let go, his mother's body fell onto the floor with a heavy thud. He would take care of it later.

Elizabeth. She was waiting for his help. She needed him.

Leah. She lay there, frozen. He poked at her, to make sure she didn't betray him by dying like Jodi. She jerked at his touch. Good, she was still alive.

He just had to put Elizabeth off for another few minutes.

Scout? Are you there? If you can't help, I understand. I know you're busy and everything.

He quickly typed.

I'm here. I just had to take care of something. I can help you demonstrate the theorem.

He typed out a simple explanation, then waited.

Thank you so much! This is great. Hold on, I need to check the test guidelines and make sure I didn't forget something. Can you wait a second?

He could wait.

Sure.

He had plenty of things to do to occupy

his time.

Brandon turned to Leah. He was still high from killing his mother. Free, liberated. He'd finally avenged his father.

Maybe now his dad would come home.

Leah squirmed on the bed.

Brandon packed up his laptop and grabbed an emergency overnight bag he'd had prepared for months. He needed money, but he knew exactly where to go for that. He had the combination to the Sand Shack safe, and he knew for a fact that Kyle never made a deposit on Saturday nights because he went out with Maggie after work.

"Good-bye, Leah."

He pulled a garbage bag from his night-stand drawer and pulled it over her head. She bucked as he tied it around her neck.

"I wish I could stay and watch, but I have to go."

Carina turned onto Burns's street and saw a white Taurus round the corner up ahead.

"That looks like Brandon's car," Carina said and started to go after it.

A black Camaro was in the driveway of the house.

"The Camaro is my mother's," Kyle said flatly from the backseat.

"Drop me here," Nick demanded. "Leah could still be in the house."

Carina didn't want to leave Nick alone — backup was still three minutes out, but she had to follow the Taurus in case it was Brandon Burns. She stopped the car and Nick opened the door to get out.

"Be careful, Sheriff."

"You too, Detective." He was already moving toward the house as Carina did a one-eighty and regained Burns's tail.

Gun drawn, Nick ran up to the Burns property. He looked left, right. Up, down. The side door was ajar. Quiet. The last time he'd investigated a house that was supposedly vacant, he'd been attacked.

He hadn't been expecting it then. This time, he was on full alert. He wouldn't be caught unaware again.

Cautiously, he entered.

The house was dim. He was in the kitchen. A suitcase was next to the rear door. "Police! Stay where you are!" He announced his presence. No answer. No sound at all.

He moved quickly through the house, eyes moving to every potential hiding place.

Lying on the floor in the rear hallway was a blue-faced woman in her late forties. Her neck was bruised, her eyes had hemorrhaged, her tongue was out. Regina Burns was dead.

Nick looked in the room across from the body and saw a naked woman tied spread-eagle on the bed, a garbage bag tied around her head.

"No." Nick holstered his gun and ripped the bag with both hands. He stared at Leah Peterson. Her eyes were closed, her mouth glued shut. He felt for her pulse. Nothing. How long? She was warm, soft. She couldn't be dead.

"Dammit, *no!*" He couldn't be too late.

A faint heartbeat.

He had to do it. If there was a chance she was alive, he had to try.

Nick ripped the gag off the girl's mouth and pried open her bloody lips. He breathed air hard into her lungs, waited, filled her lungs again. Again.

Under his watch as sheriff, the Butcher had killed three women. He hadn't found them in time to save them. And since he'd arrived in San Diego, three more women had died horribly. Leah couldn't die on him. He would not allow it.

Breathe. He willed her to come back.

He heard movement and voices from the front of the house.

"Police!" he shouted. "I need medics, stat!"

Nick focused on watching the girl's chest. *Breathe, Leah, breathe. Please.*

He continued forcing air into her lungs. His mind became blank, every molecule in his being focused on bringing Leah back.

Suddenly, she sucked in a deep breath of air and her eyes opened wide, full of terror. She started thrashing on the bed.

Nick pulled out his pocketknife and cut the ropes. His heart pounded as rapidly as hers. "It's okay, Leah. It's okay."

He found a blanket in the corner of the room and held her close while waiting for the medics. Nick wasn't a religious man, but he closed his eyes and thanked whatever supreme being was out there. Thanked the universe for not letting evil win this battle.

"It's all right. It's all right," he whispered as he rocked her in his arms. "You're safe."

Leah began to cry.

THIRTY-THREE

Carina kept several car lengths behind the Taurus. As soon as he stopped at a light, she confirmed that the driver was in fact Brandon Burns.

"Why don't you pull him over?" Kyle said, anxious.

She considered it, torn. What if Leah Peterson was in the trunk? If she was, she was most likely dead, but *what if she wasn't dead?* What if he hadn't had time to finish whatever sick plan he had for her? What if she were still unconscious in the back of the car, knocked out from drugs or a blow to the back of the head?

"He might have a hostage, I can't take the chance." Not until she heard from Nick that Leah was at the house. Dead or alive.

In addition, there was no guarantee that Brandon would pull over. If he felt threatened, he could run, speeding through residential neighborhoods causing injury to innocent people. She didn't want to endanger civilians with a high-speed chase. Criminals with nothing to lose were the most dangerous, and Brandon Burns was already destined for a life in prison.

Better to take it slow until she had backup.

Brandon drove at just the speed limit and eventually turned onto a major thoroughfare headed toward La Jolla. She continued to keep her distance to give him a false sense of security that he was making a clean getaway. Find out where he was going and trap him.

She called in two minutes later with an updated report and to ask the status of backup.

"We have two patrols on parallel streets," dispatch said, "per your instructions. One unmarked car is two blocks behind your location."

"Do we have a status at the Burns house?"

"Negative."

Damn. She had to know if Leah was in the house or in the car. The thought that she was already dead and Brandon was in the process of dumping her body made Carina both sick and angry.

I can't be too late.

She was worried about Nick. She'd left him alone, something she should never have done, but she'd had no choice. She couldn't let Brandon disappear.

Dispatch radioed a 10-78 code from the Burns address. *Ambulance needed.* Carina hoped that the medics were really needed, that Leah was alive, and that the call was not a formality. And that Nick was safe.

She prayed she hadn't made a fatal mistake.

Her radio was open for two-way communication and she heard the chatter in the background.

Female, DOA.

Female, stable.

Nothing about Nick. That had to be good, right?

Brandon drove directly into La Jolla. Why? She asked dispatch to patch Dillon into her frequency. "Dillon, I'm following Brandon Burns. He doesn't appear to realize it. He's driving into La Jolla. What's he thinking?"

"I just talked to Nick. Regina Burns is dead, apparently strangled when she returned home."

"My mother is dead?" Kyle asked from the backseat.

Carina winced. He shouldn't have had to hear the news that way.

"I'm sorry, Kyle," she said.

"Good riddance," he said, his voice ripe

with emotion. "God, Brandon, why?"

"And Leah?" Carina asked Dillon over the radio.

"Leah Peterson is alive. Burns tied a bag over her head and left her. Nick performed CPR and saved her life."

"Thank God."

"I don't like this development. Up until now, Brandon has been calm and rational in his approach. He had a plan and executed it. Now he's impulsive. I don't know if it's because his mother showed up unexpectedly — the officer on scene said her calendar had her returning Monday morning, not today — or maybe because I had Elizabeth pull him into the chat room. I don't know why, but Burns is now unpredictable."

"I didn't think he was predictable in the first place," Carina said. "Angie and Becca couldn't be more different in profile and appearance."

"But I saw the logic in his actions, even if I couldn't predict who his victim was going to be. His whole purpose was to kill. Everything going into it, the glue, the rape, the washing of the bodies — that was leading up to the finale of the kill. But it was a ritual, each step, even with the changes in M.O., had to be completed before he could kill. Until now. He didn't rape Leah. He had her body prepared as if he were going to, but then he tied a garbage bag over her head and walked out the door."

"Maybe his mother's unexpected appearance saved her," Carina said.

"You're probably right."

"But what is he doing now? Why La Jolla?"

"He's going to try to find Elizabeth. I've been reading his e-mail messages and I believe he knows she's in Atlanta. Though she never said it outright, the pieces are all there and Brandon Burns is a smart kid."

"Let's get security at the airport."

"Already done."

"Then why is he going to La Jolla?"

Kyle spoke up from the backseat. "He's going to steal money from the Shack."

Carina glanced in the rearview mirror. "You think?"

Kyle nodded, his expression pained.

"Dillon, I have Brandon's brother, Kyle Burns, with me. He thinks Brandon is headed for the Shack to grab some cash."

"If he didn't have money at his house, that's logical."

As Dillon spoke, Brandon turned onto the coastal highway. In the direction of the Shack.

"Is Patrick with you?" she asked.

"Right here," Patrick said over the radio.

"I need all units at the Shack. Code Two. Call them and tell them to lock the doors *now*. Make something up, don't panic them, but tell them not to let anyone, even someone they know, inside."

"Hold."

"Sunday at noon. The beach is packed." Kyle said.

"I know," Carina said, frustrated.

She couldn't wait indefinitely, and she couldn't allow Brandon Burns to take an entire restaurant hostage. She didn't know if he was armed, but she had to assume he was.

A family started into the street right in front of her car and she slammed on her brakes. The father slammed a fist on her hood. "Stupid bitch!"

She flashed her badge out the window. "Move it!"

They did. But when they reached the Shack lot, Burns was already making his way to the entrance. The area was crowded with people, tourists, college students. She couldn't drive fast enough. She watched as Burns opened the door of the restaurant and entered.

"Patrick, he's in. Did you get through to the folks at the Sand Shack?"

"No, I hung up when you said he's in. I

didn't want to panic them."

"I'm going after him."

"Not without backup. Three units are less than two minutes away."

"Roger. Out."

Brandon might remember her, even though he'd only seen her once. But she'd been in civilian clothes — a T-shirt and slacks. She always wore her hair back on duty.

She had an idea.

She pulled into the parking lot and reached into the glove compartment for scissors. She cut her pants high on the thigh, contorting her body to make it all the way around.

"What are you doing?" Kyle asked.

"Going undercover," she replied.

She shrugged out of her light jacket and took off her holster, pulled the fanny pack from under her seat. She didn't like wearing it, but it had a built-in holster. It also doubled as an accessory — it wasn't unusual to see people walking around with fanny packs instead of purses, especially on campus or the beach. She pulled out her T-shirt and tied a knot under her breasts, let her hair down and fluffed it up as if it were windblown, then she called dispatch and told them her plan.

Patrick got on the radio. "Dammit, Carina, don't go in there alone! Burns has nothing to lose."

"There are two patrols in the lot. I'm going to brief them and have them cover both entrances. They're uniforms, they can't come in with me. I'll be a civilian. Play the situation as I see it. Have the SWAT team cover the two entrances. I can't let him take a hostage."

She took a deep breath. "I'm going in."

"I'm coming with you." Kyle reached for the door, which was locked.

"No," she said.

"He's my brother. I can talk him out of whatever he has planned. Please let me help."

She looked at Kyle. When she agreed to let him come out to the Burns house, she hadn't believed he was one hundred percent innocent. How had he not seen what his brother was capable of? But now, his eyes, his expression, his demeanor, everything told her he was sincere.

She couldn't help but be cautious. Kyle might know more about his brother's activities than he let on.

Yet he might very well be the ace in the hole she needed to get everyone out of the restaurant to safety.

"Follow my lead. Don't do anything stupid."

Nick stayed with Leah until the medics arrived. He asked a patrol to take him Code Three — lights and sirens — to the Sand Shack. "Cut the sirens a half mile back."

He'd heard over the radio exactly what Carina had planned. She was taking a huge risk, but as he ran through the scenario he couldn't see what choice she had. At least she didn't go inside as a cop. If Burns was quietly going to steal and leave, which would be the smart thing to do, she could get behind him as he walked out the door, arrest him away from civilians.

If he took hostages, they needed someone inside.

Nick pulled out his cell phone and called Dillon direct. "Any word?"

"Carina just went in."

Dammit. "I'm at least eight minutes out."

"So far the place is quiet. A pair of customers just came out."

"Where are you?"

"En route, but we're downtown. It's going to take at least thirty minutes. But if it becomes a hostage situation I might be of use."

"Burns must know he can't disappear,"

Nick said almost to himself.

"His father did."

"Did he?"

"I don't see what you're getting at."

"How many people have you known who could just disappear?"

"It happens."

"With a lot of planning and money, yes. But with an arrest warrant out on him? One slipup . . . his prints are in the system. He'd be pulled in."

"What are you thinking?" Dillon asked.

"What if his wife killed him? Found out he was raping women again, knocked him off? The police come by and she says he just left. Been gone for days. They buy it because he screwed up, they have evidence, so they put out an APB on him and that's that. No one looks at the wife for murder."

"What about a body?"

"I don't know. Maybe she buried it in the basement. A lake. The desert."

"There may be a lot of places to dump a body in Montana, but in Los Angeles?" Dillon thought a moment. "The mountains. There are some places where you could get rid of a body discreetly. I read about a case in Utah where a husband left his wife's body at the garbage dump. It took months for investigators to sift through the roughage to find her, and they even knew the general area where she'd been dumped."

"It would explain something Kyle Burns said when we first talked to him about his father. He flat-out denied that there was any possibility that his father was behind the murders. He didn't even entertain the thought."

"As if he knew it was impossible," Dillon said.

"Because Mitch Burns is dead."

Dillon paused a long time. "You might be right. Hold on, I have a call coming in."

Nick sat still in the passenger seat of the speeding police car. Dillon got on a minute later. "That was the DOJ. I called them earlier about any firearms registered to Regina or Kyle Burns. Regina Burns has a nine-millimeter registered in her name with a permit to carry. So far they haven't found a gun in the house."

"We have to get word to Carina that he may be armed." He hung up and turned to the officer driving. "ETA?"

"Three minutes."

Carina quickly assessed the room. Thirty-five civilians, including children. Six staff within sight. Likely two in the kitchen. Brandon worked here, he would be free to go wherever he wanted.

No one appeared panicked or worried. Just going about the business of eating and talking. As she watched through the large beachfront windows, two cops were talking to the dozen or so people eating on the patio outside. The plan was to clear as many people from the restaurant as possible.

Brandon wasn't within sight.

"Talk to your people," she told Kyle. "Gas leak, have them get the customers out quietly."

She approached a waitress. "Hi, did Brandon Burns just come in?"

"Yeah, he went to the office to call his brother." The waitress saw Kyle behind her. "Hey Kyle, Brandon's looking for you. I didn't think you were coming in today."

"We have a gas leak," Kyle said. "Can you quietly tell the customers and have them leave? Don't collect any money, we just need everyone to leave the restaurant. Including staff."

She furrowed her brow. "A gas leak? Is it dangerous?"

Kyle shook his head. "Just a precaution. Liability." The waitress left and Kyle whispered to Carina, "The safe is in my office."

Carina nodded. The office was adjacent to the kitchen. "How much?"

"Saturday night's take. Over three thousand. I — I went home with Maggie instead of the bank. No one knows."

"Except Brandon."

Kyle nodded soberly.

"Help get everyone out," she began when Kyle's phone rang.

He glanced at the caller ID. "It's the Shack number."

Brandon, most likely calling from the office. Carina moved Kyle over to the front door, where she could watch the staff and keep an eye on Kyle while listening to the conversation. She nodded for him to answer.

"Hi," Kyle said into the receiver.

"It's me," Brandon said.

"What's up?"

"I'm sorry, Kyle."

"Sorry about what?"

"You'll know when you get to work tomorrow. I just wanted to say good-bye."

"Good-bye? Where are you going?"

"I can't tell you. But . . ." he paused, his voice low. "I think Dad is around. I'm going to find him."

"What?"

Carina put her finger to her lips. *Shhh.*

"Why are you mad?" Brandon asked Kyle.

"Why do you think he's in San Diego?"

"Because the police were asking about him."

"Don't go looking for him, Brandon. Why don't you come over to my house? We can kick back, talk about Dad."

"No. You don't like him. You never have. You're just going to try to tell me to forget about him like you always do."

"That's not true."

"What?" Brandon's voice was muffled and in the background of the phone Carina heard a female voice murmuring.

Then Brandon hung up.

THIRTY-FOUR

Brandon stared at the waitress. *Denise.*

"Kyle's here?" he repeated.

"He just walked in with that detective who was asking all those questions about Angie's murder."

Al, the weekend cook, called out an order. "Denise! Pickup."

"Got to get that. See you later." She grabbed the food from under the heat lamps and started for the swinging doors.

Kyle was here in the restaurant. With a cop. Brandon replayed his conversation with Kyle on the phone.

Come over to my place.

Kyle's cell phone had caller ID. He knew Brandon was calling from the Shack. He didn't say anything about being here, too.

Another waitress popped her head into the kitchen as Denise exited. "Watch it, Sherry. You almost knocked over my tray."

"Put it down, Kyle says there's a gas leak

and we have to get out."

"Gas leak?" Al said, quickly shutting off all the burners. "Are you sure?"

Sherry shrugged. "That's what he said."

Brandon stayed in Kyle's small office so Sherry couldn't see him. Heart pounding, he watched as Al and Denise exited the kitchen.

Why was Kyle with that cop? Why didn't he tell Brandon he was here? Had the police figured something out? But he'd covered his tracks so well. Hadn't he?

He was alone in the kitchen. Being alone was dangerous, he realized. He left the office and glanced through the half-open blinds next to the storage room. A cop stood half behind a tree with his eyes trained on the kitchen door.

Brandon quickly got out of sight.

Being alone was definitely dangerous. He should have called Denise back. *Something.*

He fingered the gun in his windbreaker pocket as he crossed the kitchen and peered through the swinging door window into the hallway. Beyond the hall he saw customers leaving the the restaurant. Food still on the tables. Everyone leaving at once.

Kyle had betrayed him.

He didn't know how the police had figured everything out, but somehow Kyle was part of it. His own brother. Of all people who should have understood, but instead he was one of *them.*

Movement in the hall caught his eye. Someone was coming out of the restrooms.

Without hesitating, Brandon pushed the kitchen door a foot open. A boy of about eight or nine was walking back to his table.

"Hey," he said.

The boy slowed. Slowed enough for Brandon to grab him and pull him into the kitchen.

The kid drew in a breath to scream. Brandon didn't want to hurt him. Instead, he covered his mouth with one hand and showed him the gun.

"See this?"

The boy nodded.

"I'll kill your mother if you say a word."

Carina had to get everyone out as quickly as possible. *Now.*

The waitstaff had done a good job while Kyle was on the phone with Brandon. More than half the restaurant had been cleared. She watched as two waitresses and the cook came out of the kitchen. She approached Sherry.

"Is the kitchen empty?"

"Yes," she said.

The other waitress said, "No, I think Brandon is still in the office on the phone or something. I'll go get him."

"No, I will," Carina said. "Just leave."

She started toward the kitchen, flipping her radio on and discreetly talking into the mic. "Suspect may be alone in the kitchen." She spotted a woman still sitting at a table making no move to get up. There were two sodas on the table.

"Ma'am, do you have a guest with you?" Carina asked.

"My son is in the bathroom."

"I need to ask you to leave. There's a possible gas leak."

"I'll wait for my son."

"How long has he been gone?"

"Just a few minutes."

Carina had been in the restaurant for six minutes. She hadn't seen the boy pass her to get to the restrooms, which were off the hall that connected the kitchen — and the rear office — with the main restaurant.

"I'll get him for you."

"No, I'll get him. He's my son. I don't know you."

Carina discreetly flashed her badge. "You can't go back there."

"What happened? What's wrong?"

The panic in her voice caught the attention of the remaining patrons.

"Nothing is wrong. Gas leak. We don't want anyone getting hurt. I promise, I will get your son."

The mother was clearly torn. She bit her lip. Carina motioned a waitress over. "What's your son's name?"

"Josh. He's only eight."

"I will bring him to you. Trust me."

Without waiting for an answer, Carina nodded for the waitress to escort the mother out.

Carina spoke into her mic. "All units. Potential hostage situation, minor child. Am checking status."

She glanced back to the front, where she'd left Kyle. He was nowhere to be seen.

Had she made a mistake to trust him?

She stood outside the swinging kitchen doors, back against the wall. She heard a voice in the kitchen, but couldn't make out the words.

Carina looked into the kitchen through the windows in the doors. Where was Brandon? *Where was Kyle?*

First, get the boy out. Then secure the suspect. She ran down the short hall to the men's restroom and entered. "Josh?" she called quietly. "Josh?"

No answer. She looked in the two stalls.

The bathroom was empty.

Heart pounding, she checked the women's room next. Empty. She swallowed her panic.

Her hand on her gun, she left the bathroom and walked right into Brandon. A boy stood in front of him, shaking.

"Josh," she said.

She was only four feet away from the boy, but she didn't dare rush him. Carina listened to what Brandon heard. Silence. Distant voices. Ocean waves. Then in the distance, sirens.

He turned and saw her. Did he recognize her? She couldn't tell.

"Excuse me," she said, plastering a smile on her face, "thank you for finding my son. Josh, I told you to come right back to the table. The waitress said there's a gas leak, we need to get out."

She reached for Josh and Brandon pulled the boy closer to his side.

"I know who you are." Brandon narrowed his eyes at her.

"Don't make it worse. Turn yourself in."

He laughed. "It can't get worse for me." He showed her the gun he had on Josh. "Give me your gun."

"Let the boy go. Let him go. You don't want to hurt a child."

"Put your gun on the floor and kick it to

me. That's what they say in the movies, right?" As if demonstrating his knowledge of the theater, he pointed the gun directly at Josh's head.

Against every instinct, she removed her gun from her fanny pack, placed it on the floor, and kicked it to Brandon.

"Go in the kitchen," he commanded.

She did, glancing at Josh. "It's going to be okay, Josh. Focus on me, okay?"

Josh was small for his eight years, with large, trusting brown eyes. Just like Justin's.

No way in hell was Carina going to get Josh killed.

"Josh, you with me?" she asked quietly.

"Shut up," Brandon said. Josh squirmed, but Brandon pulled the boy close.

Brandon looked her dead in the eye, gun on the kid. "Denise told me Kyle was here. Where is he?"

"I'm right here."

Kyle walked through the kitchen doors, hands up.

They stood in the parking lot behind two SWAT vans looking at blueprints of the Sand Shack. Nick, Detective Dean Robertson, SWAT team leader Tom Blade, and several cops. Dean was in charge, and Dillon was on the radio.

"We have line of sight into all areas of the main dining hall. There's only one window in the kitchen" — Dean placed his finger on the northern wall — "here."

"My men have line of sight into the kitchen and my top marksman is holding at this position." Blade pointed to an area on the map thirty yards away. "And another man here" — he pointed — "has sights on the back door. According to my men, Burns has Detective Kincaid and a minor child in the kitchen."

"What about the bathroom windows?" Nick asked.

"They're small split glass, no way an adult could fit through," Blade said.

"We've secured the main doors. I want to send men into the main dining hall, but we can't tell if he's watching. If he stands here, by the kitchen doors, he'll be able to see anyone who enters."

"So we wait," Dean said. "Let Dillon Kincaid try to negotiate a surrender. He'll be here in twenty minutes."

"Sir," Blade interrupted, "isn't that a conflict? His sister's in there."

"Not for me," Dillon said over the radio. "But we might not have the time. Burns is agitated. He feels trapped. He can and will do anything to get away. Remember, he has nothing to lose."

"I agree," Nick said.

"Do we have a line of sight on Kyle Burns?" Dillon asked.

Blade responded. "No, but he hasn't left the building."

"He's in there," Nick said, pointing to the kitchen. "My instincts tell me he's right in the middle."

"Carina said in her last conversation with me that Kyle was being helpful," Dillon said, "but we need to be cautious."

"I'll go in," Nick said.

"You're out of your jurisdiction, Sheriff," Blade countered. "My men have this covered."

Dillon said, "Sheriff Thomas has experience with killers like Burns. Wire him and let him go in."

Dean looked from Blade to Nick, nodded. "We'll position men in the main dining hall if we're able. Stay away from the kitchen window."

Nick nodded. He pushed down his fear for Carina's safety. This was part of the job. She was a fellow officer. His goal was to get the boy and Carina out alive.

Dillon said, "We'll try talking first, urge him to put down his weapon and release the hostages. But our primary goal is to separate him from the hostages."

"I understand," Nick said as Blade fitted him with a Kevlar vest and wired him. If Brandon didn't voluntarily surrender, their only choice would be to take him down.

"I'm patched through to your frequency," Dillon said to Nick. "I'll give you whatever help I can. But trust your instincts, Nick. They're solid."

"Ready?" Dean asked him.

"Ready."

Brandon stared at Kyle.

"When I was talking to you on the phone, you were here. You were here with *her.*" He waved the gun loosely at Carina, then aimed it back in Josh's general direction. He didn't look comfortable with the gun. He may never have used one before. But even the worst shot could kill someone a foot away.

"I don't know what you mean," Kyle said.

"Don't talk to me like I'm stupid!"

"Put down the gun, Brandon, please. Don't do this."

Brandon kept the gun on Josh. Carina had to find a way to distract him. Get him to release the kid. Brandon was standing close to the kitchen doors, his back against the counter. Josh was in front of him. Carina was also in front of him about four feet away, her butt up against the butcher-block-style work island. The stove was to her right, and Kyle was between the doors and the stove.

The work island was full of partially cut vegetables. A seven-inch-long knife rested on the edge, only a foot from Carina's hand. Knife versus gun and hostage. Not fair odds, but it might be useful.

Brandon had put her gun high on the shelving unit inside the doors to his left, her right. Not easily accessible, as she'd have to stretch to reach it, but not impossible if he were distracted.

"Brandon, I can help you," Carina said, diverting his attention to her as she continued to assess the situation and Brandon's state of mind.

"Shut up. You're a woman. Women lie."

"But I'm a cop. Leah's alive, Brandon."

He shook his head. "I don't believe you."

"It's true. She's on her way to the hospital right now. Right before you left the house you tied a garbage bag over her head, but you didn't wait for her to die. You left. I arrived at your house as you were leaving. Another officer jumped out and found Leah as I followed you."

"I'm not stupid," he said. It seemed to be important to him that he be seen as smart,

Carina thought. Okay, she could play with that.

"No, you're not stupid, Brandon. In fact, you're one of the smartest killers I've ever faced."

"I'm not a killer."

He said the words without emotion or meaning. He didn't believe it.

"You almost got away with it," she said, keeping eye contact with Brandon. Kyle was inching across the room, heading slowly toward the stove. "We had nothing after Angie. You did a good job cleaning her body. We had no evidence."

A small, smug smile cracked Brandon's lips, but he didn't say anything.

"It was Becca that screwed you up."

"You're lying. *Again,*" he added for emphasis.

"We have proof," she said. "DNA evidence."

"I don't believe you."

"Believe it. Plastic attracts hair. We know you covered Angie with a wool-cotton-blend blanket when you suffocated her. But you didn't put a blanket on Becca. You wrapped her in plastic wrap, but you laid on top of her as she died. Your hair attached to the plastic."

"Now I know you're lying. I shaved my

body." He moved Josh to the side and pulled down his pants just enough to show that he had in fact shaved.

"I didn't say pubic hair," she answered quietly. But her mind wasn't on what she was saying. She was staring at Brandon's navel. Four rings, including the missing earrings from Becca and Jodi, protruded. One hoop had the shell, leaf, and rose charms of the navel ring in one of Angie's online pictures.

Carina swallowed her revulsion.

"Do you know why I was asking questions about your father? Because the DNA evidence we found was a *close-blood-relative* match. That means that a brother, son, nephew, uncle, or first cousin of your father left his DNA on the body of Becca Harrison."

"Not possible." Brandon shook his head.

"It's just us," Carina said. "You, me, and your brother. No one else will know. But it's been bugging me since the beginning. Why did you kill Angie? Was it because of her sex diaries? Was it because she wouldn't go out with you? Why?"

Brandon turned his full attention to her and for the first time, Carina was scared.

There was no soul in Brandon's ice-blue eyes.

"She was the girl on the tape," he said simply.

"What tape?" she asked.

He didn't elaborate, but said almost as cryptically, "When I saw her website I knew it was her, even though she was supposed to be dead. And then she walked into the Shack and everything came together. I'd been watching her on the computer for nearly a year, and she's real. It was *meant* to happen. She already died once."

Carina didn't know if Brandon really believed what he was saying or if it was some stunt. She pushed.

"What about Becca? Becca Harrison had no Web page, she didn't look or act like Angie. Why her?"

"Because I couldn't have Jodi."

Nick was right, Carina thought. He took Becca because he couldn't get to the girl he really wanted.

"But why her and not some random woman off the street?"

"She was nice to me."

Carina forced her face to remain blank at the killer's revelation. Brandon had lowered his gun. He was still holding on to Josh's shoulder with his left hand, but his gun hand was level with his leg.

"Why Leah?" Kyle asked, turning Brandon's attention from Carina to him. "Why did you take Leah? You know her. You've always liked her, you said so after I told you Maggie and I were dating."

"Because Leah reminded me of Becca."

That didn't make sense to Carina, but she didn't push it. Brandon was getting a faraway look in his eyes and she sensed that she would need to act soon or everyone could end up dead. By this time the SWAT team had to be in place. They'd have the building surrounded. She glanced at the partly open slats in the single kitchen window on the wall between the small office and the walk-in storage unit, which led to the service entrance. SWAT would have a view of the people in the kitchen, but Brandon wasn't at the right angle. Worse, she was between Brandon and the window.

She looked at Josh. The kid was frightened, but he stood straight. The only sign that he was scared was the way his wide brown eyes darted from her to Kyle and back again. Pleading with her to save him.

For a brief moment she pictured her nephew's large brown eyes pleading with his killer, begging for his life.

Not now, Kincaid. It wouldn't do her any good to think that way. She caught Josh's

503

eye and made a connection. *Trust me.*

"Brandon, what have you done?" Kyle's voice barely registered, and Carina focused on the scene unfolding in front of her. Kyle had stepped closer to his brother, his hands out, palms up. "You killed Angie? You killed those other women?"

"You'd never understand," Brandon said.

"No, I don't. For years I've been trying to forget about our father and how he fucked up our lives, and here you are pulling the same shit."

"Don't talk to me about Dad! Don't you see? This is my chance to find him. She" — he waved the gun toward Carina — "knows where he is."

"I don't know where he is," Carina said.

Brandon glared at her. "You were asking questions about him. You're looking for him, right?"

"He's wanted by LAPD for rape," Carina said.

"No, no, you have it all wrong," Brandon said, moving the gun from Josh to Carina and back. "She lied. She had sex with my dad and then lied about it to get him in trouble."

"That's Mom talking!" Kyle exclaimed.

Brandon's attention turned back to Kyle, and Carina nodded, hoping Kyle saw her.

Keep him talking, Kyle. Keep him focused on you.

She inched toward the stove. It was off — the cook had heard about the fictitious gas leak — but the oil for the fries was still hot. If she could get Josh away from Brandon, she might have a distraction until she could get to her clutch piece, the small twenty-two she had tucked in her back waistband.

But Josh had to be safe before she made any aggressive move.

"You always talked shit about Dad," Brandon said. "You always believed the lies."

"They weren't lies! Don't you see?"

"Stop. Just stop it! I'm going to find Dad and then you'll see."

"You won't find him! He's dead!"

Brandon stared at Kyle, eyes wide and disbelieving. "You don't know that. You don't know anything.

"I know he's dead because I killed him," Kyle said, taking a step toward Brandon. "I killed him. He deserved it."

"I don't believe you. You're just saying that so I give up trying to find him."

"Our father was a rapist, a sadist. He was bad news all the way around. When he got out of prison he didn't wait long. Just a few months. And I knew he was going out at night, up to his old tricks. So I followed him."

Brandon's focus was solely on Kyle. His grip on Josh hadn't loosened, however; if anything, it was firmer. The kid winced under the pressure of his fingers.

"I watched him crawl in through the unlocked window. I stood there, saw what he did to that woman. I just stood there and didn't do anything." Kyle glanced at Carina, then looked down. "I've hated myself ever since. Hated myself for not stopping him. For not calling the cops."

"You're lying," Brandon said.

"I followed him to a bar. I couldn't go in, but I waited. He came out drunk. He saw me, came over. I had Mom's car. He sat in the passenger seat and asked how I'd liked watching.

"The bastard knew all along I was there. I pulled out Mom's gun, the one she got after the trial, and shot him. I didn't even think about it. I just shot him and he died right there."

Brandon paled, his hand shook, and he raised the gun toward Kyle. "You . . . you couldn't have. You didn't —"

"I killed him. And guess what? Mom helped me dump his body in the Sunshine Canyon landfill in Sylmar."

"No." Brandon let go of Josh and pressed his hand on his head. "No!"

Carina caught Josh's eye, and he ran to her. She had him behind her back by the time Brandon turned the gun toward her.

"He's a child, Brandon, please. Let him go."

Brandon looked confused and undecided. Carina inched toward the swinging kitchen doors very slowly, shielding Josh's body with her own. "You don't want to hurt a little boy, Brandon," Carina said. "He's innocent. You have me. Let him go and take me."

Two long strides forward and Brandon had her arm. The gun was to her head.

"Nothing stupid."

"Run, Josh," she said, not breaking eye contact with Brandon.

The boy hesitated for only a moment. He then ran for the swinging doors. Brandon followed, pulling Carina with him, looked out as Josh ran through.

"Cops are all over the place," he said, sounding surprised.

"Of course. They were at your house. They know what you did."

Carina caught a glimpse of a familiar figure crouched on the other side of the kitchen doors.

Nick.

"What do you want, Brandon?" Carina asked him, her right hand close to her gun.

"I don't know. I don't know! Don't rush me."

"Brandon, please, give it up," said Kyle. "They'll kill you."

"No. Not with her." He pulled Carina closer to him. Though he was a skinny seventeen-year-old, he was strong. He had to be, Carina thought, to carry dead bodies around.

"You let the boy go," Carina said, "they'll go easy on you if you just surrender."

"No!" He hit her over the head with the gun. She faltered, trying to fall to the floor so Nick could get a clean shot from the door, but Brandon wouldn't let her drop. He backed up to the counter, close to his original position.

Blinking back the pain in her skull, she assessed the distance between her and the knife on the butcher block.

The knife was gone.

She darted her eyes toward Kyle. His face was blank, but he had one hand behind his back. Brandon didn't seem to notice.

"Okay, this is what we're going to do," Brandon said. "Kyle, you're going to call the police. From your office. And tell them that I want a car. You'll drive it, and I'll keep her in the back with me. They won't shoot as long as we have her."

"I'm not going anywhere with you, Brandon."

Brandon shook his head, his fingers crushing her arm as he held tight. "Why are you doing this to me? It's the only way."

"It's not the only way," Kyle said. "Goodbye, Brandon."

Kyle brought out the knife and held it in both hands, the blade facing his own stomach.

Brandon was as shocked as Carina. As Kyle brought his arms up to stab himself in the chest, he caught Carina's eye. She nodded.

She grabbed her twenty-two from her waistband at the same time that she kicked back and up, aiming right for his hairless balls. Direct hit. Brandon released her and doubled over, his face a mask of ferocious pain and anger, as he jerked the gun around toward her. She dove to the left, out of the line of fire that she expected from Nick's position in the hall.

Nick rolled into the kitchen and shouted, "Police! Drop it!"

Brandon whirled around, his gun now aimed at Nick. Brandon fired. As Carina depressed the trigger of her gun, she saw

Nick take a direct hit in the chest and fall back.

Carina fired again at the same time Nick did.

But it was the knife Kyle threw into Brandon's back that hit first.

He fell forward, seemingly in slow motion, until his head smacked against the tile floor, eyes open and unseeing.

Carina retrieved Burns's gun as the SWAT team ran in through both entrances. She crawled over to where Nick was struggling to sit up, a pained look on his face.

"You okay?"

"Damn, that hurt."

Thank God for Kevlar. She kissed him, helped him remove his shirt and flak jacket. A large purple bruise was already forming. She kissed his chest lightly, tears rushing to her eyes now that they were safe. "How are your ribs?" she asked, trying to sound casual, her voice cracking at the last moment.

"Intact," he said as he exhaled and Carina helped him sit up. "I'm fine."

He stared at her, touched the top of her head where Brandon had hit her with the gun. He came back with blood on his fingers. The worry on his face matched her own.

"Are you okay, Cara?"

She nodded. "I'm okay." She wrapped her arms around him. "I'm okay."

They sat there in the corner and watched the SWAT team leader lead Kyle Burns out of the kitchen. He stopped at his brother's dead body.

"I'm not sorry you're dead," he said to his brother's inert form. "I'm only sorry I didn't see you for what you were."

THIRTY-FIVE

Carina and Nick were medically cleared at the scene and left together for Carina's house. First thing, Carina called her parents.

"I'm fine," she said into the phone. "Nothing big, just a couple bumps. I'm going to be late for dinner because I really need a shower."

When she hung up, Nick said, "I was so scared, Carina," pulling her gently into his arms. "When he had the gun on you . . . I can't lose you." Her brown eyes melted at his voice and he knew she wanted him just as much.

He lightly touched the purple bruise on her face, kissed it. "Are you sure you're okay?"

"I'm fine." Tears fell down her cheeks and Nick brushed them away with his thumbs.

"It's going to be okay."

"I-I know. It's just catching up with me." Her body started shaking. "I was just as

512

scared for you."

"And you rose to the occasion. We make a good team."

He held her close to his chest, stroked her hair, touched her, until the shaking stopped. Until her hands started reaching for him.

He wanted to be gentle, but his slow kiss grew deep, hot, needy. Carina wrapped her arms around his neck and returned his embrace with the same intensity.

He closed his eyes, sank into her lush mouth. She was alive, in his arms. Her heart beat rapidly against his chest, proving her existence.

Carina moaned into his mouth, nipping at his lips, dueling with his tongue. He teased her by pulling back, then diving back into her mouth. Their tongues mimicked sex, in and out, wrapped around each other, urgent.

Carina backed into the shower, taking him, fully clothed, with her. He stripped, leaving his soggy clothes on the shower floor. The hot water pulsed over their skin, an erotic, wet caress.

He took the soap in his hands, lathered it up, massaged it all over her shoulders, her neck, her breasts. Down between her legs and she gasped. He went down on his knees, washed her muscular thighs, her slender calves, her sexy little feet.

"Oh Nick."

Her hands grabbed his hair, kneading, as his tongue trailed up her slick body, behind her knee, scraping over her hot center to her navel. She shivered and moaned, brought his mouth back to hers. Reached down and touched him, making him moan in response. He leaned into her body, pushing her gently against the cold tile wall. She clung to him, one leg wrapped around his waist.

"The bed," he whispered in her ear.

"Here. Now." She sucked the lobe of his ear, kissed his neck, nibbled his shoulder.

He held one thigh up with his arm, and she guided him into her.

"Fast," she said. "Fast and hard and don't stop."

Her words were as sexy as her voice, deep with arousal. He gave her what she asked for, and together, too quickly, they peaked.

"Now, we go slow," he told her as he turned off the water and carried her to her bed.

"Do you believe in love at first sight?" Carina asked Nick as they lay in bed later that night.

"Not until I met you."

Her heart flipped and she felt light-headed. "My parents fell in love right away."

Nick raised his head, propped it on his left hand, while his right hand played with her hair. "Really?"

"My mom escaped Cuba when she was twenty. This was in the mid-sixties, when it was harder to escape. Not that it's easy now, but then . . . many died trying to reach Florida." They still did, but not in the same numbers.

Carina told the story as if it had happened to her. The tragic and happy tale. "My mom bribed a captain to take her and her younger sister to Florida. He only took her halfway, dumping her on a dinghy with my aunt in the middle of the ocean. My aunt didn't survive."

"I'm sorry."

"She was wonderful, my mom said. Always happy. But at sea . . . three days with no food and only a gallon of fresh water to share. There were sharks in the water, and every once in a while they'd bump the bottom of the boat.

"My father was in the army, but he was on maneuvers in the Keys. He saw the boat in the distance and took a motorboat to meet it. You know the general rule, right? If Cuban immigrants make it to land, they have amnesty. If they're apprehended at sea, they're taken to a military base and deported.

"My mother would have been severely beaten had she been returned to Cuba, probably killed, because of her escape. Made an example. She had embarrassed her father in front of his commander, Castro." She tensed, knowing the pain her mother had endured and the emotional pain still in her heart. Nick rubbed her arm and she relaxed. It was so nice to have him in her bed.

"Your dad didn't deport her."

"He brought her to land. My aunt was dead, but my mom had kept her body in the boat. To bury her in free soil." Carina's eyes watered, as they always did thinking of what her mother must have been like when she was young. Thinking about the aunt she never knew.

"My father lied to his superiors, said he found the women on an island in the Keys. On land. They were inseparable, and a week later they married."

"Fast."

"They've been married forty-one years. Not bad for a quick engagement."

"Not bad at all," Nick said and kissed her forehead.

Carina didn't know why she was compelled to tell Nick the story, except that she felt so right with him.

"You're a great cop."

"Hmmm."

"You know, we all make mistakes. I should never have left you without backup at the Burns house."

"You should never have gone into the restaurant without backup, either," Nick told her.

"But," she continued, "you saved Leah and the situation in the restaurant was contained. We make decisions, right or wrong, in a split second. We don't always have the luxury of time."

He kissed her. "You don't need to remind me. I'll never forget what happened today."

"But I can honestly say I don't know that anyone else would have done anything different under those circumstances. We trust our instincts, the gut-level impression born in the moment. When my dad broke the law to bring a Cuban immigrant to shore. When you inspected that cabin outside Bozeman. When I decided to act in the kitchen — and when I decided not to act.

"Mistakes happen. We pay the price and go on." She kissed him.

He stared into her eyes, serious. "I love

you, Carina."

She sought out his lips. "I love you, too, Sheriff."

They took their time, slow kisses and languid touches. A whisper, a murmur, skin on skin, hands entwined. *This* was making love. *This* was what Carina had been missing in her life.

She didn't want to let him go.

Nick's internal clock woke him before dawn. He leaned over, looked at Carina's silhouette, her hair sprawled across the pink pillow. He smiled. *Pink*. He'd never have suspected that Carina Kincaid had a girlie streak that included frilly linens and pink decor, but somehow it suited her. Hard and focused on the outside, all woman on the inside.

He was going to miss her. Already, he regretted having to leave.

But his duty was to the people of Gallatin County. He was an elected official who had already been lax in his responsibilities since the Butcher investigation closed.

He'd been thinking about what needed to be done, and running away was not the answer. And if he stayed here in San Diego, he'd be doing exactly that, running away from his problems and leaving the sheriff's department in irresponsible hands. He'd given thirteen years of his life to the department, good and bad, and he couldn't turn his back on the men and women who had stood by him in his darkest hour.

His flight left later that morning; he needed to be on it.

He didn't want to leave.

Silently, he rose from the bed and rubbed his knee. He also had the surgery coming up. He couldn't miss it.

He wanted Carina there with him.

"Cara," he whispered in her ear. "I need to talk to you."

Her eyes fluttered open, darker in the dim light. "Nick?" Her voice was thick with sleep.

"You awake?"

"Yeah." She sat up, rubbed her eyes. "What's wrong?"

"Nothing's wrong. I want to marry you, Carina. Come to Montana with me."

She stiffened beside him and he frowned. What was wrong? "Carina?"

She swung her bare legs over the side of the bed. "Montana?"

"That's where I live."

"But I live here!" Tears welled in her eyes. "I thought you understood. This is my family. My life. *My* career."

He swallowed, his chest tight. "You knew I was going back to Montana today."

"I don't want you to go."

"Come with me."

"I can't. For the first sixteen years of my life I moved all over the country. Every year a new school. Every year a new house, new friends, new parks. I never made a real friend until my father retired here, in San Diego. I've been here for nearly twenty years. My friends are here. My job. *My family!*"

She was right. He couldn't ask her to leave.

And he couldn't give up his career, either.

She must have seen the realization on his face. She reached for him. "Nick, please. Don't go."

He swallowed hard, tears stinging his eyes. "I have to." He touched her cheek, whispered. "I have to."

He tilted her chin up. The tears in her eyes made him ache. He wanted to tell her he'd never forget her. That he would always love her. That she had become the most important person in his life.

But he could say none of that. It wouldn't be fair to her, and Carina deserved love just as much as he did. He didn't want to trap her with some mind game.

He touched his lips to hers, tasted her for the last time.

"Good-bye."

He picked up his bag and walked out.

THIRTY-SIX

Deputy Lance Booker walked with Nick slowly across the bullpen.

"You did it. You manipulated Sam Harris out of the race."

"Manipulate is such a strong word, Deputy," Nick said, shuffling on his crutches. Today was his first full day back in the office after his knee surgery; he already felt the change in his body. The doctor said the surgery had been a miracle.

Maybe it was the change in attitude that made all the difference.

"All I did was play hardball. Just like he did to me before I left for San Diego last month." They stood outside Nick's office.

"I want to thank you for putting in a good word for me with Charlie Daniels. I promise, I won't let you down."

Nick nodded soberly. "You've never let me down, Lance. You're a good cop. You'll serve Sheriff Daniels well."

Nick had convinced Charlie Daniels, the former deputy now in charge of Search and Rescue, to run for sheriff. His family had practically founded Bozeman, and his name kept Sam Harris out of the race. He had a clear field, and had agreed to keep Nick's team in place.

"And you?"

Nick took a deep breath. "I'm going to get back into shape. And I'm moving to San Diego."

"To be closer to your brother?"

"That, and other things. You know that song 'I Left My Heart in San Francisco'?"

Booker tilted his head. "You left yours in San Diego?"

Nick grinned. "Now get back to work. For now, I'm still in charge."

Booker left and Nick swung himself back on his crutches across the rest of the large headquarters. Slowly, reminding himself not to overdo it. He needed to be in prime condition next weekend when he surprised Carina with a visit — to properly propose to her.

He was going to miss Montana; he missed Carina a whole lot more. The one thing he'd longed for his entire life was unconditional love, and when he'd finally found it, he'd walked away.

He was going to rectify that mistake.

"Hello, cowboy."

As if he'd conjured her from his thoughts, Carina sat in his chair, boots on his desk, faded jeans and black T-shirt. She wore his hat on her head and had left her thick hair down.

She was the most beautiful thing he'd laid eyes on since he left San Diego three weeks ago.

It hit him then that Carina had come to him. He wanted to pull her into his arms and hold her, devour her mouth with his, take her home to his bed. She wanted him, even though juggling their careers over the next few months wasn't going to be easy. She wanted him and she loved him, he could see it all in her expressive eyes.

"Hello," he said, unable to keep the lopsided grin off his face.

She eyed his crutches, pride and love radiating from her face. "You had your surgery."

"Incredible powers of observation, Detective Kincaid." He leaned the crutches against his desk and sat in the guest chair. "I'll admit I'm surprised to see you."

"I missed you." She was smiling, but her voice cracked. This was difficult for her, making the first move.

Nick's heart swelled. "I'm glad."

"You're going to make this hard on me, aren't you?"

"No, I'm not. Come here."

Carina beamed. For weeks she'd debated giving up what she had — her career, her family, her home — and following Nick. One minute, the thought of seeing her family only on holidays and a week in the summer terrified her. The next minute, knowing if she didn't follow Nick she'd lose something precious and rare. *True love.*

The choice wasn't easy, but in the end, coming to Nick was the only decision she could have made. She was following her heart for the first time in her life, and she didn't doubt her decision.

She sat on the edge of his desk, right in front of him, leaned over and touched his face. He pulled her into his lap.

"I don't want to hurt you," she said, mindful of his knees.

"Kiss me."

She touched her lips to his, but the sweet kiss quickly turned hot. His hands grabbed her head, held her to him, as if he were drowning.

"God, I love you, Carina. You don't know what this means to me, finding you here."

"I couldn't lose you." She feathered kisses

on his face.

"You were never going to lose me, Carina."

He was right about that. Her heart was his, no matter where they were in the world. But she wasn't so naive as to think a long-distance relationship would work. She in San Diego constantly pressuring him to move to California; he in Montana unable to leave because of duty and honor.

The same duty and honor that had attracted her in the first place.

Tears slipped out and Nick ran his thumbs under her eyes. "Don't cry, sweetheart."

"I would have lost you. I'm stubborn. And arrogant. I couldn't imagine that you could walk away. I'm always the one who walks away. I weigh the pros and cons and cut my losses. But when I started running through the checklist, the bottom line was that no matter where I am in the world, it means nothing if you're not in my life."

"Will you marry me?" Nick asked.

"God, yes. I was afraid you wouldn't ask me again!" She kissed him.

"Reach into my pocket."

"Here?" She looked around. They'd already drawn several curious onlookers from the squad room beyond the glass-enclosed sheriff's office. She didn't mind experimenting in bed, but she wasn't an exhibitionist.

Nick laughed, moved her over a bit, and pulled something from his pocket. A box. A small box.

"For you."

She blinked, frowned. Uncertain.

"You don't like jewelry?" Nick asked, uncertain.

She took the box, cautiously opened it. A solitary round diamond sparkled. Her heart thudded so loud she could hear her rushing blood. "You . . . this . . . I . . ."

"Can I quote you on that?"

"You planned this? How did you know? Did Dillon tell you I was coming?" She'd told her family two nights ago that she was going to Montana to live with Nick. It had been bittersweet, but in the end, everyone supported her, particularly Dillon.

"No one told me anything. I have a flight booked to San Diego tomorrow morning."

"You were going to come to San Diego?"

Nick lifted Carina off his lap and put her on his desk. He took her hands and stared into her eyes. "I'm not running for reelection."

"But you said you had to. That idiot who's running against you —"

"I fixed it. I found my replacement, a good man who is going to run in my place. Harris has resigned, and my duty is done here. Almost done," he conceded. "My term doesn't expire for eight months."

"Eight months."

"And then I hoped we could get married and move into your house. Of course, we have to do something about your obsession with white frills and pink." His face was stern but his blue eyes were laughing.

She wrapped her arms around his neck and gave him a loud, wet kiss on the mouth. "Redecorate to your heart's content," she said. "Except the bedroom."

"You mean I have to sleep on pink sheets for the rest of my life?" He looked to the ceiling as if weighing his choices.

She gave a loud, exaggerated sigh. "I *might* concede on the sheets, but the pillows stay."

He kissed her and said, "Deal."

She smiled, relieved and happier than she had ever imagined. There had been that tickle of fear that she'd come here and he'd tell her to take a hike.

"I'll take my house off the market."

Nick sobered up, stared at her in disbelief. "You were going to move here? *Seriously?*"

She nodded, touched his cheeks with her thumbs. "I couldn't let you walk out of my life. I gave two weeks' notice this morning as well."

"You can call your boss, right? Get your job back?"

"Yes."

"Eight months, two states isn't going to be easy."

"Nothing worth having is easily attained."

Nick kissed her again, then Carina watched as he slid the engagement ring onto her finger. She was not a weepy woman, but she felt tears in her eyes and squeezed them away.

"I love you, Nick Thomas."

"Let's go back to my place, Detective Kincaid. So I can show you how much I love you."

She glanced at his knees and winked. "Are you sure you're up for it?"

"Let's go and find out."

ABOUT THE AUTHOR

Allison Brennan is the author of *The Prey, The Hunt, The Kill, See No Evil,* and *Fear No Evil.* For thirteen years she worked as a consultant in the California State Legislature before leaving to devote herself fully to her family and writing. She as a member of Romance Writers of America, Mystery Writers of America, and International Thriller Writers. She lives in Northern California with her husband Dan, and their five children.

Visit the author's Web site: www.allison brennan.com

Contact the author:
Allison Brennan
PO Box 1296
Elk Grove, CA 95759